*

STUPID
HUMANS

STUPID
HUMANS

A STELLAR ADVENTURE IN STUPIDITY

V.R.CRAFT

DRAGONBRAE

DRAGONBRAE

An imprint of Roan & Weatherford Publishing Associates, LLC
Bentonville, Arkansas
www.roanweatherford.com

Library of Congress Cataloging-in-Publication Data
Names: Craft, V.R., author
Title: Stupid Humans/V.R. Craft | Stupid Humans #1
Description: First. | Bentonville: Dragonbrae, 2025.
Identifiers: 978-1-63373-295-7 (hardcover)
ISBN: 978-1-63373-136-3 (trade paperback) | ISBN: 978-1-63373-138-7 (eBook)
Subjects: | BISAC: FICTION/Science Fiction/Humorous | FICTION/Science Fiction/Adventure
FICTION/Humorous

Radiance trade paperback edition June, 2025

Cover & Interior Design by Casey W. Cowan
Editing by Gil Miller

PROLOGUE

"What's another word for war that doesn't sound too much like conflict?" Haylea asked the automated bartender at the Wormhole in the Wall.

"Would you like a list of synonyms for war? I can list them in —"

"No, I already had my AI pull up a list. What I want is a word that doesn't sound like it means something contentious, even though, you know, wars and conflicts and almost-wars and things we refuse to call wars because it would sound bad actually are all kind of contentious."

The bartender hologram blinked at her. "I'm afraid there is no logical solution to your problem. You want a word that doesn't mean what it means. Can I get you another drink? Usually when patrons start asking questions like this, another beverage makes them feel better."

"No, I want a word that doesn't *sound* like it means what it means, which is why an AI will never be a Director of Copacetic Communications."

"Then I guess you have job security." The holo gave her one of those creepy people-impersonating grins that never quite looked right.

"I'm not so sure about that, but three drinks should be enough for lunch. Just get me the total." She looked around the empty bar, then out through the windows onto the almost-deserted concourse. Of course there were no holes in the wall—that would be pretty dangerous on a station floating in space—and the wormhole was a safe distance away, although still close enough that tourists could capture pictures through the wall screens. Well, they could if they visited The Wormhole in the Wall, which they hadn't lately.

After swiping her finger to settle the bill, she walked out of the bar and drifted past the other empty restaurants and businesses—Earth Hearth, Two Solar Sisters Bistro, The Star Bar. Just months ago they were full of tourists and now—nothing. No surprise why her boss, Woolerton, wanted her to make the don't-call-it-a-war sound better. She quickened her step, eager to jump in the elevator and leave all reminders of her failed marketing strategy for the station behind. After downing a few Solar Slushes, she wasn't walking in a perfectly straight line, but who was around to notice?

Today, of course, not one, not two, but *four* people were around. Fortunately, none of them was remotely interested in Haylea or how effectively her central nervous system responded to the recently lowered artificial gravity—until recently it had been set to New Atlantis normal, but her boss had reduced it slightly to save on energy costs.

"I will never forgive you for this!" screamed a small blonde woman being hauled down the strip by two Guard officers. They were trailed by a tall, slouching guy who kept looking around as if he expected a crowd to gather. Fortunately he was looking back at the screaming blonde as they passed Haylea, who had paused in an alcove.

"Samantha, please," the sloucher said. "I'm doing this for your own good, and one day you'll see that—"

"My own good? You used your political clout to have me forcibly removed from my home for my own good?"

Political clout? Who was this guy? Some low level politician Haylea had tried to get drunk at a party so she could talk him into voting for lower import tariffs? He *did* look familiar.

"Sammy, listen," he continued. "It wasn't safe for you on New Atlantis—or here. The only reasonable solution is for us to go back to Earth."

Back to Earth? Haylea shuffled out of the alcove, no longer worried anyone would see her, and stared at the group as they continued toward the elevator. She couldn't tell about the blonde woman, but the sloucher didn't look like someone from Earth.

Something flickered in her mind. Something about all the Humans fleeing back to their planet since one of them started this stupid war-like situation. Well, officially they didn't *start* it, but they pissed off the people who did, so it was pretty much their fault. That was one of the things she drank to during her liquid lunch—the stupid Humans starting this stupid not-really-a-war and tanking her tourism business, because no one wanted to go through the wormhole and visit the people who were trying to kill them—and, embarrassingly, doing a good enough job that they hadn't been stopped yet.

The wormhole! That was where she knew the sloucher from—he was that Brad guy, host of some news commentary show, who kept babbling that the wormhole might collapse at any moment, leaving everyone stranded where they were. He was a real contributor to the station's bad image, too.

She ambled after the group, squinting at the blonde. It was hard to tell, but she could have been a journalist who'd debated with Brad about the possibility of someone *finally* getting faster-than-light travel to work. Brad supported government grants for those working on the drive, which he said was the wormhole of the future or something like that. Haylea agreed, but wished he could make his point without telling everyone the wormhole was going to blow up. That really wrecked tourism on the station closest to the damn thing.

"You and I are through!" the blonde screamed over her shoulder.

"When we get to Earth, you'll change your mind." He nodded as if trying to make himself believe it.

"I will never change my mind, and you're going to pay for this!"

That was the last thing Haylea heard as the group boarded the elevator. She watched as the numbers moved down, finally stopping at the station's bottom floor, where the loading docks were located. Brad must have called in some serious favors to get his girlfriend deported to Earth. Hopefully he hadn't called in *all* his favors, because a functional, widely-available FTL drive might be the only thing that could revive the tourism business here.

With a sigh, Haylea boarded one of the elevators herself. Unfortunately, she had to go back to her office and pretend to work on a plan to bring customers back to Five Alpha.

She really tried, but no one wanted to visit the station closest to the wormhole that connected New Atlantis and its various colonies to its new enemy, Earth. Ever since that idiot blew up one stupid ship, supposedly just because his girlfriend dumped him, and some other idiots overreacted and blew up a couple Human ships, and the whole debacle rapidly degenerated into a situation neither government could control, her business had *also* rapidly degenerated.

Not that it stopped the Humans. Those people continued to hang around her station, scaring off the few customers she had left. In the past, she'd been happy for their business, but now they were more of a liability than an asset. There weren't enough of them to keep her business afloat, but there were just enough to give the depot a reputation for being a Human hangout.

They weren't dangerous. In fact, most of the Humans she'd met were just as annoyed and inconvenienced by the not-really-a-war as she was. Unfortunately, the People had misinterpreted the first disaster as an act of aggression and conducted its own acts of aggression, and then the Humans retaliated, both sides claiming "self defence." Now it was a big mess that both governments refused to call a war.

Haylea arrived at her office and flopped down into her chair. After checking her messages, she determined there were no emergencies she could do anything about, and settled in for her usual afternoon nap. She had almost drifted off when something tugged at the back of her mind.

Humans! Her eyes popped open and she sat up so fast the room tilted a bit, and she remembered how many Solar Slushes she'd had. No matter, she had a good idea.

"Draft a message to Woolerton," she told her AI. "I have an idea for a new Copacetic Communications campaign."

✳   ✳

"No. Absolutely not." Samantha stared down Dr. Anderson as they stood in the dingy infirmary of the ship that was supposed to carry her and Brad back to Earth. Anderson had a husky build and a round face that made her think of a pug dog. At the moment, his head was tilted in a way that intensified her mental comparison. He looked at her like she was crazy.

"Are you crazy?" he asked finally.

"Not anymore." She shifted her gaze to the data pad he'd shoved in her face. "I'm not signing that."

"Samantha, baby, you *have* to sign it." Brad leaned against the door, thumping his head back every so often as if her refusal made him want to bang his head against the wall.

"No, *baby*, I don't," she snapped. "You can have me hauled out of my home on some trumped-up charge, you can get your government friends to deport me, but you can't have me put in cryo against my will."

Brad shoved off from the wall and took a tentative step toward her. "I thought by the time we got here you'd have calmed down and realized this was the best thing for you." He reached for her hand.

She snatched it away. "I. Am. *Not*. Going. *Back*. To. *Earth*!"

Brad scampered back to his place by the door.

"Look, Samantha...." The doctor fixed her with a pug-dog-glaring-at-a-cat look. "This ship leaves in three hours. I don't have time to argue with you. Either you sign this form, or I leave you here on Five Alpha. Remember, this is the last Earthbound ship leaving for who knows how long, considering the current... situation. Now, are you sure you don't want to sign the consent form?"

"I'm sure." Samantha's eyes drilled holes into Brad as she said it.

✻　✻

"Are you sure you want to do this?" Anderson asked an hour later, as Brad sat on a cold examination table and waited to get even colder.

"I'm positive. Put me in cryo right now. You have my instructions." Brad shoved the signed consent form and travel order back at the doctor.

✕

Could Anderson tell he was terrified his plan wouldn't work and not at all sure he wanted to do this?

Anderson stared at him for a moment and finally took the pad. "You know...." He ambled back to the row of cryocans. "You still have a few minutes to reconsider."

"I've made my decision."

"But what if your girlfriend doesn't follow you in? Are you sure you want to go to Earth, a planet you've never visited before, by yourself, in the current political climate?"

Brad took a deep breath. "She's only refusing to go back because she doesn't want me to leave my home for her. Once I'm in cryo, and you can't wake me up or take me off the ship, she'll join me."

"You're sure of that?" Anderson pushed buttons on the nearest can. Samantha called those things coffins, and suddenly Brad saw the resemblance—it *did* look like a sleek, white coffin with blinking lights. He'd never been in cryo before, and despite everything he'd read about how safe it was, the prospect of spending months in that thing was a little nerve-wracking. But cryosleep was necessary to protect travelers from the potentially damaging physiological effects of traveling through a wormhole, and a trip through the Divide was necessary to get to Earth. Besides, cryo had been used safely for years, and he had nothing to worry about.

Screw that, as Samantha liked to say. He was terrified.

"I'm sure," he said with as much confidence as he could fake.

"Her reasoning, as you've described it, sounds right." Anderson unlocked the narc box and removing a dose of anesthetic, which he slapped into a port at one end of the cryocan. "But there are a few problems."

"Problems? What do you mean?" Brad swallowed, his throat dry.

"You know she had her medchip locked, right? And the only restriction she put on it was no cryosleep?"

"She did what? Why would she do that?"

Anderson shrugged, leaned against the can, and stroked his chin. "You know the usual reasons people restrict a medchip, but nobody puts a cryo lock on it for moral or religious reasons. It can't be construed as hurting anyone else, and you still have a heartbeat—even if it is extremely slow—so you're not technically dead. People feel much more secure about their beliefs in the afterlife when they don't have to come back from the dead."

"Then why?" Brad gripped the table. The whole world was falling away from him, and they were still under AG.

"Well, I really can't speculate. But, you know, *some* people do."

There was only one other reason a person might have a no-cryo lock. "You mean she might have pissed someone off? Like a criminal who might want to put her out of commission for an extended period of time without actually committing murder?"

"Some people place cryo restrictions for that reason. Your girlfriend is a journalist—like you, right?"

Brad frowned. "Uh, yes. But she writes features about seeing this place from the Human perspective. She doesn't cover crime."

"Again, I can't speculate." Anderson shuffled over to his desk, where he stared down at a data pad for a moment. "I probably shouldn't tell you this, because it's confidential—sort of like what I just told you—but it does affect the treatment you're about to choose for yourself, so I'm making an exception. And I *didn't* tell you any of this."

"Of course. What is it?" He had no idea Samantha had so many secrets. What now?

"She placed that restriction on her medchip five years ago, shortly after she arrived here from Earth. That means she was damn sure she didn't want to go back a *long* time before she met you."

Brad sat, unable to speak, for what seemed like an eternity. Anderson said nothing more. After a few seconds, he sat at his desk and busied himself shuffling stuff around.

Brad stood and went to the view screen to look out on the space station. The brightly lit curve of Five Alpha cut through the blackness like an enormous crescent moon. Once he went into cryo, the ship would pull away from the station and head for the wormhole, whether Samantha joined him or not.

But of course she would. There might be lots of reasons for the block on her chip. She could undo it now—all she had to do was sign some paperwork, and convince the doctor and his medical scanners she wasn't making the decision under duress. If the scanners determined she was stressed, even the doctor couldn't override the block—that was what prevented criminals from abusing cryostorage.

Was she really serious, all those times she'd insisted she wasn't staying for him? She *did* say she hated Earth, that it was crowded and polluted and full of stupid Humans, and she hadn't wanted to go back since the day she'd arrived here. Could that really be the reason she was stubbornly refusing to return, even in the midst of a war that made it dangerous for a Human to remain on this side of the Divide? Or was there a more sinister reason, like an angry criminal waiting over there?

So, wait, did that mean she didn't really love him?

Brad jerked away from the window. This was ridiculous. Of course she wasn't mixed up with Earth criminals, and of course she loved him. In fact, she loved him enough to join him even if she didn't really like

Earth. And if she didn't, well, surely the people of Earth would admire him for trying. Maybe he'd even meet someone new there —

But that was not going to happen. He shook his head, trying to clear the thought away. Samantha was going to join him in cryo, and once they were on Earth she'd forgive him for manipulating her into it. He was sure of it. He hoped.

"Put me into cryo," he told Anderson.

* *

"He did what?" Samantha stared at the pug dog face again. After his consultation with Brad, Anderson had joined her in the infirmary waiting room, where their only company was a cleaner bot drifting over the already-spotless carpet.

The doctor shrugged. "I told him it was a bad idea. But he was convinced that if he was already under and slated to go, you'd go with him."

"That son of a bitch!"

"This may be none of my business, but I really think he's trying to help you."

"I didn't ask him to do that. In fact, I explicitly told him —"

"You're not going back to Earth, yes, I know." Anderson made what Samantha took as an attempt at a look of fatherly concern. "There's nothing I can do now. He signed the papers to go to Earth before being put in cryo. I can't take him out against his will any more than I could put you in a can against yours."

Inching closer to the door, Samantha shook her head, more to shake away the rising feelings of panic than to communicate disagreement. "Fine, then get his cryocontainer off this ship!"

"Unfortunately, you don't get to decide what happens to his cryo-container." The doctor shoved the form at her again. "Legally, I have to respect his wishes. Now, you have two choices. You can go with him, and the two of you can wake up a few days out from that pretty blue planet and finish up your argument. Or, you can stay here and let this guy go to a hostile planet by himself because he made the mistake of trying to help your stubborn ass. What's it going to be?"

Samantha's heart pounded. How could her disagreement with Brad have spiraled into this situation? Typical Brad, thinking the whole galaxy revolved around him, that she would forget everything she'd said about never seeing Earth again just to be with him. He was an arrogant asshole, and she loved him.

And he was going to Earth with or without her.

She pushed the pad back at Anderson. "When you wake him up, tell him to send me a postcard from Earth."

With that, she turned, grabbed her bag, and walked out the door.

"We'll be in dock until tomorrow, when you change your mind," the doctor called after her.

She did not look back.

* *

Haylea couldn't believe how well her latest Copacetic Communications stunt had turned out. To be fair, the *Travel to Exotic Lands* theme she'd tried last month had been poorly planned—every new Human attack made visiting a station close to the wormhole seem less exotic and more neurotic. Then the luxury angle failed because her funding from corporate—her mother's travel company—abruptly dried up when the non-war's effect on the travel industry cost Go Galactic a small fortune.

But the "Can't We All Just Ignore Each Other Peace Rally" on the main concourse was a huge success. She'd put out a hurried press advisory yesterday, and this morning people showed up toting signs, wearing t-shirts with peace-mongering messages — "Togetherness is overrated" was her favorite — singing songs, and reciting poetry. Some of it was borrowed from ancient Human culture, as one of the head chanters explained to her.

She'd made a deal with some of the station's artists and clothing designers to carry their crap — er, memorabilia — in the concourse gift shop. One of them had hastily produced dozens of plastic "peace symbols" from Earth, strange circle-triangle symbols that she saw as an ironic reminder of how badly the humans had failed to establish peace on their own planet. Unfortunately, the damn things were selling like Carvalian beer, so she pretended to love them.

Naturally, she was thrilled when Farley, the head chanter, invited her to host a Prayer for Peace on the concourse. Public praying was more of a Human thing, but that was okay — showing support for the Humans was acceptable as long as it was part of the "Let's All Just Ignore Each Other" campaign. She was helping both sides focus on the bigger goal.

So she found herself on a stage constructed from cafeteria tables, holding hands with Farley and mumbling to "any and all greater powers who might or might not be" — no one wanted to offend anyone — for a peaceful end to the conflict. She wasn't really religious, but she was genuinely interested in ending this stupid war.

I'm a force for peace, she mused as she watched the other chanters. About ten percent were Human, and hopefully they'd remember her station as the place where peace between their peoples started. Wouldn't helping bring peace to a warring sector of the galaxy look great on her résumé in case Go Galactic had to close Five Alpha?

As she considered how best to articulate that achievement in a job interview without sounding conceited, she saw a small blonde Human stride purposefully from the elevator, start toward the cafeteria, then pause, as if she wasn't sure where to go. Something tickled the back of Haylea's brain. Where did she know that woman from?

"Great crowd, isn't it?" her assistant, Clark, whispered in her ear. "Hey, is that another Human showing up to make peace with us?" He thrust his chin in the direction of the blonde.

"I guess so. She looks familiar," Haylea whispered back, hoping no one in the prayer circle would notice. Fortunately, they were all chanting pretty loudly.

The blonde turned around a few times, surveying the area, then shifted her overstuffed bag to the other shoulder and headed back toward the elevator. Of course! That was the woman the guards had hauled off to some ship the other afternoon. What happened to her politician boyfriend? Had she finally dumped him?

Was a young, attractive, and influential politician now recently unattached?

What a great power couple Haylea and that attractive guy from the other night would be. Maybe he could feature her on his show—

"Isn't that Samantha, the reporter from *Glass*?" Clark nudged Haylea and pointed at the blonde.

"That's right!" Haylea's train of thought veered away from the talk show host. That must be why the Human journalist was here at the peace rally. Finally, one of the news nets was sending a real reporter—not just a news-collecting drone, but a real person. Well, Human, but that was okay.

"I'm sure she'll want to interview the main organizer of this event." Haylea smoothed her hair and started toward the reporter. The other peacemakers were too busy chanting to notice.

Samantha was interviewing a shop owner, probably about the positive economic effect the "Can't We All Just Ignore Each Other Peace Rally" was having on her business.

"We've got five-cred pitchers of beer all day long, to help keep everyone in a peaceful mood," the woman practically screamed the word *peaceful*.

Haylea walked casually toward the two, not sure when she would enter the shot. Reporters usually had micro-cameras embedded in their clothing, and often roving, insect-sized camera drones flying around, too. Those were conspicuous, so most of the reporters Haylea was in the habit of plying with beer said they used them only when absolutely necessary. Unfortunately, it was impossible to know just how wide a shot the cameras were taking, so Haylea kept a perfect smile plastered on her face and tried to look like she had no idea she was on camera.

"Here's the person who made this all possible." The restaurant owner grabbed Haylea by the arm and shoved her toward Samantha. "Haylea here is the reason I'm able to offer *five-credit pitchers of beer all night!*"

"Thank you for talking to me, Sheelah." Samantha's face was slack with boredom. "I'm sure you have to get back into your restaurant and keep the beer flowing, so I won't keep you."

The restaurant owner bustled off, screaming over her shoulder about five-cred pitchers.

"I'm working on an independent piece for *Glass*." Samantha's dark eyes looked Haylea up and down in one swift glance. "You organized this event?"

STUPID HUMANS

"Absolutely! As Director of Copacetic Commun—"

For half a second, Haylea thought she heard a very loud thunder-clap, because that was what it sounded like. Then she remembered there were no thunderclaps on a space station, because there was no thunder on a space station. There were only very loud explosions. The noise went on, deafening, with no sign of stopping.

The praying, on the other hand, ground to a *complete* halt. Every-one looked around at the ceiling, the walls, the floor for the source of the noise. Samantha gripped the nearest table with one hand, her eyes sweeping the crowd of people.

Haylea looked around, frantic, trying to recall if they'd skimped on any safety measures lately due to cost. Then she realized the station was holding together, and the rumbling sounded like it was coming from outside—but how could that be? Sound didn't carry in space. Well, it did if something crashed into the station's hull.

"Oh, no!" Clark stumbled over to her, waving his data pad. Why hadn't she been looking at hers? What was she doing?

He shoved it in her face. "Look at the news!"

Haylea stared at the up-to-the-minute newsbrief, reported by roam-ing news automatons faster than any living, breathing reporter could even ask what was happening.

SHIP EXPLODES DEPARTING STATION FIVE ALPHA

DUE TO THE NATURE OF THE EXPLOSION, NATURAL CAUSES ARE DEEMED UNLIKELY (12% PROBABILITY BASED ON AVAILABLE INFORMATION). THE MOST LIKELY EXPLANATION FOR AN INTENTIONAL EXPLOSION IS ANOTHER ACT OF AGGRESSION (PROBABILITY OF HUMAN ORIGIN, 55%; PROBABILITY OF PEOPLE ORIGIN, 45%).

For reasons Haylea didn't quite understand, the second the shaking stopped, everyone ran for the exits. Hands pulled apart, feet pounded the floor in heels and soft soles, and signs fluttered to the ground as their holders fled.

"This door is locked!" someone screamed from the end of the concourse.

"So is this one!" Clark had joined the fleeing crowd. She'd thought better of him than that, but he'd been dating a Human, and while stupidity wasn't contagious, people sometimes picked up each other's habits.

Farley, running through the crowd in his "Peace for peace's sake" t-shirt, threw the first peace symbol. Samantha said something Haylea couldn't hear to Sheelah, as she flounced out the door of her restaurant and surveyed the scene. Sheelah grabbed for the nearest emergency exit door, jostling Samantha, who stumbled into Farley.

"This one's locked too!" Sheelah bellowed.

"It locks automatically after an impact to protect the inner part of the station in case of...." No one could hear her over the noisy crowd, and finishing the sentence with "a hull breach" would only worsen the panic, anyway.

"This is your fault, Human!" Farley yelled at Samantha. "I bet you caused whatever just happened, didn't you? Your people can't stand *peace*."

Two minutes earlier he'd been holding hands with two Earthers and singing some old Human song, the lyrics of which sounded a lot like, "Come buy bombs."

"Oh, that's great!" yelled a Human at the back of the crowd. "Some peace organizer *you* are."

"Seriously? *You* helped organize this display?" Samantha sneered at Farley.

"Not anymore!" He slammed his peace symbol onto the ground. Due to the lightweight plastic and the lightweight gravity, it bounced off the floor and flew up into the crowd, smacking Clark in the face.

Sheelah shoved Samantha up against the wall, grabbing the collar of her black jacket. Was that messing up one of the camera shots? "Time for you to stop asking questions and start answering them. What do you know about this Human attack? Which of your people blew up that ship, and how stupid was their reasoning? Or were *you* in on it, Human?"

"Leave her alone, or I'll make sure you stop getting an Economic Crisis discount on your rent." Haylea hoped to come off as a beacon of peace instead of a miserly manager. It was so hard to gauge these things before they hit the news nets.

Sheelah let go of Samantha and stomped back into her restaurant, slamming the door on other frantic fleers, but the Human/People clash was far from over.

While Haylea yelled at the crowd to calm down, every peace symbol in the room was lobbed at someone. Fortunately, the cheap plastic limited the damage, but a few pieces managed to leave red marks. One found its way to the mouth of a shop owner just as he yelled, "You people are sub-Human!" The peace sign drove his lip into a nearby tooth, and blood trickled down onto his "Give peace a fighting chance" t-shirt.

What was she doing? She was supposed to be in charge here, and she was gaping at this idiocy like, well, an idiot. Remembering her data pad, she called up the emergency preparedness plan she'd signed off on after Clark wrote it last month. She hadn't actually read the plan, so hopefully Clark knew what he was doing.

Going through the emergency procedures—screaming at engineering to seal off the departure dock, ensuring the station's AI had sent a distress signal to nearby ships, checking reports for life support systems in the danger zone, sighing with relief when none of them were — Haylea realized she was a lousy person. While she was genuinely concerned about the safety of everyone on Five Alpha, another part of her brain pictured the whole place going bankrupt. As the Humans and non-Humans ran around, screaming, crying, and generally melting into masses of useless hysteria, it was clear that no Copacetic Communications campaign could repair the damage the explosion had just done to her station.

✳

S T U P I D

HUMANS

ONE

Dr. Vance was drinking in the Wormhole in the Wall because he was a selfish jerk.

He knew he was fortunate to be on Five Alpha, and not on the *Traveler* when it blew up, or on the incoming *Adventurer* when most of it was taken out by *Traveler*'s debris. He knew it because every five minutes someone reminded him how lucky he was to be alive. Of course he wasn't jealous of Dr. Ambrose, the physician who was on his way to take Vance's post when the *Traveler*'s debris obliterated the infirmary and everything else on that level of the ship. In fact, Vance should probably feel guilty that Ambrose lost his life coming to take over Five Alpha's medical center.

But he didn't feel guilty. He wasn't the asshole who blew up the damn *Traveler*. Nor was he the moron in charge of *Adventurer*'s safety protocols who decided deflection shields weren't necessary so close to a space station. And yet....

He sat in the bar and wished Dr. Ambrose had been visiting one of the sex sim suites when the explosion happened, because the sex suites were on level 14, which sustained little damage. No one there had died in the explosion, and the only injury was one unlucky male whose simulation device had wound up, well, in an uncomfortable position. Vance had been able to repair the damage and expected the young man to make a full recovery—although he probably wouldn't be visiting any sim suites any time soon.

Vance brought up the holo menu. When were they going to get a damn person to work here, anyway? Frego had joined the Guard after his brother died in the explosion, but couldn't they hire someone? Sure, the computer could fetch your drink, but it just wasn't any fun complaining about your problems to an algorithm.

"Do you know who owns this joint?" A voice behind Vance interrupted his thoughts. He swiveled around on the bar stool and came face-to-face with the Human.

The Human. That was an unfair title. Her name was Samantha. She had adopted or found homes for every abandoned animal on the station, and she visited one of his patients who had no other visitors several times a week. Still. She was the only Human left on the station, the rest of her kind having fled after the explosion. She flatly refused to go, telling anyone who would listen that Earth was crowded, polluted, and full of stupid people.

Of course, it was okay for *her* to talk about the Humans like that—she was one of them. If Vance said anything about the idiots on Earth, he'd get a memo from Haylea about how *everyone* practiced Copacetic Communications *every* day and if he practiced it in a different—read better—way it would make her job so much easier, and probably his too.

"Yeah, Frego owns the bar." Conversations all around him had come to an abrupt halt. The other patrons stared, undoubtedly wondering what he could possibly have to say to The Human. "Frego used to supervise the bar, but he joined the Guard after... um...."

"I understand." She sat on the bar stool next to his, and he suddenly remembered why, in spite of her sometimes abrasive attitude, he liked her. She could have let him sit there and stammer about why Frego had felt compelled to go defend his people against hers, but instead she'd quickly ended his display of awkwardness.

"They need a new bartender in here. Someone who doesn't run on code." She flicked her hand over the holo menu.

"I was just thinking that."

"I assume it isn't strictly necessary, but it might be better for business."

Vance nodded. How did these things get so awkward? A bunch of people neither of them knew were randomly blowing up each other's stuff. Half of them shared a few more genes with Samantha than with Vance. Under any other circumstances, no one would even think about it.

"This place hasn't been the same since Frego left. I'd say business has dropped off considerably. Of course, so has the population of the station."

"Is Frego a friend of yours?"

"Yes, although I haven't seen him much lately. He's usually out on patrol with...." Vance trailed off. Conversations in the bar had just stopped *again*, although he hadn't noticed when they'd restarted. He and Samantha both turned around just in time to see Frego walk through the door and right up to the bar.

Frego's fleshy face rotated through expressions, as if trying them on then discarding them. First was a frown, which sprang elastically into a grin so quickly that it couldn't possibly be genuine. The smile faded over a few seconds, dissolving into a puzzled look, which further transformed into worry.

Finally, he peered around the bar at the other patrons. "Well, don't everyone stop enjoying The Wormhole in the Wall's fine selection of beverages just because I walked in!"

Laughter broke the tension, although most of the other customers continued looking back and forth between Samantha and Frego as he crossed the room and squeezed behind the counter.

"I trust the holo waiter didn't mess up your order?" He glanced briefly at Vance but mostly looked at Samantha when he said it.

She gave him the sort of smile Vance usually reserved for jokes he'd heard a few hundred times too many. "Of course not. Vance and I were just talking about how a non-digital bartender might be nice."

Frego looked at her sharply. "I agree, and that used to be my job. But then...."

"I understand," Samantha repeated, unfazed. "Have you thought about hiring someone?"

"I would, but business has been terrible since... well, since the explosion. Half the people on this station left — even some non-Humans," he added quickly. "I don't even know if I'll be able to keep the place open when I leave the Guard. You know, after this mess is over."

Samantha nodded. "I was a journalist back on New Atlantis. Left when things started getting bad between your people and mine — I was making a target of myself and everyone around me. I was going to do freelance work here, but there aren't that many people left to interview, so it's a little slow."

Frego's head jerked back in surprise. "You want to work here?"

That caught Vance by surprise, too. Why would she want to work in a bar full of drunk Human-haters?

"I need to pay my expenses, and the job market isn't exactly great here."

Especially for a human, Vance noticed she didn't add.

Frego frowned. "Can I ask you a question?"

"Sure, ask me anything."

"I understand why you left New Atlantis, and I understand why you stayed here when you first came — the pollution, the overpopulation, all that other stuff on Earth...."

Vance suppressed a grin at how "stupid Humans" became "all that other stuff on Earth."

Samantha nodded.

"But why are you staying here now? From what I've heard, most of the other Earthers went back to their side of the Divide. You could always come back when this is all over."

"Leaving and coming back would be a long disruption to my life," Samantha said. "This conflict doesn't have an expiration date, the closest Human settlement on the Other Side is almost three months out, and I've heard the living conditions there make Earth seem like a paradise." She sipped her drink. "Five years ago, I said I was never crossing the Divide again, and I meant it."

Frego grabbed a bottle of whiskey and poured himself a drink. "I heard your boyfriend was on the *Traveler*."

Vance stopped with his glass halfway to his mouth. "Frego!"

"It's all right. Yes, he was. He thought if he had himself frozen and packed up that I'd change my mind and go with him. He was wrong, and the ship blew up, and..." Samantha stared at the wall screen behind Frego, which showed the stark, empty expanse of space behind the station. "And he died."

Frego wiped a section of counter the maintenance crawler had cleaned thirty seconds earlier. "I'm sorry."

"I'm sorry your brother died." She knocked back the rest of her drink, set the glass down, and stood. "I should get back to my job search. If you hear of anything, would you please let me know?"

"Wait." Frego scratched his head. "I have an idea. What if you supervise this place for me, and instead of paying you I'll let you live in the empty apartment above the bar rent-free?"

She looked at the handful of half-bored, half-drunk patrons, then back at Frego. "If I improve business by ten percent in the next month, will you pay me a bonus?"

Vance nearly choked on his My Thigh, a popular Earth drink—or so one of his human patients with a damaged liver had told him. Samantha was crazy not to take the first offer Frego had given her.

Frego laughed. "If you can improve business by ten percent in the next month, I can afford to pay you a salary!"

"Great. When do I start?"

Frego swiped his hand over the main console. "Right now. I'll get your DNA keyed into the system as an employee."

Vance was about to ask how Samantha planned to bring more business into this place when his AI beeped. He pulled his data pad from his pocket, unrolled it, glanced at the message, and sighed. He was off-duty, so the medical center's AI ordinarily wouldn't have contacted him for an emergency, but....

The message specified that he was to contact Dr. Woodley, Medical Supervisor for the Five Alpha Guard Branch, about a consultation.

What did she want him to consult on? The Guard's staff of doctors and medical AIs could handle a far bigger disaster than anything he usually encountered on Five Alpha—as Woodley was fond of pointing out. In fact, after the *Traveler* explosion, she'd sent doctors and supplies to Vance's medical center to help with the unusually high influx of new patients. He hoped her message wasn't because another disaster had happened—or was about to.

Knowing Woodley, she probably just had an unusual case and wanted to give him the chance to look inept in front of the People's foremost experts on something or other.

Vance stood, swiped his thumb on the counter to settle his tab, and headed for the door, tail swishing nervously against his pants.

"Good luck with that ten percent thing," he said over his shoulder to Samantha.

TWO

Samantha knew her first night running the bar would be a pain in the ass, but she hoped to get the awkward "Oh…you're the Human?" part over with as quickly as possible. It was only a few hours into the evening when she realized it would probably never be over.

Although she was frequently gossiped about all over the station, most of the Wormhole's few patrons didn't know her on sight. Standing behind the bar blocked the guests' view of her ass, so no one could tell she didn't have a tail. But sooner or later someone would recognize her, and then the shit would hit the fan.

About ten minutes after the evening rush started—five whole customers at once!—a smirking, dark-haired kid walked in. Maybe fifteen or sixteen. She wasn't great at guessing ages. But judging by the hideously neon clothing—the shirt looked like a Sherwin Williams truck had hit a zoo with its insane hodgepodge of colors and animal prints—he was in teenage rebellion mode. He walked up to the bar and looked straight at Samantha.

"My dad *said* he hired a Human to run this place. He must be getting senile in his old age."

Conversation in the Wormhole ground to a halt. All five of Samantha's customers swiveled their heads around to goggle at her. One old barfly, who appeared as permanently rooted to his stool as a tree to the ground, actually hauled himself into a half-standing position, propping his elbows on the counter, and leaned over to look at her rear end.

"You want a better look?" She unceremoniously shoved a tray of dirty glasses onto the floor—they were made of an unbreakable polymer material and the bar's robot would collect them later—and hopped up. The counter was deep, built for a much busier bar than the Wormhole had been lately, and there was plenty of room. Turning her back to the audience, such as it was, she bent over.

"Take a good look!" She wiggled her skintight-vinyl-clad butt like a cheap stripper. "I figure you men never really get to appreciate staring at a woman's ass, what with that tail always obscuring your view."

Silence in the bar.

She stayed in her ostrich-minus-the-sand pose for a few more seconds, then stood up and whirled around. As expected, her audience of six People men—if you counted the kid, who was really more of a petulant boy, but he *was* male—stared at her in shock. After a moment, the old barfly, whose name she didn't know but intended to learn, started a round of applause. The kid joined in, then the others did as well.

As the clapping inevitably faded away, she hopped down and ordered five drinks—she wasn't going to piss off her boss/landlord by getting his kid drunk. Clean glasses slid from an opening in the wall onto a conveyor belt, where each one stopped at the appropriate tap. She'd asked for Galaxy Glue, the cheap draft beer they had on special tonight. After all five glasses had been filled and loaded onto a tray, she took it from the robo-waiter and distributed the drinks. The teenager, sulking at a table alone while furiously fingering his data pad, didn't even notice she'd skipped him.

"Tell all your friends to come by the Wormhole in the Wall if they want to see what the crazy Human bartender does next," she told each patron as she handed him a drink. "And this one's on the house. Do you know that expression?"

＊　＊

Haylea had made a lot of mistakes in her life. She'd been a highly intelligent but highly disinterested student who had about as much interest in her final few years of education as a bird has in swimming. She knew what she wanted to do and it wasn't something she could learn about in school.

Sadly, several years after she graduated, she discovered there really was no market for cartoons about cranky cats from a parallel universe and their time-traveling owner. Meanwhile, she hadn't had a "real job" since graduating, her parents constantly gave her unwanted career advice, and since she didn't have any money, she was forced to live with the unimaginative, boring people who had inexplicably produced her.

Finally, desperate to at least get her own place, she took the job with Go Galactic, which was run by a friend and business partner of her parents, a similarly boring guy named Woolerton. Her mother had, apparently, convinced him that Haylea's creative abilities made her a natural for the company's Copacetic Communications department. At the interview, lacking any relevant experience, Haylea had extolled her virtues as a writer, advertiser, marketer, and generally someone who could make Go Galactic a lot of money. She mostly did this by throwing around phrases she'd heard on her favorite drama holo about a Copacetic Communications manager with a litany of personal and professional problems. Amazingly, this tactic seemed to impress Woolerton. Or maybe it didn't but her mother had promised him a great deal on a used spaceship in return for hiring Haylea. Whatever.

When she reluctantly accepted the job, the base salary was, well, not what she needed to live on a beach planet in the Ansafari system and create cartoon holos about cats, whether anyone watched them or not. It wasn't even enough to vacation to a beach planet once every ten years.

"Don't worry," Woolerton had said with a smile. "If you do well on Five Alpha, improve the tourism rate by just five percent in the first two years, you'll advance quickly. You may even be head of our entire Copacetic Communications department."

At the time, improving the visit rate by such a small amount in two years had seemed simple. How hard could it be to improve tourism on the station closest to the most important wormhole in the galaxy?

Apparently, it was harder than she'd thought. As the People got used to the Humans, both groups became bored with the wormhole. It was still important for businesses, but most of those had well-outfitted ships. They might stop to refuel, but usually they were in too much of a hurry to hang around for long. The Divide was no longer new and interesting—and that was before the not-so-copacetic conflict. After the *Traveler* disaster, things only got worse.

There were only sixteen injuries on Five Alpha that day, only two serious, and all injured parties had recovered. Haylea had played this up for the media, but public opinion still dropped off by a few points. She understood why. What if the explosion had been closer to the station?

What if Five Alpha was the target next time? Why would anyone want to hang around so close to the damn wormhole to Earth, anyway?

Woolerton's latest memo this morning demanded an "action proposal" for improving public opinion of the station. Great. At this point, if she increased business by five percent, she'd still be well below the numbers when she'd first been tasked with improving the visit rate by five percent. Plus, the explosion had totally wrecked interest in her "Can't We All Just Ignore Each Other?" campaign. No one wanted to ignore a group of people who wanted to attack them, and vice versa. She'd even seen t-shirts screaming the message, "Look where ignoring them got us." Her brilliant Copacetic Communications stunt had gone from good to gruesome in minutes. How could she fix this mess?

"I'm going to take a long walk," she told her AI. "It'll help me collect my thoughts so I can write that memo. I'll be back after my usual lunch."

"Of course, that's a great idea."

Was it her imagination, or did it sound sarcastic? Whose idea was it to program those things with personalities, anyway?

She stomped down the hall, hoping she didn't run into anyone who recognized her as the head of Copacetic Communications, because the last thing in the galaxy she wanted to do right now was be fucking *nice* to anyone. She was terrible at this job, really awful, and her mother was going to owe Woolerton a whole fleet of used spaceships by the time Haylea's employment was terminated. The worst part was that she wouldn't even be doing this job that she was absolutely terrible at if someone had just appreciated her creative talents —

She rounded a corner and almost ran into Someone She Would Have To Be Nice To.

"Haylea, it's so great to see you again!"

Roble had a crooked grin, hair that was apparently a total stranger to his hands—or a hairbrush—and a few extra inches around his middle. Every time she saw him out—which wasn't often—he was reading something on his pad, playing some virtual game, or staring adoringly at her. That was the problem with Roble—he had a completely one-sided infatuation with her, despite the fact that they had nothing in common, and if she agreed to date him they would literally have nothing to do together except have sex.

Then again, maybe Roble knew *exactly* what he wanted in a romantic partner.

"Roble, nice to see you." Haylea looked around the crowded concourse for something, anything, that could be construed to need her immediate, undivided attention. She always had this problem around Roble because, unlike him, she wanted a romantic partner who was interesting to her in more than one way.

"I was just headed over to the Earth Hearth for lunch. Would you like to join me?" Roble's expression somehow reminded Haylea of her pet dog's face when she came home every day. Except, of course, that the dog would be content to stop at licking her face.

What to do? Despite his inability to take a hint the fifty times she'd told him they were just friends, Roble was one of the few people on the station who didn't blame her for its impending demise. Annoying the one friend she had here would be bad Copacetic Communications.

"Earth Hearth? Are they still in business?" she stalled.

"They haven't been too busy, but I think that's why they have such a good deal on pizza. Ever eaten pizza? It's the best Earth food ever!"

"I'm not really a fan of Earth food," she said, truthfully. "I was just going to walk around and get some exercise on my lunch break." *That* was sure to get rid of him.

"Wow, you're so dedicated to exercise. I wish I was more like that."

"Well, I'm sure you're busy working on all those computer problems. I'll see you later—"

"No, no, I'm not going to just sit around and eat Earth food today." Roble drew himself up to his full height, which conveniently put him at eye level with Haylea's chest. "I'm going to join you on your walk. Dr. Vance just told me I need more exercise."

"O…kay." She stretched out the Human word, knowing she might as well give up. She could ignore the guy just as easily with him as without him, right?

"But I walk very fast, so try to keep up." She strutted off in the direction of the Wormhole in the Wall, hoping to lose him by the time she got there.

"This is great exercise! Hey, look at that." Roble pointed at the wall screen, which showed the outside view of the wormhole as if the station had windows instead of radiation shielding. "There's another chunk of asteroid coming through."

"That's nice." She quickened her pace.

"Now would be a good time for me to finish explaining wormhole mechanics." He somehow managed to catch up with her.

Great. Just what she needed. The first time she'd met Roble, she made the mistake of telling him she really didn't understand how wormholes worked. What she meant was that she didn't understand them because they bored her and she had no desire to listen to anyone talk about them. What Roble thought she meant was that she wanted someone to explain it to her, which he attempted to do every time he saw her—like right now.

"See how fast that thing is going?" he asked. "That's why the station has to be so far away, because it's hard to predict the ship's trajectory as it exits, and it takes a long time for it to slow down and correct its course."

"Um... right." A large object that she assumed was a ship came flying out of the wormhole. At first it was just a blur, but as it slowed, the image stabilized and she could make out a Good Day Beer logo on the side. At least the bar was getting resupplied soon.

"That's why it'll take several days before it reaches us," Roble said. "Approaching the Divide is an interesting situation because time slows down as you approach a wormhole —"

"Are we approaching one now?" She hoped Roble's panting would prevent him from hearing her.

No such luck.

"Now? No, of course not. This station is very well-fortified, and placed a safe distance from the wormhole," he said. "There is some concern about the Divide's stability. For years, it's been stabilized with exotic matter, although we're not sure how our ancestors managed that. The prevailing theory says—are you familiar with negative energy, or would you like me to explain —"

"No, no, that's okay. Why don't we try running to the Wormhole in the Wall?" She broke into a jog. If Roble managed to keep up, she could say she had to work on an action plan for Woolerton through her lunch break....

Her line of thought suddenly turned into a squiggle as she stopped outside the bar. Roble's feet slapped the ground behind her. Hopefully he'd stop short of plowing her down.

"Why are we stopping? Don't tell me I tired you out?" He lumbered up beside her, struggling to catch his breath.

"No, I stopped to look at *that*." Haylea pointed at her destination. As usual, its doors stood open, probably to make the place seem inviting by showing people a bunch of *other* people having a fantastic time. Unfortunately, for the last few months the windows had just shown a dismally empty bar with a few miserable patrons drinking alone.

Today, however, it was actually *full*. There were people from the business offices where she worked, engineers who probably had the pleasure of working with Roble, security officers, maintenance workers from the now-deserted docks, people who ran stores. What was going on?

"Wow, they sure are crowded." Roble, master of the understatement.

"Yes, and it's my job to know why. If something exciting is happening on the station, it might be good publicity." Hopefully that sounded a lot more convincing to Roble than it did to her.

"Great, I'll go with you."

They wandered in and she found a stool at the far end of the counter, only to realize there was no place for Roble to sit.

"Um… you can have the seat." She shoved Roble into it before he could protest. "I prefer to lean on the bar anyway."

Easier to make a quick getaway.

"So are you two here to see her, too?" Gary, who ran the close-to-bankruptcy gift shop at the other end of the concourse, asked from Roble's right.

"Her?" Roble frowned.

"The crazy Human bartender." Gary pointed toward the reporter Haylea recognized from her disastrous peace rally. She shoved drinks down the bar as they came off the conveyor, and she didn't look crazy at all.

"Is that why all these people are here today?"

"Yeah, everyone wants to see her." Gary shook his head. "I wish I'd thought to be the first person on this station to hire a Human. Maybe I should get one now. There won't be as much novelty, but it still might help my business."

"I want to get one for the lingerie shop," said Carlin, who Haylea had recently overheard saying she was planning to move her store to One Alpha before the end of this year. She leaned around Gary and Roble to look at Haylea. "Don't you think it would be great for the station's public image?"

Haylea paused in the middle of ordering a drink from the automated menu. Sometimes she forgot that people thought she was an expert on these sorts of things because she was the head of Copacetic Communications.

"Well, it's obviously working well for Frego."

And, if she played the situation right, maybe it could work very well for her.

✳
THREE

"When you said you found an old Human cryocan, that might have been an understatement," Vance said to Woodley, as they stood in one of the infirmary's exam rooms.

It was bulky and awkward in a way that even the more recent Earther cryocans couldn't approach. Each end had more blinking lights than a Human Christmas tree, although not as many as it once had—years in space had left a few dents and broken panels.

"When was it stylish to decorate a glorified freezer?" He fingered the rough plating.

"Those aren't decorative." Woodley snickered. "I told you this thing was weird, even for Humans. Those are solar panels."

"Solar panels? On an object that was meant to be shot into space and float around in the void for years? Most likely far from any star?" The bulky design told him the can was meant to operate independently of a ship or power source for an extended time.

She shrugged. "You know how Humans are. You have one on your station, don't you?"

Vance bent to examine the various lights, assuming the bright red, solid one was a warning of imminent failure. "Yeah, she's running the Wormhole in the Wall now, while Frego's serving in the Guard."

"What? He joined the Guard to fight the Earthers and left one in charge of his bar?"

He sighed. "It's not *all* of them. According to Samantha—our resident Human—most of her people are as annoyed by the whole idea of a war as we are."

"Then why'd they start it?"

"Let me see the chart on this guy." He tapped the paneling and turned around to look at her. "And they didn't start it. One person carried out a personal vendetta, another one fired back, a few more people got involved, and the whole thing melted into a big mess no one wants to clean up."

The report displayed on the closest wall—heart rate five beats per minute, standard for someone in cryo. Body temperature cold enough to prevent the cells from aging at any more than a glacial rate, but not quite cold enough for them to burst, providing the right drug protocol was used. Blood pressure barely existent. Blood counts normal.

"You can see he's fine for now, but over there—" She pointed to the left of the Human's health signs, at another set of readouts. "The power source is failing."

"So what's the problem? Just haul this thing to the nearest planet and stick it out in the sun."

Woodley started to smile, but twisted her mouth back into a flat line. "We wouldn't have time to get it back to New Atlantis before the on-board power source fails."

"And waking him up is way more interesting than just hooking him up to a functional cryocan," Vance finished.

She finally smiled, but not at him. "Don't you think it's a great mystery? Who is this guy and why was he floating out here? Since we don't recognize the design, and we know all the Human models from the last hundred of our years, this thing must be incredibly old. The ones we have today aren't recommended for more than fifty consecutive years of use."

He turned back to the can and started poking the buttons.

"What are you looking for? Instructions for the thaw procedure? My AI figured it out an hour ago." Woodley's smirk reminded him that she'd been unbearably smug ever since finding a flaw in his otherwise perfect research on Human brain development at the last conference he'd attended. "If the code doesn't work, there are at least two manual overrides."

"I know that." Vance slid his hand down the side until he found the recessed panel and activated it.

One of the black panels popped open, revealing what looked like a clunky, old-fashioned data pad that was actually physically wired into the cryocan's AI.

Woodley stared over Vance's shoulder. "What is that thing and how did you know it would be there?"

"Scan this and translate whatever old Earth language the data's written in," Vance told his AI, ignoring her.

"You'll need to find some cables and plug it into my hard box. Its system doesn't support remote scans," the AI replied, and he rooted around in a supply cabinet.

"So what is that thing?" Woodley asked.

"I was bored and did some reading about Earth history during your lecture on Tarvarian Fever at last year's conference." Right before he did some other things he now regretted. Vance pulled an adaptive cable, which was supposed to work with any computational device, from the tangled nest of wires in the cabinet. He stuck one end into the AI's hard box and the other into what looked like a cable port on the clunky pad. "About two hundred years ago, they had a trend. If you had a terminal disease like cancer or something, and the doctors couldn't help you—"

"Because their doctors are such idiots." At least she was mocking someone else now.

"Well, I don't know if they're *idiots*." He faked a sympathetic tone. "They could be geniuses who spent thousands of years inventing antibiotics and pregnancy prevention."

They both dissolved into laughter.

"And then they spent another five hundred years trying to cure *cancer*!" Woodley looked at the cryocan, her smile giving way to a guilty look. "Until they finally decided to beg us for the answer."

"We should have hidden the wormhole a lot better before we left the 'less advanced' of our species behind." Was that the CC term now? He pointed at one of the half-lit panels." But before they made contact with us again, these were popular."

"Cryocans?"

"Having yourself stored in one until someone cured whatever was killing you."

"So why isn't this guy still in storage on Earth? How did he end up floating in space?"

Vance gave her his best you-should-know-the-answer look. "You know how fucked up their planet is now? I'm sure it was even worse then. The environment. Electricity. Fossil fuels. Greenhouse gases. Cryostorage was extremely expensive on Earth."

"And being stored in orbit was cheaper…" Woodley frowned. "But how did he get all the way out here? They only found the wormhole seven years ago."

"By that time orbit around Earth was cluttered. Not a secure place to store yourself while frozen."

"So they had themselves launched at… what? They didn't know about the wormhole yet."

Vance watched his AI stream through hundreds of possible access codes. "I don't think they were aiming at anything. The can probably just drifted and wound up going through the wormhole. The humans thought they'd eventually find their own cures. Every one of these things had a beacon, so it could be found and retrieved."

She studied a large, round knot on top of the floating freezer — probably the long-dead beacon. "Dying or not, you'd have to be pretty brave to have yourself frozen and tossed into space, hoping you'd be found and cured one day."

"Yeah, I guess you would. I've interpreted the data," he said as his pad beeped, hoping she'd ignore the fact that his AI had actually done all the work. "It's just like an antiquated version of the patient files we keep. This will tell us what we need to cure."

FOUR

By the time Haylea returned from lunch, she'd learned more useful information than her AI had found about the current problem since it started.

Useful fact # 1: People, in general, didn't much *like* the Humans right now, but they were still *fascinated* by Humans.

Useful fact # 2: Even *one* not-especially-threatening Human could attract the attention of half the People on the station.

Useful fact # 3: Samantha was a particularly fascinating Human, for several reasons. She had refused to go home after traveling to New Atlantis with the first group of Earthers ever to do so five years ago, claiming to find the level of stupidity on her planet as annoying as the People did.

But then the not-so-contentious conflict happened, and she *still* refused to go home—even when the rest of the Earthers fled the station. According to Carlin—who loved to gossip—the night Haylea had glimpsed her on the concourse, Samantha was being hauled off to a departing ship by the Guard.

"The boyfriend, Brad, didn't think it was safe enough and begged Samantha to go back to Earth," Carlin explained over the third My Thigh Haylea had bought her. "When she refused, he volunteered to go with her, despite the obvious risks to his own life as a Person. When she *still* refused, he assumed she didn't want to put him in jeopardy, so he had himself canned and slated for Earth and assumed she'd follow."

"But she didn't."

"Brad miscalculated somewhere. Getting Samantha deported pissed her off so much that she refused to sign the cryo consent forms." Carlin took another sip. "Now, I know someone who knows someone who's a friend of someone who was delivering supplies to the infirmary on the *Adventurer* and saw everything."

"And?"

"Samantha was so angry at Brad for trying to force her to return to Earth, she wouldn't even consider joining him in cryo. Like the Humans say, she was cold as ice about it." Carlin made a loud snorting guffaw at her own bad pun. Haylea forced a fake laugh to encourage her to continue.

"You know what she told the doctor on that doomed ship?"

"What?"

"'When you wake him up on Earth, tell him to send me a postcard.' Then she turned and walked off the ship, not once looking back." Carlin sighed. "Why is it taking so long to get a refill in this place?"

Useful fact #4: Samantha's "crazy Human bartender" routine was bringing more business into the Wormhole in the Wall than Frego had for the last half-year—which explained why the service was slow.

Satisfied she'd gathered enough information, Haylea told Carlin they'd do lunch soon and went for her quick exit plan. Roble was talking to someone at the other end of the bar and hopefully wouldn't notice her leaving—alone.

Now, how to borrow some of Samantha's success and use it to promote herself—er, the station? Returning to her office, Haylea flopped down in her chair and asked her AI to scan for recent news items involving the bar. The initial results were mostly local, but some were from as far away as Ebidor Prime.

A travel channel devoted its "Outer Fringes" segment to the "undiscovered oasis of culture" on Five Alpha, the Wormhole in the Wall. It was so favorable that she suspected Frego had quietly purchased advertising on the channel to be used later. Samantha appeared briefly in the story, but was never specifically mentioned. The Outer Fringes journalist mostly focused on the value of "meeting People—and Non-People!—from all over the sector!"

Twelve hours ago seemed to be the point when the mentions of Samantha started. The first was a local piece about "great bargains." The bar was mentioned on this segment frequently, since the downturn in business had nudged Frego to lower prices. Again, Haylea suspected an indirect payoff, and again, she didn't care if it brought publicity to the station and she officially knew nothing about it.

This report focused mostly on the exciting experience of watching a "real, live Human!" interacting with "the People her Non-People are on the brink of war with!" It was only briefly mentioned that while watching her stalk around on the bar and tell off unruly Human-haters, you could also get a pitcher of beer for only five-and-a-half creds.

The Ebidor Prime travel journalist focused less on price and more on the unique opportunity of "having a beer with someone lonely and misunderstood." Haylea was pretty sure Samantha wasn't drinking with her customers, and from what she'd seen of the Ebidor journalist, he was prone to emotionally bloated stories. Still, free publicity was free publicity.

As the stories grew more recent, they focused more on Samantha, and they weren't all favorable. Two were profiles, delving into her background as a journalist on New Atlantis, possible political motivations for her refusal to leave, and the explosion that killed Brad and twenty-two others. One reporter pointedly noted that Samantha "was the only person who vehemently refused to stay on the doomed *Traveler*." The implication was clear.

How to spin this? The media was trending toward Samantha, not the Wormhole in the Wall or the station, but Haylea could manipulate that. The important thing was not to be too obvious that she wanted to steal some of the media attention for the station. That would piss off Samantha, who was probably getting a bonus for bringing in customers, and maybe Frego, too. The safest course of action was to encourage both of them, and make no effort to overtly foist herself and the station's publicity efforts on the media.

In this case, there really was no need to divert press attention. The more the media covered the Human journalist, the more people would want to see her themselves—and that meant visiting Five Alpha. She could use the station's news log to congratulate the Wormhole and Samantha on their shared success and issue a general statement about it that the reporters would ignore. Woolerton would expect her to do that.

Meanwhile, she'd encourage the "crazy Human bartender" act, maybe even offer suggestions on how to improve it. Yes, Samantha was smart for an Earther and would probably see through Haylea's efforts, but so what? If she was truly as smart as the People, as she claimed, she'd still act in her own best interest, even if it benefited the station, too.

Shaking off the drowsiness from the My Thighs, Haylea told her AI to take dictation on her Action Plan for Woolerton.

FIVE

"Have you ever heard of that disease?" Woodley frowned at her AI's translation of the ancient data as she sat on the tattered guest chair in the exam room.

"No idea. Maybe they cured it already and the beacon failed or something. If it's some kind of cancer, he's going to a hospital closer to New Atlantis. We can't treat it here anymore because of the security risks." Vance scrolled through the data, cross-referencing it with the Human-People Disease Database. "Oh, it's some sort of dementia. Certainly preventable enough if he wasn't having symptoms yet."

"It says that his case was caused by a bad gene and... oh, crap. These people really are slow."

"Oh, because they figured out how genes caused disease and then spent another couple hundred years figuring out how to fix that? You didn't know?"

"Unlike some people, I don't spend all my time studying our annoying distant cousins." Woodley waved her hand at the cryocan. "Anyway, we can fix him. Is there a date on that thing so we can figure out how long he's been floating around?"

"According to my translation of the data, after transposing Human years into People years and figuring in the trip through the wormhole, I would feel comfortable with approximately one-hundred-fifty years," the AI offered.

"And he's still in good shape?" Vance scratched his head. Cryosleeps of more than fifty years were not recommended. Theoretically, at some point cells could start to degrade even with protective drugs. No one had tested the theory, because staying in cryo for longer than a decade or two was highly impractical—and the People weren't bumbling idiots who couldn't fix a simple bad gene, so it had never been necessary the way it apparently was for the Humans.

Woodley shrugged. "According to our scans, he's in good shape considering the circumstances. Let's wake him up."

He reached for the control panel, but stopped. Instead, he stared at the cryochamber, trying to picture the world its inhabitant had left. From what he'd seen in holos and heard from Samantha, Earth was crowded, polluted, and full of annoying morons—and statistically speaking, this guy was probably one of them.

"What's wrong?" Woodley got up and joined him at the cryocan.

Vance shook his head. "I just wish we had time to prepare before waking him up. He didn't even know about the People when he left. Everyone and everything he did know is long gone—even if we sent him back to Earth, he'd barely recognize the place. How will we ever explain who we are?"

"You mean the People?" She shrugged. "We're the better half of the Human race."

"And how are we supposed to tell him that?" He waved at the cryocan. "You know how condescending that sounds, right? And you know how angry the Humans get when they think we're being condescending."

"But it's true. You know their average—what do the Earthers call it? — I.Q. is only a hundred? A hundred!" she repeated, as if she thought he was deaf or, worse, just as dumb as the Humans. "That's equal to five on the Fefferton scale! Once we explain to him how much smarter we are, he'll understand. They *are* smart enough to do *that*."

Vance groaned. "Understanding is one thing. That doesn't mean he won't be insulted. I know you avoid spending time around Humans, but if you'd had to deal with as many of them as I have, you'd understand why simply announcing you're someone's intellectual superior is not the right way to introduce yourself."

She shrugged. "Introduce us any way you want—and, you can keep the Human here and treat him until he's ready to go home, or visit New Atlantis, or whatever he wants to do."

She phrased it as if she was doing him a favor, and in some ways, she was. Treating a more than one-hundred-fifty-years-cryostored Human would get him in all the medical databases. He could write five or six papers on this. Maybe one of these days, the medical community would respect him enough to give him a real job again, instead of stranding him on a poorly-funded station with little support for his research. His mistakes last year had cost him a lot, and he was ready to be done paying the price.

On the other hand, if he knew Woodley, she'd let everyone know that she'd found the Human and diagnosed him, while avoiding the messy problem of actually dealing with him.

"I'll initiate the thawing process." He touched the panel.

It would be almost a day before the patient could be awakened. First he had to warm up slowly, over several hours—any faster would be dangerous. Then he would be transferred to a recovery chamber, where the anti-paralytics would be weaned off, allowing him to sleep through the unpleasant twitching that usually took several hours to work its way out.

As soon as the displays showed everything was proceeding without issue, Vance headed toward the door. "Why don't we go up to the concourse and get something to eat?"

Woodley wrinkled her nose. "Do they have real food or just *Human* restaurants here?"

*   *

"What is this, harass the Human day?" Samantha was *not* responding to Haylea's offer nearly as well as expected.

Haylea tried to determine where she'd gone wrong as she sat in the crowded Wormhole in the Wall. She'd assumed Samantha would be thrilled to be Five Alpha's new spokesperson and appear in the next marketing campaign. Well, Samantha *was* Human, even if she claimed to be as smart as any Person. Maybe she'd misunderstood.

"Did I mention you'll be well-compensated?"

Samantha came around the counter and pulled out a bar stool that bore the iconic logo, "Comet Cove Beer: Drink the Ugly Away!" The logo disappeared as she sat down.

"Let me get this straight—you want to pay me, a living, breathing reminder of why no one wants to visit this station, to endorse your product? To tell people they should pay money to visit this place?"

"You don't understand—"

"Despite what you may have heard, we're not *all* stupid."

Haylea felt panic rising in her chest. Her one good idea was starting to go to crap. "I never said that!"

"Only eighty-two percent of us."

"I never—what?" Surprised by the strange turn in Samantha's rant, Haylea forgot about Rule Number One of Copacetic Communications—*never lose control of the conversation.*

Samantha smiled. "You didn't think I felt the same way you do? That Humans are a bunch of fucking idiots, with few exceptions?"

Haylea wracked her brain for the right response. Generally, it was best to agree with the person you were trying to persuade. But what if this was a trap? Was Samantha going to use her answer against her?

And if so, for what purpose?

"Of course, you have your fair share of idiots here, too," Samantha said, apparently letting the question go as rhetorical.

Haylea breathed a sigh of relief. She knew how to handle *this* conversation. "We have our issues."

"I'll admit you People don't have quite as many 'issues' as we did on Earth." Samantha slid her hand on the bar to call up the AI. "You want a drink? It's on the house."

Haylea frowned. "It's what?"

"Even after five years, I still forget the translation matrix doesn't always account for our expressions. 'On the house' means no charge."

"Oh, of course. Sure, I'll have a Wimmerman's."

Sam flicked her fingers over the holo menu. "You didn't answer my question. Why do you want me as a spokesperson?"

Jerking her head over her shoulder, Haylea indicated the rest of the bar. "A few days ago, this place would have been as empty as the Engleman Corridor at this time."

"I see. So you've figured out that I'm using every bad opinion, every piece of exaggerated or just plain wrong information about my people to attract attention to the bar."

"Yes." Haylea bobbed her head in agreement as the AI sent their drinks down the conveyor. She grabbed the hot pink Wimmerman's bottle and took a sip. "I understand you're probably expecting a bonus from Frego for that. I don't want to interfere with your work here."

"But...."

"But bringing visitors to the station will help Frego, too. In fact, I sent him a message about it earlier, and he thinks it's a great idea."

"Yes, that all makes sense. But are you sure my message will work as well for Five Alpha as it did for the bar? All the people here were already on the station. You're trying to bring new visitors here, right?"

"To be honest, nothing else I've tried has worked. You know what a disaster the peace campaign was."

Samantha shook her head. "Not entirely. It was going okay until you were the victim of bad timing. You couldn't have known that ship was going to blow up."

"I'm sorry." Haylea suddenly remembered Samantha's connection to the explosion. "I didn't mean—"

"It's okay," Samantha said. "That explosion wasn't the fault of anyone on this station. Shit, it was a Human who blew the fucking thing up."

"Well, I didn't mean to bring up all those bad memories."

She shrugged. "I think about the explosion, and Brad, every day, whether anyone mentions it or not. You might as well speak freely. Now, let's get back to your publicity problem."

"Like I said, the whole peace thing ended badly, and the previous campaign was even worse."

"Which was?"

"We had some research that showed People thought the station was unsafe, so we ran a campaign about our safety record." Haylea winced. "At least we'd abandoned that by the time the explosion happened. Even before, it didn't work. I don't know why—I guess the image of the wormhole being a portal to Earth was just too strong to break."

"Maybe you should use that weakness to your advantage. Forget about changing perceptions of the Divide, the station, and Earth. Perceptions are hard to change, and even when they do it usually takes years. I'm guessing you don't have that kind of time."

Haylea nodded.

"So paint this place as a haven for adventurers. You know, people who like to live on the edge, laugh in the face of danger. That will tie in well with the Crazy Human Bartender angle I'm already working."

"That sounds good." Haylea struggled to suppress her excitement. The dumb Human had already come up with a better idea than she'd *ever* had for selling this disaster of a space station!

"That takes care of one segment of the target market. I'm sure you know there's another untapped market?"

"Um... what?"

"Humans? I assume you didn't go after them because they're the reason the station is having issues in the first place, and inviting more of them here would exacerbate the problem?"

Haylea hoped the expression she was contorting her face into said, "That's exactly why I didn't pursue the Human market."

"But now that we're playing up the Earther angle, that's not an issue. Plus, sixty percent of Humans on this side of the Divide live closer to this station than any other, and closer to this station than any colonized world." Samantha tossed back what was left of her drink. "I did some research when I took this job."

"Of course." Haylea could have done the same research, if she'd thought to ask her AI to do it.

"More Humans, more for the adventuresome spirit to enjoy. Then more Earthers will come, and then this station will be filled with more Humans *and* People. I don't have to tell you that means more money." Samantha smiled. "Now, let's talk about how well-compensated you said I was going to be."

Haylea tried not to wince as she asked, "How much do you want?"

Samantha drummed her fingers on the counter. "The thing is, me working for the station could look like a conflict of interest if I was asked to cover a story. Working here is bad enough, but I can argue that I can be objective about any story that doesn't directly affect the bar."

"So you want me to get Frego to give you a raise?" Haylea asked. That didn't sound so bad.

"No. I'm going to tell you what I think might help you get publicity for the station. More people on the station, more customers here — which means Frego will give me more money anyway."

"So what are you saying?"

"I'm saying you don't have to pay me, and I don't work for you. I'm just giving you my opinion. How does that sound?"

"When can you start giving me your opinion?"

SIX

Having left Woodley to eat dinner on her ship—she didn't like to mingle with Humans—Vance entered the Wormhole in the Wall and went to the bar, hoping Samantha was on duty. It didn't take long to spot her, with all that blonde hair contrasting against her black shirt. She was talking to Haylea, and at first he thought he must be interrupting an argument, since Haylea didn't like Samantha—or Earthers in general, at least since the war wrecked her business plan. But then he realized they were smiling and laughing like old friends while Haylea sipped a pink-bottled beer.

As soon as he caught Samantha's eye he waved, and she yelled that she'd be over in a minute. She was sharp for a human, so he got straight to the point when she arrived.

"I was wondering if you could help me with something."

"I didn't realize you had so few patients now that you have to beg for free drinks."

He smiled. "I can pay, thanks. What I need help with has nothing to do with drinking."

"Well, I guess I'm popular today." She snagged his beer from the conveyor and plopped it in front of him, Comet Cove sloshing over the side.

"For three months, no one here wanted anything to do with me. Today, it seemed like everyone on the station had lunch here—and every one of them made an excuse to talk to me, even though ordering through the AI would have been just as accurate and probably faster. Then Haylea wanted my help. And now you." She came around the counter and sat on the stool next to him. "Interesting, isn't it?"

Vance took a swig of his beer and returned Samantha's unblinking stare. "As you might recall, I wanted your help months ago, and I was the one person on this station who wasn't an asshole to you before today. I even treated that growth-stunted lion you call a pet, even though she kept scratching me and I'm not an animal doctor. I found you someone to talk to—"

"Visiting your patient was a favor for *you*," Samantha pointed out. "But you've made your point. Just tell me what you want."

"I'd like your help with another patient."

"Another stroke victim with no visitors?"

He shook his head. "No, this is an entirely different situation. It's also sort of delicate. Could we talk in private?"

"Sure." She got up, flicked her hand over the console to put the bar on automatic, and pointed at the windows. "There's a booth in the corner."

"So what do you want?" she asked as she slid into the tattered booth and he sat across from her.

"I have a new patient—a Human one."

Her eyes widened. "Another Earther showed up? When? I can't believe that news isn't all over the station."

He hunched forward, even though no one was nearby. AIs weren't supposed to gossip, but he'd heard of a few People who programmed theirs to get around that rule. "He sort of came in the cargo bay of a colleague's ship."

"In a coffin?" She always called the cryocans that. He figured it was because Brad died in one.

"Yes, but he didn't come here recently."

"You'll have to be more specific."

Here came the hard part. "I need your promise that this is confidential for now, understood? You'll get an exclusive on a big story, but you can't release it for a few days. Do you agree?"

"Yes. Who is this guy?"

"He's a Human the Guard found floating around. Your people haven't used this type of cryocan recently enough for it to appear in any database we have. However, it does contain a Human male, and his electronic file indicates that he was—sort of stored in space until his illness could be cured."

Samantha's eyes lit up. "There were all these human-interest stories before I left, about how now that we were able to go through the Divide and come back, who knew how many of those we might find—or how many might have found their way to the People."

"According to the databases, this is the first one we've recovered." Vance sipped his beer. "As I understand it, most of those cryocans were equipped with very primitive propulsion systems, and almost no navigational equipment."

She nodded. "That's an understatement. So what do you need my help with?"

"Well, you can imagine trying to explain to this guy who I am, who the People are, what this station is, the history between the People and the Humans, the current tension…."

"Yes. I imagine that would be incredibly overwhelming."

"And once he sees the tail—well, he might panic. Who could blame him?" Vance shook his head. "He might not trust me or my colleague, Woodley—she's the one who brought him here. So I thought it might help to have a Human talk to him."

"I get to interview him and use all this information in my story, as long as I wait until you're ready to make the announcement?"

"With limitations," Vance said. "You can't use any confidential medical information without the patient's permission. And if he doesn't want to be officially interviewed, you have to respect that. You still have to answer his questions, even if he doesn't want to answer yours. In return, you'll get the story of the longest successful cryosleep. What do you say?"

"When do I get to meet him?"

✸
SEVEN

Hank Higgins thought he'd died and gone to heaven.

The last thing he remembered was closing his eyes as the cryo drugs dragged him into the vortex of unconsciousness. The next thing he knew, he was staring up at a bright light.

Then the face of a woman appeared, blocking it out. She had brown hair, green eyes, and a flawless face. The fact that she didn't have wings didn't stop him from assuming she was an angel.

So the cryo hadn't worked, and he had died, and there really was a heaven, and apparently you could get in even if you weren't really sure it existed. Hank didn't know if he should be relieved or sad. He hadn't wanted to die, but he hadn't wanted to live out the rest of his years losing his mind, either.

"Hank? That is your name, right?" The brunette peered at him, her forehead crinkled with concern.

"Uh, yeah." He sat up, finally looking to the side instead of up.

He was lying on a bed, tangled up in wrinkled sheets. Wait, they had that stuff in heaven?

"Hank, I'm Doctor Woodley. I'm one of the doctors who revived you."

"Revived? Oh my god, you found a cure!" Hank peered around the room, which didn't resemble any hospital he'd ever seen—no equipment, no beeping things, no machines with lights and numbers, no smell of disinfectant. The furniture consisted of the bed and two sleek, plastic-looking chairs. He dreaded knowing the answer, but had to ask the question.

"How long was I out?"

"We're not really sure."

He blinked and looked in the direction of the voice. There were two other people in the room, standing in shadow near the doorway. The first to step forward was a man with a mop of curly brown hair and eyes that seemed to be everywhere at once. He was followed by a dark-eyed blonde woman who stared at Hank like he was a two-headed unicorn.

"Hank, I'm Doctor Vance." The man walked up to the bed, grabbed Hank's hand at the wrist with his left hand, then gripped it with his right. It took Hank a few seconds to figure out that he was making a ridiculously awkward attempt at hand shaking. The blonde winced, obviously aware of the discrepancy. The brunette scribbled something on an electronic pad.

"Up and down, not sideways," the blonde hissed at Dr. Vance.

"What do you mean, you're not sure how long I was frozen? Celestial Futures assured me my records would be maintained on Earth and included in my cryo chamber's electronic file." Hank felt a rush of panic. How long had he been frozen that people didn't even shake hands anymore?

"Hank, you're not on Earth." The blonde stepped closer to the bed and yanked Vance's arm away. "That's more than enough hand-shaking, buddy," she mumbled.

In his concern over how long he'd been frozen, Hank hadn't even noticed the idiot was still squeezing his hand and yanking on his arm.

"Where am I?" He looked around the bare room, bewildered. "Did we make contact with aliens?"

"That's sort of complicated." The blonde scratched her head and looked back and forth between the other two. Hank suddenly realized she was here to tell him something he probably wasn't going to be happy to hear.

"What did you say your name was?" She hadn't and he knew it.

"I'm Samantha." She stuck her hand out and waited for him to shake it. Vance shuffled from foot to foot, embarrassed. The brunette scribbled some more.

For the first time in his life, Hank told a woman the absolute, un-edited, un-remixed truth. "I'm Hank Higgins, and I don't know what the hell is going on."

Samantha smiled. "Well, I'm here to help you with that. Um…" She looked at the other two. "Why don't you let me and Hank talk for a few minutes, huh?"

They looked at each other, shrugged and retreated, backing up awk-wardly as if afraid to take their eyes off him, until they made it out the door. Both wore plain shirts and pants that didn't look anything like the white medical coats and scrubs he was used to seeing on doctors.

Samantha pulled up a chair and sat next to Hank. "I don't really know where to start."

"Start with where I am. Are we on a spaceship or a planet?" The room had no windows.

"We're on Space Station Five Alpha." She looked relieved by the sim-plicity of the question. "Earth is on the other side of the Divide — that would be the wormhole your cof — I mean, your cryocan went through."

"So my can survived the trip, and you tracked the beacon even through this wormhole thing?"

"If by 'you', you mean us—no." Samantha waved an arm around the room. The look on her face said it might be easier to explain nuclear physics to a kindergarten class. "If you mean the—people here, that's also a no. The truth is, Doctor Woodley's ship stumbled onto your coffin—I'm sorry, your cryocan—by accident. Because this was such an unusual situation, she asked Doctor Vance for a consult."

Hank was so confused he didn't know what to ask next. Finally he blurted out the simplest question—the one that involved his pocketbook. "But what about the beacon? Did it fail? Because I shelled out some big bucks for that cryo chamber, and the salesman guaranteed me my money back if the relocation feature failed."

Samantha nodded. "The wormhole probably damaged it. I bet the salesman at Celestial Futures never expected that."

He got the picture. "So my ten-grand-a-pop cryo container has a beacon that just can't hold up in space?"

"Not if it travels through a wormhole. You might try for a refund, if Celestial Futures is still in business." She shrugged. "Of course, they might point out that their product kept you alive a lot longer than the fifty years they probably guaranteed."

That reminded him of the question that had been bothering him since he woke up. "You said you weren't sure how long I'd been in cryo, but you had an approximate idea?"

She nodded. "Doctor Vance looked over your chart and tried to compare the way they keep dates on Earth to the People calendar. He figures it was about a hundred and fifty years. Give or take a few."

"A hundred and…."

He had known he might be in cryo for a while. At the time he'd gone under, no one had been a slushie—was that still the slang?—for more than a few decades. But the cat-faced salesman at Celestial Futures Cryogenics Facility had been quick to tell him there was no proof a person couldn't safely stay under for a lot longer, just because no one had *tried* it. Besides, with all the medical miracles happening nowadays, it probably wouldn't be that long anyway, would it?

Hank shook his head, as if that would make the truth go away. So this was it. He really *had* been under for years. A century and a half even. That meant everyone he'd known on Earth was long dead. There would be no going back to see his friends and family again. No seeing Emily again. He'd known she would move on with her life—hell, he'd insisted she move on, despite her protests to the contrary. But when he'd gotten into the cryo container, as they put the mask over his face and started sticking him, installing tubes and wires like he was some sort of bizarre science experiment, he'd thought about seeing her again—even if she was suddenly years older than him. Now that fantasy wasn't even remotely possible.

"Everyone I ever knew is dead."

He didn't realize he'd said it out loud until he saw the look on Samantha's face.

"I'm sorry, Hank," she said. "Do you, um, want a minute?"

"No." All of a sudden, the last thing he wanted was to be alone. "No, I have to get used to it—and I still want to know more."

"Listen, Hank." She leaned forward and lowered her voice. "There's something I'm obligated to tell you."

"Uh, okay." What the hell, she might as well tell him that aliens were bad in bed and he should go back to Earth just as soon as he was cured. Nothing would shock him right now.

"I'm not a doctor. Vance and Woodley asked me to speak with you for a couple reasons."

Oh great, a therapist. Just what he needed. He just woke up, didn't even know if he'd been cured yet, found out everyone he'd ever met in his life was long dead and that he was on an alien space station, and they wanted him to immediately tell some headshrinking quack how that made him feel, when he didn't even have a clue?

"So you're like a counselor?"

"Oh, no, nothing like that. They thought I should be here when you woke up because I'm from Earth, too."

"So the other two were born here, on the station?" There was a whole generation of people who had never even been to Earth?

"Well, they were born on this side of the Divide," she said. "They may have grown up on New Atlantis—I don't know about their childhoods. I've only known Vance for a few months, and I just met Woodley. But to answer your question, neither of them has been to Earth, no."

He hadn't asked that question, but he had thought about it.

Samantha scrunched up her face. "Anyway, I'm a journalist, and I really want to cover this story, about you waking up after a hundred and fifty years."

"You're a reporter? That explains it." Hank had a feeling that sounded bad, although he'd meant that it explained why she was such a good listener.

"Look, everything you've said so far is off the record unless you say otherwise. If you don't want to be officially interviewed, I won't use anything you say to me—I promised Vance. I'll still answer any questions you have—and I'll cover the story with the official information he releases." She caught his eye and gave him what was probably a well-calculated and well-practiced smile.

"That being said, I would very much like to interview you on the record. This is such an amazing story, for both of our peoples. It's the first time anyone has spent so much time in cryo, the first time someone from your generation has visited this side of the Divide, the first time someone who was cryostored in space will be successfully cured. The press will cover it whether you give me an interview or not, but you might want to set the record straight."

Hank smiled back at Samantha. She was manipulating him, using her Earth heritage to make him feel a probably-all-in-his-head rapport to get an interview. Despite the circumstances, she was trying to wrangle a soundbite from someone who didn't have a clue what he should be feeling or why right now, and she was going to walk out of here with a scoop whether he agreed to be interviewed or not.

And he really didn't mind.

His old life was gone, he'd spent all his money—what currency did they use here anyway?—and he had no ties, here or on Earth. His medical treatment probably wouldn't be cheap, and even if they had some sort of free health care here, what would he do afterward? There wouldn't be any jobs for a computer repair tech from 150 years ago. Hell, he probably wouldn't recognize the computers they had now. If all this publicity could help him make a little money, maybe get a new job and meet some people here, why the hell shouldn't he be as much of an opportunist as Samantha?

"I'd be happy to be interviewed on the record," he said. "I promise to answer all your questions truthfully, but you have to do the same for me. Now I want to know what you're not telling me—right now. I want the truth, straight up. What the hell is going on here?"

✴
EIGHT

"You're fucking kidding me."

The guy in the bed looked like a blue-collar, NASCAR-watching, Budweiser-drinking guy from middle America. He had the name Emily tattooed on one shoulder and a crushed beer can on the other. His shaggy hair had probably never been in style, and his generally clueless expression was probably attractive to some women who went for that "aw, shucks" demeanor.

Samantha couldn't care less about any of that. This was the most interesting story she'd encountered since she'd been on Five Alpha. Aside from the fact that there was little news on the nearly-deserted station, there was another problem she hadn't told Frego the other day—much of *Glass*'s audience no longer wanted to listen to a Human journalist— but they might make an exception for a scoop like this. Not only that, but Hank's story would dovetail nicely with her crazy Human campaign—only now, there would be another Human.

STUPID HUMANS

The best way to deal with someone like Hank was to give him what he wanted—the truth, straight up. Unfortunately, as she'd expected, he was having a little trouble *believing* the truth, straight up.

"You're telling me there really *was* a lost colony of Atlantis, and they *got* themselves lost from the whole planet to get away from all the stupid people? Which would be everyone left on Earth, including me, before I left? You seriously expect me to believe that?"

"They call us Humans, Hank." Samantha suddenly felt very tired. "Although we share more than ninety-nine point ninety-nine percent of the same DNA, they think of themselves as the People and us as the Humans."

"But we're all Humans?"

"From a scientific standpoint, yes. Despite what some people here may think, we are all the same species."

Hank shook his head. "No. *No.* This is crazy. You can't expect me to believe it."

"You believed there were aliens out here. You believed they might be advanced enough to cure you of a disease that Humans can't." Samantha shrugged. "To me, that would be harder to believe than the idea that some unusually smart Humans made it off Earth and colonized another planet."

Hank gestured to the doorway. "Those other... people who were here. Did I see—did one of them have a tail?"

"I asked about that when I first came here. They tried to say they had them when they left Earth, but I called bullshit on that. I told them that Humans, in their current tailless form, had been around roughly two-hundred-thousand years, and the People—what they call themselves—only ran away from home about four thousand years ago."

"They lied?" Hank raised his eyebrows. "Why? What are the tails for?"

"They were surprised when I told them how long we'd been without tails. Honestly, I don't think it was a lie. They don't know every-thing their ancestors were doing four thousand years ago any more than you and I do. And it's not like they have a fossil record here, at least not one for their own evolution."

"So they just have tails now, and no one knows why?"

"I have a theory. I told you they didn't want us to be able to find and follow them easily, right?"

"Right...."

"I think the tails were just in case we found them anyway—which we eventually did," she said. "So they could tell themselves from us easily."

Hank shook his head like that would change what he was hearing. "And we're at war with the tailed Humans now?"

"Did you hear what I just said? We're *all* Human. What do Humans do? We get in wars over stupid shit and kill each other." Samantha had once taken a journalism class in which she was told reporters should keep their opinions out of the story. She'd never been very good at that.

Hank just stared at her, wide-eyed.

"Okay, that might have sounded a little harsh, but you have to admit it makes sense based on what you know about humanity." She didn't want to completely horrify Hank and make him clam up, even if he *had* told her he wanted "the truth, straight up." "What did we do in your era, hold hands and sing songs about love and peace?"

Hank rolled his eyes. "I guess we never did that—and we did have a lot of wars over stupid shit. What's this one about?"

"Technically, neither of our governments has declared war on the oth-er." She raked a hand through her hair. This really was a fucked-up mess to explain to an outsider. "To make a long story short, someone pissed off someone else, a ship exploded, someone retaliated without knowing all the facts, then the other side retaliated. Before you know it, you've got people killing each other, and neither government knows how to stop it."

"Religion, sex, or money?"

"It's kind of about all of those." She considered. "Basically, every crazy fringe group on Earth is throwing themselves through the wormhole and causing trouble. There's at least one group of whackos for every major religion, and several minor ones, and even a new one that was started after we found the wormhole. They claim the People are Gods who can only be properly worshipped after we make them immortal by killing them all."

Hank scrunched up his face in an embarrassed grimace. "I wish I could say that sounds like something that would never happen on Earth, but it really doesn't."

"That's not all. Some of the best-funded groups have nothing to do with religion. There's a big one called Rednecks for Reparations."

Hank face-palmed.

"Before we found the Divide, they just hated big corporations, but now they hate the People for leaving us on Earth."

"I don't see the connection."

"Big corporations pay off politicians who are voted into office by idiots, which we are because the People ditched us and headed for the stars."

Hank groaned.

"So anyway, I think their motto is 'The South's gonna do it again—in space this time.'"

"They want to secede and move to a space station or something? What are they going to do, have a rodeo on an asteroid?"

"I don't think they have that much of a plan," she said. "Anyway, there are also groups who are mad that the People won't share all their technological advancements with us."

"Why not?"

"Well, the reasons are complicated. We can talk about them later." Vance had cautioned her not to overwhelm Hank with too much info at once. "The point is, every whackjob group on Earth is trying to blow up stuff over here, the People are trying to stop them without provoking an official war with our government, the UNE is trying to stop their own People while not pissing off the People, and the whole thing is just one big mess."

Hank scratched his head. "So they don't have whackjobs over here? Did they like, remove the crazy gene from the pool or something?"

She shook her head. "No, they still have crazies. Every society does. The main difference is that the nutjobs here have no or very few followers. They don't have the herd mentality that we do, so their whackos are pretty much limited to whatever they can do on their own."

"They don't squabble over religion here? Do they even have religion?"

"Oh, sure," she said. "They have lots of different ideas about religion, kind of like we do. But when they talk about it, they consider it an interesting intellectual debate. They would never think of starting a war over it. But like I said, there are plenty of non-religious crazies running around here, too."

"So Earth's biggest export is conflict?"

"Pretty much. It all boils down to one thing—the People have stuff the Humans want, and everything else is just an excuse to try to take it."

Hank started chuckling. Then he started laughing. Samantha was a little surprised, since she didn't see anything particularly hilarious about the shitty state of humanity, but then again, look at what he'd been through in the past hour. He was probably in shock or something. Unsure what she was supposed to do in this situation, she opted for nothing.

"I'm sorry," Hank gasped, still hitching in breaths between peals of laughter. "You probably think I'm crazy."

"No, but I am curious what's so funny about what I just said."

Hank shook his head. "It's just that I've been in cryo for a a hundred fifty-something years, and not one damn thing has changed!"

✳   ✳

"What do you think?" Vance asked Woodley, as they monitored Hank and Samantha's conversation in his office.

Woodley shook her head. "I guess it's going as well as it could. There's no guide on how to handle these things."

Vance nodded his head toward the door. "When she releases this story, we'll have a huge media frenzy."

"You'll have your AI prepare a statement for the public?"

"Yes, and I'd like it to state we're close to publishing a report on the intricacies of this situation." Since Woodley wasn't leaving, he was going to have to share credit with her.

She nodded. "There are a lot of aspects to cover. His physical health after all that time seems surprisingly good—"

"And the emotional and mental aspects of waking up after so many years."

"And how simple it will be to replace the gene for whatever he's going to get otherwise."

"Which parts do you want to work on?"

She smiled. "I *did* bring this case to you."

"You want the cure?"

"And the mental health issues."

Vance breathed a sigh of relief. He really didn't want to write 5,000 words about someone else's feelings anyway. He didn't even want to *think* 5,000 words about his own. Now, if he could just keep her from taking credit for everything....

NINE

Haylea could see the press party for Hank Higgins going the way of her peace rally—right down the crapper, as Samantha liked to say.

The whole thing had sounded wonderful when the Human bartender explained it two days ago—long-lost Human from a century and a half ago, found floating in a remote area of space by People, rescued and revived right here on Five Alpha. In less than an hour, he'd learned that anyone he'd known in his previous life was long dead, there was a group of intelligent—rephrase that, *more* intelligent—rephrase that, differently intellectualized—Humans who left Earth even longer ago than he did, these Humans now called themselves People and the dumb—*differently intellectualized!*—Humans the Humans or sometimes Earthers, the Humans and the People were in the midst of a big mess that no one wanted to call a war, and not surprisingly, a lot of People just didn't like Humans.

It was a huge story, and Haylea had a hard time keeping it to herself, although Sam was right—they needed a plan before releasing the story. Also, Vance and Woodley had to make sure Hank was up to it, physically and mentally. It wouldn't look good if the guy had a breakdown in the middle of the press party, and those Earthers were so mentally unstable in *normal* circumstances.

Wait, that could be good news. Two crazy Humans would be better than one crazy Human—although Hank might not like that title. Maybe Samantha could think of another image for him. Either way, another nutty Earther would attract more adventure-seekers. Maybe the station could start a search and rescue program for others like Hank—that would be great publicity.

Who else might have been lost coming through the Divide? According to Hank, his trip had bankrupted him, so it seemed reasonable that any others floating around probably had a lot of money. Surely some of them thought to have a few valuables stuffed into the cryocan with them, right? Not all of those people would have survived 150 years in space. She was about to ask her AI to research the legalities of "salvaging" such finds when it said, "There's a news story you should watch."

The reporter, her dark hair fanning out around her head in the latest fashion, read with a deeply serious expression on her face. Did they practice that look in the mirror?

"The People Coalition released a travel advisory for the Divide region today," she said, face taut with grimness. "Security reports show an increased likelihood of Human attacks in the area within three light-years of the wormhole. A coalition representative says the Guard is working to thwart these attacks, but advises travelers to use caution when approaching the area, and to reconsider visiting it in the next few days. No specific details of the threats were given for security reasons."

Haylea let her head fall to her desk with a decidedly loud thunk. "Why did this have to happen right now when I was just starting to make progress?"

"The Humans have something called Murphy's Law," her AI said, its tone neutral. "Roughly translated, it says that if something can go wrong, it probably will. Also, Woolerton sent a memo that he wants an action plan for dealing with this latest issue."

"I have to see Samantha." Haylea stood and stomped out the door.

* *

"That's not really a problem," Samantha said in a low tone, after Haylea rushed into the bar and blurted out the bad news.

"How is it not really a problem? The government is telling people to stay away from here and the news media is blasting it all over the galaxy!"

"No, they're just suggesting caution when considering a visit to this area. And remember, we're going after the thrill-seekers who won't give a shit about that kind of warning."

Haylea pointed at one of the drinks rolling off the conveyor, a pink bottle of Wimmerman's. "You better get me one of those."

"You're missing one other very good thing about this news." Samantha swiped the bottle and slid it down the bar with one flick of her hand.

Haylea grabbed it. "Enlighten me."

"We have an expression on Earth — there's no such thing as bad publicity. There might be a few exceptions to that rule, but this isn't one of them. If it gets media attention for the station, this story is a good thing. In fact, it's probably exponentially increased the amount of coverage we'll get for the press party tomorrow. How did you pitch it, anyway?"

"I said we'd be holding a press party to announce a new medical breakthrough made by the station's Head Doctor."

Samantha snickered.

"What?"

"On Earth, a head doctor is a shrink."

Haylea frowned.

"A psychiatrist?"

"Oh, you mean a doctor who specializes in mental diseases?"

"That's it." Samantha stared over Haylea's shoulder. "Uh-oh. I wonder what she wants?"

Haylea turned around. Anna, the ship's Head Security Officer, walked up to them.

"You're really busy today." She sat next to Haylea at the bar.

"We've been busy the last few days. It's because of Haylea's new marketing plan for the station," Samantha said. "Maybe Frego mentioned it to you?"

Anna nodded. "Briefly. We don't get much time to talk since he's out in the Morvallian sector. With this new threat to the Divide, he probably won't be back for a long time."

"Is that why you're here?" Samantha asked. "I want you to know I've set the AI security to its highest level."

Anna nodded. "I'm glad to hear that. I did want to talk to you about security, but not about that. I'm concerned that your crazy Human routine might make a target of you, the bar, and even the station—especially with the latest threats."

Haylea nearly choked on her Wimmerman's. She didn't like where this was going.

"I appreciate your concerns," Samantha said smoothly. "Like I told you, I've increased the threat level here at the bar, and I'm sure your department has increased security station wide, right?"

"Yes, of course," Anna said. "But you might want to ease off on the campaign for a few days—just to be safe."

"Are you saying your staff isn't adequately prepared to protect the station?" Samantha asked.

Haylea winced. This conversation was going down like a shooting star and she had no idea how to stop it.

"I'm sure that's not what she's saying," she stammered.

"Of course it isn't," Anna said through gritted teeth. "I just thought you might want to avoid exacerbating an already volatile situation."

Samantha shrugged. "There's already been an alert for the whole area. If someone is planning an attack, they're going to do it regardless of what I do. We can't go around living our lives in fear forever."

Did Anna have any authority here? She and Frego had been romantic partners for years, but as far as Haylea knew, the bar had always been Frego's business. However, she really had no idea what the formal agreement was. Could Anna order Haylea to stop the campaign?

Anna stared at Samantha for a moment. Samantha stood behind the bar, arms crossed, mouth pressed into a firm line. Anna tapped her fingers on the counter, watching her. Finally, she shoved back her stool and stood up.

"Right. Well, I just came to warn you and make a suggestion. Frego didn't like it either, but he said it was your decision since you're responsible for the bar. Just make sure you keep security measures to the full standard."

"I'll do that."

"Thank you." Anna turned and walked out.

"Was that an implied threat?" Haylea asked when the head of security was out of hearing range.

"Yes—if anything happens, Frego blames me and I get fired. Now, let's get back to planning the press party, okay?"

"Should we still go through with it?" Woolerton could *definitely* end Haylea's employment if he thought her plan put the station at undue risk.

"Of course." Samantha flapped her hand in the air as if swatting a fly. "I wasn't making shit up just now—if an attack is planned, it'll happen no matter what. Look at the *Traveler*—there was no security alert for the area, and no one was exercising a crazy Human marketing scheme. Besides, with Vance's announcement about Hank tomorrow, this station is going to get all kinds of attention, and it's all going to be about Humans."

"I guess you're right," Haylea admitted, making a mental note that Samantha's logic would be a good way to cover her ass if anything *did* go wrong.

"Now, tell me about the press advisory Vance released to the medical community," Samantha said. "How many quacks are we expecting?"

TEN

The lights dimmed and the dallying reporters dragged their mini sandwiches and champagne—the People didn't have any dumb rules about drinking on the job—to their tables. Haylea had borrowed extras from some of the less-popular restaurants, like Earth Hearth—for a significant rental fee, of course. It didn't look like they were all necessary at the moment, but Samantha suspected that after the announcement reporters would flood the station. Hank, Vance, and Woodley sat beside her near the podium.

Vance got up, stumbled through a few remarks about what an historic occasion this was, then said his patient would tell the story in his own words. The holo Samantha had helped them prepare appeared in the space between their podium and the audience.

The recording opened on Hank, one day after he woke up. His hair had been trimmed into a current People style—as he requested, having admitted to knowing nothing about hair and fashion—and he was freshly shaved for the first time in a century and a half. Haylea had built him a wardrobe—she had a deal with one of the station's struggling stores—and for the shoot she'd suggested a blue shirt, probably because its sleeves were long enough to hide the beer can tattoo.

"My name is Hank Higgins," Holo Hank said, "And this computer"—he held up a data pad Haylea had given him—"just calculated my age. Guess what it is? Adjusting for a lot of factors I don't really understand, I am one-hundred-eighty-five years old."

Some audience members stirred, while a few whispered or tapped their data pads. Youth-regeneration treatments were very effective, but there was a limit. It was one thing for a seventy-year-old to look thirty-five, but a hundred-eighty-five-year-old was another story. Besides the usual hallmarks of aging—wrinkles, sagging—there were more subtle signs. Older people tended to get slower, even if their joints were replaced and their aches and pains cured.

Dr. Vance had told Samantha once that it wasn't really physical. "After a century, most people just aren't in a rush to do *anything*."

But Holo Hank was talking as fast as a used-spaceship salesperson. "The thing is, I've only been awake and, uh, animated, for about thirty-five of those years. Until yesterday, I had been in cryosleep for a little more than a hundred fifty years."

This aroused the audience a bit more. The longest anyone, Human or Person, had been in cryo was fifty-seven years—and that was the consequence of a tragic filing error, resulting in the victim winning ten million dollars in a lawsuit against the storage facility on Earth.

"This seems weird to me, to have to say this, but—I'm Human," Holo Hank continued. "A hundred fifty years ago, on Earth, we hadn't found the wormhole yet. Even if we had, it would have taken years to get there with our tech.

"My mother had several family members, including her own mother, who died young of a kind of dementia, something you've probably never heard of here — I've been told you solved genetic problems centuries ago.

"Usually this disease doesn't happen until much later in life, but if you have a particular bad gene, the symptoms can start as early as your forties. What happens is that your memory starts to go, and I mean in a big way. At first it's just little things, like forgetting what you walked into a room to do, or where you left your keys." Hank smiled. "I was telling this to my doctors the other day, since they'd never heard of it either, and Doctor Vance didn't know what keys were. Apparently, now you lock and unlock your door with a DNA scan."

Smiles and chuckles around the room. Just as Samantha had expected, the audience was warming to Hank. Human or not, he was non-threatening, unassuming, just a regular guy in a crazy situation.

"Anyway, forgetting little things quickly turns into forgetting big things." Hank's smile dissolved into a grimace. "You don't recognize people you've known for years—even your significant other, your children, your best friends. Eventually you need round-the-clock care, or else you won't remember to eat.

"It's an awful way to go, losing your mind like that—my mother suffered for four years before she finally died. She begged to be euthanized, but at the time, it was only legal for people who were terminally ill and in severe physical pain.

"The thing is, we couldn't cure genetic diseases then, but we could identify the genes. My mother chose not to receive testing, and she decided to have a kid, knowing that she could have this disease and, if so, she could pass it on."

The room went very quiet. Samantha didn't think anyone here had ever considered such a problem. If you had a bad gene, it got switched off or replaced at birth, problem solved. No one had to worry about passing an awful disease on to their offspring.

"I don't think I'll ever forgive her," Hank said. "She could have gone to a fertility clinic and asked to have any harmful genes removed, but then she would have had to admit she might have a problem, and she refused to do that. She was a free spirit, one of those positive-thinking idiots who go around babbling if they *believe* everything will work out great, it will. So she didn't go to a fertility clinic when she wanted to have a baby. She had a one-night stand with some dope I never met, and I was born doomed to suffer the same horrible fate she did.

"When my mother started to have symptoms, I was only nineteen, but I was just old enough to make the decision for myself—I got genetic testing. I knew there was nothing that could be done if I had it, but I also knew I could at least avoid screwing up someone else's life like my mother did to me. I told myself it wasn't necessarily an early death sentence—they were making medical advances all the time back then. Even the doctors I talked to seemed confident that there would be a cure in twenty years.

"Even so, I really hoped that test would be negative, and I was devastated when it wasn't. I'm not proud of this, but I didn't visit my mom much after that." Holo Hank looked down, shaking his head. "If she had had cancer or something, I would have been there with her. But I didn't want to watch my future—the future I was sentenced to because of her. That probably makes me a bad son, and I'm sorry for that—but doesn't recklessly passing on bad genes make you a bad parent, too? You're responsible for that person. That life."

The reporters stared at their data pads in a way that suggested they were either broadcasting live or sending video back for immediate editing. Those who weren't looking at their pads stared at the holo, riveted.

"Anyway, I spent the next twenty years hoping a cure would be found. I thought about getting married and having a family, but I always decided to wait for a cure. Yes, I could have had a genetic counselor filter out the bad genes for me. But I didn't think it was fair to have kids when I knew there was a good chance I wouldn't be around for very long.

"Then I met a wonderful woman named Emily. She was beautiful and smart and I could talk to her for hours without getting bored. I tried so hard not to fall in love with her." He shook his head. "But I just couldn't help it, and unfortunately for her, she fell in love with me, too.

"I tried to push her away. I told her about my situation, about why I really couldn't get into any long-term relationships. I hoped that would let her down easy, but she said she wanted to be with me even if we didn't have that long.

"As much as I loved her, I tried everything to get rid of her. I took a job on the other side of the country, hoping I could lose her that way." Hank half-smiled and half-grimaced. "But Emily followed me! She said she could spend the next ten years miserable because she wasn't with me, or spend most of it happy because she was. Then she said she was going to try to find me a cure, whether I helped her or not.

"Against my better judgment, I finally gave in. I knew it was the selfish thing to do, but I guess I thought, if I'm going to die sixty years ahead of everyone else, I deserve to be happy for a few years before I go, right? And it wasn't like I didn't *try* to get rid of Emily for her own good. Besides, she said she'd be miserable for years either way, right?"

Samantha scanned the news feeds. Stories from half a dozen media organizations bubbled up on the screen. *Glass* streamed her live feed, several bubbles down, with a link to the longer story she'd filed just before Vance introduced the holo.

It didn't matter how hard journalists tried to focus on just the facts — news was almost always equal parts fact and opinion. The opinions on this story, of both reporters and readers, were all over the board.

"Obviously Human propaganda! They stuck this guy in a can and told him to make up some lie about being a hundred-eighty-year-old victim of his species' stupidity just to gain our sympathy."

"So sad. Maybe if his people hadn't spent so much time in the last four thousand years thinking up new ways to kill each other they could have cured this poor guy in his own time period...."

"If curing a genetic disease is the big breakthrough Vance wants credit for, he's going to be disappointed. Didn't we do that right after we got away from Earth?"

"Hank Higgins just put a Human face on the Human-People conflict."

Samantha blacked her pad and looked at Hank. Like the audience, he stared at the holo, transfixed, as if he didn't know what was going to happen next.

"After that, Emily became obsessed with finding a cure for me, hassling every geneticist she could find. No matter how many times they told her they could only prevent future generations from getting my disease, that there was nothing they could do for me, she wouldn't give up.

"It was my worst nightmare. My problem had become Emily's problem, and she was going to waste her life trying to cure me. I wished that I'd never let her back into my life. I wished I'd never met her." Holo Hank smacked himself in the forehead as he relived the frustration. "I wished I didn't have this goddamn disease!

"Then I saw a news story about a man with cancer that had spread. Stage four was what they called it. I guess that means write your will and pick out a coffin.

"Euthanasia was allowed for terminal cancer, but this guy was on the news because instead of being euthanized, he was going to be put in cryostorage. Because of the low temperatures and very low levels of oxygen, the doctors at the Celestial Futures Cryogenics Facility were confident his condition wouldn't deteriorate for years in the can.

"The idea of putting a terminally ill person into cryo until his illness could be cured wasn't new, but it wasn't as popular as you might think—a lot of people figured there wouldn't be a cure until everyone they knew was dead, if ever, so what was the use? Some were afraid it wouldn't work and they'd lose the few healthy weeks or months they had left, just to die anyway.

"The thing was—I don't know how this works here, but at that time, you still had to be relatively healthy to go into cryo. The risk of death was pretty low for someone really healthy, but if you were in bad shape, there was a good chance you wouldn't survive. So you had to go in before you got too sick, if that was what you wanted.

"Well, this guy with cancer wanted to do it. I remember him telling the reporter he'd rather take a chance that he could come back to his loved ones, ten or twenty years from now, than spend a few more weeks dreading the inevitable.

"So I saw that and thought maybe that could be the solution for me. At least I might have some slight chance at the life I'd always been denied. Even Emily might feel better if she thought I might be cured *eventually*. In reality, I knew she'd probably be an old woman by the time anyone got around to finding a cure, and I sure didn't want her to wait around for me.

"That's why I decided to get stored in space, so she'd *have* to accept that I was gone. Celestial Futures offered both services—storage on Earth or in orbit, or being shot far out, past Mars. The first option was bigtime expensive, and orbit wasn't much cheaper, certainly nothing I could afford for more than a few years. The last thing I wanted was Emily struggling to pay for it, which I knew was exactly what she'd do even if I told her not to.

"Besides, the space idea didn't seem that crazy. You could be tracked down with the beacon if they found a cure. Most importantly, it was a one-time fee, versus paying a fortune for long-term storage.

"So I took the chance. I didn't tell Emily what I was going to do. I know I should have, but I chickened out. Couldn't do it. So I went to the clinic, signed the papers, and wrote Emily a message explaining what I was doing and why. I made their administrator promise he'd wait until several days after I'd been ejected from the facility in orbit before forwarding the message to her.

"I have to admit, it was scary. The doctor at the facility told me it was very safe, that they would use a combination of drugs to preserve me. He said one of them came from some sort of zombie fish toxin that lowers your metabolism and puts you in a state of near death. By itself it can be fatal, but they give you these other drugs that prevent cell damage. The doctor told me this drug cocktail could prevent cell damage indefinitely, but only if my body was in a state of really, extremely low metabolism, from the fish poison or whatever. They also give you medication to thin your blood, keep your cells from exploding or something, and, uh, put you to sleep. I'll be honest, the whole thing sounded insane, and if slowly dying while losing my mind wasn't the alternative, I never would've considered it. But those were my choices.

"So I got into this cold, scary-looking box, and I lay there as the doctors hooked me up to all these tubes and wires, like I was Frankenstein or something. I started feeling sleepy, and I wasn't cold anymore. I felt like I was lying on the beach, and this peaceful, warm wave washed over me. That's the last thing I remember before everything went black.

"And then I woke up here, on this station, in the infirmary with Doctor Vance and Doctor Woodley. Now I expect you'll all have some questions."

The holo faded and every face in the audience stared through the space where it had played to the podium. Haylea nudged Hank and he got up, straightened his shirt, and shuffled to the center of the stage as reporters screamed questions.

✳
ELEVEN

The next two hours went by in a blur for Hank. Reporters—and, he suspected, some regular people who had showed up for free food and decided they were interested— shouted questions so fast he couldn't keep up.

Haylea stood and slammed her palm on the table. The thud echoed around the room, thanks to all the microphones floating around, and questions stopped in mid-air.

"If you'll all return to your seats, questions will be taken in an orderly fashion, one at a time. We'll start with you." She pointed at a portly guy with a beard.

He sort of half-rose, looking at Haylea like he was waiting for her to sit down. After an awkward few seconds of silence, during which she stood her ground, he finally straightened up and asked, "What do you plan to do now?"

Haylea and Samantha had prepared Hank for all kinds of questions: *How do you feel about the don't-call-it-a-war? Are you a Human sympathizer? What do you say to those who think your sudden appearance and extraordinary story are just a little too convenient? Do you plan to go back to Earth as soon as you're cured, or would you like to visit New Atlantis? How does it feel to find out you're part of the dumb half of your species?*

None of those questions would have caught him off guard. But what did he plan to do now? He didn't have the slightest idea—so he said so.

After that, answering questions got a lot easier.

"Look, I wasn't that interested in Human politics on Earth a hundred fifty years ago, and I don't have a fucking clue what's going on now." Haylea had assured him that no one here was offended by or attempted to censor profanity. At least *that* was a relief. "I never understood why we had so many damn wars on Earth. I always figured we should all be able to get along, but I wasn't naïve enough to believe it could actually happen, so I just wasn't interested. Right now I have more than enough things to sort out in my life before I worry about Human/People politics."

"If I'm part of a big Human conspiracy to take over New Atlantis, no one told me about it."

"Yes, Dr. Vance believes he can cure me. He wasn't familiar with my disease, but after scanning my DNA he found the problem and replaced the bad gene with a healthy one."

At that point, Vance and Woodley jumped in, both trying to talk at once. After they discussed some boring medical mumbo-jumbo that Hank didn't begin to understand, they sat down, and the reporters went back to shooting questions at Hank until Haylea yelled for them to wrap things up. He took one final question.

"Will you go back to Earth or do you plan to stay here?"

"You know, I'm not in any big rush to go back home," Hank said.

"It would be interesting to see how it's changed, but everyone I knew there is gone now. I think if I went back right away it would just be sad. Besides, I want to spend time here, getting used to all the new technology. Then I'd like the visit some of the other planets and space-ports out here—I think I'd like to be a tourist for a while."

*   *

Anna had been running station security for Five Alpha for more than twelve People years. There were the usual problems—petty theft, public intoxication, occasional robbery or vandalism. After the Humans showed up five years ago, though, threat levels had been raised insanely high. Given the circumstances that had been under-standable, but there hadn't been any real threat until the let's-not-call-it-a-war-because-that-sounds-bad situation began.

Until then, she'd enjoyed her job. No two days were ever the same, most of the crimes were more laughable than harmful, and she met a lot of interesting people. There were the Humans, a new addition, but there were also traders, travelers, and tourists from every corner of the galaxy—on both sides of the Divide now. She loved telling stories about her adventures on the job—the one about the drunk teenagers who managed to turn off the artificial gravity in their flyer *before* puking everywhere always got a good laugh.

But since the damn Humans started the conflict, everything had changed. Now she spent most of her time worrying about the station being attacked. Not that it wasn't heavily defended—the local Guard unit prowled the sector every day, checking ship authenticity, scanning for weapons, poking every piece of space junk with a robotic stick to see if it poked back. Two other units from the station covered the same area, and the automated Protector guarded the wormhole.

The station itself was as well-fortified as she could manage on Woolerton's security budget, with weapons scanners and guards on every dock. Incoming ships were checked thoroughly, and every doorway on the station scanned for weapons, explosives, and now, Human-only DNA, so Anna and her staff could track any Human "visitors." Although perfectly legal, this might be problematic if word got out to the public — some Human or Human sympathizer would start whining about how unfair it was — so she made her staff sign confidentiality agreements for the first time in twelve years.

For years, her equipment had checked DNA against the latest wanted-criminals list for every visitor to the station. There was no law that said she couldn't give Humans extra attention — for their own protection, of course. Earthers had such a combative nature, they were likely to start a brawl and hurt themselves, and possibly others. Everyone was safer if her AI followed the Humans in the station's public areas with extra diligence.

Even after the fighting started, the station remained secure due to her extra measures. She just wished Woolerton didn't feel the need to complain about how she did her job every chance he got. Instead of being grateful for how well she'd secured the station, he invented problems.

"Every reporter in this sector is converging on our station right now," he yelled from the patio of his beach home on New Atlantis. His AI's comm system always took a wide shot when he was outside, undoubtedly at his instruction. Who wouldn't want to make the underlings jealous of his holo image?

"Isn't that what you wanted? More people on the station?" Anna asked from the fifteen-year-old chair in her cramped office.

"Of course I want that!" He frowned as if she was some dumb Human—like that bartender. "But my main concern is the safety of the station, and that's *your* job."

"Of course, but I don't see any reason for concern." She kept her voice smooth. No worries here. "As I stated in my daily report, we're on the highest alert, scanning every ship, resident, and traveler, verifying identities and checking for unauthorized weapons."

"You need to track the authorized ones." A bird winged behind Woolerton's head, swooping down to snag something from the water.

"Yes, *and* we get an alert when any weapon, anywhere on or *near* the station, is activated."

His forehead wrinkled in concentration. "There are ways around that. Veiling devices, scramblers—"

"There's a way around everything, with enough time and money and expertise. Nothing can ever be wholly secure, and we both know that. I'm doing the absolute best that I can here, and I see no reason for concern."

He leaned forward, hunching over on the table. "No reason for concern? What about this Hank Two-Name guy?"

"Hank Higgins? He has two names because he's Human." Anna's patience was wearing down. "Samantha has a second name as well, although she has no reason to use it here. I can pull it up, if—"

"I don't care about their names!" Woolerton pounded his fist on the table. An orange-colored drink sloshed from a laser-cut crystal glass. "Don't you think that guy's a threat?"

"Hank?" That took her by surprise. "Of course not. The guy just woke up, he has no idea what's going on, and he doesn't know the first thing about our technology. Even if he had bad intentions against us—and I have no evidence of that—he wouldn't even begin to understand our systems well enough to breach them, and he's probably never seen the kind of weapons we have. I'd say he's the least threatening person—well, Human—on this station."

"So you just *believe* all that nonsense about him floating around in a cryocan for years? I thought you were smarter than that."

"Well, of course I considered the alternative." She struggled not to ask if he wanted to do her job for her. "My team thoroughly checked out his story. If that cryocan is newer than he says, it's the best fake antique anyone has ever seen. I also analyzed his body language on the recorded interview and during the press party—"

"Body language can be faked." Woolerton waved his hand dismissively.

"That's more difficult than you'd think—much of it is unconscious. If he was faking, he did an incredibly good job, *and* he got someone to make the best fake cryocan, *and* he had some idiot Human doctor who managed to make him appear, to every medical test Vance and Woodley did, like a Human who spent one hundred fifty years in a cryocan. *And* that brilliant *Human* doctor also gave him a genetic disease we've never seen before, at least not recently enough for it to appear in any of our medical journals since we fled from Earth.

"So yes, I've *considered* the possibility he might be lying. I found that while it might be remotely possible, it is highly unlikely. Even so, I am watching everywhere he goes, everything he does, and everything he says."

Woolerton raised an eyebrow. "Everything?"

Anna heard the unasked question. Legally, she couldn't spy on the guests. She could track the signatures of registered weapons and their locations when they were engaged. She could track people in public areas of the stations, like the concourse, hallway, or a business. She could not, however, watch people once they went into their rooms and shut the door.

Because guest privacy was a concern, public access systems like Five Alpha's were, in some limited ways, more vulnerable than personal ones. Guests' devices couldn't access information that would interfere with station security, like the view of another guest's room or the security codes that protected the station. A personal AI could, however, monitor all interactions between it and the station's system. It could alert its owner that the room's camera function had been activated and how it was being used, how long various information was stored, and how and when such information was accessed. At the end of a guest's stay, his or her system could ensure that all information recorded about the guest was deleted from the station's files.

As a result, Anna and her staff spent most of their time trying to make sure they didn't accidentally do anything that would piss off a guest. Explaining that it was necessary to monitor a wild party to prevent damage to the room never went over well. It was easier just to charge them for the repairs later.

There were, of course, ways around any "perfect" system, and Anna knew all of them. Woolerton knew that she knew them, but officially knew nothing. They both understood these things posed a lot of risks and were only to be used under extreme circumstances.

Woolerton wanted to know if Anna considered this one of those circumstances.

"Everything is possible." She knew the conversation was likely being monitored. Her answer was noncommittal enough that it could mean anything, but the message should be clear to Woolerton—everything was in place in case she needed information on Hank, and that situation was likely to arise soon. Very soon.

✷

TWELVE

The Wormhole in the Wall never officially closed, but it rarely did any business at this hour, which was either very early or very late depending on whether you were a morning person or not. Dr. Vance was not, but he had been so busy in the two days since the press conference that he couldn't remember the last time he'd had anything to eat or drink. As he'd expected, colleagues congratulated him, offered to "consult" with him—which really meant they wanted to get some of the money and attention coming his way—and asked questions about his treatment protocols for the Two-Hundred-Year-Old Human, as Hank was now known, not quite accurately. Plus he still had to deal with patients, one of whom was convinced he had Hank's illness, even after Vance told him five times he didn't have the gene in the first place.

When he finally finished dealing with dummies—an apt phrase he'd learned from Samantha—he left the infirmary in the care of his staff, stumbled straight to the Wormhole in the Wall, and collapsed at the counter.

He'd expected Samantha to have left by now, but she was behind the bar, lounging in a chair, and drinking a bottle of Wimmerman's. Oddly enough, she didn't look nearly as happy as most people did when drinking an overpriced designer beer. With a flick of her hand, she sent a dish of peanuts flying down the counter in his general direction. It clattered to a stop two feet away.

"What's the matter with you?" he asked.

She raised an eyebrow in his direction. "The AI will get your order. I'm off duty."

Vance selected the "Daily Deal!" because it was the first thing he saw on the holo menu. "I didn't ask you to get my order. I asked what was wrong, because you look pissed off."

"Why do you care?" she snapped.

He was far too exhausted to think of a snarky comeback. "What is your problem? You've been having a great time playing the crazy Human bartender, then being the journalist who got the big story on Hank. I'm sure you've convinced Frego to give you that extra ten percent, if not more."

Samantha sighed, shook the beer bottle as if she couldn't remember if she'd drained it or not, and tossed it in the general direction of the nearest trash can. It hit the floor and rolled, coming to a stop at the other end of the counter. An automated cleaner would collect and recycle it later.

She got up and hoisted herself onto the counter, settling opposite the stool next to Vance. "Look, you've always been okay to me. You never lied or tried to convince me I was wrong about how everyone else on this station sees me. So I want you to answer a question, and I want you to be as honest as you've always been, okay?"

Vance nodded, trying not to look too distracted as his drink slid down the conveyor belt toward him.

She looked out the window at the now-deserted concourse. "Since I've been here, I assumed everyone didn't like me because of what I am."

He frowned. "But you knew that when you started the crazy Human campaign, didn't you?"

"Everyone here knows who and what I am. The station was already getting publicity because of it—the campaign was just to change the tone of that publicity. Anyway, the point is that I assumed everyone hated me because I was Human."

Vance couldn't think of an especially delicate way to phrase his next question. "And now you think you were wrong? Why?"

She did that creepy eye-rolling gesture that Humans did when they thought they were smarter than you. "Why do you think? Look at Hank! Everyone loves him. Yeah, a few People have suggested he might be a threat, but no one took them seriously. I've watched him, the past couple days, walking around the concourse, eating and drinking here, talking to People—and I've watched the People interacting with him. They're *nice* to him, Vance."

"Maybe they secretly think he's a threat and don't want to piss him off."

"People are constantly accusing me of being a threat, but no one cares about pissing me off!" She slammed a hand down on the counter, startling the almost-asleep patron a few stools down. He gave her a suspicious look before diving back into his drink.

"Is it me? I realize I'm not necessarily the nicest person around, and I don't care if I have a reputation for being a bitch, but most People respected me back on New Atlantis. Until the crazy bartender campaign, no one here wanted anything to do with me. Even after, no one wanted to get to know me—they just wanted to watch the show. But with Hank—I see all these People trying to be his new best friend. He doesn't have any money, his fifteen minutes of fame will be gone soon, and I've gotten almost as much publicity with the crazy Human act. So what's the difference?"

Vance took a long drink and plunged ahead. "You really want to know?"

"Yes."

"Please remember this is just what *some* People think—what I've heard them say. It's not what *I* think."

"Understood. Tell me."

He took a deep breath and blurted it out as fast as he could, too tired to spend a lot of time on this tonight, even for a friend. "Samantha, everyone here knows the story of how you wound up staying on the station instead of going with Brad to Earth. Think about that from an outsider's perspective. Consider how it could look to some People—you stopped at nothing to get your ass off the *Traveler* hours before it was destroyed by some... other Humans. There are a few people here who think that seems... suspicious."

Her brows pulled together in anger. Vance responded by taking an avid interest in the arrangement of peanuts on his plate. He was actually seeing a nearby star constellation when she finally spoke.

"They actually think I had something to do with that? My boyfriend was *on* that ship. If I *was* some sort of Human spy, wouldn't I have arranged for us *both* to be somewhere far away from here when the explosion happened?"

He shrugged. "I told you, I never believed you would do something like that. But, the People who do—well, they think you didn't know it was going to happen until just before. Information doesn't always flow evenly in both directions with spies, you know. Also, there's a rumor that when he tried to have you hauled off the station, you screamed at him on the concourse, something about making him pay."

"I was angry, but I didn't want him dead. They can't possibly think I blew up a ship full of people just to get even with Brad!" Samantha shook her head. "I've been on this side of the Divide for more than five years on your calendar. I've never done anything to hurt the People—or the Humans. I had nothing to do with this war-ish situation and I want it to end as much as anyone here!"

"I know that." Vance stuffed a handful of peanuts in his mouth.

"How many is 'some People here'?"

He should have just gone back to his apartment for dinner. "I don't know. Honestly, I don't think it's very many."

"Who?"

Vance shook his head. "This really isn't productive, and I don't think I'd be helping you by—"

"Fuck helping me," Samantha snapped. "I'm not one of your patients. I like to think we're friends. And as a friend, I'm asking you to tell me the truth. If you really don't believe I'm capable of violence, then there's no risk in telling me, is there?"

Vance slumped down over his beer, defeated. Sometimes he forgot Samantha was as smart as any Person he'd ever met. Smarter, in many cases.

"I heard Anna and some People from Station Security discussing it as a remote possibility." He touched the AI menu to order another beer. He was damn well going to need it. "I don't really think they believe it, they were just discussing possibilities, right? In fact, one of the guys who works for Anna was laughing about it. He said...."

"He said what? That I wasn't smart enough because I'm Human?"

"Something like that," Vance mumbled.

"Who else?"

"I've heard a few People talk about it here in the bar. I honestly don't know their names. A few tourists, a while back, but I don't think they're here anymore. That's really it."

"Those are all the People you've overheard talking about it." She stared at the concourse again. "But there are probably more who think it."

"I told you, I don't think anyone *seriously* believes it," he said. "I think it's occurred to a few People as a *distant* possibility, and they probably all dismissed it as unlikely. Now please, *please* don't make an issue of this with Anna. She would have talked Frego out of hiring you if she considered you a threat, right?"

"Yeah, I guess." She snagged his fresh beer off the conveyor belt and took a sip. "This tastes bad. You should order another."

"I assume there's no charge for that one then."

Then the conversation took a weird turn.

"Do you know anyone on the HirshMed ship?"

Surprise, fatigue, and alcohol combined to make her face a little blurry. HirshMed was a hospital ship that was currently docked outside of Five Alpha, because so many of its doctors wanted to meet Hank. The floating hospital was a research leader, and chose to treat patients on a ship instead of in a building so they could travel to the most interesting and urgent cases. "Sure. I have friends over there. Why?"

"I might need a favor."

"You have a medical problem you don't think I can fix?" Vance was hurt. He had, after all, revived a guy after 150 years in cryo, and Samantha didn't appear to be in bad shape.

"No, nothing like that." She shook her head, blonde hair obscuring her expression. "I need to go visit someone there."

"This doesn't have something to do with what I just told you—"

"No," she said sharply. "I saw someone today that I used to know.

He was in a video taken on board the ship. I, ah, have some unfinished business with this person."

"What kind of unfinished business?"

"Nothing you should worry about." She plucked his third beer from the conveyor and handed it to him. "I just have to ask him a really important question. Can you help me?"

"I assume he doesn't want to see you?"

"Let's just say it would be better if I showed up unannounced."

Vance nodded. Getting into Hirsh was tough, due to recent security concerns. If you weren't a patient, or someone a patient wanted to see, you weren't getting past the gate.

"I might be able to help," he said. "But you have to tell me why. Not because I don't trust you, but because there are a lot of issues involved here—privacy, safety, politics. I need to know what you're getting into."

"Okay. But I need your word you won't repeat anything I'm about to tell you."

"By the time I'm done drinking tonight, I probably won't even remember it."

"Let's talk over there." Samantha pointed to a table in the corner, and he reluctantly picked up his bottle and followed her, sloshing beer on the table as he sat down.

"Why don't you start with why it's so important for you to see this person at Hirsh?"

She leaned forward, speaking very softly. Vance figured she probably scanned the place for spots—a Human term short for spybots—hourly, but it never hurt to be careful.

"I assume that since you've been a doctor for a while, you've probably accidentally killed someone."

Vance raised an eyebrow.

"I mean, you did your best, but if you had done something differently, your patient would still be alive." She picked up the nearest salt dispenser and turned it around in her hands. "You know what I mean?"

Vance shrugged. "They tell you to expect that in medical school. Sooner or later you're going to kill someone, and if you can't deal with that you should find another job. Is this about Brad? I know everyone has probably told you that wasn't your fault, and maybe you don't believe it, but it really —"

"Everyone has *not* told me that," she snapped. "A few of my friends from New Atlantis said it when they called after the explosion, but no one here has. Some of Brad's friends have told me the exact opposite, actually."

Vance shook his head. "They're angry and grieving. You can't listen to them. You're smart enough to know there was nothing you could do after Brad had himself put in the can."

"There *was* something I could do!" she hissed, her head snapping up. She leaned forward and continued, her voice barely above a whisper. "There was something I could do, and I did it, but it didn't work, and I think I got a second person killed in the process. Now do you understand?"

He really should have gone home. He was too tired for this. "No. Explain it to me."

Samantha squeezed the salt dispenser, knuckles turning white around it. "I wanted Brad off that ship, but you have to believe me, I knew *nothing* about the explosion. I just didn't want him going to Earth without me. As mad as I was, I didn't want him going to a hostile place alone."

"I understand."

"I tried to get him off that ship, but there was no legal way to do it." She went back to rolling the dispenser between her fingers. "So I acquired the services of someone who was very good at breaking onto ships when everyone was in cryo and... acquiring things."

"Like a cryocan?" He frowned. Cryocans were usually stored in the most secure part of the ship, so they'd be safe not only from the situation Sam was describing, but also in the event of an accident or explosion—not that it always helped.

She nodded. "Yeah. He'd retrieved a few in the past, so I knew he had the expertise to do what I couldn't."

"And he was willing to take the job."

"It wasn't exactly a job."

"What was it then?" Vance was now completely confused.

"Blackmail."

"I know that's a Human phrase, but after the extremely long day I've had I don't remember what it means."

"Sometimes, in the course of researching a story, I come across information that isn't really interesting enough to write about, but it might be useful if I ever need a favor."

"Oh. Extortion."

"You want to say that a little louder? I don't think they heard you back on Earth."

"Sorry." He looked around the crowded, noisy bar. No one seemed to be paying them any attention.

"I had no idea about the explosion. I thought the worst that could happen was that he'd get caught—in which case, his story would be that he was acting on his own, or he'd be in worse trouble." She set the dispenser down on the counter. "He assured me, though, that he never got caught."

"So he was on the *Traveler* when the collision happened?"

She shook her head. "The thing is, I don't know. He didn't give me a schedule, just a date when he expected to meet me. It was about seven days after the explosion."

"So he could easily have been on board when it happened."

"Yeah." She sighed. "Afterward, I scoured every news report, every statement by the Guard, looking for some mention that they'd found an unidentified body, or parts from a small ship, or *something* to suggest they'd found him. But I couldn't come up with anything."

"You hoped he'd gotten away with the cryocontainer?" Many of the cans, including Brad's, were never recovered and were assumed to have been obliterated in the explosion.

"Yeah, but I didn't hear anything from Jake—the guy I black-mailed—and I finally realized he'd probably gotten killed doing that job for me," she said. "You're right—Brad would have been on that ship no matter what I did. But Jake wouldn't have. He wasn't a bad guy, either—just someone making the best of a bad situation."

Vance nodded. "And you think you saw him today?"

"Yes, and if he's alive, then there's a chance he got that coffin." She inhaled sharply. "I want to think that so badly. But the truth is, if he had Brad, he'd have found a way to contact me. If he's avoiding me, it's because he didn't get what I wanted, and he's afraid I'll use what I have on him—which I wouldn't, not after what happened. But I guess he doesn't know that. I just want to see if he's alive, ask what happened, and apologize."

They were silent for a moment as she ordered another drink and Vance contemplated her problem.

"I have a friend—Barry—at Hirsh who shares my interest in neurological regeneration," he said finally. "He did a really fascinating study, but he's having trouble getting the funding he needs to continue with his research."

Her eyes flickered with shared understanding. "An interview by the journalist who broke the Hank Higgins story would bring a lot of attention to Barry and his pet project."

Vance smiled. "That's right! Hirsh would appreciate that sort of helpful publicity, so they'd give you a visitor's pass right away."

She lifted her glass. "I'll drink to that."

"Yes." He nodded vaguely, unable to recall what he was supposed to do when a Human said "I'll drink to that." Take a sip of his own drink?

"You still might encounter some problems," he warned her.

"What do you mean?"

"Well, some of the People who run Hirsh will be happy, and so will Barry, but a lot of other People there are *very* unfriendly toward Humans." Vance sighed and rubbed at his eyes, which felt like they were full of sand. "Worse than here, I mean. They treated a lot of People who were hurt in the *Traveler* explosion, and some of the earlier attacks. While most of us are rational enough to remember that you didn't personally have anything to do with any of it, well… some People aren't."

Samantha nodded. "I know just how to deal with *those* People."

✷
THIRTEEN

Hank had never been so happy to get a hard-on in his life. He'd been worried that Dr. Vance was wrong, and his extended stay in the freezer really *did* damage his equipment. After his exam with Vance the day he woke up, the first question he'd asked was, "Can I still have sex?" Closely followed by, "Can you fix my brain?" of course. The doctor assured him everything was fine in both departments, but he was still worried about all those years of inactivity.

At least picking up women was a lot easier than he remembered. Apparently he was a minor celebrity here on the station, and the Wormhole in the Wall was full of attractive women who were a lot more attentive than the ones he used to meet in bars back on Earth. He was honestly amazed at how fast he managed to convince a pretty brunette named Lala to join him in his room—a suite that Haylea had generously provided free of charge, because obviously she wanted her latest cash cow to be comfortable. Not that he was complaining.

The problems started when Lala took off her dress. She had a fantastic figure, with curves in all the right places and an ass that looked like something he'd seen in a gym commercial on Earth.

And she had a tail.

It wasn't like it came as a shock to him. He'd seen people walking around with tails for more than a week now. He just hadn't pictured himself having sex with a woman who was wagging her tail like a dog.

"You like what you see?" Lala apparently took his staring as a sign that he was impressed by her body. She pushed him down onto the bed and climbed on top of him, reaching for the zipper on his pants.

"Uh... yeah." Her tail swished against his legs, and he suddenly remembered a news report he'd heard back in Texas about some guy who got arrested for fucking farm animals.

But this wasn't like that at all. He wasn't with a horse, he was with a beautiful woman who... had a tail.

"Could you move your tail out of the way?" he asked as he fumbled with her bra. Apparently they had some new kind of clasp here that he didn't understand. Just when he finally figured out the ones back on Earth.

"What am I supposed to do, take it off? It's attached, you know." She giggled as she slid down into a horizontal position and started nuzzling his neck. As she worked her way south, Hank tried to forget about the tail.

Then he felt the damn thing flicking around his legs again. A memory popped into his head — hanging out in a filthy bar on Earth, leaning on a beer-puddled counter and telling his buddies he was "going to get some tail tonight." He was pretty sure he'd never use that particular phrase again.

"Can you at least stop moving it?" he asked as she wriggled out of her underwear, probably assuming he was too dumb to figure that out, too.

"Damnit, Hank, what is your problem?" She wrapped her legs around his waist and rolled over, pulling him on top of her. Now he could *really* feel the tail between his legs. "Forget about it."

"I... can't. It's bothering me."

She unwrapped her long legs and used one of them to shove him away as she sat up. Damn, she was limber. He could have such a good time if it wasn't for the....

"This is ridiculous. Your lack of a tail doesn't bother me, why should my having a tail bother you?" she asked.

"That's a real fair question, but it's not that simple. I realize those are both, whatchamacallit, social — *things* — that are normal, in, uh, our cultures — "

"So if I'm willing to accept your lack of a tail, you should be willing to accept that I have one."

"But it's not about being *normal*, it's about...." He groaned. "Your people don't associate lack of a tail with being a member of the animal kingdom. *My* people associate having a tail with being an animal. So having sex with someone who has a tail — even someone as gorgeous as you are, babe — it just makes me feel like... like... well, like one of those people I used to see on TV, back on Earth, you know, one of those goatfucking rednecks who got arrested for bestiality."

Lala's face twisted in disgust. "You Humans fuck goats on Earth?" She jumped off the bed and grabbed her dress. "I heard your people were uncivilized — barbarians even — but you seemed so normal. I guess I should have believed what I heard. It's even worse than I thought!"

"No, no, we don't have sex with animals, at least most of us don't, just a few, um...." How the hell was he supposed to explain goatfucking rednecks to someone who already thought Humans were uncivilized idiots?

"I don't even know anyone who would do that in a sex sim, let alone with a real goat!" She rehooked her bra and yanked the dress back over her head.

"I don't either, I think it's disgusting!" he yelled, trying to salvage the situation. "That's why I can't have sex with you if you can't get your tail out of the way!"

"Now you're calling *me* disgusting? You come from a planet where people fuck goats, and you think I'm gross for having a tail? My friends were right. You Humans really do need to just stay on your own side of the Divide!" She grabbed her bag and stomped out the door, slamming it behind her.

✳
FOURTEEN

The Hirsh security guard who greeted Samantha took his time. She could tell by the way he kept a fake smile plastered on his face as he peered at her ID and scanned the chip in her palm that he was trying to act like a Person who didn't hate Humans. Obviously, his bosses had instructed him to do so if he wanted to preserve both their financial well-beings.

Unfortunately, the patients waiting in the lobby had no such reason to avoid being rude to her. Everyone stared—people in flimsy hospital gowns—a universal problem, apparently— people abandoning their data pads to stare at her, people forgetting their conversations to point at the Human.

At the Visitors' Desk, she was confronted by a tall, dark-haired man holding the hand of a little boy. The kid was wearing a shirt with dinosaurs on it. What were kids taught about dinosaurs in school here, anyway? That they went extinct before the Great Escape? Did the Humans get blamed for that, too?

The boy's eyes widened when he saw Samantha.

"Daddy, look." He tugged on his father's arm.

"Just a minute, Taran," the father said placidly, not turning his attention away from the sign-in menu. "We'll go see Mom soon, don't worry."

"Daddy, there's a Human behind us!" the kid yelled.

At that, every noise in the lobby died. If People hadn't been staring before, they sure were now.

For a minute, she thought the guy might have enough sense to chastise his child for being rude and make him apologize. But then the man turned around and stared at her. His lip curled up in a sneer of disdain, and he pulled his son closer to him, as if he thought she posed some threat. The boy ducked his head into the crook of his father's arm.

"You shouldn't be here," the dad snarled at Samantha. "My wife is in this hospital because of your... species. Her ship was docking with that station, the one you're making a media disaster of, Five Alpha, when the *Traveler* explosion happened. So if you have a problem, Human, I suggest you go home and let the idiots on your own planet treat you. This hospital is for People. Most of them are here because they were injured by the Humans."

That was a vast overstatement.

She stared him down. "Did it ever occur to you that I might be a Person who lost her tail in that damn explosion and came here for treatment? Maybe you should use all the intelligence that I assume you have as a *Person* to think before you open your mouth."

The little boy stared at her, wide-eyed. His father's face wasn't so static. His anger dissolved into surprise, which was quickly replaced by shame. He hastily stepped back out of her way, pulling the kid with him. "I am so sorry... I had no idea."

"Of course you had no idea. You made a quick assumption based on what you saw. It's something Humans do all the time." She gave him a final glare, then stormed past him to the elevator. It was probably too much to hope he'd learn anything from the altercation, but at least she'd embarrassed him in a crowded lobby.

She was scheduled to meet Barry for a lunch interview in an hour. While arranging her media clearance, he had given her access to far more of the hospital's AI than she would need to research any story, thanks to whatever the hell Vance had told him. She asked the AI a number of general questions in the elevator, to make it think she was actually working on a news report.

"I understand Hirsh has more research projects than any other hospital in this sector. Which one has been most successful so far?"

"None are completed yet, and the board and staff of Hirsh are proud of all our projects," the AI spat back predictably. "However, Dr. Barry recently received the highly coveted Millerton Grant for his work on neuron regeneration. I understand that's what you're here to learn about?"

"Yes, that's right." She was careful to keep her stance open and her arms uncrossed, knowing the AI would be studying her body language.

"You're a little early for your appointment," it observed.

She shrugged. "I'd just like to walk around and get a feel for the place. Don't worry, I won't bother anyone who doesn't want to talk to a reporter."

Twenty minutes later, she sat in a lounge with view screens tuned to an outdoor park scene. Trees swayed in the breeze, and happy, healthy People were out walking their dogs, playing with their children, or lolling on the grass. She wondered if that made the patients feel better, or if it made them feel worse because they were stuck in here.

The lounge was open and the door to Jake's room was just to the right. She milled around, asking a few patients general questions about how much they were enjoying their stay at HirshMed, while keeping an eye on the door.

When Jake approached his room, she politely disengaged from her conversation and slipped into the hall. He looked at her and took a step back toward the door. At first she wasn't sure if it was him, but then she saw the caterpillar tattooed on his neck. Not too many of those around.

"It really *is* you," she said.

"Who the hell are you?" He was now recovered enough from his surprise to at least try to lie convincingly.

"Let's not play this game, Jake," she said. "You know who I am. Oh, I know you told the doctors you remember nothing for the week surrounding the explosion. But I also know you remember what I know about Iris, because—"

"I don't know what you're talking about!" He turned and bolted for the door.

Great. This wasn't how she wanted things to go. She ran after him, glad the AI's cameras were not active on this floor for the patients' privacy—a fact she'd learned from asking the hospital's AI "How do you ensure security without compromising patient privacy?" The cameras would, however, turn on if a patient was yelling for help or if a medchip indicated distress. Hopefully Jake's chip would just think he was running for exercise. According to Vance, they were generally programmed to record vital signs constantly but only sound an alarm for severe, life-threatening medical problems, so unless she gave the guy a heart attack, it probably wouldn't initiate increased surveillance.

She hoped.

"You could call security on me," she yelled, just loudly enough to be heard as she swiftly gained on him. "But then you'd have to explain why you're afraid of someone you don't know. And I might have to remember some details about the Iris project." She hated to threaten him, but she didn't have a better idea, and she needed to talk to him.

Jake kept running, but the limping slowed him down considerably. She broke into a light jog.

"I know this probably isn't a good copacetic communications thing to say," she called, as his green jacket flickered around a corner. "But I know damn well I can outrun you, so why don't we just quit this bullshit now?"

She bounded around the corner and snagged the corner of his jacket. They were in a storage area for linens, which the hospital apparently didn't much care about. They were stacked up on all three sides, ripe for stealing. But who would want to steal hospital sheets?

He tried to jerk away, but she yanked him back, easily pulling him off balance. Snagging his other arm, she slipped an autocuff on him. She'd borrowed it years ago from a cop contact and sort of forgotten to return it. "I didn't want to do this, but I have to talk to you, just for a minute, okay?"

"You caught me," Jake snarled, trying to pull away. She pulled back, just hard enough to stop him, but he tripped and fell against a linen rack. Although she scrambled to grab him, he wound up on the floor in a pile of ugly sheets. Suddenly, she remembered why she didn't apologize very often — it was because she sucked at it.

He writhed around, still trying to escape, but couldn't get up with his arms behind his back. "Are you happy now that you outran a guy with a bad leg? Who the fuck are you and what do you want from me, anyway? And what do you think you know about Iris?"

She sank to her knees next to him. "You know what I want, Jake. I just want the truth."

He gave a resigned sigh. "They Hazed me. It — "

"I've seen your file, and I'm familiar with Hazing."

"Then you know it erases memories for the past several days, but sometimes up to two weeks if a large enough dose is necessary."

"It can, but it doesn't always. If you don't remember anything for two weeks before the accident, why did you jump three feet in the air when you saw me?"

"You startled me! You were a stranger who acted like you knew me, and you were waiting for me."

"Why not just call security?"

Jake rolled his eyes. "Because you knew about Iris, remember?"

"I thought you didn't know anything about Iris?"

"Fine, you caught me. What are you going to do, Samantha?" He looked her right in the eye, and she could see some of the work his doctors had done. All those white marks were fading stitches, according to Dr. Vance. To her they just looked like clouds in a blue sky.

"Are you going tell about the Iris job?" he pressed. "Are you going to do something worse?"

"What?"

"Do you want to me to do another job? You're still trying to extort me?"

"No!" she snapped. "I'm done with extortion. I just wanted to — ""

"Get back at me? Look at me!" he yelled. "I've had twelve surgeries. The doctors tell me it'll take at least four more to fix everything. My ship was destroyed. Most of my former business associates are pretending not to know me in case the authorities get interested in my... accident. You already blew up my life, what more do you want from me?

This wasn't how she wanted the meeting to go at all. "I destroyed everything I had on you and the Iris job a long time ago. All I came here for was the truth." She reached behind him and tripped the autocuff. "I just needed to know if you were alive, and what happened to Brad's coff—cryocan. Why couldn't you just call and tell me what happened?"

Jake's mouth dropped open. "Are you crazy? I didn't contact you because you extorted me into doing a job that I couldn't finish, that I can never finish. I didn't get your cryocan out in time, and now...."

"Then he really is...." She couldn't finish the sentence.

Jake shook his head. "I assume. Look, I really *don't* remember the day of the explosion, okay? The last thing I remember is getting ready to leave the station after you gave me my assignment. My craft was destroyed, so if I did get the can, it probably was, too. I'm really sorry I don't know more."

She let out a breath she didn't remember holding. "I figured, but I hoped I was wrong. But if your ship exploded, how did you get out?"

"Apparently I was in a space suit when it happened, near the airlock. The Guard officers said they found me floating in the wreckage. The suit's built-in repair function made it reseal around the piece of metal in my leg, so I didn't lose air too fast."

"But why couldn't you contact me after? Even just—just to tell me what happened?"

He gave her the familiar are-you-stupid look. "Tell you that I failed, that you had no reason not to tell everyone that I—why would I?"

Samantha groaned. "You think I would do that? After everything that happened when you were trying to get Brad out?"

"After I failed to get your boyfriend off that ship, and it blew up and he died? Yeah, I thought you'd be pissed about that. I thought if you knew I was alive, you'd release the info. Or worse, what if you thought I deserved to die, too? Is that what you're really here for? To kill me?"

Samantha jerked backward, stunned. "You think I want to *kill* you?"

Jake took an interest in the ugly sheets. "Losing a loved one... it can make you do some crazy things. Let's just say I know about it."

She shook her head vehemently. "You didn't know that ship was going to blow up any more than I did. I blame the morons responsible for Brad's death. And sometimes, I blame myself for his being on the *Traveler* in the first place — and for *you* being there."

"Then what are you doing here?"

"First, I wanted to make sure you were alive, so at least I could stop feeling guilty about that." She squeezed the autocuff until her knuckles turned white. "I still feel badly that you got hurt doing something for me, but at least you didn't get killed."

"And the other reason is that you wanted to know if Brad might still be alive," he said quietly.

She nodded.

"I'm sorry, Samantha. Either he was on my ship when it blew up, or he was on the *Traveler* when it blew up. Either way, if they haven't found his cryocan by now...."

"I know," she whispered. "He's dead, and I have to accept it."

They sat in silence for a few minutes. Finally, Samantha broke the quiet as she stood up. "The third reason was so I could apologize to you."

"This is how you apologize? By beating up a guy with a bad leg? You're really fucked up in the head, you know that?"

"I didn't beat you up, you ran into the linen rack yourself." She raked a hand through her hair. "I chased you because it's sort of hard to apologize to someone who isn't in the room with you, and I was also desperate to get an answer about Brad. I really am sorry for all the problems I've caused you."

Jake shook his head. "You had what you had on me for a reason. I did some things I'm not proud of, and I've had a lot of time here to think about it. I'm as responsible as anyone else for where I was when that ship blew up."

"Still—"

"Were you telling the truth about destroying the evidence?"

"Yes." She offered him a hand and helped him to his feet. "I only brought up what I know to get you to talk to me. As of this moment, I don't remember a thing about it, okay?"

Jake nodded, and they headed back into the corridor.

"By the way, you'll find that all your medical debts at this hospital, and the one on Five Alpha, have been written off, and your future expenses have also been taken care of," she said as they reached the lounge.

"You paid my medical debts?"

She suppressed a snort. "I don't have that kind of money. But I have some... unfortunate information about the hospital's board of directors."

"I thought you were done with extortion?"

"I am! But I grandfathered in extorting people to fix my previous extortion mistakes."

"Of course you did."

"If you ever want a job on Five Alpha, I can twist a few more arms."

He shook his head. "I actually like what I do, even if it isn't always legal. Legalities don't always protect the innocent. Anyway, I think I can get my former associates to come around—I just need to pull one big, impressive job. If you hear of anything like that, let me know."

✳
FIFTEEN

"You have fourteen messages from Lee," the AI reminded Samantha as she walked back into her apartment on Five Alpha.

"Do any of them say anything other than 'call me immediately'?" She tossed her bag on the floor and flopped onto the couch.

"No, they all say that."

"Then call him immediately, I guess." She looked down at her rumpled clothes, then ran a hand through her hair. "Audio only on the outgoing."

Lee's image flickered on right next to the couch. He was a short, portly man who probably saved a lot of money on wrinkle treatments since his forehead was always creased in a frown anyway.

"Samantha, where the hell have you been? Your AI tells me you've been off the station."

"I was looking into a lead on another medical story. I'll send you a report soon, don't worry."

"Have you seen the press advisory your friend Haylea just released?"

"I have a message from her, but I haven't read it yet. Or yours."

"Read it now."

Press Advisory: People Representative Council

Officials from both the Human and People governments have agreed to meet to discuss the current peace challenges in an informal setting. Both governments have been eager to hold such a meeting since the current issues began. Due to security concerns, the meeting place was intentionally not chosen until the day before the meeting, and the date was also withheld.

Delegations from the Human and People governments will meet on space station Five Alpha. All interested members of the press should immediately contact Five Alpha's Copacetic Communications Director Haylea for entrance credentials.

"Informal meetings are how the People solve most of their diplomatic problems, right?"

Lee scratched his head. "Unfortunately, it isn't as simple as just signing a treaty with... well, you know. But maybe it's a start, right?"

"Nothing would make me happier than to see this stupid fucking war come to a screeching halt, so I could go back to New Atlantis," she said. "But I'm not naïve enough to believe that a couple politicians from both sides shaking hands and eating together is going to fix anything, and neither are you. Best case scenario, they smile and nod and make polite conversation. Worst case scenario, they get in a fight and someone throws wine on someone else. We could lead with that."

"I was hoping one of your officials might punch one of ours. Wouldn't that make a great image to share on our nets?"

"Our politicians are more likely to get caught banging hookers in a taxpayer-funded hotel room than punching each other. The press advisory doesn't say specifically who's coming, does it?"

"I asked Haylea. She said even she doesn't know, and she was told the names of the delegates won't be revealed until the meeting for security reasons." Lee leaned forward. "Listen, I've been hearing some things... unsubstantiated, of course."

Samantha sat up. "What kind of things?"

"Interesting theories about what else might happen tomorrow. One involves some civilian showing up with a bomb, or a gun—"

"You don't have a lot of wars on your planet, so let me help you with this, Lee. During times of heightened tensions between two groups of people, like a war that no one wants to call a war, rumors like that always fly around. I'm not saying they never amount to anything, but usually they don't. Do you have anything credible?"

"Not really. But Five Alpha's been on high alert for a long time. Just keep digging."

"If I overhear someone plotting to blow up the station, you'll be my next call after security."

"Of course." Lee rolled his eyes. "There *is* another angle you should pursue. I got word that a guy named Morriss, some Human bazillionaire who thinks he can save the world, will be one of the delegates." Lee probably thought *bazillionaire* was a job title.

Samantha groaned. "You know, when we first made contact seven years ago, there was a tabloid rumor that he was actually one of what we thought were the 'aliens' out here. Poor guy can't catch a break with the media."

"You thought he was an alien who just happened to look exactly like a

Human?" Lee snickered. "Anyway, he might show up."

"It was just the cheap tabloids calling the People well-disguised aliens, and they gave up after a couple months. Any other interesting Humans who might make a cameo?" According to Haylea, the official gala itself would be invite-only, but that only stopped people from getting into the station's Event Hall. The main concourse and the rest of the station were still wide open, and the party wasn't going to stay contained to one floor all night.

"A what?" Lee frowned at her.

"That's what we Humans call making an unexpected appearance."

"There was a rumor about some fringe Human political groups sending members out a while ago," Lee said. "Some strange-sounding groups. You'd probably know more about them than me. Who are the Sisterhood of Mother Earth?"

"Some people — I mean, Humans — who object to all the pollution and crap on Earth."

"You mean there are Humans who don't?" Lee's forehead tightened, and the crow's feet turned into pterodactyl feet.

"Well, no one's in favor of it." Samantha rubbed her forehead. Trying to explain Earth situations to People always gave her a headache. "There's just a lot of disagreement about how to deal with it."

Lee looked down and away, scratching the back of his head. He tried to keep his political beliefs out of the office, but Samantha suspected he was one of those who saw the Great Escape as a moral failing, like leaving a bunch of toddlers unsupervised with a gallon of gasoline and a box of matches. He probably felt guilty about the huge mess the Humans made of Earth. "What about the Medical Responsibility League?"

She winced. This list wasn't getting any better. "You know our medical technology didn't advance very fast for centuries, and even when we first crossed the Divide, there were a lot of diseases we couldn't cure — still can't, in most cases."

"That's why Hank ventured out." Hank had been *Glass's* biggest story for two days after the press party.

"Well, there are still a lot of desperate Humans. Not all of them handle the situation the way he did," she said. "We don't have cures for a lot of things, but that doesn't mean we haven't done a lot of research. This is kind of embarrassing, but before Humans could come here for a cure, there were... problems."

"Like what?"

"I guess a lot of Humans thought they shouldn't have to wait any more. Or they really didn't have time." Samantha ran a hand through her hair, limp and tangled after hours of travel. "Most medical research was funded by the government or private donations. There were a lot of political arguments that held things up — funding, safety, you name it. But when a cure seemed so close for some peop — Humans, well, some researchers tested drugs that hadn't been approved for testing. Others went so far as to give untested medications to Humans who were so desperate they didn't care how dangerous that was. You can understand the ethical problems — there were a lot of injuries and deaths."

"So the Medical Responsibility League wanted to end those problems?"

"It started out that way." She tried to push away thoughts of Earth. "Unfortunately, like a lot of organizations designed to help people, it all went to crap. A power-hungry, self-serving asshole got control of the organization and made a mockery of what they were trying to do. Somehow, he started blaming the victims, claiming that people were only encouraging these non-legit companies by paying them in the first place."

"Why weren't people doing their research and avoiding these...."

Lee's face turned tomato red.

"Most of them were desperate and wanted to believe in a cure for whatever their problem was. And many of them were… on the less intelligent side of Humanity." Samantha smoothly let Lee off the hook without completely agreeing with his assumption that all Humans were idiots—even though most of them were.

"Of course." Lee cleared his throat and finally met her gaze again, if only briefly. "Well, it's rumored one of these Medical Responsibility Humans will be at the dinner tonight. As I understand it, they have a few members who don't mind using violence to make a point."

Samantha stood and made her way toward the shower. "I'll look into it and let you know if I find anything."

"One more thing. You know the rumors about an anti-Hazing drug?"

She groaned. "We have a phrase for those on Earth—urban legend. I didn't realize *Glass* was pursuing Earth tabloid-quality stories now."

"First of all, your p—ah, Humans, have way more government conspiracy theories than we do. But this one's different. We got an anonymous tip saying the Humans have this drug. We can't get anyone in the government to confirm it, but this tip looks like a page from a classified report."

"We've been getting anonymous tips like that for years. Are you saying the People finally think the Humans are smart enough to—"

"Oh, no," Lee said quickly. "The rumor is that the Humans stole it from our government."

She sighed. "Do you want me working on this or a real story?"

"A real story, of course. But I do need a quote from some governmental-type Earth person confirming it's untrue."

"I'll see what I can do."

✳
SIXTEEN

Haylea had a million things to do and the last thing she needed was to run into Roble—so of course she ran into Roble.

"I heard you were going to be in charge of tonight's party." He ran up to her from the other side of the concourse. Maybe "run" wasn't the right word. It was more like shuffling quickly while panting.

"Yes, so obviously I'm very busy."

For once it wasn't a lie. She had to confirm the approved guest list for Anna, return calls from reporters, tell some of them why they hadn't made it into the party—"Limited space"—and figure out what she was going to wear. While she was deliriously happy the delegation party had chosen Five Alpha for all the publicity and money it would bring the station, she wished they'd told Woolerton sooner. Now he expected her to plan the party of the year!

In one day.

"I ran into this Human back there." Roble flailed his left hand behind him. His right was busy holding what looked like a badly disfigured doughnut close to his mouth. "He said the strangest thing."

"Yeah, Humans say strange things sometimes. Like I said, I'm a little busy —"

"I checked with the station's AI, and there's nothing wrong with our cleaning automatons or laundry service." He licked his fingers. "Is there any more free food?"

"Of course there's nothing wrong with our laundry service. I would have heard about it." Haylea pulled up the next list on her data pad. "And we won't be putting out any more free food for the *journalists*" —she looked pointedly at Roble— "until late this evening. Now, I really have to —"

"But this Human, he kept saying something about dirty laundry at the party. Why would he say that?"

She frowned. "Dirty laundry at the party? I have no idea. I'm sure he was just confused. The cleaning crawlers are working fine, the tablecloths are beautiful, and if anyone is wearing dirty clothes it's because they didn't call the laundry service in time, that's all."

She was hurrying toward her office when Roble said, "Wait, do you have a date for tonight?"

Haylea winced, glad her back was to him. *Just keep walking and pretend you didn't hear.*

"I said, do you have a date for tonight?" he asked again, loud enough that some of the reporters stopped munching on their doughnuts to stare.

"No, and I don't need one." She stopped and turned around. "I'll be much too busy to spend any time with anyone for non-work reasons. You understand."

"Haylea, I've never told you this before, but...."

Oh, crap, he's going to tell me he's wanted to be with me for years, because he doesn't realize I already know that. What to do? She didn't want to make him feel bad, but she didn't have time to give him a speech about how she really wasn't looking for a relationship right now, she wanted to focus on her career, and no, she really wasn't interested in a casual sex thing either, and it wasn't him, it was her, and —

Wait, there was an easier, faster way to deal with this problem.

"If you want to come to the party tonight, I'd be happy to put your name on the list. But like I said, you won't see much of me because I'll be really, really busy."

A big grin spread across Roble's face, reaching almost all the way to the farthest doughnut crumb. "Great! I can't wait!"

"Me, neither." She wasn't sure if she'd just made things worse or better.

* *

Hank had never liked doctors' offices. They tended to be places where he got bad news handed to him by cold, impersonal people in white coats. Those same people made you wait, sometimes for an hour, because they felt their time was so much more valuable than yours, then they gave you bad news and told you they were sorry but there was nothing they could do.

He didn't like Vance's infirmary any better — it was a dull shade of beige, no furniture except the exam table, no magazines, no pictures, not even any brochures on healthy living. Did they still have brochures here? He hadn't seen any paper since he'd arrived, only those data pad things. They were similar to the tablets he'd had years ago, except that they were almost as thin as a sheet of paper and could be rolled up, like a joint. Not that he knew anything about that.

At least Dr. Vance didn't keep him waiting. He entered the room less than a minute after Hank sat down awkwardly on the exam table.

"Hi, Hank." Judging by the mouth-smiling-eyes-sad look on Vance's face, there had to be something wrong.

"You didn't cure my disease, did you?" Hank's mouth was moving before he even thought the question.

Vance sighed and sat down in a chair opposite the table, his tail tapping nervously against the wall. Hank was still trying to wrap his head around the tail thing, but at the moment that was the least of his concerns.

"As I told you a few days ago, replacing the gene with a healthy one wasn't a problem," the doctor began.

"You said there might have been permanent damage already." Hank's fingers gripped the edge of the exam table.

"Yes. We'd hoped it would be negligible, since you weren't having any symptoms yet when you went into cryo. The process drastically slows cellular degradation."

"So I was in cryo too long?"

Vance shook his head. "No, we don't believe there was any significant progression while you were under. It's the amount of damage that occurred *before* you went in, Hank. The cellular changes that eventually lead to your disease start in childhood. Just because Humans with this untreated gene don't have symptoms until they're later in life doesn't mean the disease isn't active."

"So... I'm shit out of luck?" *Please tell me I'm wrong.*

"I'm sorry, Hank. We scanned many of your individual neurons. The damage is extensive, and within a few years, they will start to destabilize, at which point your symptoms will begin."

Hank scratched his head, trying to process what Vance had just said.

"But... can't you regenerate the neurons? Samantha told me you grow people new body parts all the time. I watched an interview she did with this one guy who lost all four of his limbs in the war thing that we're not supposed to call a war. The doctors regrew them all in a few weeks and you can't tell the difference. He doesn't even have any scars!"

"We can do that with most body parts, but we're talking about brain cells," Vance said quietly. "Yes, I could grow you some healthy new ones. But even if I could get them all into your head and get enough of the old ones out without killing you, which no one's ever successfully done, you would lose all the memories you have now. You could make new ones, but you'd have to relearn everything, as if you were an infant. You'd lose every trace of who you are—and that's if we could even do such a procedure without killing you, which we can't."

Hank swallowed. He remembered hearing something like that from the doctor back at the clinic on Earth, when he asked if it was even worth being put in cryo. The doctor had said that while replacing brain cells wasn't the answer, he hoped fixing them would be—eventually.

"What about fixing the damage?" he asked.

"The type of 'fixing' your neurons would need, in this case, isn't currently possible," Vance said. "But I've personally done a lot of research on the subject—not on this particular illness, of course, but neural regeneration. My main area of research is injury to the brain—usually caused by accidents, but occasionally illness. I currently work with a patient who suffered a blood clot to the brain, what you call a stroke, I think, extremely rare, but we're trying to—"

"Strokes are rare here?" Back on Earth, stroke was the second leading killer of men older than forty, after heart attacks and tied with cancer. Or at least it had been when he left.

Vance looked surprised. "Oh, yes. You know that tiny med chip we installed in your hand, under the skin? I told you it monitors your health, right? If a clot formed anywhere in your body, even a very tiny one, it would let you know right away. You'd have time to get to a doctor and have it treated before it could travel to your brain and cause damage."

"Not that a blood clot is necessary."

"I don't want you to be discouraged," Vance said. "The research I'm doing is much more advanced than what they were doing on Earth when you left, and most of my colleagues are doing similar work. There aren't hundreds of diseases to cure like there were when you went into cryo. I believe we'll find a solution."

"Before I lose my mind in the next couple years?" Hank asked.

The doctor shook his head. "The type of research we're talking about is focused on reversing damage. So if it worked, we might be able to reverse the problem even after your symptoms start."

"You're saying I could come back from not knowing who I am or who anyone else is?"

"I honestly don't know. It's possible. Probably you'd have permanent memory loss from the months after you started to deteriorate, but you might get back older memories."

"Can you put me back in cryo?"

"Yes."

Hank nodded. "Then I want you to do it as soon as you can, and wake me up again whenever you find that cure."

"I understand why you feel that way, but I recommend you take some time to think about it," Vance said. "If you stayed with us, I could work not just on this type of research in general, but on your case in particular. It would be easier for me to formulate a treatment if you were awake."

"You want me to be a guinea pig?"

Vance crinkled his nose. "You still use animals for research on Earth? No wonder you can't cure anything. Their systems aren't enough like ours to have any predictive value."

"That doesn't answer my question," Hank snapped.

"No, I don't want to *experiment* on you," Vance said. "With your permission, I would be studying your case and devising a treatment plan. Then I'd use computer models to predict potential side effects—those are more than ninety-nine percent accurate. Any treatment would still have risks, of course, and we would discuss them in depth before you made a decision. That's how research is done here—we don't sit in a lab and watch mice run on a wheel. We work specifically with the people who need treatment. Sometimes, after we've cured several patients of a similar ailment, we look into whether a standardized course of treatment can be developed, but usually we don't take a one-size-fits-all approach. Just think about it, all right?"

"Yeah." He wouldn't be thinking about anything else for a long time.

✷
SEVENTEEN

Richard Swinton had come through the wormhole in search of his first wife, Angela. Like that Hank Higgins guy, she'd elected to have herself frozen and stored when modern medicine could do nothing to prevent her from developing a terrible disease. Unlike "Hank", as he was now calling himself, she hadn't fucked up a scientific trial, stolen medical records, and cost one of the best neuroscience researchers at Berkeley funding for a project that might have led to a cure.

Richard gripped the champagne glass in his hand so hard he worried it would shatter. He had to focus on what he'd come to this damn party to do—find Hank, humiliate him, and kidnap the jerk.

But in the meantime, he had to pretend he was here as the head of Good Day Beer. Despite his personal concerns, Richard had legitimate business reasons for his trip. He represented a consortium of businesses that hoped to expand trade into this side of the Divide, if only the wormhole wasn't the only way to get there, with its long travel time—three months to reach it from Earth—and the costs associated with cryostoring passengers and shielding cargo. In the last few years, with rumors swirling that the People had secretly developed FTL technology, businesses from Good Day Beer to Zip-a-Dee-Doodah Condoms to Cosmic Cruise Tours found a renewed interest in developing the Other Side. But that hinged on the uncertainty of the drive, which the People claimed they didn't have—and naturally, the Humans didn't believe them.

He took a seat by the "window," where he would be out of the way without appearing to be hiding, swallowed a sip of champagne, and stared out at the stars. There was so much room for expansion out there—if only the damn People weren't so greedy about their technology. New business opportunities, expanded trading, finding Angela's cryocan and who knew how many others'—all those things would be possible if they could wrestle FTL away from the People.

One of the reporters approached him, doughnut in hand. "Richard Swinton? You're the CEO of Good Day Beer, aren't you?"

Richard put on his usual dealing-with-the-press smile. "Yes, that's right. I'm here supporting many Earth businesses that trade with the People. We're all hopeful that the delegation can settle the current hostilities so we can continue to trade peacefully with our friends here on this side of the Divide."

That part was true—it just wasn't the *only* thing he came here to do.

* *

Xenia had been friends with Brad before he got himself killed trying to save his idiot Human girlfriend. She had watched him leave a job he loved—even if his parents disapproved of their son being a junk journalist instead of a business leader—so he could run off to Earth with Samantha. She had stared in horror at the news reports following the blast, grieving at how unfair it was Samantha was still alive while Brad was dead. Everywhere she turned on this station, she remembered that awful day.

She tried to push away the memories as she walked into the Woolerton Hall. Reminding herself that she was here as a delegate for the People, not as a grieving friend, she led her group into the room, which was garishly decorated with very different but equally tacky looks on each side. On the Human half, the walls were transformed into some sort of island getaway, with sandy beaches and waves. An old-fashioned ship sailed across the blue ocean. On the People side, a white backdrop represented peace, while pictures of diplomats and politicians who were remembered for being more successful than not rotated across the wall. In the center of the room, the delegation table was half-and-half, the decorator having apparently chosen the ugliest elements from both sides.

Xenia, as the leader of the party and highest-ranking Council member present, went to the People side of the table and sat down first. Next in line behind her was Tom, Vice President of Trade and Industry, followed by a couple low-level politicians who were there simply because they were owed favors. Their job was to nod, smile, and look like they were contributing while saying nothing.

Tom was one of those People who had gone into politics because he liked to see himself in holo. He certainly had the looks for it—twinkling blue eyes and a dimple in just the right corner of his face. Unfortunately, his skill-set was limited to spouting off pithy epithets that meant nothing and keeping his embarrassing romantic romps out of public view. He would have been more suited to acting in fictional holos than pursuing a career in politics, but unfortunately the voting public of New Atlantis didn't think so.

"Will the Humans be mad because we sat down before they got here?" he asked.

"Why would they? We're on our side of the table," Xenia said. "And we haven't even opened the wine yet."

"Well, you know how weird Humans are about their 'customs'. They get offended over the silliest things. You wouldn't believe the crazy stuff they've used as an excuse to start a war. I heard there was one over the price of tea or something—"

"They're here," Xenia's AI announced in a hushed tone.

"Are we supposed to stand up?" Tom asked.

"What for?"

That was when the doors at the other end of the hall flew open, and the Human procession entered.

"It's so nice to meet with you," Kyle Howard, President of the United Nations of Earth, said as he looked at the three of them. His lips were curved up in a smile, but the tightening of lines on his forehead suggested he was anything but happy and this meeting was anything but nice.

"So nice to meet you, too." Xenia jumped up so fast her chair toppled behind her. Keeping her own faux smile in place, she ignored the clattering, knowing one of her aides would fix it.

"I see you've already been seated," said the tall, dour man just behind President Howard. Xenia knew him as the head of one of Earth's self-defeating charities.

"Yes, please join us."

Howard took a seat directly opposite Xenia and the dour man reluctantly followed, flopping down in his chair like a sullen teenager. Beside him sat the other expected delegate, Susan Marshall, whose biggest accomplishment was inheriting a controlling share in the largest energy company on Earth. The entourage behind them remained standing, shifting from foot to foot or checking data pads.

Xenia quickly skimmed Morriss's dossier on her eyeplant. He ran End Hunger Now, what the Humans called a "non-profit" organization dedicated to "ending hunger worldwide." Upon the establishment of Human-People communication seven years ago, his organization had demanded that the People assist Earth in feeding its hungry, a problem that hadn't been seen on New Atlantis in centuries.

Back then it was considered an opportune time for the Humans to ask favors, since most of the People felt their ancestors, however far back in time, had treated their less-advanced distant cousins unfairly. Some claimed Earthers were only slightly less intelligent and shouldn't have been shut out of People society. Others took the opposite side, saying that leaving Humans alone on Earth was horribly irresponsible, like leaving a room full of toddlers alone with no AI supervision. Public opinion skewed toward regretting the decision to leave the Humans behind.

Unfortunately, once the Governing Council looked into the Humans' requests for "aid", attitudes shifted. End Hunger Now was one of several popular examples of the Humans' flat refusal to help themselves. One of its biggest donors was a large cattle company that made the money it donated by farming cattle on land that could easily produce far more food if it was used to grow grain. Tom, assuming the Humans simply missed this fact due to their own stupidity, proudly sent them a memo explaining that he'd found a solution! All End Hunger Now had to do was tell the major meat producers to start producing plant foods instead and there would be more than enough food for everyone on Earth within months.

He'd taken some backlash for, as one political columnist put it, "assuming that stupidity is the only cause of problems on Earth and forgetting that dumb people can be hypocrites, too." That gaffe was soon forgotten after Tom sent the UNE a memo detailing several highly effective methods of pregnancy prevention—with projections of how hunger could be reduced simply by stopping the population's exponential growth. He then suggested that moving to a plant-based diet without fixing "the excessive reproduction problem" would derail efforts to end hunger in the short term, by causing Humans to live longer when there were already too many of them.

For reasons no one on the Council quite understood, the Humans took offense again, and none of the suggested solutions were implemented. President Howard had assured the People that Humans understood "birth control," as they called it, they just couldn't force anyone to use it. At that point, Tom publicly asked why the Humans would have to be forced to do something that made sense, and the situation deteriorated again.

"Appetizers and drinks will be served shortly." Xenia blinked away the text on her eyeplant and refocused on her Earther guests.

"Thank you for your hospitality." Howard glanced around the hall as if looking for some random thing to compliment. "The decorations are nice."

"Thank you." It was normal for Humans to waste time on ass-kissing bullshit, but Xenia was already ready for this dinner to be over.

Fortunately, the expensive wine from New Atlantis's Moralia region arrived then, just ahead of the appetizers. As the servers handed Xenia her plate and glass, she dove into the political discussion.

"We're very happy to hear the United Nations of Earth is as committed to peace as the New Alantean Governing Council." She paused to take a bite of her appetizer while waiting for Howard to respond.

"Yes, of course, we've *always* wanted peace." Howard speared an artfully seasoned carrot with his fork. "Everyone in the UNE agrees that the events leading to our current... situation were very unfortunate for everyone."

"Glad we all agree continued attacks on either side aren't the answer."

Howard spread his hands. "You realize our own armies really have nothing to do with those."

"By 'our armies,' he means those belonging to countries in the United Nations of Earth." Marshall upended a salt shaker and violently shook it over her plate.

"But you have sent troops through the Divide," Xenia said.

"Believe it or not, we were trying to stop the... unauthorized militia. And to protect ourselves from retaliation—which, under the circumstances, we certainly understand," Howard added swiftly. "We still have to protect ourselves."

"Of course. We have to protect ourselves too," Tom said.

Xenia looked around the room, picturing the reporters and lower-level politicians and People with agendas to push and Humans with agendas to push, all straining at the doors. Soon the crowds would stream in, and both sides of the delegation would take questions from the press.

She stole a glance at the time on her pad as the servers appeared with the main course. They would only have another twenty minutes or so.

"To clarify your last point, President Howard, you don't condone any of the violence on your side?" she asked.

Howard shook his head. "Aside from anything our troops have done in self-defense, no, we don't condone any of the... unfortunate actions taken by some Humans without the knowledge or approval of the UNE or the respective governments of those Humans."

STUPID HUMANS

And if you can follow that, you can unravel a Tivioli puzzle in five flat.

"So you're saying you can't control your citizens?" Tom asked, and Xenia nearly choked on a bite of broccoli.

"Can you control all of *yours*?" Morriss crinkled his nose and pushed a piece of potato around his plate, as if looking for something better underneath it.

"Obviously, the actions of a few individuals have created problems for all of us," Xenia said. "From an official, military standpoint, neither side has done anything that wasn't in self-defense."

"From a bunch of individuals — on both sides — who took things personally," Marshall agreed.

Now the ass-kissing was going around in circles. "What we're here to do is put an end to the violence," Xenia said.

"Unfortunately, it's damn near impossible to convince millions of peope — individuals on both sides to just forget all the reasons these attacks have happened." Tom stuffed a forkful of noodles in his mouth with one hand and thumbed his data pad with the other.

"And if anyone is an expert on doing the damn-near-impossible, it's Tom here." Xenia gave him a swift slap on his back. "Tell us how you propose to do it."

He gulped and grabbed his water glass. "Right. You just have to... convince everyone that nothing can be gained by more senseless violence and death and destruction."

Howard stared at him as if he had just said Earth was the third planet from the Sun in their solar system. Morriss make a coughing noise that sounded very much like someone suppressing a laugh. Marshall stared off in a way that suggested she was reading on her eyeplant. Fortunately Tom and the favor-collectors were better actors than the Humans.

"Please elaborate on how we should do that," Xenia told Tom through clenched teeth.

He twisted his fork in the noodles again. "We just need one terrific copacetic communications plan to reach everyone with the right message. Wars are won with words, not weapons. You Humans must know that, with as many wars as you've had, right?"

"Get us another bottle of wine," Xenia hissed at the server.

✳
EIGHTEEN

"Why am I here?" Hank asked Haylea. He was outside the Woolerton Hall, wearing a blue tailored suit that made him feel like he was in a very bad old movie. Haylea had sent it over right after informing him he had to make an appearance at some public political spectacle.

"I told you, this is an important meeting of delegates from both sides, and more importantly, everyone important will be here."

"But that doesn't explain why *I* need to be here." Hank wished he was back in his room watching this mess on the holo.

"Because you're a celebrity Human. Everyone will want to know what you think," Haylea said. "Isn't that right, Roble?"

The goofball who had been drooling all over himself staring at her put his tongue back in his mouth long enough to say, "Absolutely." The guy probably couldn't have repeated the question if asked.

"The really important celebrity Humans are in there." Hank waved at the closed door. "I don't even know what we're fighting about."

"No one does." Samantha popped out of the crowd behind him.

"I hope you're here to be the first reporter to get Hank's official statement to the press," Haylea said.

"My official statement is that I just woke up from a century-and-a-half long nap, I don't have a clue what's going on politically, and I wasn't even that interested in Earth politics before I left." Hank inched toward the doors. "When are they going to at least let us in to eat? I'm starving, and the sooner we eat the sooner I can leave."

Haylea shrugged. "They've been in there more than an hour, but who knows? They're having peace talks."

"Is there a way to sneak out of this place?"

"You can't leave because we haven't introduced you to the delegates yet," Haylea said through gritted teeth and a forced smile.

"There's a rumor their president is here," Roble said.

"The president of the planet? Is that what they have on Earth now?" Hank looked at Samantha. She had been there more recently than anyone else in the room.

She snorted. "Don't overestimate our level of togetherness. It's more like the UN you remember than one big country."

"They still have wars," Haylea clarified.

"Whoa, I'm meeting President…." Hank trailed off. "Shit. I have no idea what his name is."

"Kyle Howard, and it's an unconfirmed rumor," Samantha said. "That reminds me though, I ran into someone who says he knows you."

"Really? Who?" Hank tried to be polite, but he really just wanted to go back to his room and continue his research on brain cell regeneration. He still hadn't given Vance an answer about using him as a guinea pig, although he was leaning toward yes. What did he have to lose?

"Richard Swinton," Samantha said. "He told me he's looking for his wife — she went through the wormhole like you did."

"I bet Hank's story gave him hope." Haylea's eyes lit up, and Hank thought he saw dollar signs flashing in them, but it could have just been the glaze of champagne. "Maybe you could do a feature on that, Sam. Think how many media agencies would pick it up."

"He's the CEO of Good Day Beer, right?" Roble asked.

Hank was still reeling over hearing the name Richard Swinton. It was just a coincidence, right? Richard couldn't know anything. But then why would he claim to know Hank?

"You know, I don't think I remember him."

Samantha shrugged. "Well, he seems to remember you. Says he met you during a clinical trial. I think maybe his wife had the same illness."

Hank shrugged. "I knew a lot of patients who were trying to get into trials. I never got into one myself, but I guess it's just as well — they never found a cure."

"But you're better now," Haylea said. "There's another good angle, Samantha. 'People cure man where Humans failed.'"

"I don't know about that," Samantha mumbled.

"Since you two Humans are here, can I ask you something?" Roble said.

Hank shrugged. "What?"

"I've been trying to learn more about the Humans by reading their most famous pieces of literature. Have you read *Romeo and Juliet*?"

Hank groaned. "I was assigned to read it in school but I really just read the *Cliff's Notes*."

"Me too," Samantha said.

"It's supposed to be the greatest romance in Human history. But I don't think it's romantic at all."

"What's it about?" Haylea asked.

"It basically says you should get married at the age of thirteen to someone you've only known for three days, and if that relationship doesn't work out, you should just kill yourself."

Samantha snickered. "That's a pretty good interpretation."

"Wow, no wonder your society is so messed up." Haylea's face twisted in horror.

Hank felt obligated to say something in his people's defense. "Well, it's not really like that."

"You don't want to defend Shakespeare," Samantha said.

"I mean, at the time that thing was written, it was normal for people to get married at the age of thirteen." Hank realized just as he said it why she had tried to stop him.

Haylea's nose crinkled in disgust. Roble's jaw fell open so far it dislodged a donut crumb from his chin.

"You people let children get married?" he asked.

"Not for centuries. It was a thousand years ago and we're embarrassed by it too." Samantha looked around as if hoping no one had heard their conversation. "We all think it was totally barbaric, don't we, Hank?"

"Oh, uh, yeah." How did he get into these messes?

Just then, Haylea's AI beeped at her.

"That's a reminder that I need to go check on the drink distribution for the party—right after the delegation talks finish, we're going to have a lot of thirsty reporters flooding the hall. Don't go *anywhere*," Haylea told Hank, then she took off, Roble trailing in her wake.

"Do all the insults like that bother you?" Hank asked Samantha, desperate to steer the conversation away from Richard and his own problems. "I mean, it's not just Haylea and Roble. Some of the news commentators here are really rude. They say things that would be completely offensive on Earth."

"The thing is, they *are* smarter than us. Their average IQ is one forty."

"So? Some humans have a higher IQ than that. They can't just judge us all by an average number. There's a word for that. And some of their insults make it sound like we're even stupider than we really are." Crap. That didn't exactly come out right.

She shrugged. "Don't you remember dealing with dumb people on Earth? I do. I like it better here."

"But Haylea told me the security chief wanted to kick you off the station just for being Human."

Samantha snorted. "She's had it out for me since I got here. Haylea told her boss, the station's owner, that it would be bad copacetic communications—that's what they call PR here—to kick me out if I hadn't broken any laws or station rules. He begrudgingly agreed, so I stayed. Anna wastes a lot of time following me around, like she thinks I'm going to blow the place up any minute, though."

"Isn't that harassment or something? Don't these people have anti-discrimination laws if they're so enlightened?"

"Why would they have those?"

"Because that's what enlightened societies do. They make laws that say everyone is equal and has to be treated fairly. Or are they less enlightened than they would have us believe?"

Samantha waved a hand at the party guests, sipping drinks and chattering about the weather on New Atlantis. "But that's just it. They're enlightened enough not to have had any of the things that prompted the need for those laws on Earth, Hank. They didn't have slavery or a holocaust or any of the reasons that we have anti-discrimination laws."

"What about their dispute with us, back when they left?"

"What about it? They left. They walked away. That's the worst thing they ever did, and they still manage to feel remorse about it." She frowned. "I've always felt like there was more to it than that. It's one of my pet projects—investigating why the People *really* feel guilty about the Humans."

"Why? They let us have the whole planet."

She smiled. "Yeah, that's how I see it too. But some of them feel it was irresponsible to leave us alone instead of trying to fix us."

"Can they?" Hank suddenly realized there was an important question he'd never thought to ask. "Can they genetically engineer us to be like them?"

"There's another one of those issues I mentioned when I first met you," she said. "As far as you and me go, no. They've identified the genes that make them slightly more intelligent, and they could be transferred into our DNA. But those only affect brain development in early childhood—it would be pointless for us."

"Yeah, I understand." *Better than you know.* "But our children...."

"Yes, a lot of Earth politicians are pushing for them to give us the genes so future generations could benefit." Samantha sighed as if she'd explained this a million times and didn't feel like doing it again, but.... "There are a few problems. For one thing, genetics is only half the equation. Apparently living with dumb people makes you dumber. The People estimate that if all future Earth children were given the genes, the average IQ would only go up to only about one hundred and ten due to the society they're raised in."

"Over time, that would change, right?"

"Not necessarily, because not everyone on Earth would agree to give their kids the genes." She rolled her eyes. "You remember Earth. People refuse medical treatments for all sorts of reasons—and there's a *huge* amount of mistrust for the People. Plus, you remember how overpopulated Earth was when you left?"

"That's why it was cheaper to be stored in space."

"Well, it's even worse now. Almost half our population is starving. The People are afraid we'd start reproducing at an even faster rate in the hopes of changing society faster, and more of us would starve."

Hank was starting to get the picture. "A lot of... Humans probably don't like that, do they?"

"That's just one of the real reasons we're having a... war-ish situation," she said. "That reminds me—I know this can't be true, but you should know there's this rumor going around that you—well, that you're telling people we fuck goats on Earth."

"What?" How the hell did she hear about that? "Don't tell me that got around."

"You did?"

He shook his head. "No... well... not exactly. It wasn't like that, I just...."

"You just what?" Samantha looked as horrified as he felt. "These people already think we're uncivilized idiots, Hank!"

"I never said that we all fuck goats!" As people turned around and stared, Hank realized he was yelling in a crowded room and lowered his voice. "I was trying to explain—oh, hell, this is really embarrassing."

"More embarrassing than telling people we fuck farm animals?" She rolled her eyes. "Fine, there's a meeting room over here. Let's finish this conversation somewhere private."

She dragged him down a hallway to a small meeting room with a couch and a collection of mismatched chairs. Random gadgets he didn't recognize were piled on a table. Five Alpha's staff must have had to move everything in a hurry after finding out about the delegation party.

"Can I ask you a personal question?" Hank asked after they sat down.

"That's only fair. I make a living asking people personal questions, you included."

"Does it ever bother you—you know—having sex with someone who has a tail?"

"Oh, of course. I still find it weird, but I've gotten used to it." Her eyes widened. "Oh no, you didn't tell some woman that having sex with her was like screwing a goat, did you?"

"No, of course not! I never had sex with goats!" he snapped. "It's just... well, okay, I was about to get laid for the first time in a century and a half. And this girl, she was really beautiful. But when she took her clothes off and I saw the tail, it freaked me out! She said it shouldn't, because I didn't have a tail and that didn't bother her, so I tried to explain that to Humans, tails make you an animal, right? Then maybe I said something about her tail making me feel like one of those rednecks I used to see on the news back in Texas, you know, the ones who get arrested for fucking a goat or a horse or something...."

"Oh no," Samantha groaned. "Tell me you didn't say that."

"Then I couldn't figure out how to explain goatfucking rednecks to someone who already thinks Humans are cavemen or something...."

"Hank, please stop talking. You're just making this worse."

"So she told everyone what I said?"

Samantha sighed. "Not really. There was a drunk woman at the bar saying she screwed the two-hundred-year-old Human, or at least she tried to, but he said he'd rather have sex with a goat. It sounded so ridiculous, I just figured she was on something in addition to the drinks. If it makes you feel better, though, I really doubt anyone else is going to take her seriously. She's kind of a drunk."

"So how do you get used to the tails?"

"Well, I usually get on top or wrap my legs around the guy so I don't have to feel it swishing between my legs." She thought for a minute. "Then there are some fun things you can try if you're on a small ship and you can adjust the gravity."

"Oh, right, sex in zero-G. Never thought I'd get to try that."

"Oh, I don't recommend *that*. Low gravity is better. There's this one position you can try..." She then launched into an explanation of something that sounded like it would only be appropriate if an acrobat and a yogi were shooting a porno in low-G.

"I just woke up from a century-and-a-half nap. I don't think I'm limber enough for that," he finally cut her off.

"Well, Brad and I used to enjoy...." She stared into space.

"Brad was your ex?" he asked.

"Well, yeah, you could say that."

"Did you break up recently?"

"Yeah, we broke up and... then he died. On the *Traveler.* I'm sure you heard about that."

"Oh, I'm sorry. I didn't know."

"Now everyone thinks...." She trailed off again, then shook her head. "Well, it doesn't matter. Let's talk about something less personal—like your sex life. Just use the sim suites on deck two until you figure out how to avoid the tail problem. And *please* stop talking about goatfucking rednecks on Earth, okay?"

"I swear, I wasn't trying to give her the impression we were all like that."

Samantha opened her mouth to reply, then closed it again as she squinted at the blank space in front of her. She must have one of those implants where you could read stuff on the inside of your eyeballs. Vance had offered to give him one, but Hank had told him to worry about fixing his brain first.

"My AI just told me they're about to let everyone into the hall." She jumped up and headed for the door.

Hank reluctantly followed. How bad could this party be?

NINETEEN

As the crushing wave of reporters and politicos carried her forward into the hall, Samantha literally bumped elbows with Richard Swinton, one of Earth's most successful business moguls.

"Pardon me." He flashed what he probably thought was a disarming smile. "Say, you're that reporter who got the exclusive on Hank Higgins, aren't you?"

"That's right. And you're Richard Swinton, here to bring peace to both sides of the Divide by handing out free samples of beer."

Swinton grinned sheepishly. "I make no promises, but drinking Good Day Beer has brought a lot of people together. Surely you remember the jingle—"

"Yes. No need to sing it for me."

"I know you think I'm just here to peddle a product." Swinton kept pace with her as she weaved through the room, trying to get a closer look at the delegates' table. "But I, like the others at Good Day Beer, really do want to make the world—the whole galaxy—a better place. That's why we're the official beer sponsor of this historic event—"

"Where everyone is drinking champagne."

"It was nice meeting you. I've sent a copy of our latest press release to your AI. Hope you enjoy the speech." Swinton waved at someone across the room and moved on.

Like most reporters, Samantha hated people trying to use her for free publicity, but she suspected Richard might have a few interesting skeletons in his closet. He had been one of the first Humans to open trade relations with the People, and one of the first to seek regeneration treatment here. According to news reports, he'd retired from Good Day Beer at the age of 70, then had himself put in cryo in the hopes of one day joining his similarly stored wife. Instead, his kids had woken him up thirty years later, after The Divide was found. Richard immediately bought a ship and went through the wormhole, returning with a younger face and a new mission—to establish trade between the Humans and the People. The board of Good Day, which at the time had been suffering from floundering sales, voted unanimously to fire their current CEO and re-appoint Richard.

"Perhaps we could do an interview later," she called after him.

He turned, looking surprised. "I'd like that. I'll have my AI contact yours to schedule something tomorrow."

Samantha agreed, then edged toward the delegates' table as Richard hurried off. She couldn't get closer than twenty feet, thanks to the neon-colored warning lights indicating an expensive technology frequently used by government officials and VIPs. It consisted of DNA and infrared scanners plus a "mild electrical deterrent." If you brushed the field once, it was indeed mild, somewhat like being shocked by static electricity when touching metal. If you brushed the field repeatedly, it became more like a tasing incident where someone ended up getting sued afterward. Haylea had promised to get Samantha behind the blockade later, but she didn't know how much pull the CC director really had in this situation.

An automated server glided up to her with a tray of Beach Breeze. Canned beer at a political event — Earth really had gone down the crapper since she left. She grabbed one and popped it open.

Her AI buzzed in her ear to let her know she had a message. Taking a sip of the Beach Breeze, which tasted like a regular Good Day Beer drowned in coconut, she read Haylea's message. "Meet me in Hallway B. We join the delegates in ten minutes. Have you seen Hank?"

* *

Hank told himself Richard Swinton wasn't the reason he'd taken the first opportunity to disappear from the party. He really didn't like crowds, and after all the media attention he'd had to deal with lately, he was getting tired of answering questions. No, Richard didn't scare him at all.

He was at the edge of the outer hall, almost to the elevators, when that dope Haylea was dating caught up with him. "Hey, where are you going? You have to come back to the party!"

Pretending not to hear, Hank stepped closer to the elevator, which made the door open. He still wasn't used to that.

"I'm serious, Haylea needs you for this event to be a success." Roble jumped between Hank and the elevator.

Hank pasted on a fake smile. "That's nonsense, and if you stop thinking with the wrong part of your anatomy, you'll realize I'm right. People are here to see the delegates, and while I might make an interesting side show, the main event will be fine without me. Now I'm sure you can understand that the last few weeks have been very hectic for me, and—"

"That's not true!" Roble stepped to the side as Hank tried to go around him. He wondered if they had football here, and if Roble had ever played. He was a good blocker.

"You don't understand," Roble said as Hank looked around the lobby for alternative escape routes. "Haylea was about to lose her job before Samantha invented that crazy Human bit. Then you showed up and made the whole Earther thing even more interesting!"

"I've done my part then, haven't I?" Hank pointed out. "I've already told my story to every reporter here. The delegates are their main focus tonight, not me."

"And why do you think they're here? You know they didn't announce the location until yesterday, right? Do you think they were even considering Five Alpha a month ago?"

"How the hell should I know? I was in cryo a month ago." Should he make a run for the elevator at the other end of the room?

"If it wasn't for you and your story, they never would have picked this place," Roble said. "And in order for it to remain popular after the delegates leave Haylea needs something that will cause the viewing public to forever associate Five Alpha with you and the Peace Committee."

Hank spread his hands in an honest gesture of bewilderment. What the fuck was this guy talking about?

Roble rolled his eyes. "She told you she wanted you to make a speech, right?"

Hank groaned. "Did she write it for me, too?"

"Not exactly." Roble scratched at the back of his head. "She just thought it would be great if you could talk about all the positive things

Humans and the People have achieved together, in a general sort of way. The People came up with a cure for your disease, Hank. But they couldn't have helped you if the Earthers hadn't developed a way to store you in space, then found the wormhole and established communications with us."

Hank stared at him in horror. "She wants me to use *that* as an example of Humans and People working together to achieve greatness? You've got to be kidding me."

"I know they didn't work directly together to cure you, but both sides contributed," Haylea's doormat said. "Listen, you can put this in your own words. In fact, she was just going to let you say whatever you wanted, then edit it together like that after your speech. She'd be really mad if she knew I was telling you...."

Hank considered telling Roble that he really wasn't cured. That Richard Swinton might be after him for fucking up a clinical trial more than a century ago. That even if he made the greatest speech ever, Haylea still wouldn't love Roble. He thought about saying a lot of things, but found he couldn't say any of them.

Richard Swinton couldn't hurt him in a crowded room, after all.

"All right, Roble," he said with a sigh. "Where do I go to make my damn speech?"

* *

Richard watched the crowd as they sipped their Beach Breeze, knowing he had only a limited window in which to grab Hank. The benefit of using a twenty-minute rufie was the reduced potential for anyone to notice, because most people only remembered the highlights of their day, not the second-to-second minutiae. People rarely thought twice about a ten- or twenty-minute blank spot—it was simply one of many less interesting things that happened. There were ten- and even five-minute pills available now, but Richard wasn't sure how long the grab was supposed to take and wanted extra time.

He was starting to think he was going to have to search the whole station when he finally spotted his mark heading toward the podium. Hank was flanked by the Human reporter/bartender Samantha and the station's beleaguered Copacetic Communications Director, Haylea. Richard glanced at all their hands to make sure they were holding cans of Beach Breeze. Samantha had cracked one open and taken a sip a few minutes ago. He hadn't seen Haylea drink any but she had one in her hand. As for Hank, it didn't really matter—Richard wanted him to remember what was about to happen.

After politely disengaging himself from the trio of colleagues he was discussing import strategies with, Richard moved toward the podium. He walked slowly, greeting people and shaking hands, because sudden, direct movement in one direction might trigger the station's security bots, and they weren't so easily drugged into forgetfulness. The delegates probably wouldn't touch Beach Breeze, but they were distracted by bigger problems, and Richard wasn't going to do anything too problematic here—if he could avoid it. Of course the room was full of recording devices, and Richard wouldn't do anything he didn't want anyone to know about. He just wanted to make sure the reporters didn't feel like chasing him out the door when he left with his mark.

Hank stood at the podium, shifting from foot to foot, hands in pockets. For a brief moment, Richard considered just leaving him there and letting him suffer through the speech—that would almost be punishment enough.

"I, um, wanted to talk about, uh…." Hank glanced down at his data pad. "Cooperation between our people… peoples… species. Es."

Haylea winced and downed another slug of Beach Breeze.

Good call, you won't want to remember this disaster of a speech. Not that it would matter—the media's floating cameras were impervious to rufies and everyone would see it tomorrow.

Which was why he needed to handle this situation very carefully.

"What I'm trying to say is, um…." Hank grabbed the edges of the podium like a drowning man clutching a lifesaver. "I'm grateful for the excellent medical care I received here at Five Alpha. When I had myself put in cryo, I could never have expected to wake up here, so many years later…."

The security bots were designed to thwart violent attacks, not spotlight stealers, so Richard had no problem waltzing on stage and slinging an arm around Hank, whose expression went from deer-in-the-headlights to politician-caught-with-a-call-girl.

"Many of you don't know this, but Hank and I are old friends." Richard gestured magnanimously with the hand that was holding his un-sipped Beach Breeze. "And I hate to interrupt, but I also wanted to express my gratitude, to those on both sides of the Divide, for curing my dear friend of such a dreadful disease."

He paused to ride out the applause, turning to shake hands with Hank. Oddly, Hank's expression was no longer deer *or* politician, it was more… well, that was odd. Hank just looked sad. What was that about? Well, he'd worry about it later.

"You may not know this about me," Richard said. "But my first wife Angela had the same illness as Hank. She also eventually had herself cryostored in space. As many of you know, a solar flare on our side of the Divide destroyed the beacons for many such cryocans. Unlike

Hank, my wife has not been found yet. That's why I asked Good Day Beer to give me this assignment — so I could come here and look for her. And Hank, I apologize for interrupting, but when you started talking about your struggle, I was moved to say a few words as an individual. I hope you'll allow me the privilege."

Hank nodded and mumbled something that might have been, "Of course." He looked eternally grateful that he didn't have to finish the speech himself.

"What I wanted to say is that there are enough problems and pain and loss in the galaxy," Richard said. "There are other medical problems to conquer. There are thousands of cryocans to find. There are new worlds to explore, on both sides. Hank here is proof that when People and Humans work together, there is no obstacle we can't overcome. I hope that everyone here tonight is as dedicated as I am to overcoming the biggest obstacle we all face — senseless fighting."

While waiting out the obligatory applause, Richard briefly turned his attention to the delegates' table. Xenia, Vice President of International Relations, wore a smile that didn't come within light-years of reaching her eyes. Tom, VP of Trade Relations, stared at the stage as if Hank had just pulled Richard out of his own asshole.

Then there were the Humans — President Howard, that Marshall woman who never smiled, and End Hunger Now's resident windbag, Ron Morriss. Howard's practiced poker face revealed nothing as he stared raptly at the podium, while Morriss sloshed wine around in his glass as if waiting for it to get better with age. Marshall poked at a data pad.

Keeping with the let's-all-get-along theme, Richard launched into his favorite speech about how Good Day Beer could solve the world's problems. Despite the fact that he spent ten minutes waxing poetic, it was fairly simple—about three Earth years ago, the big news story was a live, on-air, knock-down, drag-out fight between two musicians at the Global Music Awards. A punk rapper known as The Cootie—real name John Smith, because his parents obviously lacked imagination—stormed on stage during the lackluster performance of neo-country artist Roger Rogers—real name Roger Rogers, because his parents also obviously lacked imagination.

The Cootie then proceeded to smash his guitar, which wouldn't have been unusual for a punk rapper, except that he chose to smash it into Rogers' face. To be fair, the Woodley 500 was almost all plastic and Cootie really did more damage to the instrument than the neo-country artist's face, but the situation still devolved into a fistfight between Rogers, Cootie, and a couple of Rogers's bandmates.

In between punches, the two screamed at each other about an attractive female pop singer named Ooh La La—real name Amalaya Amadalea, because her parents obviously had too much imagination—who had apparently been romantically involved with both of them in an uncomfortably short period of time. The security bots failed to break up the fight because their programming read the situation as a normal stunt for that type of awards show.

One week later, both Rogers and Cootie were ridiculously overpaid to shoot an ad in which they drank Good Day Beer together in a bar while talking about how hard it was to understand women. It was the most-viewed commercial on the nets within minutes of its rush release a few days later, and Good Day Beer went from being the twenty-seventh most popular beer in the world to being the third most popular.

Of course, when Richard told the story, he left out the part where Rogers and Cootie were overpaid and the part where Good Day Beer made millions, focusing instead on the part where his company brought about peace and tranquility.

"And I am so thrilled to be here, representing the whole Human race, on this historic occasion, as we work toward galactic peace," Richard finished, pausing for what he thought would be a wild round of applause.

Unfortunately, when he'd been rehearsing the speech, he hadn't expected the People to be such experienced and enthusiastic hecklers.

"If your drink is so great at bringing everyone together, why do you have so many wars on your planet?" a reporter called from the press table, apparently assuming he was finished.

"I'll, ah, take questions in just a moment, thanks," Richard said. "Right now I want to draw everyone's attention to the servers you see gliding by with trays of Good Day Beer. Those are complimentary samples of our newest beverage, Beach Breeze.

"As you're enjoying the new flavor, I'd like to thank the organizers of this evening's festivities for giving Good Day Beer the opportunity to sponsor this historic event. We know that peace is coming to both sides of the Divide, and we want to be there for all of you. Please enjoy the Beach Breeze."

"I agree with my, uh, friend, uh, Richard," Hank said, and Richard thought he actually meant it.

"I know there have been individuals on both sides who have tragically made misguided mistakes," Richard continued. "But I'm hoping that we can all get past that, and work together to improve life for everyone. Thank you for indulging me."

Hank started the applause, and soon everyone in the room was standing, although the People appeared confused as to why. Richard waited out the laughter and clapping before striking the final blow.

"Now if you'll all excuse me, I'm going to buy my friend here a drink and no one's going to stop me!" He slapped Hank on the back and left the stage to another half-hearted, confused smattering of applause, without bothering to take any questions. That did not, however, stop the press from shouting at him.

"So, why are there still so many wars on Earth?"

Halfway to the door with Hank in tow, he had to stop and address the question. This was the moment the media would be talking about tomorrow, and he wanted to keep it that way. "We're not miracle workers, but we like to do our part to facilitate peace and cooperative dialogues. Besides, much as we wish it weren't true, there are a few Humans who don't drink Good Day Beer."

This earned him a round of laughter, and he continued out the door with an easy smile. Hank, however, didn't look relaxed at all.

✳

TWENTY

Samantha knew the Beach Breezes were spiked—obviously with one of the new-generation rufies—after the first sip. Standing in the hallway with Haylea, she noticed the subtlety, the way the effect was almost barely noticeable—just a slight slowing of her movements. Probably no one else noticed at all—she wouldn't have if she wasn't a) used to having catlike reflexes and b) very familiar with the effects of tranquilizers.

Contrary to what most people thought, downers did *not* impact the ability to think clearly—or at least, they never had that effect on her. So it didn't take her long to figure out that if a sealed can—and she was sure her can had been sealed and she hadn't taken her eyes off it—contained something other than sunscreen-flavored beer, it must have been put in during the canning process. Could the drug have been on the rim of the can? No, she always wiped off cans with a napkin before drinking out of them, because who knew where those things had been?

Was Richard Swinton behind this? He had encouraged everyone to drink this crap, but it could still have been one of his lackeys. But why? There were hundreds of recording devices in the room, so what could Richard do without anyone noticing? If he attempted anything violent, security would be on him in seconds.

The intention had to be more subtle then. Maybe he didn't want anyone to think too much about what he was saying or doing. As a reporter, she knew that most liars got caught because someone — sometimes a journalist, but sometimes a snoopy friend or enemy — remembered one little thing that didn't seem right and investigated further.

But Richard had just ensured that everyone would be scrutinizing his behavior tomorrow with that tacky little speech. The media would be talking about nothing but how Richard Swinton had steamrolled over Hank and —

Maybe that was it. He didn't want the press thinking too clearly right now, but he wanted them focusing on the speech later. What was he trying to divert attention from? Did he think he could get past the electric fence and chat up the politicians?

Samantha leaned over and whispered to Haylea, "Am I ever going to talk with the delegates?"

"After they wrap up the private dinner, they'll mingle with guests, then take questions from the press."

"You've been saying that for an hour. I'll be working the room when the politicians get their shit together." There was more going on here than just government types kissing each other's asses, and she was going to find out what it was.

*   *

"Where exactly are we going?" Hank asked as Richard and the goons ushered him into an elevator. He couldn't put up a fight when Richard led him out of the hall—not with all those reporters around.

"Back to my ship, where we can talk about old times in private," Richard said, still keeping up that cheerful public persona.

"You'll have to forgive me." Hank plastered what Emily used to call his "aw, shucks" grin onto his face. "I was unconscious for more than a century, and I was always terrible with names...."

"Obviously!" The elevator doors opened and he herded Hank into another indistinguishable gray hallway. They started toward a massive archway marked "Airlock 14." "You can't even remember your own."

Hank produced a confused frown, but wasn't sure if he did it fast enough. "What are you talking about?"

"I think we both know that, John." Richard stopped at the airlock and passed his hand over the sensor panel. Hank hadn't paid too much attention to the nickel tour Vance had given him, but he recalled that the airlocks had some of the tightest security in the building. People attempting to pass through either way were scanned down to their DNA. Getting onto the station required security approval, and getting on a ship required approval from the craft's system. There were some other protocols too, something about people being kidnapped or dragged off the station against their will, but Hank couldn't quite remember what they were....

"Don't worry, the security system won't block you." Richard gave Hank a friendly slap on the back. "I slipped a little something into the Beach Breeze to help you relax, so it won't be concerned by your high blood pressure."

That was it—the scanners could detect signs of stress, like high blood pressure and heart rate, sort of like those old polygraph machines on Earth.

The system wouldn't automatically lock you out, but it would alert a security officer to investigate the situation before the ship could un-dock.

"Look, I don't know how I know you or what you want from me, but I'm tired of whatever game we're playing." Hank stalled while trying to think of an escape plan. "Clearly you think I'm someone else that you don't like very much, so if it's all the same to you, I don't think I'll be joining you for drinks."

The goons immediately moved in closer. They didn't touch him, but they came close enough that Hank noticed one of them had atrociously bad breath. Apparently that was another medical problem they hadn't quite licked here.

"I have no intention of hurting you." Richard crossed his arms over his barrel chest, a pose Hank recognized from a news article he'd read earlier. Richard had been portrayed as blazing a trail for Earth companies in the "new frontier" on this side of the Divide.

"Then you won't mind if I leave," Hank shot back.

Richard returned a tight smile. "If you go back to that party, I'll be forced to release the evidence I have against you, Mr. Halbrooke. Or can I call you John?"

"I don't know what you're talking about." Hank tried to imitate Richard's tough-guy pose.

Richard shrugged and reached into his pocket, extracting and unrolling a data pad. "Very well. It'll just take me a few seconds to send the info to the authorities."

"What authorities?" Now that Hank thought about it, surely the statute of limitations on what he'd done had expired. Besides, if Earth and New Atlantis were having an almost-war, did that mean they weren't extraditing each other's criminals? Shit, he should've done more research.

Richard flashed him that magazine-cover self-assured smile. "Yes, New Atlantis and Earth have an extradition treaty, and yes, they *are* still enforcing it in spite of this... scuffle. Both sides want peace, remember? And just to get you caught up on Earth laws, since you left I mean, let me tell you about the Fortieth Amendment. I'll cut through the legalese for you. It basically says that a person can't escape the statute of limitations by having himself put in cryo...." His voice trailed off as the lights went out.

Immediately, Hank felt one of the "security personnel" grab his arm and twist it behind his back. "Don't get any ideas."

"Have you ever considered breath mints?" How could he use this situation to escape?

"What the hell is going on?" Richard's voice sounded like he'd just been told Good Day's stock had dropped five points. "I thought these People were geniuses with technology far beyond ours! And they can't even keep the fucking lights on?"

"Look, the airlock console is still working," said one of the goons. "Obviously they have backup systems for the important stuff."

It was true. When Hank turned toward where the console had been to his right, he saw several small but dim lights.

"Then I guess we're all going in. There won't be any power problems on my ship," Richard said, and Hank was tugged toward the console. It was a little like being pulled behind a motorboat on waterskis — except, of course, that he was horizontal and not wearing skis.

What the hell, he wasn't going to get a better opportunity to escape. He leaned toward the goon, holding his breath, in the hopes that the guy would loosen his grip. No such luck, but it was worth a shot. What else could he do?

"Oh my god, this must be the Human attack they were talking about on the news!" he yelled.

"Then we'll be safer on my ship, and ready to take off if the station looks like it's about to explode," Richard's voice said from somewhere in front of them. Hank heard thumping and figured it was Mr. Mentos trying to find the right button on the console. Were they still clear or did they need to be scanned again? Haylea had said something about a scan being good for two minutes, unless security saw a reason to be concerned. Security might be a little busy right now.

And so was Bad Breath. Hank kicked at where he assumed the guy's leg or hip would probably be, based on where his hand was on Hank's shoulder. He got lucky and hit... something. He'd never know what, but the goon groaned. He did not, however, let go of Hank's arm.

"You don't think that's going to work, do you?" Richard's voice suddenly sounded right in Hank's ear, and a new hand clamped down on his shoulder. "I have an infrared scanner, John. So do my associates, but unfortunately this development with the dark has apparently caused them to forget. Now, let's all go inside and have a chat, huh?"

*　*

The interior of Richard's ship lit up as soon as Bad Breath crossed the threshold, Hank in tow. Neither he nor the goon with the scar touched the console, so Richard must have set it to let everyone in for a brief time period. The beer baron's fingers flickered over the pad inside the door—locking them in, Hank assumed.

They were in a large atrium with three curtained archways. Hank figured one led to the guest quarters, one to Richard's work area and one to his personal space, which had to be even more opulent than the room they were in now.

The gallery "windows" currently showed the curve of Five Alpha to the left and the vast, inky blackness of space on the right. Hank had been told these "windows" in space were really just sophisticated view screens, but they looked so much like windows he had a hard time believing it. In the center of the room, an actual chandelier dangled from the ceiling. He had never seen one before in real life, although he had glimpsed a few in old movies he'd seen as a kid. Had those things come back on Earth while he was in cryo?

Below the chandelier was a U-shaped grouping of sofas, which Bad Breath shoved him toward. Hank reluctantly sat on the one closest to the airlock hatch, although proximity probably wouldn't do him much good. He tried to think of an escape plan, but nothing came to him.

Richard sat at the other end of the sofa, as close to opposite Hank as he could. Bad Breath sat uncomfortably close to Hank while Scar stood between him and the hatch. Figuring he had nothing left to lose, Hank reached into his pocket and pulled out a roll of breath mints.

"Mint?" he asked Bad Breath.

"You're making this hard for me, Hank!" Richard's smile rapidly dissolved into that hard, unyielding grimace from the magazine article. "I want to like you, but then I remember that you ended the trial that could have saved my wife from being put in cryo and lost in space."

Well, what could Hank say to that? That the drug probably wouldn't have worked anyway? That no one should be forced to lose their mind when even the remote possibility of a cure existed? That if Richard was the one faced with going crazy he might feel differently? Those arguments had been made before, by more eloquent people than Hank. Maybe he should just continue denying the whole thing. What kind of proof did Richard really have, anyway?

He was just about to ask when he saw Richard's grimace change to a look of shock. He was staring over Hank's shoulder at the leftmost curtained archway. Hank and Bad Breath both followed his gaze.

Hank didn't recognize the man who came through the curtain. He was Human — no tail — with a forgettable face, forgettable features, and dull, neutral clothing that likely blended into most wallpaper. Only his eyes were memorable — they were tiny, cold blue marbles.

"That trial shoulda never happened." His voice was hard, with a distinct southern drawl.

"How did you get in here?" Richard growled. Bad Breath nearly knocked Hank off the couch jumping to his feet. Scar was already moving toward the intruder.

The gun appeared so fast Hank thought he must have blinked and missed the forgettable guy whipping it out. Then he realized guns had gotten a lot smaller and more portable since the last time he'd watched a bad movie on Earth.

"I wouldn't do that if I were you." Forgettable's eyes fixed on Scar, whose hand had moved almost imperceptibly toward his jacket pocket. It occurred to Hank that he wasn't a big enough threat for Scar to bother with a weapon. Should he be insulted or relieved?

Scar stood, frozen, Bad Breath a few steps behind him. Richard also remained still, staring down Forgettable.

"There sure are a lot of relics floating around out here." His voice cut through the silence like a knife. "There's Hank here, and there's you, and you both got out of your boxes okay and you're walking around. But Angela — I still don't know where she is."

"Cry me a river," Forgettable said. "That trial she wanted to get into, that treatment he stole —" He looked at Hank as if he was dog shit on his shoe. "It shoulda never been developed. Not by a multi-billion dollar corporation that was only going to string people along to make money."

Hank almost groaned, but thought better of it. Now he knew why Forgettable was here — he was one of those whackjobs who had slowed progress down in the first place.

Unfortunately, the Medical Responsibility people inspired a lot of fringe groups, and one called Stop Big Pharma had been big when he left. According to some reading he'd done after waking up, they'd never convinced Congress to take charge of all medical research — thank God — but they continued to harass anyone who conducted private research — or might benefit from it.

Richard stared down Forgettable. "I'm sorry that you feel people should suffer and die to prevent companies from making a profit."

"Why do you think I was so desperate to get my hands on that treatment?" Hank saw an opportunity to align himself with Richard. "That trial would have happened years earlier if it wasn't for people like him buying their way into the FDA and slowing progress."

"I agree." Richard's eyes never even wavered. "And if you think you're using that gun on me, think again, genius. I have the best protection money can buy."

What was that? Probably some ultra-light bulletproof vest or something. Hank really needed to get caught up on that stuff if he was going to keep getting into messes like this.

"That's all right," Forgettable said, unperturbed. "After my associates killed the lights, I slipped in here while you were fumbling for your infrared scanner and made some alternative arrangements."

"The station would've scanned you for weapons," Richard said warily.

A shrug. "I knew you'd have plenty of guns on board. Station security only scans ships for large explosives—as long as you don't bring your guns on the station, they don't care what you do with them on your ship. We in the Redneck Reparations League are real good with guns."

"The what?" Hank was completely confused. Had Samantha said something about them the day he woke up? It was such a blur.

Richard rolled his eyes. "They're like the Medical Responsibility League or Stop Big Pharma, except run by rednecks and opposed to most big business. When we made contact through the wormhole, they decided the plight of the oppressed blue-collar worker was the People's fault, so now they hate them, and people like me."

Forgettable sneered. "You big businesses have been keeping down the little man long enough. And it's all because the People left peop— Humans like you in charge."

"I'm not sure I follow your logic," Hank said.

"Dumb people vote in the politicians who let big business do whatever it wants," Forgettable said. "Big business keeps simple people like us down, forcing us to slave away for the pittance of food and medicine they dole out."

"Did somebody bring a violin?" Hank mumbled.

"So what exactly are you planning to do?" Richard asked Forgettable. "You might be able to shoot me, but my associates here will take you out."

Forgettable smiled. "I got my own associates, Richard. Some of them are guarding the exits out in the hallway, others are making sure the lights stay out for a few more minutes, and some of them are where you can't see them. You're outnumbered."

"So you're just going to kill us? Because I didn't want my wife to die? Because Hank here didn't want to die a horrible death himself?"

Richard was obviously stalling for time. Hank figured that was a good plan, because he sure as shit didn't have a better idea.

"Because that research was wrong!" Forgettable yelled, and Hank finally understood what Richard was doing. "Cain't you understand? A pharmaceutical company don't make money if they cure someone. They *only* make money if they make a drug you have to keep takin' and takin'. They make more money if the drug only slows your symptoms, because then they can create another drug and call it better. Your wife woulda never been cured by that trial."

"Maybe not, but your group didn't save anyone's life by blowing up buildings where research was conducted. Also, my company sells beer, not drugs."

"Alcohol is the second most commonly used drug on Earth, right after caffeine."

"What was it, the thing Big Pharma couldn't cure you of? Or was it a loved one?"

"You don't know what you're talking about! You're flying around on a ship with chandeliers and shit, representing every corporate crime ever committed." He gestured around the room with his gun hand.

That was the opportunity Richard needed. He grabbed at Forgettable's gun, lunging to the side and out of the line of fire at the same time. Unfortunately, Forgettable hadn't been kidding about his associates. Hank threw himself down on the couch as he heard a muffled popping sound behind him. Scar yanked out a weapon and fired toward the center archway. Bad Breath yelped as something grazed his arm. Hank wondered, obscenely, if they had stain-resistant shirts here as a red blossom appeared on Bad Breath's shirt sleeve. Richard and Forgettable were on the ground, still wrestling for the weapon.

He wasn't sure why, but he found himself crawling off the couch and reaching for the gun in Forgettable's hand. For a split second, his eyes met Richard's, and Richard gave an almost imperceptible nod.

Their animosity was suspended for the moment.

There was another muted popping noise as he tried to pry Forgettable's fingers off the gun, which was smaller than his hand but still ominously gun-shaped. Finally, he zeroed in on the criminal's trigger finger and, unable to ply it from the gun, he dug his own fingernails into it.

He had never spent a lot of time getting manicures. The rate of hair and nail growth in cryo was incredibly slow, but over the course of 150 years, his nails had grown a good quarter of an inch, and he hadn't put any thought into trimming them since he'd woken up.

"Son of a bitch!" Forgettable yelled, loosening his grip as Richard snatched the gun away. Relieved of his weapon, the redneck avenger scrambled to his feet and ran for the door. Richard tried to run after him, but Bad Breath and Scar blocked him.

And that was when things got *really* weird.

Voices drifted through one of the archways. Only they weren't associates-are-lying-in-wait voices—one of them sounded familiar.

Hank very carefully sat up and peeked over the couch. He hadn't heard any popping sounds in a little while. Maybe Forgettable's friend in the center archway had run out of bullets, or whatever these little guns fired—or maybe he realized he was outnumbered and was trying to find a way off this ship—

—Which sounded like a hell of an idea to Hank.

There was no movement in the left and center archways, not even the fluttering of a curtain. The voices came from the right-most hall.

"Well, thanks for letting me interview you for this feature," the familiar voice said, loudly, as the curtain pulled back. "Let's see what Hank and Richard are up to."

With that, Samantha and another man walked into the room.

Hank suddenly realized that there were no guns in sight. Richard had pocketed the one he'd extracted from Forgettable. Bad Breath and Scar must have stowed theirs as well. Forgettable was disappearing through the front exit, having yanked free of Richard in the commotion. Bad Breath hastily yanked a jacket over the bloody shirt sleeve, while Scar looked down at Hank and offered him a hand.

Hank just sat there, staring at him. What was Samantha doing here?

"Are you all right?" She came around the couch to join them. The dark-suited man with her mumbled something about business he had to attend to and raced for the exit, which opened for him without incident. Bad Breath and Scar tore after him, no longer concerned with keeping Richard from the door.

"Hank here is still adjusting to the artificial gravity," Richard said smoothly, taking Hank's arm and jerking him to his feet. "It's a little lower on the station."

"It's definitely different," Hank managed.

"How did you get in here?" Richard asked Samantha.

"I hope you don't mind." She flashed her best PR smile. "I wanted to cover this historic event—Hank meeting up with an old friend. It's the first time you've met with someone from your old life, isn't it, Hank?"

"Security let you onto my ship without permission?" The stonewall expression returned to Richard's face.

"Well, it wasn't without permission," she said. "You signed a waiver allowing the press access to all Good Day Beer facilities as part of the publicity blitz Good Day is getting out of this event, remember?"

Richard winced, ever so slightly, before a fake smile spread across his face. "Of course. We're always happy to speak with reporters about our product. I just wasn't prepared to have such a private moment recorded. I mean, this is my first meeting in decades with a good friend."

Samantha put on her best fake-apologetic smile. "I understand completely. I'll have my AI stop broadcasting this live right now."

Suddenly Hank understood why Forgettable's associate had raced off in such a hurry. Samantha had probably introduced herself as a reporter who wanted to interview Richard and Hank about this momentous occasion, and how did the dark-suited gentleman know them and would he like to be interviewed for her live broadcast as well? He couldn't shoot someone on live TV—unless he wanted security or the Guard to intercept him leaving.

"That's all right." Richard smoothed his jacket. "You just surprised me. I'd be happy to be interviewed, so long as it's all right with Hank."

"It's fine. Samantha, you're just in time to join us for that drink Richard promised to buy me." *Holy shit, do I need one now.*

"Good Day Beer, of course!" Richard sauntered over to the bar.

✳
TWENTY-ONE

The station's security sensors and cameras were monitored by Anna's AI, which would alert her to any potential problems. Meanwhile, her team watched everyone, despite the fact that anyone allowed into the Woolerton Hall had been triple-scanned for weapons. Two guards were posted near each of the entrances, while Anna and her assistant chief, Baumgarden, remained rooted by the delegates' table. The other six guards swept the room, looking for potential problems.

The alerts on her data pad showed that at least half the people in the room were exhibiting "suspicious" body language, which just meant they were acting nervous. It was one of those situations where a person was smarter than a computer—nervousness was not uncommon at political functions, especially where public speaking was involved. While Anna and her team had taken a closer look at all the "suspicious" individuals, none appeared to be a real threat.

Most of the anxiety tapered off after the free beer started circulating.

Anna and her people couldn't drink on duty, of course, but she had a pretty good idea why a lot of other people in the room relaxed. Besides the alcohol, everyone probably figured they couldn't look any dumber than Richard when he made that humiliatingly Human speech.

A soft chiming noise in her earplant told her another alert had appeared. She casually glanced at her pad to see what it was now. Probably just another twitchy person eagerly awaiting the right moment to pitch his business proposal at a politician… what?

POWER OUTAGE ON DECKS 1-3.

Well, at least it didn't happen up here. Anna scrolled through various station systems, looking for the source of the problem. It probably had something to do with the fact that not one but two extra generators had been hooked up to this deck, just in case. That was more of a CC move than a security measure, since the data pads and many of the cameras and sensors ran on battery power. And yet, for some reason, the expense had been charged to her budget….

She suppressed a frown as a potential problem glared at her from the screen. Less than a minute before the power outage occurred, the cameras on Deck 1 had all failed, due to a power surge. Who was on that deck at the time?

A few seconds before the failure, Richard Swinton had cleared entrance to his ship for himself and "guests." Six people entered in the darkness that followed, although the last shot from Deck 1's cameras only showed four people in the hallway.

A team had already been dispatched to fix the problem. Anna directed them to check on Swinton's ship first, although she doubted he had anything to do with the issue. She was more concerned that someone might have taken advantage of the situation to rob his fancy ship. Woolerton would be sure to blame her for *that*.

Most of the other consoles showed no activity, although three other ships had guests entering or exiting within two minutes of the outage. One was owned by the catering service, accessed by workers Anna had cleared for the event after an extensive background check. The second ship was a freighter that docked with Five Alpha about once a month — both low risk, but worth a quick check.

It was the third ship that really concerned her, because it was registered to a Human named Leon Fisk, whose background check had turned up nothing since the Earther databases claimed no knowledge of him. Scans of his ship showed no weapons, and he claimed to be a "tourist," so her team couldn't find a reason to prevent him from docking with the station earlier. Haylea said it would be bad Copacetic Communications to turn away Humans without a good reason.

Anna sent another team to check on Fisk's ship.

✳ ✳

Leon Fisk and his "associates" — two high school buddies named Earl and Bubba — left Five Alpha in their rented ship without waiting for clearance. When he was sure security wasn't pursuing them — probably too busy with their la-de-da rich people party — Leon set a course for the wormhole, with a brief detour to an asteroid where he'd stored a special package.

"Are you sure this shit ain't gonna blow us up too?" Earl scratched his head as he looked at a display of the capsule now mounted to the front of their ship. "I ain't no kamikaze pilot, man."

STUPID HUMANS

"I told you, the Redneck Reparations guy promised me this thing was safe. We just wait for that light to go green, then we use the device to stream antimatter into the wormhole." The RR rep *had* said that, but it kind of worried Leon, too. From what he'd heard, antimatter was some unstable shit, and he had important work to do.

"Why don't we just throw an antimatter bomb in there and run?" Earl asked.

"Because we can't keep the Protector shut down for long, and if it comes back on before the bomb reaches the wormhole, we're screwed." He rubbed a hand over his forehead. "Also there's a good chance a bomb would detonate before it got far enough into the wormhole to damage it. Gravitational forces or sumthin. Some science-y shit I don't understand."

"If we're going to shut down the wormhole, how do we get home?" Bubba asked. "Shouldn't we do this from the other side?"

Leon gritted his teeth. Bubba never had been bright. "No, I've received my orders. We're to stay here and colonize one of these nice terraformed planets the People don't need. We'll start a new colony here, where there's no Earth government to get in our way."

"So all the other RR people are on this side already?" Earl asked.

"Some of them. Some had to stay behind on Earth to do other important work." *Please stop asking questions, both of you.* The light went green and he triumphantly hit the button. "There. We're streaming antimatter. As it disrupts the exotic whatchamacallit, particles or whatever, the wormhole, you know the vortex or whatnot, is gonna start to close—now don't be making any dirty jokes, this is serious shit here."

Bubba wasn't laughing. "The RR didn't appoint you to start no new colony. This is your idea, isn't it? You want to be the bigshot runnin' a planet we probably don't even own!"

"Is that true?" Earl reached behind him and scratched his ass.

Leon gripped the armrests of his chair with sweaty palms. "The RR can't see it, but we'll never be able to live the lives we want on Earth. Out here, we really do have the opportunity to start a new colony. Anyway, the People are gonna probably eventually build a new wormhole, they've known how for thousands of years. You buy that shit that they 'forgot how to do it'? Cuz I don't."

"Then why bother blowing up this one?" Bubba asked.

"Because it will shut down *everything* for a while. Earth will blame the People, the People will blame the Humans, and when the People make a new wormhole, our government will know they lied. They'll all have a big war and be too busy to stop us from colonizing a planet the People aren't even using. By the time they settle shit and the rest of the RR gets over here, we'll have too big of an army to be stopped, and the RR will be begging to live on our planet."

"This don't sound so bad," Earl said.

"I don't know." Bubba shook his head. "Doesn't seem right. We came here to steal Richard's ship and make it look like *he* blew up the wormhole."

"That didn't work out, but we can still carry out the most important part of the mission —"

"Going back through the Divide and blowing it up from that side!"

"No!" Leon yelled. "Listen to me. That was *never* the plan. If we blow it up from there, we won't be able to influence the conflict. This way, we have tons of important people from both sides a few miles away — any of them could be to blame."

"So you knew you were stranding us over here, away from our friends and family, and you didn't tell us?" Earl grabbed Leon by the collar, lifted him out of his chair, and slammed him against the wall.

"Get your hands off me." He tried to shove Earl away, but Bubba grabbed his arms and pinned them to his sides.

"I can't believe this punk thinks he gets to start his own kingdom and put hisself in charge." Earl pulled him away from the wall and Bubba yanked his hands behind his back and tied them with a bandanna he pulled from his pocket. He used another to gag Leon, presumably so he couldn't give the AI any commands.

"Guys, we're so close, please don't fuck this up," Leon begged around a mouthful of cloth, but it came out as gibberish.

"We didn't agree to be stuck here forever!" Earl shoved him into the nearest chair, then went to the console and punched a few buttons. "I'm going to take us through the wormhole and do this the right way."

"Nnnnnnnn!" Leon thrashed in the chair, trying to stand up. What were those morons thinking? They were going to blow themselves up, possibly before they even made it to the damn Divide.

"Don't we like, have to be in cryo to go through that thing?" Earl asked.

"He's right." Leon tried to say around the gag. If he could slide to one side enough, maybe he could kick Bubba....

"Okay, we'll go get in the emergency cryocans. I've plotted a course for the Divide." Bubba reached over to grab Leon, and he took that as his chance, kicking Bubba as hard as he could. Bubba was leaning over, and Leon's foot caught him right in the gut and sent him flying.

Earl rushed over to help, and Leon kicked him, too. Using one elbow for leverage, he stumbled to his feet, even though he was bent over. Bubba got up and headed in his direction.

Earl groaned on the floor.

Leon had one chance to get this right. He stumbled to the console, turned around, jumped in the air, and slammed his ass down on what he sincerely hoped was the right button. He probably hit some other buttons too, but at the moment he didn't care.

Fortunately, his butt managed to hit one of the right controls. As Bubba advanced toward him, he looked down in surprise. "What the fuck?"

The floor was slipping away from him as the artificial gravity slowly disappeared.

Leon dragged his knuckles over the console behind him. "Do you want to make a complete stop?" the AI asked finally.

"Mmmhmmm," he said around the gag. The RR should have sprung for a better model of rented ship, something with a truly smart AI and not just a mindless automaton that couldn't see what was happening.

"I'm sorry, I didn't understand. Did you say yes, you wanted to come to a complete stop?"

"Yrrmmmmm!" he yelled around a mouthful of bandanna. At least the ship wasn't set to take voice commands from anyone but him. Why hadn't he set the manual controls that way, too?

A disoriented Bubba tried to stumble his way. Leon kicked his legs, trying to get himself between Bubba and the console. Surely there was a way out of this, if he could just stall long enough to think of it.

Just then, a bright red display popped up and Bubba stopped to stare at it, wide-eyed.

"Payload will release in five, four, three...."

"YMMRNN!" he tried to yell. Crap, he had hit another button. They were about to jettison the antimatter device, which was probably going to explode before it actually made it into the wormhole.

"No, we haven't gone through yet!" Bubba yelled, flailing at the console. His finger almost touched the blinking Stop button before the countdown ended.

But, as Leon liked to say, close only counted in horseshoes and hand grenades.

The capsule launched, zipping toward the wormhole. Although he hadn't grasped everything the RR's scientific guy had said, Leon knew it was full of antimatter, which had to be contained in some sort of electric field, since it couldn't be exposed to normal material for some complicated reason he didn't understand. The field was inside the capsule, but it might not hold up if the capsule entered the Divide's gravity well, allowing the antimatter to —

"Nnnnnnn!" Bubba yelled, as a bright flash of light exploded from the vicinity of the wormhole.

Then the flash of light blotted out everything in the windows, and a few seconds later, everything went black.

*　*

The problem with trying to end the war, Xenia thought as she sipped her wine, was that it was being discussed by government officials. "Government," on both sides, consisted of individuals who got their jobs because they weren't particularly good at anything else, but that wasn't the worst problem here — the real issue was the fact they were trying to stop a war that had never been officially declared by either side.

It had all started with one of the People — yes, that was embarrassing — declaring war on the Humans. He wasn't anyone important, his "declaration" was more of a statement in a journal, and no one took him seriously at the time. But then he decided to start blowing up Human ships.

Of course the People government condemned his actions, and the Human government didn't hold one unstable — what did they call it?

Whackjob?—against them. But the Earthers had their own unstable whackjobs, and some of them *did*. Reports that war had been declared were rampant. People on both sides—but mostly the Humans—failed to verify these stories, and before anyone knew what had happened, Earthers and People were firing weapons at each other on both sides of the wormhole. It was exactly the sort of widespread disaster the People had—mostly—managed to avoid since leaving Earth behind.

The situation came precariously close to resolving peacefully when the UNE voted not to declare war on the People, but then the Humans' warlike nature got the better of them. Several countries decided the Earth government wasn't doing enough to protect them and sent their own troops through the Divide to "secure our side." Their unexpected arrival and attempts to police ships near the wormhole rapidly degenerated into violence. Meanwhile, Howard and the UNE apologized and promised to get their people under control, which led to a big war on Earth. The Guard eventually stopped the rogue Humans' "security force" and sent what was left of it back through the Divide in a hurry. Once again, the Council voted not to declare war on the Humans, but issued a stern warning that if anything like this happened again, they would not be so lenient.

The Earthers eventually settled their civil disagreements, promised to get the situation under control, and the UNE posted a large security force around the Divide to prevent a repeat of the incident. Unfortunately, that made the "individual nutcase" problem worse, as every crazy on Earth decided the politicians weren't doing enough to protect them. Attacks by ordinary civilians with a few blind followers had been steadily increasing since then.

That was one thing the People had in their favor—sure, they had a few nutcases, but their nutcases didn't attract tons of followers. The Humans called this "herd mentality," but they had never been able to fix it.

"I know we all hoped that if we did not make this conflict a military matter any more than necessary, it might resolve on its own." Howard brought Xenia back to the depressing present. "That's why we agreed to intervene only when necessary to prevent the conflict from spreading, but it's been almost a year now, and the attacks are only becoming more frequent. I will admit it's just as much on our side as yours."

"We hired the best communication experts to create an anti-violence campaign," Tom offered. "Unfortunately, it wasn't as successful as we'd hoped."

"I'm afraid we've had the same problem," Howard admitted. "What if we undertook a joint campaign? We could use both People and Humans in the ads, presenting a united front."

"I think that's a great idea," Xenia said, honestly.

Morriss snorted as he twirled his spoon in his mashed potatoes.

"You disagree?" Tom asked.

He shrugged. "I just don't think a communications campaign will do any good if it doesn't address the real issues."

"Let's address them." Xenia wasn't sure if she was making a huge mistake or taking a step toward progress. "Why don't you start since you seem to know so much about them?"

Tom silently handed his empty wine glass to the server for a refill.

"Great." Morriss let his spoon clatter noisily onto his barely-touched plate, and crossed his arms over his chest. "The real problem on our side is that *our people*—" He put heavy emphasis on the words. "—don't trust *your people* due to a lack of communication on *your part*. I'm not talking about touchy-feely, can't-we-all-just-get-along-and-appreciate-each-other's-differences ads. I'm talking about real transparency—sharing your technological progress, for example. *All* of it."

A heavy silence settled over the group like snow blanketing a rooftop. Howard kept an expression of neutrality frozen on his face. He wasn't agreeing with Morriss, but he wasn't telling him to shut up, either, and that spoke louder than words.

Tom studied the remains of his dinner as if looking at an undiscovered work of art from the Mulanean Period. Xenia sat mutely, unsure of how to continue. What could she say that hadn't already been said?

"With all due respect, Mister Morriss," she addressed him in the way Humans preferred. "We have been transparent. In instances where we felt sharing certain technologies might be harmful to your people, we explained why. We may have made mistakes in the past, but that was centuries ago. In my lifetime, my government hasn't lied to your people."

"You won't give us the cure for cancer," Morriss said, and Xenia suddenly realized why he was here—to say all the things Howard *couldn't* say, for political reasons.

She sighed. "Our research indicates that more people on your planet are starving to death than dying of cancer. You have ten *billion* people on Earth, more than your planet can support with your present agricultural situation. If Humans stopped dying of cancer, more would die of starvation! We're sorry for what our ancestors did to your people, Mister Morriss, and for that reason we don't want to cause them any more harm. Surely you can understand that?"

"We do appreciate your position on that." Howard finally spoke. "We increased funding for off-world colonization projects and hope to have at least a million people living off-planet in the next ten years."

"As soon as your population is stable and better distributed between

Earth and other colonies, we will share our medical knowledge with you." Xenia didn't point out that one million would barely make a dent in Earth's food and population problems.

"How about the FTL drive then?" Morriss plowed right on to his next issue. "That would help us move off-world a lot faster."

"I don't know where you got the idea that we were lying about that," Tom said. "We really don't have one yet. We've been working on it for years, and we hope to have it one day. But you must understand we're dealing with the same problems your scientists are."

"Why should we believe you?" Morriss asked. "A recent poll by a well-established research center on Earth shows that almost eighty percent of Humans believe your People have FTL technology, but you think we'll just misuse it, like the cure for cancer."

Again, that awkward, heavy silence fell on them, and Xenia had no idea how to deal with it this time. How could they prove they didn't have something they didn't have? She glanced down at her plate, trying to buy time, and noticed an alert on her pad. Very subtly, she tapped the screen.

UNUSUAL RADIATION AND GRAVITOMETRIC LEVELS MEASURED IN THE WORMHOLE VICINITY AFTER UNCONFIRMED REPORTS OF AN EXPLOSION IN THE AREA. THIS IS MOST LIKELY A NORMAL FLUCTUATION, BUT VISITORS ARE WARNED TO AVOID THE DIVIDE UNTIL READINGS RETURN TO NORMAL. GUARD PATROLS WILL BE DISPATCHED TO MONITOR THE SITUATION.

Ten feet away, Anna stared at her own pad, and Xenia knew she had the same news. She rolled the pad, slid it into her sleeve, turned and walked toward one of her guards, her calm, in-control expression never wavering.

✱
TWENTY-TWO

"Someone just tried to blow up the wormhole!" a woman in a green dress screamed from one of the Earth-side tables. "They're saying it was some sort of antimatter weapon!"

Panic spread through the room. Samantha, who had just received an alert about the possible wormhole explosion a few minutes earlier, dispatched her tiny cameras to capture every minute of unnecessary hysteria. When she got the news alert back on Richard's ship, he'd insisted they would all be safer near the center of the station, "if this wormhole thing blows up." Samantha wanted to get back to covering the party anyway, since her exposé on Richard amounted to nothing more than him and Hank kissing each other's asses.

"What if this delegation meeting is the target?" a man in a dull gray suit asked. "I know the wormhole fluctuates, but the readings from the last few minutes go well beyond normal variations. This really could be the result of someone using a large weapon near the wormhole."

"We can't leave, and we're safer in here than anywhere else right now. Besides, it's probably nothing." Richard snagged a can of Good Day Beer from a passing tray. Samantha noticed the interactive holo label was now red-and-white checkered, with a tiny icon encouraging the drinker to "Let us know which new design you like best!" That was probably how he knew which cans were rufied.

"Yeah, you don't want to be sitting in a ship if the wormhole goes supernova," said Richard's bodyguard, the one with the breath you could smell ten feet away. "Now, if someone got a bomb into *this* room—"

"A bomb? I thought the wormhole was erupting or something?" Hank asked a bit too loudly.

"A bomb?" someone screamed at a nearby table. "They're bombing us?"

"What about the Protector? Doesn't that deflect weapons that could damage the wormhole?" a woman in the back asked.

"Who?" someone at the next table yelled. "The damned Humans?"

"You know, now would be the perfect time for them to attack the Divide," said a man sitting next to her. He tugged at his ill-fitting brown jacket. "Because of the security concerns for this party, virtually all the station's security and the Guard patrols for this area are encircling the station, leaving the wormhole vulnerable."

Samantha was thinking he had a point when her earplant chimed and she swatted at it to answer. "Yeah?"

"Are you prepared to go live?" It was Lee's voice, sounding as excited as everyone in the main hall, except that in his case it was a happy kind of excited—the kind of excited that really good journalists got over unsubstantiated bomb threats and possibly exploding wormholes.

"I assume you want public reaction?" Repeating the same two sentences about what little was known bored the crap out of her, and she tried to avoid it as much as possible. But Richard was probably right about the report being meaningless, so she might as well cover the party guests' hysterical reactions. Some of this stuff was going to be pretty funny once the threat turned out to be nothing—take that moron who thought a wormhole could go supernova, for example. She hoped one of the Human networks played that soundbite *ad nauseam*.

"Yes," Lee said giddily. "Even with the Divide instability report, a lot of people are still watching the Good Day Beer guy and his old friend catch up. Now that you're back in the hall with both of them, this live feed will get millions of watchers. Try to use Hank as much as possible—the viewers love him!"

"All right." She didn't know exactly what she'd interrupted earlier, but she was pretty sure those two weren't really old friends—but that was a story for another day. "The bombed wormhole thing—that couldn't happen, right? If someone fired an antimatter torpedo at the wormhole, the Protector would shoot it down, right?"

"It's always worked in the past. They set it up before the Hu—your people were allowed to visit the first time, one ring on our side and one on theirs. I don't know that it's been tested much, but it's supposed to be impenetrable. Oh, look, there are Hank and Richard, why don't you get their reactions?"

"Hank, Richard, just a few minutes ago you were talking about the old days, more than a hundred fifty years ago, and the more recent search for Richard's wife, who went through the wormhole like Hank. Now, in light of these recent developments, how do you feel?" she asked as she caught up with them.

"Well, first of all, I don't think anyone should panic." Richard put on his I'm-the-CEO-and-I'm-in-control face. "This could be a normal fluctuation, and I know the Guard patrols and station security here at Five Alpha are well-equipped to handle whatever problem we might be facing. In fact, I think everyone might be a bit more relaxed if they kicked back with a nice Good Day Beer here—"

Samantha abruptly turned away as Richard raised his can. Media organizations only stayed in business because of *paid* advertisements, and Richard had gotten more than his share of free publicity already tonight. Plus, the guy helped start the panic, and was trying to paint himself as calm and cool thanks to his product.

She consulted the feeds from her cameras. The delegates' table was empty, as the politicians had been rushed into the next room for "safety." This hall was already the most secure place on the station—in fact, the whole level was in the very center of the Five Alpha, ostensibly the safest place to be—so obviously they just wanted to talk about the situation in private. Or get away from the cameras. Or yell at each other without reporters around. At this rate, she wouldn't get to see them for hours, if ever—they might take this as an opportunity to leave early, the lucky bastards.

On another feed, a woman in a ridiculous red feather ensemble pointed in Samantha's direction, waving and wailing and obviously making a spectacle of herself.

Now that looked like news.

Samantha trotted off in her direction. As she walked closer to the ridiculous red woman, the conversation grew louder.

"Matilda, would you please keep it down," a timid-looking man, probably her boyfriend, was saying. He had dull brown hair and a face that appeared permanently stretched into a frown. Easy to see why.

"It's all their fault." The woman waved her arms around in a blur of feathers dyed a hideous shade of fire-engine red that made her look like an overgrown cardinal. "Those damn Humans *made* that idiot start this stupid war, and now we're all paying the price. Do you hear me, Reynold? We're all going to *die* because of *them*—" She stopped short, her gaze skipping over the reporter she was addressing and landing on Samantha. "And *you're* one of them!"

"I'm doing a special assignment for *Glass Media*. Would you like to comment on these most recent events?" Samantha paid no attention to the woman's rudeness.

"*Glass* still has a *Human* journalist?" Reynold, a reporter from one of *Glass*'s top competitors, *Know News*, was better known for his ego than his journalistic skills. He had a habit of standing straight as a board with his nose in the air, and Samantha's colleagues joked that he must have a rod up his ass to maintain that look.

"Yeah, they hired her right after those fucking Humans started immigrating in *hordes*." Ridiculous Red flapped her hand dismissively at Reynold, who had to jump back to avoid a fingernail to the eye. She didn't notice.

"So would you like to comment on the situation?" Samantha ignored Reynold, who crinkled his nose at her, as if she was moving in on his prey. "Since I see you've learned our jargon and everything."

"Damn right I'd like to comment." Ridiculous Red ignored the jab. "This is all you *Humans'* fault. You made that poor man crazy, and he blew up a space station. Then we had to respond to protect ourselves, and the rest of you popped out of every asteroid and uninhabited moon, where you'd all been waiting for this sort of opportunity. And now your People... I mean, you *Humans*, are out there again, firing weapons into our wormhole. Are you in on it? What a great ruse, posing as a reporter...."

"Let's just slow down and address your comments one at a time. First of all, I'm curious where you got the intel that there was a bomb heading straight for us. I get up-to-the minute feeds from my media organization, and I haven't seen *anything* about a *credible* bomb threat to the station, and we don't have a firm answer about what happened to the Divide. Where did you get your inside information?"

Ridiculous Red stood there for a moment, her mouth working but no sound coming out. "If anyone has inside information, it would be *you*," she stammered finally.

"If I had inside info that a bomb was heading this way, why would I be standing around interviewing people?"

"Because you're all a bunch of idiots!"

"Matilda, please," moaned the boring man at the table.

"It's true that on average my people have lower IQs than yours," Samantha agreed. "But if we were all *complete* idiots, why would *you* be so worried about an attack? *Your* People, your very *intelligent* People, have handled security for this event. Earlier, this station's security chief told me her patrols are checking every ship within half a light year of the station. With such good security measures on the part of *your own* People, why would you be so worried about an unconfirmed attack by idiots?"

"You see what she's doing?" Ridiculous turned to Reynold. "She's trying to make me look like the stupid one!"

"And doing a damn good job," the boring man grumbled from the table.

That was when the whole room trembled.

Samantha had never experienced an earthquake back on Earth, but she'd seen vids of them. The hall looked eerily similar right now. Glasses fell from tables and trays. Wine sloshed on expensive suits and gowns. People tripped and tumbled to the floor. Samantha caught her balance by grabbing the nearest ugly sturdy-looking thing, which in this case was a hideous ice sculpture of two globes melting together.

Ridiculous stumbled against a table, her ample rear end knocking over a wine glass. Without appearing to notice, she sat down on the table, as if that could stop the room from shaking. It didn't.

Another wave of vibration rippled through the room. Were those explosions? Samantha couldn't shoot her mouth off about a bomb unless she had confirmation.

"You see?" Ridiculous screamed at Reynold, who was gripping a chair for support, his knuckles white. "I told you those Humans were going to bomb us!"

"We don't even know why the room is shaking," Samantha yelled. "Or who is responsible."

"It's confirmed," Lee said in her earplant, and she hurried away from Red so she could talk to him. "But the station wasn't bombed, at least not directly. The Guard just confirmed an antimatter weapon detonated either in or near the Divide, causing it to shrink. That's what caused the event here—a gravitational wave pushed some of the ships guarding the station into the station. They're not sure if this had a permanent effect on the wormhole's stability"

"You mean it could collapse?" Samantha whispered, glad she wouldn't be overheard with all the background noise. *Glass* automatically stopped broadcasting live audio when she talked to Lee.

"The experts aren't sure yet, but it could," he said. "It looks like someone wanted to stop both sides from using the wormhole."

TWENTY-THREE

Before her stroke, between teaching classes at the university, dealing with faculty waste-of-time events, and her work on the Lightning Project, Merelyn never had time to think. Now, she had all the time in the world.

Here she was in a medical facility, unable to speak. She tried, but the words didn't come out right, so she refused. Dr. Vance said if he ever found a solution to her brain damage she'd want her vocal chords to be in good shape. If she could, she would have told him that after a month of vocal therapy and no progress she was not fucking speaking anymore. But the words wouldn't come out right, so she just rolled her eyes.

Well, she rolled *one* eye at him. The right side of her body didn't work very well, either. After months of physical therapy, she could *move* her right arm, but only with a jerky motion that made her feel she was looking at a puppet's limb and not her own. For the most part, she'd started using her left hand to pick things up, or eat, or make that hand signal that the Humans favored when pissed off.

She was always pissed off now, and not just about the stroke. Oh, she was plenty pissed about that—of all the health problems in the world, she had to have one that medical technology hadn't conquered yet. Worse, it could have been avoided, if she'd taken the doctor's advice and gone straight to the hospital when her medchip alerted her that she had a clot. But no, she was in the middle of a test for the Lightning Project, she was making history, and medchips always alerted you to problems hours or even days before they became serious, right?

"No," she'd told the physician when he called. "I'll be fine for the two hours it takes to complete the test, then I'll go straight to the nearest medical center for treatment."

As she ended the call, he babbled about the risks, about how high her blood pressure was, how the clot could break off at any moment and go to her heart or her lungs or some other vital organ....

Apparently she'd disconnected before he got to the part about her brain. Would that have scared her into abandoning the experiment? She wasn't sure. Hearts and lungs could be regrown, but brain damage—that wasn't an easy fix. But what were the odds the clot would break off and go straight to her brain in the two hours it took to test Lightning?

Merelyn's left hand clenched into a fist. Why hadn't she listened? The project test could have been rescheduled. Sure, it would have meant waiting several months, but at least she could have continued her work. She could hardly do that now, sitting in a medical suite, tended by automaton nurses and that idiot Vance. She was unable to speak, write her own name, or, most importantly, continue the highly detailed work of designing and testing the prototype.

But she *hadn't* taken the time to think about it, because she was finally testing an FTL drive! Eight years working on it, running into problem after problem, fighting for funding, hitting technical obstacles, then fighting for clearance to test the damn thing, convincing unthinking government types the prototype was safe, that it wasn't going to blow up half the star system — all of that had come down to a few hours, and absolutely *nothing* was going to stand in her way.

Certainly not some tiny little clot that formed in her leg because she'd been spending eighteen hours a day sitting in a chair, poring over test data and graphs and projections, her blood pressure spiking every time she spotted a number that seemed slightly out of place, because any damn little thing could screw up eight years of work. Well, any damn little thing except a blood clot — that problem had never occurred to her.

But that paled in comparison to the things she had to be angry about after her stroke. Worse than her predicament, worse than her prognosis — Vance hoped to have a solution within the next ten years! — worse than the fact that the Lightning test's miserable failure, was the fact her so-called friends and family disappeared. She understood why her friends stopped showing up — most of them were people she worked with, and they didn't want to make her sad by talking about the job she couldn't do anymore. She could maybe forgive them for that.

But then there was her daughter. Merelyn hadn't seen or heard from her since she'd been transferred here, but from what she'd heard, Shannon was out spending her mother's money at a rapid rate.

Thinking about her predicament and her daughter's abandonment had deeply depressed Merelyn. According to Dr. Vance, most of the better antidepressants would alter her brain chemistry in such a way as to negate the effects of the treatments he was likely to try for her stroke damage. He then suggested that a milder antidepressant and animal therapy might be a better alternative. Merelyn would have laughed, but her laughter sounded like a choking seal now, so she let it go. The one good thing about her daughter's negligence was that she couldn't be bothered to spend a lot of time talking to Vance about treatment options, so she'd signed over control of her mother's care to him. Merelyn thought the doctor was a useless idiot, but he was the only person who seemed genuinely dedicated to helping her get better.

As for her depression, she just pretended the dog visits and half-assed pills were helping so Vance wouldn't reconsider a more aggressive treatment plan. She did like the dog, a large, friendly breed with eyes like liquid chocolate. At least he was silent.

The dog's owner, the damn Human, well, that was another story. She would sit there for an hour, repeating every gossip story that had circulated through the station since her last visit. Merelyn, who had never taken much interest in the personal lives of others, who in fact hadn't even taken that much interest in her own personal life if she was being honest, now knew that Roble was in love with the station's CC Director Haylea, who had no interest in him whatsoever. She knew that Anna had thousands of drunken tourist stories, and the more she herself drank, the more embellished and interesting they got. She knew Anna said she wanted the war to end so the tourists would come back and life would go back to normal, but what she really wanted was for Frego to come home. She knew Vance was pissed at some doctor who'd died in the *Traveler* explosion because it meant he was stuck here, and that made him mad at himself, and that wasn't a new feeling for Vance. He'd been mad at himself ever since he made the mistake of falling in love with one of his brief girlfriends and she hurt him badly.

But the Human and her dog only visited a few times a week, and Vance was often busy with other patients, so Merelyn found herself with an awful lot of time to think, and tonight was no exception. She could watch any of the five hundred or so entertainment channels available — including about forty from Earth — but most shows quickly bored her, so she set the view screen to window mode. As she stared at the wormhole, her thoughts went where they usually did — back to Lightning's failure.

Everything had been going so well with the test. She had developed a plan to encase a ship in a protective bubble, shrinking space ahead of the vessel and expanding space behind it. Unlike a wormhole, which would be limited to travel between two points in space, Lightning would allow travel anywhere at superluminal speeds. The protective bubble should, theoretically, shield normal matter from exotic matter, protecting the ship and preventing a messy explosion. All the projections and preliminary tests showed it was much less likely to blow up than her colleagues' failed attempts at recreating a stable wormhole, but just in case, she'd found the most remote area possible for testing and spent months proving there wasn't so much as a microbe to be harmed out in that asteroid field. After receiving final clearance, her team successfully sent a probe through to a position a tenth of a light-year away in minutes.

Then the device self-destructed, taking the probe with it.

She'd gone over every piece of data she could remember. It had taken her most of an hour, but she'd sent a message to her colleague Harak asking for the data from after the test. She told him that if she didn't have something to keep her mind busy she'd wind up insane. Fortunately, he understood what it was like to spend years working on a project only to see it fail, and he'd sent the data the next day. He also promised to visit the next time he was in the area, although she doubted that would be any time soon.

So she pored over the material, day after day. None of it made sense.

At first, Lightning worked. Then the bubble destabilized, causing a large explosion. Today, like every day before, she pondered one question — Why had the projection numbers been so far off from what actually transpired?

When she looked at the wall screen and saw the wormhole contracting, saw the bright flash of light, felt the tremor rocking the station, at first she thought it was another memory of the seconds in which the bubble failed. But then the lights flickered, stuttered, came back on, and the automated nurse warned her not to panic, calmly repeating that everything was fine. That was not like the script in her head at all.

Merelyn tapped on her data pad until she reached the menu to direct the room's AI, since she couldn't give it verbal commands, and asked for an outside view of the station.

"Those images have been cut off from public viewing. Would you like to see the last ones available?"

"Yes," Merelyn tapped into the screen, although she already knew what she'd seen. But she watched again. Something had gone very, very wrong with the only stable, functional wormhole in existence. It would take someone as skilled and clever as she was to fix it — except, of course, that she wouldn't be doing anything like that anytime soon.

In her empty, lonely hospital room, under the dim lighting that indicated the station was running on its backup generators, Merelyn started to cry for the first time since she'd had her stroke.

TWENTY-FOUR

Ignored by Haylea—and everyone else—Roble was feeling alone in a crowd of people when the room trembled. He immediately looked for Haylea, and he found her fast—despite the shaking, she was up near the podium, talking a mile a minute.

"There's nothing to be alarmed about, the wormhole fluctuates from time to time." She would have been more convincing if she wasn't shouting quite so loudly and didn't sound quite so panicked. "It's one of the many fascinating attractions here at Five Alpha. At any given time, you might see the wormhole spit out a chunk of asteroid, or a piece of history. It's like an intergalactic garbage collector—"

Roble's AI dinged in his ear and he looked at his data pad with a sigh. His boss wanted him down to Engineering immediately. Well, he couldn't do any good here, except correct the scientific inaccuracies Haylea was spouting about the wormhole—and that wouldn't improve his standing with her.

So he trudged down ten flights of stairs—almost all the elevators were shut down when the station was on backup generators, except a few designated for emergencies—and found himself in the middle of *real* hysteria.

"All the primary generators are down. What happened?"

"Are we really under attack by the Humans?"

"Did some suicidal idiot actually toss antimatter into the wormhole throat to destabilize the exotic matter? How did they get it past the Protector?"

"What the fuck is an exotic matter discharge? That sounds like something you catch from a night with—"

"I know you're all busy with the communications system and the defense grid, but shouldn't we be concerned about this failure on the Life Support panel?"

That one came from Roble's right. He turned around and saw Molly, a technician he'd met a few times. He didn't spend much time in Engineering, but he remembered her singing drunkenly at the last office party while Haylea took pictures "for the employee morale update."

Roble didn't see his boss anywhere, so he wandered over to Molly. He had already determined on his way down the stairs that the station AI was working and the only problem was in the communication system, which wasn't technically his problem—although he had a feeling it would become his problem soon.

"What's wrong with Life Support?" That had to be a top priority for *everyone.*

"The impact did more than knock our generator offline," Molly said. "Look at the station diagram." She pointed at a display, lit up in various colors. "See all that black? Guess what's in that section?"

Roble shrugged. "Something important?"

"Those big cylinders are our air recyclers." She pointed at one black section, then another next to it.

Roble glanced around at all the people yelling and poking at screens and displays. "Does everyone else know?"

"I don't know." Molly looked at the melee. One woman was batting at her station display, as if she could fix the black areas that way. "I think the other problems may be distracting them."

Roble pulled out his pad and checked the life support system. Sure enough, there was a whole page of alerts:

COMMUNICATION WITH RESPIRATION POD 1 IS OFFLINE.

COMMUNICATION WITH RESPIRATION POD 2 IS OFFLINE.

COMMUNICATION WITH...

"Well, I don't see any other necessary life support systems down." All he had to do was tell his boss that the comm system problem with Respiration Pods 1-4 was caused by a hardware failure in the pods, not a software issue directly involving the AI, which made this someone else's problem. Maybe he could go back to the party and see what Haylea was—

And then it hit him what his diagnosis meant. "Our air is going bad?"

It just so happened that the room went silent at that moment. As he looked around at all the frightened faces, he vaguely recalled hearing his boss, Baldor, screaming at everyone to shut up, calm down, and wait for instructions just a few seconds earlier. It hadn't registered as important to him at the moment, because he heard Baldor yelling that stuff all the time. But apparently it had had an effect on everyone else in the room, and they all shut up, just in time to hear his question....

Which was now being interpreted as a statement.

The silence ended almost as abruptly as it had started.

"What did you damage now?" Baldor yelled at Roble.

"It wasn't me this time, it was the gravitational wave," Roble stammered, then realized he should clarify that point when he saw everyone looking at him like he was a particularly stupid Human.

"*This* time?" Molly asked.

"What I mean is—well, it's not that things are always my fault. It's just that Baldor always blames me for things that are rarely ever actually, technically my fault...." Things were going from bad to worse.

A tall, tight-lipped woman near the back of the room looked right at him and broke the second silence. "I'm sorry, but *who* are you?"

Roble suddenly wished that a gravitational wave would hit him right now. Based on his admittedly limited knowledge of the subject, it would either send him somewhere a few light-years away, or kill him, either of which would be preferable to his current situation. He tried to speak, but found that his mouth was, thankfully, failing him this time.

Molly stood up. "His name is Roble, he works in AI Support, and he just discovered a big problem that the rest of you were ignoring."

"We weren't ignoring anything, we just had more alerts and alarms than we could deal with at one time." The tight-lipped woman sat back down at her terminal and fingered a display. "I'm sure the Life Support alert is buried under all these security notices."

Roble breathed a sigh of relief. It was his job to make sure the AIs prioritized alerts properly, but that was based on the list Haylea gave him. He remembered a lot of boring meetings in which the problem had been discussed at length, with Anna arguing Security alerts should take priority over Life Support alerts because Security problems could lead to more Life Support problems faster than Life Support problems could lead to Life Support disasters. Some boring guy whose name Roble couldn't remember had droned on that LS should take priority because the People responding might not get to the LS problems before they became disasters. Anna had said that was ridiculous, and Haylea concurred, voting down the boring businessman. Roble had a feeling that guy was going to be saying "I told you so" at the next meeting — if they all lived that long.

"I want you to get to work on this problem immediately." Baldor clapped Roble on the shoulder like he suddenly *wasn't* the department's worst employee.

"But I work on the AIs, not the Respiration Pods," Roble stammered.

"You've done a good job catching this problem, and I think we would all feel better with you working on it." Baldor smiled and nodded, probably hoping everyone would forget what Roble had blurted out earlier.

"I'll send crawlers to check the pods. I want to make sure they're actually damaged and it's not just a sensor failure." Roble sent the order from his pad. "Now, who knows where to find the replacement Respiration Pods?"

✳   ✳

Still at the party, Samantha remembered one of the many things she disliked about being a journalist — dealing with hysterical people during a crisis. When she'd settled on this side of the Divide, she'd hoped the tendency to go off the deep end was a Human deficiency, a problem of the IQ-challenged — roughly 82% of the Human population, last time she'd checked. When covering crises here, at least she wouldn't have to put up with so much screaming, crying, and complete irrationality, because she would be dealing almost exclusively with People, right?

When she was seven, she'd hoped for a pet unicorn, but that didn't work out either.

"We're all going to die!" A dark-haired woman lunged at Samantha out of the semi-darkness. The latest statement from Security said power availability would be reduced until they were off the backup generators.

"They're trying to kill us by cutting off our air supply!" Ridiculous Red's husband shouted. Samantha was once again surprised he was able to speak.

She wasn't sure how the air-running-out story had started, but all she'd read on the nets were unconfirmed rumors. Lee had nothing conclusive, and Haylea hadn't answered any messages since the wormhole spazzed out.

There were other rumors feeding on the broiling panic—the wormhole had been destroyed. The Humans did it, of course. The People did it to protect themselves from the Humans—who could blame them? An antimatter explosion had disturbed the exotic matter that propped open the Divide. The wormhole was temporarily fluctuating unpredictably because the tech that kept it open and stable was failing after all these years, and it would probably collapse soon—giving the People very little time to get all the Humans back on the Other Side where they belonged, of course.

Of the rumors, Samantha thought the one about the wormhole destabilizing probably had the most credence, since the station's AI was blocking all outer views "due to technical difficulties." She had long since given up trying to interview People, most of whom thought she was to blame for the evening's events. Instead, she sent her cameras around the room.

Ridiculous Red stood up, nearly knocking over the table, and stomped toward Samantha. Since she'd already done the Idiot Person interview, she decided to insert herself into any conversation that didn't involve the feathered freak. She scanned the room for anyone remotely interesting who did not appear to be sweating, hyperventilating, or rewriting a will.

Hank was at a table in the corner, talking to Richard. Now that might be interesting. Just what kind of unfinished business did they have?

She was halfway across the room when she felt a tap on her shoulder.

"Excuse me, Little Miss Human?"

Gritting her teeth, Samantha turned around to face Ridiculous Red, reminding herself that she was working and had to act like a professional. "What can I do for you?"

"I was wondering if you could tell me just when the big explosion is going to hit." Red gestured toward the wall with her nearly-empty wine glass. "We all know that first bomb was just the beginning."

Samantha tried not to roll her eyes, but they seemed to have a mind of their own. "There's been no confirmation of a bomb near this station."

Red tossed her head back and roared with loud, drunken laughter. Reynold moved closer, cameras buzzing like bees around him. Samantha hoped he was running this live on his station's main feed. Let everyone see what an idiot Red was.

"I know you know more than that." Red narrowed her glazed eyes at Samantha. "I did a little research on you, *Miz* Human."

Samantha pushed the corners of her mouth into what she hoped resembled a smile. "I'm glad you've mastered the art of conducting a net search. My people managed that years ago."

"I'm not talking about the stories on the nets." Red stepped closer. "I heard gossip from some People who live here on the station."

"So you've heard that I like to tend bar. So? Everyone needs a hobby."

"Actually, what I heard was how desperate you were to get off the *Traveler* five minutes before it exploded." Red stammered a little on *exploded*. Any more than two syllables, and drunk People got confused.

But she was blundering into territory Samantha *really* didn't want to revisit. Grateful her years in journalism had given her a good poker face, she stared down the inebriated woman with all the emotion of a rock.

"I chose to stay here rather than return to Earth," she said calmly. "It wasn't the first time I did that, and it probably won't be the last."

"But it was the time that your people blew up the ship you were supposed to be on five minutes after you deserted it." Red looked at Reynold. "Don't you think that's suspicious? Maybe you should poll your viewers and find out what they think?"

"The man I loved was on that ship." Samantha was unable to hold her tongue any longer. One part of her brain was screaming at her to shut *the fuck* up, to do the smart thing and make no further comment validating a drunk woman's ramblings. But another part of her brain told the first part of her brain to shut the fuck up itself, and that was that.

"Do you know how I found out my boyfriend was dead? One of *your people* shoved me up against a wall and asked why *my people* blew up the *Traveler*. Not a day goes by that I don't wish that ship was still intact, that I don't wish I could get my hands on whoever was responsible for the explosion. Did you lose anyone that day? Did you?"

She tried to make eye contact, but Red jerked her gaze away.

"Why would anyone believe her, anyway?"

Samantha stared at the crowd of People, wondering if they believed Red over her, and forced her face back to its normal, calm veneer. There was no point in talking further—it would only weaken whatever position she might have established.

She was thinking about going after Hank and Richard again when a hand on her shoulder made her whirl around. Anna stood there, tight lipped.

"Haylea sent me to escort you to the meeting room in Operations," she said, her face as expressionless as Samantha's.

✳
TWENTY-FIVE

The first thing Samantha heard as she walked into the meeting room on the station's first level was someone screaming, "We're all going to die!"

"That is not true!" Haylea ran up to Samantha. "And that's what I need you to help me communicate to all these People we finally have here on the station!"

Roble, the guy who was obviously hopelessly in love with Haylea, looked up from his display. "We need to evacuate everyone who came on their own ship."

Samantha snagged the nearest empty chair with her foot, dragged it to her, and flopped down in it. "How does the number of People on the station affect the wormhole destabilizing?"

"The wormhole vibrated or something, but it probably wasn't an explosion, it was just a gravitational discharge from, uh, whatever happened. It pushed that clump of Human ships into the station. Hard. But that's because the Human delegation only docked one of their ships, and kept the others floating at a distance." Haylea's lip curled in disgust. "If they hadn't been too paranoid to dock all their ships, there would have been no impact. The only major catastrophe was caused by the Humans' refusal to trust us!"

"That's all very interesting, but if the wormhole isn't the problem, what's going on?" Samantha asked.

"No one was hurt because this station is so well-shielded. We need to stress that in our communication." Haylea tapped her data pad. "But the outer hull and the Life Support systems on the side closest to the wormhole sustained a small amount of damage. We're fixing it."

"Shouldn't our Life Support systems be in the better shielded areas?" Samantha asked.

"Life Support has to be housed in the same layer as the generators for safety, stability, and ease of maintenance," Roble said.

"So it's in the middle layer, better protected than it would be in the outer hull but not as well protected as we are?" Samantha asked.

"That's right," Haylea said. "Besides, we have backups for all essential Life Support systems, so in the unlikely event that one of them is damaged, normally there isn't a problem."

Samantha *really* didn't like the sound of *normally*. "Aren't backups on opposite sides of the station?"

"Yes, but perpendicular to the wormhole, so both are the same distance away," Roble explained. "A gravitational discharge of this impact wasn't anticipated."

"What about replacement parts? Surely you have spares that are housed somewhere safe, right?"

Haylea smiled through gritted teeth. "Yes, normally we keep spare parts for everything essential to Life Support in the centermost part of the station."

Again, *normally.*

"That's near the Woolerton Hall." Samantha had a bad feeling she knew where this was going. "Let me guess—you had to move some things out of storage for the party?"

"I knew nothing about this, of course," Haylea said. "The staffers who moved the backup equipment out of the closet didn't even know *what* they were. One of them said they were spare parts for the kitchen equipment."

"They were moved to a non-essential storage area near the outer hull, on the wormhole side of the station," Roble finished for her, probably because she was wincing with every word.

"So you're saying our air is going bad," Samantha said. "Surely someone can bring new recyclers or something?"

"We've already checked, and the nearest spare recyclers are on a ship six days out," said a woman with curly dark hair and a frumpy purple sweater. "I'm Molly, by the way. Also, the ship can only spare two recyclers, and they're designed for a facility one-fifth the size of this one."

"So... that won't fix our problem." Samantha suddenly felt as panicked as the guests in the party room. Her mind raced. There had to be a way out of this, right? "How long until our air goes bad?"

"At our current capacity, about one day." Molly consulted a display. "But many of the party guests can be evacuated back to their own ships."

"What you're saying is that all our recyclers are completely cooked?" Samantha looked at her data pad, where a message from Lee was flashing.

WHAT'S GOING ON? WHY DID YOU STOP TRANSMITTING?

Inside this room, according to Anna, outgoing transmissions were blocked, though she was still receiving incoming messages.

"One is still functioning at about forty percent," Molly said.

"So we're not totally screwed?"

"One recycler running at forty percent is nowhere near capable of recycling air for the three-thousand twenty-two People on this station." Molly squeezed a column of numbers on her display and a graph appeared in the air over her desktop. "If we evacuated ninety-two percent and moved the rest onto one level we might make it six days, assuming most of us don't use oxygen faster than the average person these figures are based on. Ninety-three percent would be better. Ninety-four, better still."

"I have that data on docked ships." Roble flicked his hand in Molly's direction to send it to her.

Of course, they could just evacuate people. That didn't sound so bad. Samantha stared down at Lee's message. The station AI blocked transmissions out of the room without clearance, and asking for it now would probably lead to Haylea seizing her recorded video. She was just the type to panic and insist they couldn't tell the public anything.

"So that other ship is on the way with the spare recyclers?" she asked instead.

"Yes, and we have to assume their expenses for going so far off-course, and the fuel costs for getting here so fast," Haylea said with a sigh that said she was no longer worried about imminent death because she had returned to worrying about money, which meant....

"How should I spin this for the press?" she asked, right on schedule.

Apparently it had not yet occurred to her that Lee was expecting a news report, and that he still considered Samantha an unbiased source as far as everything other than the bar was concerned. Samantha had known walking this tightrope wouldn't be easy, but her relaxed attitude toward professional and journalistic ethics was a big help, at least.

"I am the press, and I would expect a statement detailing the evacuation plan," she said carefully, hoping Haylea wouldn't suddenly remember to ask if she could keep this off the record.

"This is a *disaster*," Haylea said. "I finally get people onto the station, and now I have to ask them to leave. Woolerton's going to blame me for this."

"He can't blame you for the wormhole situation," Samantha said. "I've covered stories where events beyond anyone's control caused a problem, and the venue offered guests some free amenities or services on their next visit, ensuring they would return. That usually prevents people from demanding a refund."

"Stupid wormholes! You think they might demand refunds?" Haylea's fingers scrambled for her pad. "We were profitable for two days!"

"We have bigger problems!" Roble yelled. The whole room went quiet.

Samantha had never heard quiet, goofy, eager-to-please Roble yell before. Worse than that, she'd never seen him say or do anything to contradict Haylea. This must be worse than she'd thought.

"At slightly-more-than safe capacity on all docked ships, we can evacuate seventy-six percent," he said. "At significantly more than safe capacity, eighty-seven percent. That's the absolute best-case scenario."

The room suddenly felt very claustrophobic to Samantha. She should have stayed on Richard's ship and listened to his stupid sales pitch for beer.

Molly raked a strand of curly hair off her face and it popped right back. "Is someone bringing the station doctor in here? We need to confer with him about this."

Just then Samantha heard a commotion in the doorway. "Well, I got here as soon as I could. It wasn't easy with my ship being damaged by one of those flying Human death traps. Damned Humans are behind all of it, I'm sure."

The man was dressed in a suit she recognized as an Altarian, made from a rare and highly expensive material that was probably on a par with 1,000 thread-count Egyptian cotton from Earth. He stopped and cleared his throat as his eyes landed on Samantha.

"Anyway, I, ah, got here as fast as I could once the station's patrol picked me up." He ambled toward Haylea at the center of the room. "What's going on here?"

"How badly was your ship damaged?" Haylea asked, her eyebrows popping up. Samantha knew what she was thinking—maybe Woolerton's big ship could hold the overflow.

"I don't know—it wasn't moving, that's for sure." He shrugged. "My crew will see that it gets fixed. Now, please tell me what the emergency is. I understand power has been restored to most of the station. It's embarrassing that this happened during the Delegation Meeting, but it was only a temporary glitch. One day, this event may be remembered as—"

"As the day the Humans blew up the wormhole and put our lives in jeopardy!" the tight-lipped woman in the back of the room interrupted him. "Do you know our air is going bad right now?"

Woolerton's brow knit as he whipped his head around to look at her, his jowls swinging like a suspension bridge. "What in the Civilized Sector are you talking about?"

Haylea pressed her lips together so tightly it almost looked as if her face would swallow them. "Our air recyclers were damaged by the impact after the wormhole incident. One is completely dead, the other functioning at about forty percent."

Woolerton glanced behind him at the nearest chair, then thought better of it and paced the floor in a small circle instead. "Forty percent should be okay until our automated crew replaces both recyclers with the spares we keep on hand. If it's that dire of a situation, we can always send a People crew if that would get it done faster?" He looked at Molly and Roble for confirmation.

"Well, you see, that's sort of the problem." Roble shifted from foot to foot. "We don't have any backup recyclers. They were fried by the impact."

"Fried by the impact?" Woolerton looked at Roble as if he'd just said that the recyclers had been affected by a magic curse and could only be fixed by unicorns. "That can't happen. All spare parts for Life Support essential equipment are kept in Storage One, near the center of the station. It's one of the best shielded, safest areas, and it's right next to the meeting room, which I understand was undamaged."

Haylea gripped the arms of her chair so hard the knuckles went from white to nearly transparent. "Prior to the Delegation Party, all the spare parts were moved out of storage — completely without my knowledge or consent — to make room for some catering equipment."

"Moved where?" Woolerton bellowed.

"To the Life Support ring, not far from where the operating air recyclers are... were," Haylea stammered.

Woolerton's face turned so red Samantha thought the next step might be either purple or blue — after he passed out. "So what are we going to do about this?"

For a few seconds, the room was completely silent. Samantha inched toward the door, hoping she could leave before Haylea asked her not to repeat everything she'd just heard. Woolerton turned his head from side to side, looking at everyone in turn.

"What am I paying you People to do here, anyway?" he demanded. "Besides store spare parts right next to the parts they're needed to replace? Not one of you has a plan? What are you, a bunch of stupid Humans?"

✳

TWENTY-SIX

"Where have you been?" The holographic display of Carlton's face hovered inches from Xenia, like an angry dog barking in her face.

"As you might recall, I was meeting with the Human Delegation when the wormhole... incident happened," she said. "Five Alpha put us in a secure room, but I didn't feel comfortable having a high-security-level conversation there, and my ship wasn't declared safe for almost an hour. You do realize a fleet of Human vessels just slammed into the station, right?"

"Which is what we need to talk about. The Humans intentionally planned to attack us!" The Council leader slammed his fist on the table before him, causing coffee to slosh out of a cup. One of his Human friends had introduced him to the beverage, and he'd been hooked ever since.

"We don't know that," Xenia said. "All the reports I'm getting show the only ship close to the wormhole was a small, rented vehicle. This looks like the work of an individual whackjob. We can't prove the Humans knew their ships would be flung into the station—which caused them a lot of damage and several injuries."

"Well, we didn't do it!" Carlton roared as though this should be obvious to anyone who wasn't a dumb Human. This, from the guy who was constantly telling the Council they had a "moral responsibility" to "help our disadvantaged cousins from Earth."

"We haven't identified the person or persons responsible for releasing the antimatter weapon. Isn't it possible this was one of our people?"

"Possible? Sure. Right after the Humans show up here, *claiming* to want peace?" Carlton grabbed the coffee cup and knocked back a big gulp.

Xenia's fingers flew over the display, pulling up data. "We lost the info on how the wormhole was stabilized thousands of years ago, and we've never replicated those results. We don't know if it will continue to destabilize, but it appears the vortex is shrinking, which suggests it will eventually collapse if we don't intervene.

"I know it seems suspicious because the Humans are here, but we can't just make assumptions—"

"But it's not just the wormhole!" With a flick of his hand, he sent the cup flying down the table, presumably for a refill. "All of our ships were docked during the incident, except a couple unmanned news vehicles, and those were too small to cause any damage. The Humans insisted on keeping a fleet of six ships free 'for their own protection.' They only docked two security ships with the presidential vessel, and practically stationed an army between us and the wormhole."

"We did agree to those terms," Xenia said. "We had more ships between the station and the Divide than they did. Remember, we agreed because *they* came *here*. Wouldn't you want a contingency plan if you went to visit their side?"

"Yes, but I'd know I didn't blow up the damn wormhole. The delegation group is requesting immediate clearance to leave! That looks guilty. I don't think we should let them."

Xenia felt a groan escape her lips before she could stop it. "The Guard can't stop them without cause. Where are they even going to go? Trying to make it through the wormhole right now would be very dangerous. Why don't we just follow them, call it a security detail for their own protection?"

"We don't know what else they had planned. They may be trying to escape before the whole station goes up in flames!" Another Human phrase, oddly ironic considering that the station wouldn't burn for long in space.

"Let's not make things worse here. They're probably thinking we did this. Why would they strand themselves on this side? "

"We can't let them leave. I've been told that we have sufficient Guard ships around the station to stop them."

Xenia gripped the edge of the table with sweaty palms. "And what if they resist? Are you going to have the Guard shoot them?"

"Let's hope it doesn't come to that."

"I vote against holding them here."

"I vote for it, and so does the majority of the Council."

"This is going to end badly," she said as his image faded.

*　*

"So you see, with Emoralian Fever, there rarely is any fever at all. Generally, the effect on sexual desire is so pronounced that the disease becomes obvious very quickly," Dr. Vance said to the two attractive women who'd asked him to explain the difference between two afflictions. "With Haubshegan Syndrome, increased sexual desire is mixed with other behavioral symptoms, many of them much less pleasant. Frequently, victims start hallucinating—"

"During sex?" Vericky asked. She was tall, blonde, and as she kept telling Vance, very limber.

He gave her his best smile. "You know, I've never asked."

"Do some patients refuse treatment for Emoralian Fever? I mean, is it true it heightens the sexual experience?" Clarmore was dark-haired and fidgety, and right now her fingers were playing with Vance's collar.

"Well, ah, I can't say I've ever asked a patient that, either." Vance plastered on his best nice-guy smile. "But according to all the research I've read, no, it doesn't. It simply gives the patient an insatiable urge to—"

"Dr. Vance?" said a low female voice behind him, and he could almost hear the smirk.

"I'm a bit busy right now." He turned around to face his former lover, Jill. Not long after she'd dumped him—saying she'd rather date an Andalian Male-for-Hire than look at Vance again—she'd transferred to a station half a light-year away. Or so he'd heard. He didn't blame her for being pissed—she'd been his first romantic entanglement after Iris, and that was a lousy position for anyone to be in.

Well, it could be worse. At least his two female companions were interested in him.

"Good to see you again," he said, in as professional a tone as possible, as he took in her station security uniform. "I didn't know you'd transferred back here."

"It's just temporary—they needed extra people for the Party." She gave Clarmore and Vericky a look that could melt the ugly ice sculpture of two globes Haylea had ordered for the party. They were supposed to represent two worlds coming together peacefully, but they really looked like two worlds being populated by tasteless idiots.

"Well, it was good to see you again, but if you'll excuse me, I'm in the middle of an important discussion about exotic diseases." Vance turned back to Clarmore. "Now, as I was saying, treatment protocols—"

"I didn't come to socialize." Jill stepped up beside him so she was roughly between Vance and the girls. "I was sent to escort you to the meeting room downstairs."

He knew the meeting room was generally where Haylea, Anna, and several department heads liked to discuss a crisis, and he could see how the current situation constituted one, but he didn't see how it involved him. As far as he knew, there were no serious injuries, and when he'd checked with his staff, they'd assured him everything was fine.

"If there's a medical emergency, I have people on duty in the infirmary," he said.

Jill shrugged. "I was told they needed you personally, in the meeting room. That's all I know."

Vance pulled his pad from his pocket, unrolled it, and scanned the messages. He would have been alerted if his staff paged him about an emergency, but Haylea was not on his list of approved interruptions. Sure enough, he had multiple messages from her, one from Anna, one from Roble and two from someone named Molly. All said roughly the same thing—they needed him to consult on a medical situation immediately.

Vance glanced longingly at Clarmore and Vericky. "I'm so sorry. I'll take care of this as quickly as possible so I can get back here." Then he turned and followed Jill toward the guarded exit, wondering what kind of medical emergency had happened that Haylea felt she couldn't take to the infirmary.

Once Jill ushered him into the meeting room, a dozen frantic conversations died at once.

"What seems to be the trouble?" Vance hoped to get this over with as quickly as possible. Say, before Clarmore and Vericky found someone even more interesting than him at the party.

The two seconds of silence that followed his entrance quickly turned back into a dozen conversations—but they were all one-sided and directed at him.

"Can you give us all some drug so we use less oxygen?" Haylea asked.

"What if you put us all to sleep for six days?" A woman in a purple sweater demanded.

"What's your action plan for fixing this problem?" A big guy Vance didn't recognize, with a bulbous nose and a neck that could benefit from regeneration therapy, challenged.

"Would someone please tell me what's going on here? What's wrong with our air filtration system?" Based on the questions, that seemed the most likely concern.

"Both our recycler units were damaged by the impact." The dark-haired woman waved her hand at him. A priority message blinked on his pad. Oh, she was Molly. "One is completely useless, the other functioning at forty percent."

"What about the backups?" He opened the data file and flipped through numbers and charts. "Why are both the spares showing zero percent capacity? They're brand new, right?" It occurred to him that Haylea might have attempted to save money by getting used recyclers. But surely she'd still have bought ones that *worked*, right?

"They've never been used," Haylea said through gritted teeth. "But they were damaged by the event, too."

"But I thought they were stored near the center of—"

"They were moved without my consent!" she screamed.

Roble consulted his pad. "The nearest ship that can spare a compatible extra is... six days out."

Vance looked around for an unoccupied chair, didn't see one, and sat on the nearest desk instead. Something pointy poked him in the ass, and he turned around to see that he was on someone's Spiked Sea Monster figurine. Suddenly the whole situation seemed as absurd as someone keeping a statue of an ugly creature like that on a desk where someone might sit on it.

Choking back completely inappropriate laughter, Vance tried to focus on the problem, which wasn't very funny at all. "You're telling me we stored the spares with the in-use recyclers and they all got fried? Why aren't we evacuating everyone off the station?"

"We are but there aren't enough ships." The big guy whirled around to look at Haylea. "You did put out the advisory for everyone who came on a ship to return to it, right?"

"Absolutely, Woolerton." Haylea's eyes stayed on her screen.

"But you've instructed them they can't leave yet, right?" Vance asked, louder than he'd intended because he'd just gotten to the best case scenario.

"Yes, an advisory has been sent to all docked ships that it's unsafe for them to leave due to damage from the impact," Haylea said. "I've also sent a station-wide message telling guests that we apologize for the lack of amenities on our station right now, and hope they'll be more comfortable on their own ships until we get the situation fixed."

"You *what*?" Vance couldn't believe what he'd heard. "What if some of them think they're comfortable enough here? Why haven't you told anyone what's going on? Those people are sucking up oxygen as we speak!"

"She's trying to manage the station's image, which is important," Woolerton said. Vance had never seen Haylea look relieved before. "Besides, we'll have a full statement explaining the problem in an hour or so. We have to protect ourselves, legally, financially, and image-wise."

"You have to protect the lives of the People on your station," Vance snapped. "Issue the evacuation order. *Now!*"

"But a full, beyond-capacity evacuation may not be necessary." Haylea's voice was calm and reasonable. "Molly's data suggests if we were all put to sleep for the next six days, oxygen consumption might drop enough that—"

"You want to put out a press release telling people 'Everything is fine, we just need to knock you out for six days so we don't run out of oxygen'? Don't you think that's going to sound worse than an evacuation order?" Vance hoped he could reason with Haylea and Woolerton, who was obviously some sort of management asshole here.

Samantha winced. "He has a point. You need to evacuate as many People as possible as fast as possible. If everyone thinks that will solve the problem, they'll be less panicked while we work out the details."

Haylea flopped back in her chair and stared at the ceiling. "I'll send the evacuation order now."

"Make sure you emphasize that we're handling the problem and developing a dynamic solution!" Woolerton said in her direction.

Vance studied the plan Molly had sent him, which included data about how much oxygen the average person used in a day, with the assumption that People slept eight hours in that time frame.

"I don't think these calculations are accurate," he said finally, and the room fell silent again. "There are a few problems."

"Like what?" Woolerton demanded.

"Like using averages. Oxygen consumption varies a lot from person to person. In order to calculate this right, we'd need to know the weight, health, and physical fitness level of everyone currently on this station."

Molly's eyebrows shot up. "I can use sensor data from the airlocks. Everyone had to pass through them to get on the station. I think I can tell you how much everyone weighs and their general state of health."

Vance closed his eyes, trying to think. "That helps, but we need more. Maybe there's another way to use the data. You have sensors that monitor air filtration in each room, right? In case the local unit breaks and stops filtering air through to the main recyclers?"

Molly bobbed her head without taking her eyes off the display. "I can use that data to determine how much oxygen each room uses in a given time period, then add up all the rooms."

"For now, that sounds like a good plan." He looked at his pad. "But aside from the lack of oxygen, we also have to worry about toxic gases building up as people exhale. Even in the best case scenario, with eighty-two percent evacuated, everyone else using oxygen at no higher than the average rate, and all of us sedated and sleeping, we would still run out of air about twelve hours before the ship with our spare parts arrives."

Once again, the room greeted him with silence. Molly looked at Roble as if she thought he could come up with a better answer. Roble glanced at Vance for a second, his face scared, then looked back at his display. Haylea had stopped working on the evac order and she stared at Vance as if hoping he'd say, "Just kidding!" the way Humans liked to do all the time.

"Is there a way to reduce the workload on the remaining recycler to slightly increase its efficiency? Or fix whatever brought it down to forty percent in the first place?" Samantha asked.

"I'm working on that now," Roble said grimly.

Woolerton glanced around the room, down at his pad, directly at Vance, and then back around the room once more. "In the interest of reducing oxygen consumption, I'm going back to my ship right now. I will continue to monitor the situation remotely, of course."

"You'll be taking some of the evacuees with you, right?" Samantha yelled after him as he moved toward the door.

Woolerton turned to look at her. "What?"

She held up her pad. "I see your ship can safely hold forty-five people, fifty-seven in short-term emergency situations. I'd say this constitutes an emergency, wouldn't you?"

Woolerton grimaced, looked around at the room full of angry, terrified faces, then somehow twisted the grimace into one of the most fake-looking smiles Vance had ever seen. "Of course. I will be happy to welcome fifty-three People onto my ship, in addition to me and my assistants."

"Wonderful. I'll be sure to include that in my report. It really puts a relatable, personable face on things." With that, Samantha scurried out the door.

✳
TWENTY-SEVEN

"I need everyone to just calm down for a minute!" Vance screamed. Ordinarily, people might have noticed and shut up. But with most of them also screaming, yelling, or crying hysterically, his voice just got lost in the melee.

From what Vance had overheard, the few People who seemed to be thinking clearly were focused on trying to make extra recyclers from the attached ships work on the station. The idea had been dismissed earlier because most ship systems were much smaller than those intended for a station like Five Alpha, and due to design features couldn't interface with their equipment. Roble was trying to make it work anyway.

The really frustrating thing for Vance—aside from the fact his own People were acting like panicky Humans—was that he actually thought he might have a solution in case the recycler repurposing idea didn't work, but he couldn't get the noise level down enough to talk. He was considering a mass message to everyone in the room when he had a better idea.

Gritting his teeth, he threaded his way through the crowd to Jill, who was calmly telling a fidgeting short guy that he should concentrate on finding a solution, not making matters worse. "I need to make an announcement."

She left the anxious guy with a reassuring pat on the shoulder and followed Vance into an unoccupied cubicle, eyeing him coolly, like she thought he was going to ask for help reconnecting with Clarmore and—whatever the other one's name was, he couldn't remember at the moment.

"About what? The open dates on your social calendar?"

Vance bit back a smart remark, and forced out instead, "No, I think I may have a solution, but I'll need the attention and cooperation of everyone in this room for five minutes. Can you help me?"

Jill raised an eyebrow, but she tapped into her pad, and within seconds a loud, blaring alarm filled the room. She let it run for ten seconds, during which time everyone finally shut up.

"Doctor Vance has something important to say about our problem," she said, using the AI's loudspeaker function. Then she gestured for him to talk.

"I know you're all focusing on making ship recyclers work for us," he said. "That's the best idea we have right now. However, I have another idea in case it doesn't work."

He had thought the room went quiet a moment ago, but it hadn't, really—people had still been sniffling and snuffling and sobbing in a slightly quieter way. But now, the room actually went so silent he wasn't sure anyone was even breathing.

"Sedating everyone won't slow down our use of oxygen enough to last us six days," he said. "But putting almost everyone in cryo will. We only have fifty unused cryobeds in the infirmary, which we keep on hand for... well, emergencies like this one.

"Each bed puts a person into a very deep sleep, while lowering body temperature. Metabolism slows to an almost nonexistent state, allowing the patient to survive with only a few heartbeats per minute, for years if necessary, with extremely low amounts of oxygen, which are simply recirculated by the bed itself. The embedded recyclers are highly energy efficient because long-term storage is often necessary, so they are not capable of sustaining a person breathing normally—even one who is unconscious.

"What I need from you is help collecting data on how many cryocans all the nearby ships have available. For my plan to work, we would need to get almost everyone we can't evacuate into cryo within the next day or two—the sooner, the better for anyone left awake."

A flurry of activity started in the room, as sobs hitched short, people sucked the snot back into their noses, and everyone started talking again.

"If you'll wait just a moment," he shouted before he could be drowned out again. "There is one more matter of importance. I know you're all working on an evac plan, and I don't know what criteria you're using to determine who evacuates, but before randomly choosing people we have to remove some from the pool. First, you need to find out who has a medical condition that would prevent them from going into cryo—recent heart problems, most implants necessary to treat otherwise life-threatening conditions, pregnancy, and any recent serious illness."

"Don't we have medical info on file for all station visitors?" Haylea asked.

He shook his head. "Not unless they've come to my infirmary for some reason. The doorway scanners don't check for anything except infectious diseases."

"I'll draft a letter saying it's imperative that we know the medical history of all our guests, due to our current problem with the air recyclers," Haylea said. "If I word it right, some People might think they'll get evacuated first, which they will, and will be more likely to tell us the truth. I'll be sure to mention that all their info is confidential."

"Good," Vance said. "Once we know how many People can't go in cryo, and how many additional People can be evacuated, then we'll have a better idea how many cryocans we need. I'll start calling the ships and find out how many cans they have."

Roble glanced around, looking conflicted. "I *could* keep working on repurposing the ship recyclers...."

"But what?" Vance asked. "Did you just have a better idea?"

"Well, I looked at this data on your infirmary cryobeds." Roble handed Vance his pad. "Those things are rated to keep one person alive, in cryo, for up to fifty years — better than that in at least one case. Anyway, two People in a cryobed would overwhelm it in a long-term situation, but this would only be for a few days."

"So you think these things could fit two People each?" Molly asked.

"The power cells are the main reason cryocans are rated for one person, over fifty years," Roble said. "But if we connected these things to the station's system, I don't see why they couldn't work at double capacity."

Vance turned off the loudspeaker function. "Now I just need to find enough cryocans to hold everyone with two people in each one," he mumbled to Jill.

✳
TWENTY-EIGHT

Roble was contemplating using spare parts from a crawler to build a converter for the power cells when a shadow fell over his display. Probably that damn reporter, back to bug him when he was trying to work.

"What do you want now?" He didn't bother to look up.

"Hello to you, too," said Molly's voice.

Roble turned to look at her. "I'm sorry, I thought you were Samantha."

"I understand." Molly pulled a chair next to his and sat down. "The preliminary reports suggest we'll have almost enough cryobeds for everyone—if you can adjust each of them to fit two People."

"How are you and the others coming on the recyclers?" Molly was directing that project while he worked on the power cell problem.

"If every nearby ship gave us their spare recyclers, and every one of those could be made to work successfully with our system, at their full capacity, within the next twelve hours, and we barricaded off all but a small section of one deck and only recycled the air there...."

"With that many ifs?" Roble groaned. "Would it work?"

"There might be enough air for four or five smallish People to survive six days. The air wouldn't be great quality, towards the end, and Doctor Vance says they might suffer some hypoxia, but if they're all in good health, they'll probably survive."

Roble leaned back in his chair and stared up at the ceiling. "And that's assuming we double-pack everyone into the cryocans."

"Triple-pack some of the children and smaller adults." Molly stared at his display. "Building a converter out of crawler parts, that's a good idea."

"There's no way it's going to be done successfully in the next twelve hours. I don't even have one good working model yet, and it would have to be tested before we could implement —"

"To make sure we don't just short out every working power cell on every cryocan." Molly fingered her pad and popped up a display. "But what if we left the cryocans on their own crafts? Most of them are designed to run on the ship's power, and only switch to battery if that fails. We wouldn't need to convert anything."

Roble frowned. "Why doesn't the infirmary have that kind?"

"Vance said he wanted them, but Woolerton purchased the older, cheaper type instead. Said the infirmary wouldn't use them enough, and it would save money on power."

Roble looked at her numbers. "So what do we do about the fifty cryocans on this station that have to hold at least one hundred People?"

"I've been working on that," said a voice behind them. Roble turned to see Dr. Vance.

"I'm still considering the power cell problem —"

"That may not be necessary." Vance sat on the desk, shoving the displays out of his way. Roble knew they weren't technically in the way, but they looked better against a non-living background. They all shrank in size and shifted to the wall.

"What do you mean?" Roble asked.

"I looked over the detailed specifications on the beds. Each one is safety rated to hold one person, weighing up to forty gravs — about three hundred fifty pounds, to the Humans. The specs are based on power usage for someone that size."

"And most of us weigh less than forty gravs!" Molly's eyebrows disappeared under her hairline.

Vance nodded. "Also, that was a safe limit for fifty years. Going over by a few gravs would probably be fine for six days."

"So we might even be able to fit three People, even four, into some of the cryocans," Molly said. "Let me run the numbers —"

"No, I don't think that will work," Vance said. "We still have space restraints inside the cans. Each person is going to have tubes running into them, recycler masks over their faces, and electrodes on their skin."

"Are the electrodes necessary?" Roble asked. "As I understand it, they're intended to constantly stimulate the muscles, so they won't degrade over time. Is that necessary for a six-day stay?"

"Probably not, and it would save us time. I still don't think we can fit three adults into a cryocan, though. Maybe if we had three People who each weighed ten gravs, but even then it would be a tight squeeze, and most People weigh more than that."

"But as long as we don't go too much over the weight limit, we won't need to refit the power cells?" Roble asked.

"I don't think so," Vance said. "You can go back to repurposing the ship recyclers. And work fast, because we're still going to have a few extra People left over who will have to breathe *something* on this station for six days."

✳
TWENTY-NINE

Wandering through the meeting room, Vance found an empty cubicle where someone had left a newsfeed running on the desk. As he sat down, he reached to turn it off, then decided to watch for a moment—he wanted to make sure Haylea had communicated the urgency of the evacuation order. If she didn't, he was going to call Woolerton and ask if he had an action plan for dealing with the CC fallout of people asphyxiating on his station.

"Lee here with a special report on the wormhole incident. I'm being joined by our Human Affairs reporter, Samantha, reporting live from Space Station Five Alpha. Samantha, I understand there are some new developments to the situation, since the station was affected by the gravitational wave?"

"That's right, Lee. At the time the historic Delegation Party was meeting to discuss ending the Human/People hostilities, the unanticipated wave slammed the Human party's ships into Five Alpha, causing damage to both the vehicles and the station.

"Due to the severity and unexpected nature of the impact, key life support systems were damaged on Five Alpha, including the station's main air recyclers, as well as backup systems. Copacetic Communications Director Haylea says that crews are working to correct the problem, and the station's guests and inhabitants are being evacuated as a precaution until it's resolved."

"What do you think, Samantha? Is the situation worse than the CC Director's press advisory would have us believe?"

"I think it would be prudent for guests to follow evacuation instructions immediately. I should note that the press advisory cautions people not to leave the station, as further evacuation efforts may be necessary. My contacts at the Guard tell me there is no threat to the station itself, and remaining here will not endanger anyone on the docked ships."

"So you believe the situation is serious?"

"Yes, Lee, I'm afraid so. Normally the backup plan for recycler failure is to replace the recycler with a spare, but that isn't an option here. Evacuating the station is the only option."

"What about getting another new recycler?"

"As I understand it, Lee, the nearest one is on its way but won't be available for about six days, and the remaining recycler function won't be able to clean the air for that long at the current level of population. Following evacuation protocols will reduce strain on what's left of the system and allow it to clean the air for the remaining inhabitants."

"Let's turn now to speculation on who is responsible for the antimatter explosion. Authorities for the Guard and the Federal Investigative Board, or FIB, have not yet ruled the explosion as an act of sabotage, and accidental antimatter explosions are rare."

"That's true, Lee, and there is a lot of speculation. As you can see in this video recently released by Five Alpha security, this is the last ship seen approaching the Divide from our side before the incident. I'll direct your attention to that blurry cylinder exiting the vehicle, which has been confirmed as a Human design, although its ownership has not been established. See how the cylinder hurtles toward the wormhole, right before the video ends? That's when the explosion happened."

"Could this have been an accident?"

"It's possible, but my sources in the Guard tell me that antimatter is a very dangerous substance, difficult to find or produce, so it's rarely transported by individuals. There are very strict safety standards that apply to moving antimatter for industrial uses to avoid just this sort of situation. There hasn't been a reported accident with antimatter in hundreds of years. It seems unlikely that this was unintentional, but it can't be ruled out at this time."

"That leads us to who might be responsible. Most speculation reported on our website leans toward the Humans, although there doesn't seem to be any evidence other than the fact that it was a Human ship carrying the antimatter. Have you found that to be the case on Five Alpha as well?"

"Yes, Lee, most of the partygoers seem to suspect the Humans of plotting to destroy the wormhole, although the UNE and People governments have both issued official statements claiming no responsibility. Both would stand to lose a lot if the wormhole continues to destabilize and collapses, and it seems hard to imagine that the UNE would want to strand its president and several other leaders over here."

"Have any fringe groups taken responsibility?"

"No, but there were rumors before the delegation party that an attack might be imminent from one of Earth's fringe groups, like the Medical Responsibility League, the Mother Earth Protective Society, and

Rednecks for Reparations, to name a few. It is possible one of those reports was correct, but with a different target."

Vance dismissed the news and asked his AI to prepare a message for every ship docked with the station or close enough to deliver a cryocan in the next few days. At least she seemed to realize the important of evacuating the station, even if Haylea didn't. Now he just had to hope they could find enough cryocontainers—and that none of those groups Samantha just mentioned were planning a second attack on Five Alpha.

✳

THIRTY

A million years ago—or so it seemed—on a sleepy, small-town college campus on Earth, Samantha had taken Principles of Public Relations as a journalism elective. Its professor, Dr. Baker, was a tall, dark-haired woman who might have been attractive if she'd ever bothered to comb her hair, which frequently could have passed for Einstein's if she hadn't at least dyed the gray away. She lectured sitting on a table at the front of the room, where she rambled about various things that had happened to her in the last six decades, some of which were vaguely related to public relations. Although Dr. Baker came off as such a ditz that nobody believed she really had a Ph.D., her crazy stories always managed to be entertaining, and Samantha remembered most of them.

One point Baker tried to make was that public relations practitioners could never really be business executives, and they could never really be journalists either, because they had to be trusted by both. For Samantha, that seemed simple. In her years as a journalist, she never trusted PR people—or Copacetic Communications directors, as they were called here.

Haylea trusted her completely, which made her as dumb as most Humans. Samantha had been shocked when she came and went from the room three times without Haylea asking her once if she was recording. Now, sitting in her apartment and staring at the footage from the meeting room, with everyone arguing about how to solve the air crisis, she wondered what to do with it.

Haylea—not to mention that stuffed shirt Woolerton—would use up the rest of their oxygen screaming if she released it. She could argue that it didn't reveal anything the public couldn't figure out anyway, that it put a relatable Person face on things, but Haylea would probably still be pissed. Worse, she would go back to handling things herself, which would be a disaster for the station right now. Despite her own self-serving interests, Samantha had come to think of this place as her home.

The vid should absolutely be released—just not until it would have the most impact, probably after the crisis was resolved. In fact, this was the sort of inside-the-disaster thing that usually earned great ratings a few weeks after said event. Whether Haylea liked it or not, showing what *really* happened to the backup recyclers would prove that the stupid *Humans* weren't completely at fault, should they take the blame. Samantha suspected they would, but wanted to see how the situation played out.

She finally set aside her pad and reached for the sedatives Vance had been handing out like candy to anyone who passed a brief medical scan. The situation was still precarious, more so than anyone who read that press release would believe.

Calculations for the salvage plan hinged on the one remaining recycler continuing to function at forty percent for the next six days. Even though they had shut off eighty percent of the station, the one filtration system was still struggling to scrub far more dirty air than it could handle at one hundred percent. The extra strain could make its efficiency drop from forty percent to thirty, or twenty, or lower. Roble said that if it reached ten percent, it would almost certainly fail completely within twelve hours.

Lee said he'd try to find a way to sneak her onto *Glass*'s ship, a roomy *Galaxy*-class liner parked just outside the station. He was aware of the evacuation protocols, and had already accepted the maximum safe number of evacuees, but thought he could squeeze her in. It wouldn't be comfortable, but they wouldn't run out of air—probably.

She said she'd get back to him after Vance figured out the cryo-can situation. Security was watching her like a hawk, and as much as she wanted off this floating death trap, she also sort of wanted to stay here and cover the story. Anyway, it no longer seemed that dangerous with Roble's new plan. Also, the overstuffed ships could have recycler failures, too, and they'd all donated their spare recyclers to the station already.

She tossed the pad aside and flopped back on the couch. Lee had promised to call and wake her up if anything interesting happened, but she was exhausted after covering the party and the wormhole disaster. Hopefully nothing interesting would happen while she was sleeping off the pills.

A pounding on the door startled her just as she started to drift off.

"Samantha? Are you still awake? Hello. It's me, Hank," flooded from her intercom.

She opened her eyes. "Yeah, I'll be there in a minute."

Stumbling out of bed, she looked down at her rumpled plaid nightshirt and pink fuzzy socks, considered finding a robe, and then decided she really didn't give a crap right now.

"What's wrong?" she asked after getting her door lock code right on the third try. The sedatives made her clumsy.

"I just don't have anyone else I can talk to—I mean, really talk to. Can I come in?" Anxiety creased his brow.

"Oh… sure." She shrugged.

Hank sat down on the sofa and gave her a wary look as she flopped down next to him. "This is all off the record, okay?"

Honestly, Hank was no longer a hot story anyway. Despite the strange circumstances of his meeting with Richard, no one was going to care about a few skeletons in the golden boy's closet when the wormhole was destabilizing and the station was struggling to keep its inhabitants breathing.

"Of course. Whatever you want."

Hank stared down at the carpet for a moment. If Samantha had cared about appearances, she might have wished that she ran her cleaning bot more often, but fortunately she really didn't care.

"I'm going to volunteer to be left out of cryo," he said finally.

She blinked, shook her head, and looked at him again. "What? Why would you do that?"

He shrugged. "I'll probably be all right. Doctor Vance says that oxygen deprivation won't worsen my condition—in fact, it might temporarily slow the degradation of neurons."

She rubbed her hands over her face, trying to wake herself up again. "Degradation of neurons? I thought… you were cured."

"They fixed the gene." He sighed and leaned his head back on the couch. "Doctor Vance ran some more in-depth tests. It turns out the disease has been causing damage my whole life, and it's not reversible."

"Oh, Hank, I'm so sorry. Why didn't you tell me before?"

He groaned. "I didn't want anyone to know at first—that made it too real, and I wasn't sure what I was going to do. Vance thinks he might be able to develop a treatment, so he says I shouldn't rush back into cryo. I don't know why I shouldn't. I mean, what's the point of making friends and getting back into my life if I have to get frozen again in a few years? The doctor can always wake me up if he thinks he has a cure."

"So why do you want to be left out now? If you might be going into cryo soon anyway—"

"Because I'm in no rush to go back in after a hundred and fifty years. Besides, on the off chance something goes wrong, it's better if it's me who runs out of air than someone who actually has a future," Hank said, so complacently that he sounded like someone discussing the price of hydrogen fuel. "Thanks for listening, Samantha."

"Hank, wait!" She grabbed his arm. "Wait a minute, let's talk about this. Are you sure—"

"Relax. Chances are, I'll be fine and so will everyone else." He stood up and headed for the door.

She didn't think anyone would be fine any time soon.

THIRTY-ONE

"Why the fuck are we backing up?" Frego screamed at his AI. He was in a Guard patrol ship, on what had started out as a routine mission to ensure other vessels didn't leave Five Alpha. It had now turned into a massive confrontation with the Human delegation party.

"There appears to be a problem with the navigational array. It may have been damaged by the gravitational wave earlier."

"Which is why we ran a complete diagnostic before moving!" Frego yelled. The one good thing about the Guard's outdated, frequently inaccurate AI was that he could yell at it all day and never hurt its feelings. Best of all, he never had to apologize to it. "Didn't you check the nav system then? What part of 'complete diagnostic' didn't you understand?"

"It was thoroughly checked during the complete diagnostic," the AI said blandly. "But sometimes damage can occur that doesn't become evident until the systems have been running for a while. This is one of those situations. Now, I'd like to direct your attention to another—"

"I'd like to direct your attention to the fact that we need to fix this!" Frego waved at the wall screen in front of him, which showed the Human ships dodging around the other Patrol vessels and, as the Earthers liked to say, making a break for it—something they couldn't do if he wasn't moving rapidly away from them.

"I am attempting to repair the problem, but it appears that a part will need to be changed, which will require us to shut down the engines. I assume you don't want to do that right now?"

"Do I want to be unable to go anywhere with Human ships shooting at me? No, of course I don't want to do that." Frego slammed his fist down on the console. "You know what, I'm just going to switch to manual control. The propulsion systems are working correctly, right?"

"Yes, but I wouldn't advise that, and we still have another—"

"Thanks for your input. I'll let you know when you can complete the repair." Frego flipped the switch and grabbed the controls. Just as he was about to make the much-needed course correction, he glanced at the display that showed where all the other Guard ships were. Several he could already see on the wall screen, trying desperately to catch the Humans. But three were now....

"Why are you guys following me?" he yelled after opening a channel.

"Your orders were to follow you," came the reply.

"That's what I was trying to tell you about," his AI added helpfully.

Frego did, in fact, vaguely remember telling the three patrol ships to follow him for backup as he dealt with the Human problem. He'd been instructed to try a blockade first, only shooting at them if absolutely necessary and only using his weakest weapons, in an effort to avoid a full-fledged fight. Having the other ships flank him had been the best option for blocking the Earthers.

Now, it was the best option for letting them go.

"Well, stop following me and go back to stopping the Humans, but try not to shoot at them unless they shoot first!" He adjusted course. Unfortunately, the ship didn't respond as he'd hoped. He didn't have a navigation display anymore, since he'd taken the controls and shut down the non-functioning system, but he could still use the wall screens to navigate manually.

And at the moment, he was moving sideways. "What's wrong with the propulsion system?"

"Nothing, but without the navigational system it can't calculate which way forward is. I can recalibrate using the edges of the ship as directional points, but that will take a few minutes," the AI said in its irritatingly calm voice.

"Maybe I can just figure out which way it thinks is forward." Frego randomly moved his hands over the controls, making a quick correction after he almost crashed into one of the patrol ships.

"Why aren't you guys going after the Humans like I told you?" he yelled at them. The line of Human ships zipped past them, heading in the direction of… the Divide? That was a dangerous proposition right now. Were they crazy? He aimed one of the lasers at the lead vehicle, hoping at least his targeting system would still work. It did, but the Human craft bounced around in an evasive pattern, making the weapon ineffective. He could try a targeted torpedo, but that would probably start an international incident, and his commander thought it was more important to avoid bad CC than stop the Humans from leaving, so he reluctantly let them go.

"We're having trouble going after them," one of the pilots said. "My AI is trying to diagnose the problem, but there seems to be some sort of gravitational pull coming from the wormhole."

"Yes, I'm getting that," said Frego's AI. "It's dragging us toward the Divide, even though we should be far enough out to avoid its gravity well."

Frego looked at his displays. They were all headed for the wormhole, but on parallel paths. Since the controls weren't responding right, he adjusted course manually and aimed for the wormhole, hoping that would send him in some other direction, any direction. Looking at the speed display he saw, to his relief, that the move had slowed them down.

But as he turned his attention to the wall screens, he realized they were still heading toward the wormhole.

"Is there something there?" He looked for the usual lights, then remembered they'd been demolished by the wormhole event.

"The gravitational distortion is growing. That could indicate the Divide is fluctuating again, but I have insufficient data to be sure," the AI said.

Frego looked at the wall screens in dismay. All three patrol ships were now following him into—what? He had no idea.

"I'm going to try a full stop." He reached for the controls. "Hopefully the emergency braking system can override our progress toward...."

He trailed off as a bright, milky swirl filled the blackness on the wall screen behind him.

"It's too late, we're getting pulled in," the AI said. "You need to get into an emergency cryopod, now!"

THIRTY-TWO

Dr. Vance stood in the huge hall that hours ago had been full of the delegation party. Most of the decorations hadn't been cleaned up yet, and it looked like his apartment the morning after a big party. Dirty dishes were still on the tables, some knocked askew—no one had wanted to waste energy running the cleaning bots during a crisis—streamers still dangled from the ceilings and random clothing items—hats, coats, even a skirt, who knew what that was about—lay on chairs or tables or even the floor. Vance, Anna, Haylea, Woolerton, and Roble were clumped on the podium where Richard had made his tacky speech. It seemed to Vance as if it was a lifetime ago.

"The latest shockwave was less intense than the first, but several ships docked with the station were damaged," Vance said, after Anna once again shut everybody up for him. "Fortunately, since they were all docked none of them hit the station this time. Unfortunately, one of them is no longer able to accommodate any of its thirty-two passengers—including twenty-seven evacuees, who will now be forced to return to the station."

Groans went up all around, and people shouted questions.

"Are we all going to die now?"

"Can we get stuffed into those coffin things?"

"Can we have their air recyclers if their ship is a loss?"

"What happened to using extra ship recyclers for the station, anyway?"

Roble stepped up beside Vance. "I think I can answer that last one," he yelled in a surprisingly confident tone, and the crowd quieted. Vance moved aside.

"We can convert only about ten of the recyclers, the ones from the biggest ships. The others are too small to even function with our systems," Roble explained. "They would short out and fail. We're converting the others and should have them installed within a few hours."

More screaming, some of it congratulatory this time, more questions. Anna silenced them all just by reaching for the alarm icon on her screen.

"This will help slow the degradation of our air, but multiple small recyclers can't come close to the function of the two large filtration systems that were damaged. Even with the new recyclers, we'll still only be at about fifty percent of normal efficiency for *one* recycler. That's assuming the remaining respiration pod doesn't lose more efficiency—and there's a high probability it will." Vance noticed he left out the possibility of total failure. "Dr. Vance tells me that if we load all the cryocans available well past safety limits, we will be short spots for five People."

"However," Vance said, loudly, to drown out the sudden hum of chatter in the room. "If those People are sedated, there will probably be enough air to last until the new recyclers get here and can be installed." He pointedly didn't mention the higher risk of cryocan failure for those being stuffed in past capacity. Or the fact that they would be overstuffing the cans even more than planned. Or that there were more overweight Humans than People and there were a lot of Humans on the station right now.

Anna stepped forward. "I will remain out of cryo to oversee the security of the station."

Vance cleared his throat. "We have already relocated anyone who can't go into cryo for medical reasons. Since cryosleep is not recommended for children younger than fifteen, all children were evacuated to other ships. An algorithm determined the most efficient way to assign cryobeds to the remaining people here, based on size and weight.

"The computer model also considered physical health, based on the scans I gave everyone when prescribing sedatives yesterday. I used those not only to ensure that sedation and cryosleep were safe for the patients involved, but also to measure how efficiently each person uses oxygen. It's easier and safer to awaken someone from regular sleep than it is to awaken them from cryo, which takes several hours. For that reason, like Anna, I will remain out of cryo in case of a medical emergency.

Roble jumped in at that point. "Don't worry—the crew bringing the recyclers will evacuate everyone awake immediately upon arrival, and they will install the new recyclers—you don't have to worry about one of us trying to fix the life support systems while suffering from hypoxia!"

He started laughing, apparently finding this funny, but stopped when he noticed he was laughing alone.

"So we're all going to be fine?" a woman in the back of the crowd asked.

"Assuming things go as planned, there's a high probability of that, yes." One of the first things Vance had learned in medical school was how to avoid lawsuits—never, ever, guarantee anything to anyone.

"And what if things don't go as planned?" asked a man Vance thought he recognized as one of Samantha's colleagues from *Glass*. It was his ship that had been damaged after the last wormhole event. "What are the risks to the People you've selected to stay out of cryo?"

Woolerton cleared his throat and stepped up beside Vance, Roble, and Anna. "Our decision was based on the results of computer modeling. We carefully studied the problem and all alternatives, then chose the option that was the most likely to result in everyone surviving for the next seven days."

"So are you going to stay out of cryo?" the *Glass* reporter asked. Normally, at this point in a press conference, other reporters would be clamoring to ask questions, but this time they all remained silent to hear the answer.

"I've been told I would not be a suitable candidate because of my size," Woolerton said smoothly. "As you might recall, they chose only People who were very small and in top physical condition. It's in everyone's best interest for me to return to my ship."

"So who is staying here and awake?" asked another reporter.

"And you never answered my question about risks to those on the station and staying out," persisted the *Glass* reporter.

"After the first few days, oxygen levels will drop, and carbon dioxide and other gases will begin building up." Vance struggled to sound calm when the situation was even making him feel panicked. "This will happen slowly and won't pose any immediate danger. Our bodies can adjust, especially if we don't do anything strenuous.

"When oxygen levels start to fall below twenty percent, some people begin to experience symptoms of hypoxia. These include lethargy, dizziness, and poor coordination. Too much carbon dioxide in the air can cause increased blood pressure and heart rate —"

"Both of those things can cause death!" someone in the back yelled, and then the tidal wave of questions Vance had anticipated earlier finally hit.

"Were your victims given any choice if they wanted to be left out?"

"What's the probability of death for each person staying awake?"

"What about long-term brain damage in those who survive? Could they end up as stupid as the Humans?"

Anna finally got everyone under control with another blast, but it took longer this time.

"Yes, hypoxia and carbon dioxide poisoning can be fatal, *but—*" Vance practically yelled the word, trying to put as much emphasis on it as possible. "Death usually doesn't occur until oxygen levels drop below eighteen percent, and the models don't predict that happening for about seven days. The new recyclers will be here before then."

"You said usually—that means death can occur before eighteen percent, right?" the *Glass* reporter pressed.

"It's extremely unlikely in healthy, compact individuals like those chosen to stay out." Vance tried to steer the conversation back to the part where *everybody was fine.* "I want to emphasize that we studied not just size, but lung capacity, heart health, blood composition, and every health factor that could possibly influence additional problems in even the most minor way."

"But are these People being given a *choice*?" demanded a frizzy-haired, frazzled-looking woman to the left.

"We have not released the names of those selected yet." Vance felt like he was walking on a tightrope of dental floss. "My name is on the list because I volunteered. It is my responsibility to be available for any medical emergencies that might occur. Keep in mind, there are also risks associated with cryosleep. Normally those are very low, but computer models suggest they are a bit higher when the cryobeds are being used outside of normal circumstances."

"So being stuffed into a cryocan with two other People might kill you too?" asked another voice.

"Cryosleep normally carries a risk of death of slightly less than half a percent." Vance could hear the strain in his own voice. "Our predictions suggest the risk might go up to about one percent, still extremely low. To minimize that risk, all cryobeds monitor the health of the inhabitants. In an emergency, they will be pulled out of cryo, and I will be alerted."

"So is the probability of death higher for someone in or out of the freezer?" The reporter from *Glass* again. He was a short but muscular man, whose short-sleeved shirt and half-length pants revealed the muscles of someone who exercised regularly. Vance considered suggesting that he volunteer to stay on the station and let someone less fortunate have his place on the now severely overstuffed caterer's ship, but thought better of it.

Instead, he said, "Honestly, we calculated the probabilities to be very close — one point one percent for those in cryo, and one point four percent for those out. There really is no significant advantage either way."

"So will you be forcing People to stay out if they want to go in?" The *Glass* reporter yet again, his eyes burning into Vance.

"That's not up to me. I only make medical recommendations." Vance knew he was shirking the question and didn't give a crap.

"I don't believe that would be necessary," Woolerton said, after an uncomfortable pause in which he, Haylea, and Roble looked expectantly at each other. "If anyone is determined to go into cryo, I suppose we could ask for volunteers to stay out or... well, if there aren't any volunteers, I guess we could pack more People into one of the ships. The probability of death in that situation, however, might be more than one point five percent."

"The more we overload ships past safe capacity, the more that probability goes up. Right now we're looking at two to three percent on the most crowded ships. Why don't I release the list of recommended names now?" Vance asked, looking around at a roomful of angry, scared faces. All he wanted was to get this mess over with so he could take a sedative and hope like hell an alarm didn't wake him up before the six-day mark.

THIRTY-THREE

Anna had more problems than she could count, but the biggest and most pressing one was her son, Will.

"Will, I am not leaving you out of cryo," she said in her best do-not-mess-with-me voice.

"But I can do it, Mom." He flipped through a full-dimensional model of a school project. "I'm smaller than you and use less oxygen. Besides, cryo is dangerous for someone my age. I read about it on the nets."

Anna gritted her teeth. "What you read on the nets can't compare to what Doctor Vance told me himself—"

"Did he tell you they don't let anyone under twenty in cryo, except in emergency? It could stunt my growth, weaken my brain like the Humans—"

"First of all, those are slight risks." Why did he spend so much time reading non-entertainment information on the nets? That wasn't normal for a kid his age. "Cryo is usually a procedure done for convenience, for space travel. It's rarely necessary to save anyone's life."

"I thought we would all be fine if left out of cryo."

She sighed. "Probably. But if the last main recycler fails, that could change. And if it does, you are the first one going into cryo, Vance and I agree. Do you understand?"

Will stared at her incredulously. "You want me to go through life as stupid as a Human?"

"First of all, calling them stupid is insulting and it really upsets them," Anna stammered, trying to remember the appropriate parental things to say in this situation. "Second, your life is the most important thing here. Third, Doctor Vance says that your brain development is ahead of schedule anyway. Even if it was stunted by cryo, it's highly unlikely there would be any measurable difference to your long-term intelligence."

"But what if there is?" Will whined. "What if I wind up being dumber than my friends all of a sudden? I'm used to being the smartest one in class. I *know* Marina would lose me if I got stupid."

"If she really loved you, she wouldn't." Anna knew how trite that platitude sounded as she said it. Will turning his back to her and going back to his model just drove that point home.

"I am not going into cryo, and you can't make me," he mumbled. "I looked it up on the nets."

Anna had looked it up on the nets too, and it was true — at fifteen, children couldn't be forced to have medical procedures they objected to without a judicial order. And where was she going to get one in the next six days?

"Let's just hope it doesn't come to that anyway." Her voice sounded hollow in her ears.

✳ ✳

Samantha was both surprised and not surprised that her name wasn't on the list of those left out. She was in excellent health, and she never saw anyone besides herself and Vance running laps around the station rings. He'd even said she was in "really excellent health, especially for a Human," and she was smaller than most of the People on the "out" list.

On the other hand, if Vance hadn't thought of the political ramifications of putting her on the waking list, Haylea or Woolerton surely had, and pointed it out to him. She knew how her friends in the media — Earthers and People alike — would spin the situation. "Human conspicuously excluded from cryosleep." "Why was the only Human still on the station left out of cryo?" "With no function as a security or medical officer, there was no reason for her to remain awake."

As she entered the meeting room again, two hours later, it was empty of people who were not on The List. They had all run off in relief, presumably to get ready for cryo treatment. Vance stayed behind to discuss the plan for the next five-and-a-half days with the others on The List, Haylea, Anna, Anna's son Will, and Roble. They all stared at her.

"Do you mind if I stay?" she asked. "I would like to chronicle the next few days."

"You want to leave your cameras with us when you go into cryo? I don't have a problem with that. Do you?" Vance looked at the others.

Samantha looked at all of them in turn. Haylea nodded eagerly — she understood the publicity value. Hell, she was probably already considering what shade of makeup would make her skin look less blue when she became hypoxic. And yet, under her forced smile, she looked scared, too.

Anna's face was tight, expressionless as usual. She must be damn good at her job. Her son, on the other hand, looked scared, angry, and petulant in a way that only a teenager could manage. His arms were folded over his ripped t-shirt and his neon-orange boots nervously tapped the floor.

Roble stared adoringly at Haylea as he had every time he'd ever seen her.

"Actually, I'd like to volunteer to trade places with one of you." Samantha tried to ignore the feelings of panic that stabbed at her chest. This was another of those awkward situations where one part of her brain knew she was doing something stupid, but another part was screaming so loudly she couldn't ignore it. "I don't want to go into cryo. I want to stay out here and cover the story."

"Are you crazy?" Haylea asked, but she was fighting a real smile now, which was ironic considering she'd been forcing a fake one five minutes ago.

"You know I'm the ideal candidate," Samantha said to Vance. "And we all know I wasn't left off the list for *medical* reasons. You said yourself I was the healthiest non-Person you'd seen in years. I weigh less than everyone else here, probably even Will. Put him in cryo and let me stay out with all of you. Don't worry about how it looks—you left my name off the list and I volunteered."

There was a moment of silence, in which Samantha could have sworn she couldn't hear anyone else breathing. Haylea's face fell, then she looked at the kid, then she looked guilty about wanting to go into cryo herself. Anna looked torn between hating the idea of leaving a Human out in a potential crisis and hating the idea of leaving her teenage son out even more.

"Well, medically you're really the best candidate," Vance admitted, finally. "If you're volunteering, I see no reason why we shouldn't—"

He was cut off by the sound of an alarm screeching loudly. It seemed to come from everywhere at once, filling the room. Everyone scrambled for their pads. Samantha's flashed an automated station alert.

STUPID HUMANS

"This looks like an automated message that was written well before the current situation." She had to scream to be heard.

Anna frantically tapped her screen, and finally shut down the alarm. "It's standard-issue when air quality levels dip below a certain point." Her voice was low and strained. Had she always had so many crow's feet on her forehead, or were those new?

"Our remaining recycler's efficiency just took a major dip," Roble said. "It's at thirty percent and likely to fall off again within the next fifty hours. That means two more of us have to shove ourselves into a cryocan somewhere. *Right?*"

Vance nodded, his head moving mechanically. "We've crammed them as full as they can get with any semblance of safety. I guess...." He looked around the room, as if hoping the answer was written on the nearest wall. "I guess we can cram one more into a few of the lightest cryocans. But there aren't many with any room at all. The others are so full there won't be room to close the lid, and without the lid closed the cold process won't work."

Anna whipped her head around and looked at Samantha. "Is your offer still good?"

Samantha's heart pounded in her ears. This was her last chance to back out. A part of her brain screamed, "What the fuck are you doing? Shut up and get in the freezer!" But another part screamed even louder, "No!" and somehow it won.

"Yes. I'm still the best person to stay out, and I still prefer to remain out here and document everything that happens until the crisis is over."

Anna turned back to Will. "You're going into cryo, Will. Get down to the infirmary now."

"But Mom—"

"I said now! You're going into cryo if I have to cuff you and shove you into the can myself!" Anna screamed, and even Will lost his intentionally unaffected pose over that one.

THIRTY-FOUR

"So how much worse can this get?" Anna asked, in her matter-of-fact way, as they sat in the deathly quiet infirmary a few hours later.

"You mean, what happens if the last recycler gets worse or fails completely?" Vance gripped the arms of his chair. "I've filled every can beyond capacity. We'll be lucky if none of them malfunction as it is."

"None of them?" Haylea asked.

"There's barely enough room in the one we're putting Will in, and the one we'll put you in. Beyond that—"

"Me?" Haylea couldn't avoid sounding hopeful.

"Since Sam opted out, I doubt anyone else would fit," Vance said. "Almost all the cryocans barely closed."

"You said almost all," Samantha pressed.

"There are three that I *might* be able to add someone to, but it would be dangerous. You have to understand that your blood flows very, *very* slowly in cryo. Add to that compression, and you could suffer serious injury—bruising, blood clots. Normally we use low-dose blood thinners to reduce the risk of clotting from cryo treatment. I could increase the dose, but that would increase the risk of hemorrhaging from compression injuries. It would be dangerous, and I would never recommend it unless there was absolutely no other option."

"Like if the last recycler died," Anna said.

"Yes." Vance stared at the simulated window, which showed the wormhole. Now it was only inky blackness. "But I suggest we all hope that *doesn't* happen."

And then something swam out of the dark —surrounded by several more somethings. Tiny points of light, almost like shooting stars, rapidly grew bigger.

"What are those?" Samantha asked.

"I don't know, but I don't think it's anything good," Anna said.

*　*

Commander Carroll was not a guy who acted on rumors, appearances, or what he thought might be going on. That could be dangerous, or worse, make you look like a thoughtless Human. He only acted on what he knew for a fact was the truth.

What he knew, as he sat on his ship in the Flomboggan sector, wasn't much, but there it was—just minutes ago, the struggling wormhole spit out five Earther ships—but not the ones that escaped with the delegation party. Four were Human military, while one appeared to be a scientific research ship, based on its identifying marks. In the command center of his ship, Carroll watched the situation unfold through camera and sensor feeds from every Guard ship anywhere near the Divide. Put together, they provided a panoramic view of the wormhole, Five Alpha, and all the People ships in the area—plus the intruders.

"One of them just powered up its engines," his second-in-command, Marlene, said, as she studied the visual feed of the ships.

"Did we scan for weapons?" Carroll asked. Marlene was a good officer, very smart and capable of making connections a lot faster than he ever could. But she sometimes liked to make decisions faster than he would, and sometimes that wasn't a good thing.

"Yes. The military ships are loaded, but their main weapons are in standby mode, unaimed." Marlene sounded suspicious. "That could change in less than—"

"I'm aware of the Humans' capabilities. The science ship is unarmed?"

"A couple small laser weapons toward the front, standard defensive stuff. Nothing compared to what the defense ships have."

Carroll frowned as a red light began to glow beneath Marlene's freshly-chewed fingernail. "Did they just arm weapons?"

"No. They just powered up their engines."

"Have we attempted contact?" He found that sometimes in situations like this, the simplest things yielded the best results, and many people forgot to try them first.

"No. Carlot is waiting for your orders." Carlot was commander of the Guard patrol surrounding the wormhole.

Carroll conferenced him in.

"Attempt contact with the Human vehicles," he said, then broke the connection.

He and Marlene watched the visual feed, waiting for any indication the ships were starting to move or activating weapons, but none came. A moment later, Carlot reappeared over the desk. "No response."

"Understood." Carroll ended the connection. There was no need to tell Carlot to keep him posted.

Marlene stabbed her hand into her display and zoomed in on the middle ship. "One of the weapons just moved—wait, two of the launchers have moved."

"Pointed at what? One of our ships?"

"One is, at least close enough to hit with ninety percent accuracy." Marlene paused. "Two more torpedoes are moving, although those are on the back of the ship, pointed toward the wormhole."

"The wormhole?" The display indicated the Protector was active. They still hadn't figured out why it had failed to detect the antimatter weapon that kicked off this mess, but no one could find anything wrong with the huge ring that had guarded the wormhole for years.

He looked at the ship that was apparently aiming some sort of torpedo at the Divide. The launchers would be tucked under the rounded hull at the front of the ship, in a hidden overhang—he knew the model well. He knew all Human ships well. It was his job.

"Where it was and could reappear," Marlene said. "It's not like them to aim so poorly, but their navigation systems were probably shaken up in the trip through the wormhole."

That was when Councilmembers Xenia and Tom stormed through the door, and Carroll wished he'd locked it. He was used to his own crew respecting boundaries. Why had he agreed to speak with politicians today, of all days?

"I demand to be part of this meeting." Xenia took the third chair in the room, leaving Tom looking around uncomfortably. Carroll only had two guest chairs because he really didn't want to encourage anyone to hang around in his office. Maybe he should get rid of one.

"This is classified—" Marlene started.

"We are diplomats, the highest ranking government officials to attend the delegation meeting." Xenia cut her off. "We both have high-level clearance. We have every right to whatever information you're discussing."

Marlene raised an eyebrow in Carroll's direction and he nodded, having unfortunately been appraised of their access.

"Fine," he said. "To catch you up, the wormhole just ejected five Human ships, four of them military and armed. One launcher is aimed at us, two more at the wormhole, one toward the station, and the others appear to point at random points in space. They are not answering our attempts to communicate. We're discussing how to proceed."

Xenia opened her mouth, closed it, took a breath, and opened it again. Then, looking from Marlene to Carroll to Tom and back to Carroll again, she re-closed it.

Tom was the first to speak. "Exactly what possibilities were you discussing?"

"I recommend firing a warning shot in their direction," Marlene said.

"Head of Council Carlton gave us explicit instructions that we *cannot* fire at ships that have not fired at us—*again*," Carroll grumbled. "He said the Humans would use that as an excuse to officially declare war on us and claim *we* started it—*again*."

"Yes, the delegation party's exit was... unfortunate," Xenia said with a grimace.

"But doesn't that make those poor People on the station ideal targets?" Tom asked.

"The station!" Xenia had left hours after the failed meeting. "Those Human ships could possibly evacuate people off Five Alpha. Or, they could overpower the security system, especially with everyone in cryo or sleeping."

"They can't do that if they won't respond to attempts at communication." Marlene crossed her arms and leaned back against the wall.

"Well, shooting at them isn't going to persuade them to help us, either," Xenia said. "What if some of those cryocans fail from having too many occupants? What if—"

"We're aware there are risks with that situation." Carroll cut her off, trying to keep the conversation on track. "There's also the possibility the Humans found some way to control the wormhole, and this is the first wave of an attack."

"Commander!" Marlene sat up and speared something in a display. She enlarged the image and popped it up over his desk.

"Explain." He frowned at what looked like the usual murky blackness of space.

Marlene added a second display, one with lots of numbers and charts and graphs. "I could take you through the details—"

"Just tell us what it means." Marlene was much better with technical details than he had ever been.

"This"—she pointed at an area of blackness that seemed, strangely, like a slightly lighter shade of black. Maybe. Looking at this thing was giving him eyestrain—"suggests a ship masking their heat signature with ion redistribution—"

"I don't care how, get to your point."

"There are a couple smaller areas, but those are more likely to be false indicators based on their size."

"Are you sure the big one isn't ours?" Carroll ignored the surprised looks from Xenia and Tom.

"No, we have tracking on ours," Marlene said. "Also, our newest technology covers this type of leakage from the ion masking."

"Are any of our hidden ships close enough to rescue those People on the station?" Tom blurted out.

Carroll gritted his teeth. "Aside from the fact that diverting those vessels from a critical mission could get a lot more People killed, aside from the fact that those ships are necessary to protect us if the Humans invade, they are tiny and unmanned. The cabin is only pressurized when someone is on board, and then it can only support one Person, for a few hours at most."

"The leakage." Marlene pointed at something undecipherable to him. "It's spreading."

"You mean a masked ship is heading for Five Alpha?" Xenia yelped.

"Commander, we have ships in the area," Marlene said. "They need instructions, now. If that thing gets much closer, they will automatically fire in self-defense."

"Tell them to disable the masked ship with as little effort as possible," Carroll said. "Can you target its masking system?"

"We don't have a good enough image to know where it is."

The team of Guard vessels unmasked and pounded at the murky area with high-intensity lasers. Xenia and Tom both flinched as the ship shuddered, like they thought the pieces breaking off could hit them in the face. Politicians, what could you do?

Unfortunately, his ships had to keep moving to avoid two of the other Human vehicles, which were advancing toward the melee. Carroll was about order them to use the torpedoes when the fogginess started to resolve into something—

"That's huge!" Xenia said unnecessarily. "But it's marked with the UNE seal. Wait, that looks familiar."

"It looks like it has a number of armed weapons," Marlene said. "Should we launch the torpedoes?"

"Yes." Even as he said it, Carroll knew they'd waited too long. The ship bobbed around in an evasive pattern. Even with targeted torpedoes that could readjust their course, they would have a hard time hitting a randomly moving target from that distance.

"Wait, I think we finally made a dent with the lasers." Marlene pointed at a spot near the back of the ship, from their point of view. "That damaged area is crucial for their weapons targeting. Now if one of the torpedoes hits —

"We haven't slowed them down at all." Carroll sank into his chair. "And the Human military ships just disabled two of our craft. We don't have the resources to chase the escaping ship and deal with the remaining ones. I say we let it go."

"You should definitely let it go!" Tom yelled, and Carroll turned to stare at him. What did this suited moron think he knew about the situation anyway?

"You have a strong opinion about this?" Carroll asked as one of the manned backup ships swooped onto the view screen, bouncing around as lasers hit it from three of the Human ships.

"Do you know what you just did?" Tom yelled. "That ship that just escaped — I recognize it. That was the main Delegates' ship, you idiot! We just shot at the peace party from Earth!"

THIRTY-FIVE

"Welcome to *Lightspeed News*, I'm Lee, bringing you the latest on the Wormhole Disaster. I'm told we are standing by for a statement from President Howard—ah, yes, there's the transcript on your screen.

"I'll paraphrase for those of you who don't wish to read the two-page document. The United Nations of Earth have officially declared war on the People, less than two days after our delegates held peace talks on Space Station Five Alpha.

"And here's the President now, taking questions from Earth reporters."

Samantha tried not to breathe too fast as she watched Lee's presentation on *Lightspeed*. She was wondering how much the news had raised her heart rate and how that would affect her respiration when she noticed a sudden quieting of the station. Glancing at Anna and Vance, she realized they'd noticed it too, because after the president's address they'd muted the broadcast—everything after the president's speech was just a reporter repeating what he'd just said. Samantha had done that job enough to know they weren't learning anything new for the next few hours.

"Something just stopped humming," Anna announced.

"I hope it's not the something I think it is." Samantha looked at the air-quality measurement graph Vance had set up. Oxygen levels were hovering at 19.4 percent.

An alarm sounded, and Anna turned to her pad. Samantha had a bad feeling she knew what the alarm was for.

"The last station recycler just died." Vance's face was calm, completely emotionless. Doctors were probably trained to do that, but in this situation, she wished he'd act a bit more normal.

"And the other ships all took off after the Humans escaped—again. Why the hell did they come back? The Guard didn't stop anyone after that. The few that were left disappeared after the president's war declaration." Anna looked in Samantha's direction but didn't quite meet her eyes, as if she thought Samantha had control over what the President of Earth did.

"That wouldn't have been an option anyway," Vance said. "They were all crammed way over capacity. Several were getting warnings that their own recyclers could die soon."

"Sooner than ours? Sooner than the relief ships can get here?" Anna's face still looked calm, but her voice was starting to shake.

"Someone had to stay awake in case of emergency," Vance said, his voice quiet and a little angry. Samantha saw a guy who really hated his job right now. Not only that, but he probably felt guilty about wishing he didn't have to be the responsible doctor who stuck around in case of emergency.

Or maybe he was grimacing because he wasn't getting enough oxygen.

"What about... the recyclers that were too small, but we used them anyway?" Samantha heard how jumbled her thoughts sounded as she said them aloud. Well, if her brain wasn't working right now, who could blame her? It was a strange sensation, panicking while feeling drowsy and sluggish all at the same time. Efficient panicking required a normal oxygen supply, but then again, a lack of oxygen required a panic attack, didn't it?

"Without the main recycler working at least at twenty percent capacity, they'll barely make any impact on our air quality," Vance said.

"So the other ships just left us here to die!" Anna yelled, her voice raspy. "How could they do that?"

"They... didn't want to get caught in the crossfire. And adding more People to an overcrowded ship could have gotten everyone killed." His face said he didn't give a crap about that, either.

"What about all those military ships flying around?" Samantha asked. "I know the tiny, unmanned ones don't have room, but there must be bigger ones somewhere. You can't tell me one of them can't get three People out of here!"

"I already contacted the Guard—I know people there!" Anna said. "Frego is a captain. His brother was an assistant commander. My contact said he couldn't promise anything with everything else they had to deal with, but they'd re-task a ship to get us out of here as soon as possible. Yes, even you too," she said to Samantha. "The biggest problem is that most of their fleet in the area was dragged into the wormhole with the UNE ship."

Samantha gritted her teeth but forced herself to hold her tongue. At least until she was off this fucking station. "Why do you think they came back?"

"I don't think it was intentional," Anna said. "You know how the Guard didn't mean to get pulled in? The wormhole is becoming less predictable as it destabilizes. Maybe the UNE ship should have been clear of the gravity well, but got sucked in again when it fluctuated."

Vance looked at the wall screen showing the destabilizing wormhole, at the data pad showing their oxygen levels, at the tiny cameras buzzing unobtrusively at the edges of the room, then back at the row of coffins. "I... should stay here... in case of an emergency... but if I'm unconscious, I can't help my patients anyway, right?"

He was asking for permission to do what he wanted to do anyway... no, he wasn't asking. He just wanted to justify his going to sleep or into cryo, so he'd look good when this footage aired. Samantha didn't blame him.

But if Frego and the brother-in-law and the friends couldn't help them, maybe the live feed from her cameras could.

She was considering whether to go live with the footage now or wait for the result of Anna's calls when she glanced at the wall screen and saw the wormhole expand one more time.

THIRTY-SIX

Vance had always thought of space as lifeless, cold, and, well, dull, so he didn't know a lot about wormholes. He knew they were rare, that the Great Divide was the only stable one known to exist and the only one large enough to allow travel, and that no one was really sure how their ancestors had stabilized it.

He stared, mesmerized, at the whitish swirl in space that had, just seconds ago, been a bigger white swirl. "What just happened?"

"I think the military ships all masked themselves as protection from whatever came through the wormhole," Samantha said.

Vance blinked at her. "So masked ships could be coming through the wormhole too, right? I mean, from the other side?" Damn, it was hard to think straight when oxygen was scarce. Until Samantha opened her mouth, he'd been under the impression they were alone out here, with the crazies from the Other Side. Was this what it felt like to be Human all the time—having a brain that didn't work right? How awful.

"Could be, but I don't think that's what happened." Anna shuffled past Vance to stand inches away from the wall screen. "Did you see it? Did either of you actually see it?"

Vance rubbed at his gritty eyes. His head throbbed, undoubtedly the result of not getting enough oxygen. Was his eyesight a little blurry? Probably. "I don't know what I saw. The room was shaking. I looked over at the wormhole and… I don't know, there was a big, bright flash of light."

"That's about what I saw," Samantha said. "But my cameras record-ed it, if you want to look at it again?"

Anna nodded, turning away from the wall. "I swear I saw those Guard ships get sucked in."

Samantha scrunched her face up as she pawed lethargically at her pad. "I thought… they were at a safe distance."

"They were." Vance looked over her shoulder at the video feed. She scrolled back through it with one finger, and had passed the event twice already. The whole thing really did happen in a few seconds.

"Right there!" Anna jabbed her arm at the screen and almost took out Samantha's nose in the process. Samantha managed to pull her head back in time. Vance had to admire the fact she had any reflexes left at this point.

They watched the sequence in slow motion once, then twice, then a third time. First, everything was normal, the Guard ships advancing toward the Human ones, all of which were well outside the clearance area for the wormhole.

Wormholes, Vance vaguely remembered from the last non-medical science class he'd been required to take, were really just black holes with unusual properties, and as such, they were deep gravity wells—get too close, and you get sucked in. When the wormhole had first been redis-covered, the safe distance had quickly been mapped. In case of unusual wormhole activity, it was recommended that any ship not planning to go through the Divide add twenty percent to that distance.

The Human ships were almost twice the safe distance away when they were sucked in, the Guard ships, slightly more.

Five-Alpha was located five times the safe distance away.

"I guess they won't be able to re-task that ship now," Samantha said.

THIRTY-SEVEN

"Are they on the Other Side?" Anna asked.

"Who cares? We're now stranded here... almost out of oxygen... and there's no one left close enough to rescue us!" Samantha had to pause for breath three times, but she still managed to yell all of it. Probably a waste of oxygen, but at the moment she didn't care.

"Because if they come back, we might be a little less stranded." Vance frowned at the image.

"If the wormhole is destabilizing…." She forced herself to stick to this train of thought. "If it opens wider, wouldn't the pull be stronger?"

"And grab ships that ordinarily would be far enough out for safety," Vance said. "That's as good a theory as any. But overall, the event horizon is still shrinking—the Divide will eventually collapse completely if it continues to destabilize."

"She was right the first time," Anna growled. "It doesn't matter. We need to think of some alternate way to breathe. What about being sedated?"

"No, *you* were right the first time." Samantha hated saying it. "What if we took a shuttle and made a run for the wormhole? I know it's unstable and could collapse at any time, but we'd still probably get through, right?"

"If we still had a shuttle, we'd have a way to breathe and wouldn't need to get through the Divide," Vance interrupted. "All our shuttles were filled far over capacity and they're gone. Most are trying to dock with larger ships because they're suffering from oxygen deprivation problems of their own."

"And we don't know... where those ships ended up," Anna said.

"Could we move the whole station?" Samantha asked. "Assuming we make it to the Other Side, one of those ships could come get us."

"But how do we move it?" Anna asked. "It was intended to be as fixed as the wormhole—we only have enough propulsion capabilities to keep us in one position. It's possible the wormhole might swallow us anyway, but there's nothing we can do to increase our chances. Besides, the Divide's throat shrank a lot before the weapon detonated—something the size of this station probably couldn't get through safely. That Human delegation ship was damn lucky it made it."

"So, back to sedating us all." Samantha looked at Vance, who appeared to have aged in the past three days —hell, the past three hours. He covered his face with his hands, rubbing the skin as if increasing blood flow to his head would help him think.

"I don't think that alone will help, based on these projections." One hand slid down his face and slapped his pad. A new graph popped up opposite the outside view.

This time, the arrow plunged below eighteen percent roughly fifteen hours before *Long Voyage* arrived.

Samantha wracked her brain, trying to think of an alternative. When

Anna walked over and gave her a hug, she was so surprised, she momentarily forgot everything else.

"What are you doing?"

People weren't that into hugging—it was more of a Human thing, and when the People did hug, it was only with family or close friends, never strangers or new acquaintances.

Anna had never even *liked* Samantha.

"Thank you." She let go and walked away. It took Samantha's air-starved brain a moment to realize it was a thank you for taking Will's place out here.

"This isn't over yet," Vance said, getting her thinking back on track. "You know that emergency kit I've been working on?"

She did remember the box he'd been tinkering with all day. She'd seen some syringes and patches going in earlier. "Do you have a drug that can help us function with less oxygen?" The answer had to be no, he'd have said something earlier if that was the case, but she asked anyway.

Vance shook his head. "No. But I can arrange for us all to make more oxygen-carrying blood cells, much faster than we normally would."

"So we could do more with less?" Anna asked.

"For a little while," Vance said, and Samantha had a feeling his next projection would get them farther than fifteen hours, but not all the way there. "There are big risks, mainly blood clots. We'd need to take something that would increase the risk of bleeding."

"If we're sleeping, we probably won't be bumping into things," Samantha pointed out.

"That's true. The risk of bleeding would be better than the risk of clotting," Vance said. "But this would be a lot more effective if I'd given us the shots yesterday, or even twelve hours ago, or if the recycler hadn't already died. Even at an accelerated rate, we can't make that many new blood cells in the next twenty-four hours."

"So where are we on the projection?" She pointed to the wall, and Vance tapped his pad again. The new arrow showed nine hours and seventeen minutes.

"That's with us being sedated?" Anna asked, and Vance nodded mutely.

"Is there any oxygen left in the tanks you have here?" Samantha asked. The medical center kept some around for emergencies, and Vance had been slowly using the supply on patients suffering the effects of bad air.

"We have maybe enough left for one person to breathe for four or five hours, two people maybe two hours. I'd recommend using that air ten minutes at a time to stretch it out while the rest of our supply worsens," he said. "Maybe we can convince the Guard to send three of those little masked ships for the last six hours."

"I've messaged everyone I know in the Guard, but I haven't heard anything else." Anna looked down. "I think the only ships close enough just got sucked into the wormhole. Well, hurry up and dose us now, and we can try to think of another solution while the drugs are getting to work."

"You understand there are risks—" Vance started.

"Please skip the ass-covering speech just this once." Anna rolled up her sleeve. "We know there are risks, and we know the risks of asphyxiating, too. I for one will take the risk from the drugs."

Anna's pad beeped, and they all turned to look at it. "It's a priority communication from *Long Voyage*," she whispered.

"Maybe they're getting here faster than expected," Samantha said, and she felt like she could breathe better already. Vance hadn't even pressed the patch to her skin yet.

"Put them through," Anna half-whispered and half-yelled.

THIRTY-EIGHT

Captain Warford looked like he would be more at home in an office with a lot of books on the wall—old-fashioned, paper books with pages that were basically like dollar bills without the presidents' faces. But instead, he sat in a crowded, cramped, windowless room full of navigational charts, shifting uncomfortably in his chair like he was doing a hemorrhoid cream commercial.

"You understand my concern," he said. "The wormhole's gravity well is fluctuating, and not at predictable intervals. We don't know where it's dumping the ships it pulls in, and it could collapse at any time."

"We have the same concerns." Samantha had a sinking feeling she knew where this was headed.

"So you can understand that, as much as I want to help you with these recyclers, I can't take my ship—with forty-two passengers—close to an unpredictable, possibly destabilizing wormhole when its opening can't be controlled or predicted."

"We are still well beyond the safe distance," Vance said. "And I have to say, I'm less afraid of being dumped out on the Other Side than I am of running out of oxygen here! Not to mention that we have almost seventy People in cryo, and they can't stay there for long the way we've overloaded the beds."

Anna shoved Vance to the side so she could get into Warford's field of view. "You and the People on your ship won't die if you wind up on the Other Side. We're running out of oxygen within the next day and a half!"

"You don't know that!" Warford's head snapped up, his nostrils flaring. "The Guard attacked those Human ships almost as soon as they popped up here. Who's to say the Humans on the Other Side won't do the same? This is a passenger ship—I have only basic defense systems. I wouldn't stand a chance against a heavily armed military ship."

Vance looked like he was wracking his oxygen-depleted brain for a good response. "The odds are... nothing will happen... while you're here. Uh... you have shuttles on board, right? Could you put the extra recyclers in two of your shuttles and send them ahead? Then you won't have to get as close."

"Won't that take longer?" Anna asked, and Vance shot her a shut-up-please look as Samantha moved up behind them.

"In order for you to have the recyclers by the time we were scheduled to arrive," Warford said, "I'd have to get closer to the wormhole, and the recyclers would be later than planned. I understand even if they arrived on time, you'd still have barely enough oxygen left."

"Holding out for another hour or two is better than never getting the recyclers at all," Vance said.

Samantha wondered how any of them could replace a recycler that was almost as big as a shuttle in their current state, let alone a worse one.

"There's very little risk at three times the safe distance." Anna's voice was strained. "That would improve the time."

"Let's be honest here, we don't know that there's very little risk," Warford said. "I'm not even sure four times is safe. I'm not comfortable with less than six or seven times the safe distance."

Samantha somehow managed to run the numbers in her head. "That would put us almost a day behind schedule!"

Warford shrugged his already-hunched up shoulders. "It's the best I can do. You have to understand —"

"Of course we understand that, Captain," she said, her voice as calm as she could make it right now. "But you should know that all of this is being recorded and beamed back live to *Glass* Network, which you agreed to when you accepted Five Alpha's communications link." She was pretty sure this sort of situation was, at best, vaguely hinted at in some way by the station's general terms of communications, which included the right to record conversations held on an unencrypted channel, for "purposes of serving you better." All of which was buried in some legalese everyone agreed to without reading it.

Warford's face went paler than his shiny forehead. "I never gave you permission to rebroadcast this conversation!"

"Well, you can sue me later," Samantha snapped. "But I want you to know that right now, everyone on this side of the Great Divide is seeing you as the Person who would rather let *at least* three People die of asphyxiation when you could save them. I say at least because, as Anna pointed out, those overloaded cryobeds could go at any time."

Warford stared at them, his jowls quivering, and for a second or two, Vance actually thought he was going to cave. Instead, he abruptly cut the transmission without another word.

"He'll rethink that position," Samantha said, not sure at all.

"Maybe we can somehow squeeze into the cryobeds," Anna said. "Even if they're almost critical now, they'd last a *few* more days, right?"

Vance groaned. "It would be risky, if one or two of us could even fit. But I guess it's better than the risk of staying out here."

THIRTY-NINE

Anna went in the first coffin with any extra room, and it was a tight fit. Vance said she was the largest and in the worst shape, and therefore the least likely to survive a low oxygen situation the longest. Getting the security chief, already sedated and limp as a rag doll, into the coffin was a bitch, even though they started with her on a stretcher right next to it. With both of them pushing, they managed to roll her on top of the two smaller bodies already inside, but then they had to close the damn thing again. Samantha sat on top, wondering if she was crushing anyone's bones. Vance assured her that broken bones were easier to fix than asphyxiation, and the cryobed was designed to cushion its occupants from outside forces, so a serious injury was unlikely.

Even so, he had to join her on top of the coffin, where they both leaned to the side to struggle with the latches. Neither of them could do it until Samantha had an idea. She dragged herself to Vance's side, and they both leaned over and squeezed the latch shut, then moved to the opposite end and did the same. Afterward, panting, Vance glared at her, and she knew he was pissed that the Human had a good idea.

"Good thinking." He scrambled off, stumbling as he landed on his feet.

They checked the other coffins, finding almost all of them far too full to fit anyone else.

"See this red light? That means the cryobed is failing, probably due to overfilling. It's got a…." Vance squinted down at a display. "Ninety percent chance of going critical in the next forty-six hours. If it goes critical, it automatically starts the warming procedure and alerts me."

"What if you're in cryo too?"

Vance sighed. "At that point, it won't matter. There's not enough air for both of us, let alone anyone else. The warming procedure takes six hours, and the cryocan will sustain the occupants for that long. Honestly, we only need it to hold for another thirty-two hours or so, anyway."

"Assuming Captain Warford comes through. We still haven't heard anything since I threatened him," Samantha said as Vance moved to the next cryocan. He undid the latches, lifted the lid, and peeked inside, sticking his hand in to poke around while leaving the lid as low as possible to preserve the cold. She had a random memory of herself as a child, feeling around in the freezer for a popsicle, her mother yelling at her to hurry up and close the lid because electricity was expensive.

"At the very least, I think we can rely on him to send the recyclers in a shuttle." Vance jerked his arm out, letting the lid close with a thud. "There's room in this one, I think."

Samantha nodded dully.

He continued to the next coffin, squinted at a red light, moved on to the next. "I'm still hoping some of our ships will come back through the wormhole. Overloaded or not, getting onto another vehicle has to be an improvement over this."

He stopped at the last coffin, which had a green light, and looked at her. "I see it."

"Should we draw for it, as your people like to say?"

"What?" She blinked at him. "No, we're not going to do that. You're going in the last coffin, and I'm staying out here."

Vance shook his head. "That isn't fair."

"The way I see it, there are just as many risks with getting into one of those things, as overloaded as they all are," she said. "I may not be doing you a favor."

"What if that ship doesn't get here on time? Or at all? What if the wormhole opens and sucks in the shuttle? What if you're stranded here for who knows how long? Your air supply won't last more than two or three days, at the most. And that's if you're lucky, and the medication works."

"Well, every Guard ship on this side of the Divide is headed here right now. This station is strategically important. If Warford doesn't come through, someone else will eventually and I'll get out of here."

"Why are you doing this?" Vance asked. "Is it because I'm the only friend you have here who doesn't walk on four legs?"

"No, that's not it. Months ago, I chose to stay on this station even though I knew it wasn't the safest place for a Human. I chose to stay out of cryo so I could see this story through to the end, and I'm doing that again. And don't look at me like that," she added, seeing the are-you-insane look pushing up his eyebrows. "I don't believe staying out here is that much more dangerous than undergoing a potentially risky medical procedure under far less than ideal circumstances."

"If for some reason that ship doesn't arrive, your chances are better in cryo," Vance said, and she could barely hear him, because the voice in her head was back, screaming at her. *He's right and you know it, let him put you in that coffin!* But there was another voice in her head, and it was even louder, and it was just repeating one thing, over and over and over.

No! I'm not going into that thing, and no one can make me.

Vance shuffled to the nearest AI terminal. He pulled up a display and scrolled through what looked like pages of text. "I saw the no-cryo rider on your medchip, you know. I can try to deactivate it."

"Not without my consent, and you know that too," Samantha snapped, thumbing off the recording button on her data pad. Good thing she wasn't broadcasting live since her conversation with Warford—she and Lee agreed the footage would be worth more later.

"Yeah, I've heard the story of how your lover tried to get you deported back to Earth, and how they had no choice but to leave you here when you wouldn't sign the consent form." Vance narrowed his eyes. "You've had that rider since shortly after you arrived here, five years ago. You couldn't possibly have anticipated the situation with Brad then, let alone this one."

She winced at the mention of Brad's name and wrapped her arms tightly around herself. Was it cold in here or was that just an effect of too little oxygen? "What does that have to do with anything?"

He walked away from the display and approached her, slowly, as if his feet were made of lead.

"It doesn't make sense, Sam." His voice was low and calm, probably something he'd practiced in medical school.

"What doesn't? And what does it matter right now?" Her fingers dug into her forearms. Why couldn't he just give up on this conversation and get in the damn coffin?

"There are lots of reasons People put riders on their medchips," he said. "If there's a medical reason, it's always noted by the physician. The doctor you saw on New Atlantis only indicated that it was put there at the patient's request."

"So what?"

"People with religious or ethical objections to medical treatment always have a list a light-year long of things they don't want done. No rejuvenation treatments, no extraordinary measures, no artificial life support post-brain death, no stem cells, no abortion—that one's just your people. I had to look it up, since no one *here* has had an accidental pregnancy in a couple thousand years—"

"This is a fascinating discussion about your people's technological superiority, but what does it have to do with—"

"Because your medchip only has one rider—no cryosleep."

"So?" The cold seeped around the edges of her clothing, puckering her skin with gooseflesh. If he would just shut up and get in, she could go put on a few more layers of clothes.

"So you didn't request the rider for religious or ethical reasons." Vance's eyes flickered over her face, searching for some reaction.

Well, he wasn't going to get one. She had one hell of a poker face and she wasn't afraid to use it.

"And you don't have cryophobia, because the only reason to develop a phobia about something you've already done is if you had a bad experience, and it's pretty much impossible to have a bad experience while unconscious. The only *other* reason people get that particular restriction is because they're afraid someone will try to put them in cryo against their will, to get them out of the way," Vance said. "Mainly that means criminals or people who have pissed off criminals."

She rolled her eyes. "If you're trying to change my mind by pissing me off, you're going to have to try harder than that."

"I'm not implying you're a criminal. I know you're not, because if you were the kind of high-level criminal who needs a no-cryo block, you wouldn't have had to blackmail a low-level crook like Jake to do your dirty work for you—you'd already have a professional on the payroll to do that."

"I don't know what you're talking about, and what's your point?"

"You got the rider *ten days* after you arrived here," Vance persisted. "Most of that time you were being followed by cameras, much as you are now. You were with the Human party and a bunch of diplomats trying to kiss your ass. I can't imagine how you would have encountered, let alone seriously pissed off, a dangerous professional criminal."

"We're wasting time and oxygen here." She suddenly felt as exhausted as Vance looked. And yet, her mind was still thinking about all the editing her video was going to need when this was done. She looked at the display. "We're down to nineteen point three percent."

"So there's only one other explanation for why you're here."

"And what's that?"

"Your people—the Humans—sent you to do something, in spite of the demands against it, and in spite of our best efforts to ensure they followed our instructions," Vance said. "You were a spy, possibly a saboteur. You were supposed to accomplish something—maybe plant some infiltration tech we don't know the Humans have yet, maybe stash some new weapon we're not aware of, maybe build one or steal one or steal some of our tech that your people want. Whatever."

Samantha rolled her eyes. "You sound like a bad holo show. We didn't even know all the things you were going to refuse to give us at that point."

"If there was another possibility that fits the evidence, I would agree." He shrugged. "But there isn't. Anyway, I said that's what you were *sent* here to do. Whatever it was, for whatever reason, when you got here you found you couldn't do it. That's why you can't go back to Earth, no matter how dangerous things get for you here."

"You're an idiot." For the first time since this conversation started, she felt completely confident.

Vance shook his head. "No, I don't think I am. It's the only thing that explains why you refused to go back to Earth, why you had the rider put on your medchip, why you wouldn't go back with Brad despite the current political situation, *and* why you won't get into the cryocan now."

That took her by surprise. "What the hell does *that* have to do with your ridiculous theory?"

"You think I haven't figured it out? Once I'm in cryo, you're going to get rid of something you don't want anyone else to find."

She allowed a laugh to escape her tightly pressed lips. "You can't actually believe that!"

"It's less ridiculous than my other theory," Vance said. "That you're still working for your people, and as soon as I'm in cryo you'll signal them to join you and take the station. It is strategically important, as you just pointed out. Of course, I also know you and I don't believe that you're working for your government... anymore."

"I think the lack of oxygen is affecting your brain." Samantha sucked in a breath of stale air. "At least I hope it is. The alternative is that you're *always* a paranoid whackjob who thinks I'm some sort of character in a bad spy movie."

"Then give me another explanation that makes sense!" Vance yelled. He paused, gulped down a few big breaths of bad air. "*Why* are you here, Samantha?"

"My reasons for staying here are personal and none of your goddamn business!" she yelled back. It left her panting for breath in the thin air.

"Oh really? It's none of my business? I'm the closest thing you have to a friend on this station, Samantha!"

She must have let some of the hurt seep through her façade, because he frowned and looked down at the floor.

"I'm sorry," he said softly. "I really am your friend here. I don't believe you're a threat to this station, or anyone on it. But I'm supposed to stay out of cryo, and if I leave you out and anything happens, my career will be over. I won't even have a middle-of-nowhere job like this. I'll be lucky if I don't go to prison."

"Then get in the coffin." Samantha forced the words past lips that felt frozen and numb. "Because I'm not going to, and even if you could overpower me—and I'm not sure that you could at the moment—the bed would reject me because of the chip. Then it would shut down and kick out the other occupants too, and we'd all die. So if you really think of me as a friend—if you really trust me—then you'll get in. And if you don't trust me, you still might as well get in, because you really have no other choice. If you stay out here, we'll both probably die. If you get in, there's a halfway decent chance we might both get out of this alive."

Vance stared at her for a few seconds, his eyes flicking over her face again, as if still looking for some sign of… what? Guilt? A threat? Finally he sighed, turned around, and walked to the coffin.

"I know you're not a threat," he mumbled over his shoulder.

She watched as he stripped down to his underwear, scanned himself with several medical devices, and tapped an override command into the panel. Finally, he went back to his workstation and retrieved a medical kit.

"Do you have any questions about what to do?" He removed a patch and walked back.

"No, I paid attention when you explained everything earlier." She helped him undo the latches.

"If you can't get it closed, get the crawlers to help you." He climbed gingerly over the two bodies beneath him. One belonged to an attractive blonde woman. Of course he'd end up sleeping with her.

"I remember." She followed the procedures he'd shown her earlier, initiating a sequence to disperse electrodes and monitoring devices.

Only one IV was necessary, and that was the one that carried a powerful cocktail—the anesthetic that should knock Vance out, the solution that slowed metabolism to an almost-deathlike state, the drug that prevented cell damage during the metabolic slowdown, the cooling solution that would turn his blood into a not-quite-frozen sludge, and the blood thinners to prevent the sludge from clotting. The IV snaked out of a port and wormed its way into a vein on Vance's arm. With the other, he reached for the mask that would deliver the very limited amount of oxygen he would need in cryo.

"Before the anesthetic takes effect, would you tell me the truth?" he asked.

"What?" She looked at him in surprise.

"I probably won't remember this conversation when I wake up," he pointed out. "And it'll be at least two minutes before I'm out. You have time to tell me."

She sighed. "Never count on anyone not to remember."

"I scanned you with my medical imagers earlier. That makes you my patient, so I can't tell anyone anything you say. Please, Samantha. You're my friend, and I can't help you if I don't know why you're really here."

She looked at him, lying there in the dimly glowing coffin on top of a macabre pile of bodies, like some serial killer's victim, and for just a moment, she thought how nice it would be to finally tell someone the truth. But it was a long story, and two minutes wasn't enough time, and she didn't want to do something stupid while her brain was foggy from stress and lack of oxygen.

"There's a flaw in your logic," she said at last, reaching for the button that would dispense the anesthetic. "Figure out what it is and I'll tell you the whole story."

He reached out and grabbed her hand. "But... what if... I mean, if we don't both... I'll never... know the truth."

"Then I guess we better both survive this, huh?" She pushed the button, and his eyes slipped closed. Then she waited for the display to indicate he was asleep with a blue light. She pulled up the brain-wave pattern on his pad, read the AI's interpretation—that he was indeed fully unconscious—and checked the blue light again. Then she reached out and poked him. He remained unresponsive, his face slack and peaceful.

She climbed up on the lid and reached for the nearest latch.

* *

Afterward, she wandered among the coffins for a while, looking at the occupants' faces through the foggy lids. Most of them, despite having their arms and legs smushed awkwardly into another person, looked strangely peaceful. One woman's face was pressed up against the glass, like a kid looking out the window—except that her eyes were closed and the breather mask distorted her nostrils so she appeared almost piglike.

Samantha finally left the infirmary and trudged back to the bar, where she had a little plan of her own waiting.

She knew Roble had rerouted the air filtration system to flush the clean air left on the other levels down to this one, and that most of the deck had been shut down so the remaining oxygen would get where it was needed. She swiped her fingerprints and stared into the ocular scanner at the bar. Fortunately, the Wormhole in the Wall was in the small section that had been left open, so at least she could wait in her own room.

After directing the crawlers to grab all the potted plants in the Wormhole and follow her, she crossed the bar, which seemed so strange without people in it. Her room, once she'd dragged herself up the five stairs and slumped through the door, was even worse, because her dogs weren't there to greet her. Not that she wasn't glad to have gotten them off the station—even if they were sedated in some crowded cargo hold, at least she knew they'd be all right. But it was still lonely in her apartment without them, and she couldn't help but think she'd been an idiot not to get off this station when she had the chance. Then again, if she'd joined her friends on *Glass*'s ship, she would have been right back here anyway when their air recyclers failed.

She walked through her main living area, past the kitchenette and into the tiny bedroom. Despite its size, the room felt spacious to her, probably because she had all the wall screens set to a panoramic view of a beach in Tahiti. At the moment though, all she could do was grimace because instead of lying on that beach, she was sitting in a tin can in space, waiting to run out of air.

At one end of the room, she directed the crawlers to dump the plants. At the other, she placed the articulating fans she'd found in the bar's storage closet. Would this work? Green plants cleaned the air like a recycler, eating carbon dioxide or monoxide or whatever the hell was bad for you and shitting out nice, clean oxygen. What she wasn't sure about, however, was how fast that happened and how many plants she'd actually need to clean the air for one Human. Roble's notes suggested collecting a large amount of plants in a small place might help preserve the quality of the air for a slightly longer time, although without knowing the exact number of shrubs she could get her hands on he couldn't calculate exactly how long. Maybe a couple extra hours.

Maybe this wouldn't be necessary. Maybe Warford would take her threat seriously and rush his ass over here with the damn air filter. Maybe the Guard ships would reappear. Maybe purple pigs would fly through the wormhole with a new recycler.

She took a deep breath of air that wasn't nearly as refreshing as it should be and flipped the fans on. Then she left the bedroom, shutting the door behind her. Exhausted as she was, she trudged out of the apartment, back down the stairs, and out onto the concourse to look for stores that might have living plants hanging around.

* FORTY

"How did we get here?" Xenia asked.

Staring at President Howard's image on the wall screen, she knew the diplomatic thing to do was stammer on about resolving their differences, but she couldn't think of anything else to say. She could deny that her People had anything to do with the wormhole disaster—and it would be true—but there was no reason for Howard to believe her. Pointing the finger at the Humans would be even worse. As for shooting at the delegates' ship, there was no way to deny that, although she had already explained multiple times that it had been a grave error. If she hadn't, she didn't think the UNE president would have agreed to this remote meeting.

"You mean, how did we go from peace talks to declaring a war that neither of us wanted?" Howard rubbed at a small crease on his forehead, the only visible sign of aging on his whole face.

"Yes." Xenia sighed, the exhalation ruffling her bangs. It didn't matter anymore how she looked, or what Howard thought. They were two tired, frustrated people who couldn't make their constituents stop fighting.

"I wish I knew how everything went wrong so fast." Howard shuffled pads around his desk. "But the truth is that my people have been getting into these messes for centuries."

Xenia said nothing. Agreeing with Howard was the wrong move, and she didn't want to point out that her own people shared some of the blame. What if one of *her* People, acting on his or her own, committed an act of sabotage?

"I apologize again for the confusion when your ship was... detained," she said finally. "I understand now that you were just trying to get home safely, but when the Guard saw a masked ship moving toward the wormhole area, which was sabotaged earlier, it *looked* like a credible threat."

"I suppose it's our fault," the UNE president said diplomatically. "Since our cultures rejoined, your people have probably picked up on some of our barbaric bad habits, like shooting first and asking questions later. We should never have assumed that your superior intellect would protect you from picking up our poor problem-solving skills."

She smiled tightly. There was nothing to do but take the insult, since they had shot at the damn delegation ship.

"Have you made any more progress in understanding why the wormhole is fluctuating?"

"Not yet." There was no harm in sharing the truth. "I've been told exotic matter is poorly understood, as is the mechanism that keeps the Divide stable. We're trying to communicate with our ships on the Other Side, but the destabilization of the wormhole has scrambled our signals. Very little is getting through. I'm sure you have the same problem."

"Yes."

"I suppose there was confrontation on the Other Side, too?" Xenia hoped she didn't sound as hopeful as she regretted she felt.

"Surprisingly, we were able to avoid too much violence." Howard sat up straighter and folded his hands in front of him, a very presidential pose. "Our reports are limited. From what we can piece together, the ships that came through the wormhole more or less together—ours and yours—started shooting at each other fairly soon after arriving. Fortunately, the best-armed ones apparently weren't interested in such a small skirmish. They took off, employing masking technology to discourage others from following. The Human military stayed out of the conflict, hoping it would resolve on its own, and it did."

Xenia took a deep breath. Unfortunately, her reports were about the same as Howard's—she hated to admit it, but the Humans were doing better at staying neutral than the People, so far. Or at least they had been before declaring war on the People.

"I know what we both want is to go back to a few days ago." She let the composed look slip off her face. Although she actually had no idea what she looked like right now, she had used this gambit before, always successfully. "But since we can't do that, what we want right now is to keep the violence to a minimum, and eventually end the fighting. We want to work together to fix the wormhole, if possible, or build a new one."

Howard nodded, his face relaxing slightly, but not all the way. "Of course. I know you and I still want to end this war so our people can accomplish great things together."

"What will it take to get there, now?" Xenia already knew the answer, but she wanted to hear it from Howard.

"In the long run, we would need to build trust between both sides." Howard's face rerouted itself into campaign-speech mode, chin lifting, half-smile coming dangerously close to reaching his eyes. "In the short run, we would need proof the People aren't responsible for the wormhole's collapse, at least not in an official capacity. If it *is* an individual or fringe group on your side, we would want to see those People caught and brought to justice."

"As would we. I can assure you that we did not intentionally cause this collapse, and we are doing all we can to determine who did, and bring that person or persons to justice. To that end, I will send you all the data we have currently." Well, maybe not *all* the data, but Howard didn't know that... although Xenia was sure he suspected. "I'm sure you would want to do the same."

"Of course. Transparency will help us resolve the situation faster." Howard glanced at something off screen. "I understand the situation at Five Alpha has worsened in the last few hours. Can we offer any more help?"

Xenia kept the smile plastered on her face. Of course, she was supposed to thank Howard for the assistance eight Human ships had provided in evacuating the station. "We're very grateful for your help. At this point, though, none of your ships are any closer to the station than ours... to the best of my knowledge, at least."

"Nor to the best of mine." Howard politely ignored the subtle implication that her people might have improved their masking technologies without mentioning it to their "allies" in an undeclared war... which had now been declared.

"Well, we are still grateful for all the assistance you provided." Xenia looked down at the display on her desktop and saw that only one box remained unchecked. "President Howard, I've been asked to tell you that the governing Council has taken a vote. Given that the cause of the wormhole explosion is still unknown, and our unfortunate error in attacking your vessel was just that—an error caused by not knowing that masked ship heading for the wormhole was yours—we have decided not to declare war on your people. That being said, we will still defend ourselves against attacks. I'm hoping we can work together so it doesn't come to that."

Howard put on a let's-be-friends smile. "So am I, Councilmember Xenia. I hope in the future you'll consider the possibility that a masked Human ship might simply be trying to get home without being destroyed by your superior technology."

Yes, we'll just assume every veiled vessel heading for our recently-attacked-through-no-fault-of-our-own wormhole is perfectly innocent. Not.

"Of course," Xenia said. "We'll give it very careful consideration in the future."

✳ ✳

"We always suspected our ancestors would have left tech in place to keep the wormhole open." Frego's friend Anders leaned back in the chair of his small, well-equipped ship, and rested a beer can on what the Humans liked to call six-pack abs. Frego was impressed to see he could actually balance the can. No way his own abs of flab—another handy Human phrase—could do that.

"We couldn't study anything inside the wormhole, because its radiation and gravitational forces rendered most our instruments useless inside. And by we, I mean our scientists, of course." Anders paused to lift the can and take a sip. "We've always been afraid someone would try something like this—but we hoped the Protector would prevent it."

"You're not a scientist. What were you doing out here?" Frego wasn't sure what had happened, but one minute he was diving into a cryopod, and the next he was waking up from a rapid thaw sequence on the Other Side with Human ships shooting at him. He was fighting the losing end of that battle when an unmarked craft appeared out of nowhere and sent the Human ships scattering in a haze of torpedoes.

Enter his old friend from the Guard, Anders, who Frego hadn't seen since he went away on an undercover assignment months ago.

Anders shrugged. "I was protecting some scientists. Officially they were studying the Divide. Mostly I was trying to protect the wormhole."

"So you couldn't stop whoever it was?"

Anders gave a quick shake of his head. The beer can didn't move. "I didn't know what they were doing until it was too late. I might have a lead on who was in the ship—I'm almost positive it was Humans, not here in an official capacity, but I'm still working on that."

"Using this new toy of yours?" Frego waved around the ship. The insides were sleeker than anything he'd ever seen on a patrol vessel, with walls and counters that swallowed control panels when they weren't in use.

Anders chuckled. "It's definitely not a toy. My commander will have my ass if I don't get this top-secret prototype back in one piece. And yes, it was helpful in both uncovering other masked ships and disguising myself. The second I realized I was being pulled into the wormhole I activated it and hoped like hell it would work as well as promised."

"So you've been here since the first event?"

"Second. I was just far enough away to avoid being hit after the initial explosion. Gravitational wave sent me flying, but I managed not to hit anything. I went back to investigate, and when I got pulled in, you guys in the visible Guard had everything under control. I assume you still do."

"When I got sucked in, the situation on Five Alpha was degrading. The last recycler was failing faster than expected. I was going to evacuate some more people, but then there was this situation with the Human delegation party trying to leave in a hurry. We were trying to stop them when the wormhole fluctuated again. It's too bad that...." Another idea occurred to him. "Wait, at least one science ship came through last time. In fact, when you found me it was in the middle of that engagement. Was that the one you were protecting?"

"Yes, and they're fine." Anders reached for a display, the beer can teetering precariously for just a second before resettling. A new display appeared in the air between them, showing the science ship and the other Guard vessel drifting near the edge of an asteroid field. "My new 'toy' has a pretty good range, so I was able to confuse the Humans' sensors long enough for our People to get away. As I predicted, they both headed for the asteroid field and hid themselves here. We can contact them discreetly."

"And say... what exactly?" Frego had a hard time keeping up.

"That we're with the Guard, which we are, and I was on a covert mission when I stopped to assist them." Anders picked up the beer can and chugged the last of it. "Helping citizens in distress is part of my job description."

"Then let's say hello." Frego frowned at the display. "And ask if anyone has a spare recycler—just in case we can get back safely."

FORTY-ONE

Since her discussion with Howard, the idea that had been tickling at the back of Xenia's brain had turned into a surety. In order to keep Carlton from, to borrow a Human phrase, throwing her under the bus—whatever *that* was—she had to blame *someone* for this mess, and it *had* to be a Human.

Finding the actual Person/Human responsible would take too long, and what if it was someone on their side? She grimaced at the thought of discovering one of the People, pissed off at those damn Humans for whatever stupid thing they'd done last week, had made a misguided attempt to help everyone by closing the wormhole. It would be a di- saster—just like when that stupid Human had pissed off that guy who started the war. Ever since then, the Humans had been whining about how, despite being "less civilized" and "less evolved" and "*supposedly* less intelligent"—that last part because they obviously didn't understand *what* intelligence numbers *were*, they were so dumb— they weren't the ones who started the first Human/People war!

Apparently, they were assuming it wouldn't be the last.

But Xenia had to deal with the present. The only way to achieve peace was to prove the Humans started this mess. If she could do that—legitimately or otherwise—then her people would be reasonable. There might be a few holdouts, but the vast majority would want the war to end as soon as possible so they could go back to looking like the civilized, evolved, rational People they thought themselves to be. Reporters and commentators would drone on about ending the hostilities, stopping the violence, and all the other phrases both sides liked to toss around during an era of aiming-for-peace. If the Council was appropriately apologetic and willing to punish the guilty, hopefully the Humans could eventually let this thing go.

Hopefully.

Eventually.

Well, it was the best option she had.

Now, who to frame? One of the politicians from the delegation party? A lower-level Earther government type? No—too hard to frame and too much political baggage. If she was lucky, the media might help her crucify a politician, but it was just as likely they'd see through the ruse and attack her instead.

The media, now there was another possibility. There were quite a few Human talking heads constantly blathering about how this war was the People's fault. Was it conceivable that one of the more outspoken commentators took matters into his or her own hands? She could think of three or four names who might qualify as the most inflammatory on the subject. Journalists were far less careful about covering their asses than government types.

On the other hand, they were usually trailed by insect-sized cameras or recorded by their AIs most, if not all the time. Any journalist near the vicinity of the wormhole would have been reporting live at the time of the incident. Could one of them have faked a live report somehow? She'd have her AI look into the possibility, but whatever set off the explosion could have been automated.

The media also tended to back each other up when one of them was accused of wrongdoing. Plus, they had good investigative skills. What if one of them found proof the accused didn't do it?

Of course, that problem went away if the accused was someone most of the Human population didn't like much—especially her fellow reporters. Someone who was seen as a deserter, who insisted on staying with the People when all the other Humans fled back home. Samantha had gotten more attention than any other Human journalist during the delegation party, due to her position with a People network. Everyone on both sides was suspicious of her motives.

Yes, Samantha would make a nice target. For all Xenia knew, the woman could be guilty. There were legitimate reasons people were suspicious of her. If she wasn't guilty of anything else, she was still the one responsible for Brad's death, whether she'd known the *Traveler* was going to explode or not—and Xenia thought she did. Besides, she'd been a constant pest to the Council since she arrived, always trying to get at "the truth about what the Ancestors really did to the Humans."

Now that she had an appropriate target, all Xenia had to do was enlist some help. She tapped a high-level security code into the nearest display.

✴
FORTY-TWO

I must be crazy. Warford followed the automated carriage into Five Alpha's airlock. He could have ridden on the cart with the humongous recycler, which was so big it took up almost the whole shuttle, and it had taken him five minutes to climb around it to the pilot's chair. But when he thought about how he was going to look in that damn Human's documentary, he decided he'd rather be seen striding onto the station ahead of it.

Once again struggling around the recycler's girth, he stumbled up to the authorization booth, placing his palm on the scanner so it could read his fingerprints and sample his DNA. Three days ago, when he'd first volunteered for this damn rescue mission, he'd spoken with someone named Anna who promised to add his profile to the security system's Accepted list. Well, she better have, or she wasn't getting her recycler, and it wouldn't be his fault.

Fortunately, she had passed his information along to the AI. It prompted for the passcode he'd been given, and he entered it into the keypad. "Authorization granted," the automated voice said, and the doors slid open.

STUPID HUMANS

Warford straightened up, squared his shoulders, ran a hand over his hair. Confident that he was ready to redeem himself to *Glass*'s viewers, he marched into Space Station Five Alpha.

It didn't take long to notice the change in air quality. Not only was there a stale odor, like the cleaners had run out of air fresheners, but his breathing became faster and more labored. He'd packed a breather unit with extra air just in case, but didn't think it would be necessary for the brief time it would take him to replace the recycler—unless the station's air supply had worsened more than expected by the time he arrived. Anyway, they'd apparently turned down the artificial gravity, probably to make things easier on those struggling to get enough air.

He glanced at his pad, trying to look nonchalant and in control of the situation as he checked the air quality levels. Right now they were well below ideal but sufficient for him to breathe short term without problems. No way was he going to put on that breather unit and look like a wimp—unless he had an unexpected problem with the installation. But that shouldn't happen.

"Hello?" he called as he approached the maintenance room where the recyclers were housed, according to the navigation arrow on his screen. One dull gray hallway looked the same as the next on these space installations. From what he remembered, there was supposed to be at least one person left out of cryo—possibly two or three, depending on how badly the situation had degraded. Based on the oxygen levels, things hadn't gone well.

Would the remaining person still be awake? No, he or she was probably drugged on sleeping pills to conserve oxygen. That explained why no one had greeted him at the gate, even though he'd started sending messages as he approached.

He stepped through the maintenance room doors as they slid away. The cleaning crawlers were apparently on vacation during the crisis, and the floor was strewn with discarded tools, empty water bottles, and food wrappers left behind by whoever had tried to fix the faulty system. He didn't see any cameras, but knew the station was still recording him. That annoying Human was probably broadcasting their camera feeds live, or at least recording it for his future embarrassment.

Flicking a hand across his pad, he sent the oxygen levels and navigation icons into the background—if the air levels dipped dangerously low, he'd be alerted, although he had a feeling he'd know by then. Quickly skimming the instructions for replacement of the Breathe Easy 550 Air Recycler, he couldn't believe how simple it was. He just had to access the room's security panel, enter a code and the crawlers would do most of the work. In fact, it was so straightforward he'd have to work at making himself look like a hero in the damn documentary. Well, he had to do something—his boss had been pretty pissed after seeing his explanation of why he couldn't deliver the recycler on the news. Said it made the whole company look bad. Suggested that was bad for Warford's career objectives.

He found the recycler's control panel, swiped his hand, blinked into the retinal scanner and entered the appropriate codes. As he initiated the shutdown sequence and hit "yes" after each of ten or twelve variations on "Are you sure you want to perform this shutdown? Air recycling will cease completely," he thought about what he was doing here. He wanted to think that he wasn't afraid of a little wormhole that would probably just dump him out to the Human side of the Great Divide, anyway. Also, he didn't want to look like a guy who left a bunch of innocent People to die. But that wasn't the real reason, he told himself as the screen showed the shutdown process completing—he really wanted to save all those people.

The instructions indicated that shutting down the main recycler should take a few minutes, but the process ended much sooner. Well, of course it wouldn't take as long when the respiration equipment was already off— he should have known by the lack of noise in the room. The crawlers unplugged the nearest failed recycler, and as soon as the movement icon lit up—letting him know everything was correctly detached—he helped them wrestle it out of the way to save time. He'd selected the "emergency mode installation," which meant they'd move the old one just enough to get the new machine in, and deal with removing it from the room later.

The new air system was on a wheeled cart, and it automatically moved flush with the wire box as soon as the old one was clear. The crawlers unceremoniously shoved it into a corner and zipped back over to the new one to connect the wires. This time Warford stayed out of the way, since he figured he'd look like an idiot if he plugged something in wrong and it ended up taking longer to get the damn thing started. In less than a minute, the automated helpers attached more than twenty wires. Another green light showed on his screen, letting him know he could safely start the new equipment.

"Please move all remaining personnel back behind the safety line before commencing startup," the computer's irrationally calm voice stated.

Warford rolled his eyes. The safety line was twenty feet behind him, and someone could be gasping for breath in one of the rooms on this level while he wasted time. How would that look on the news? Besides, that was just one of those excessive safety precautions, in case the new machine malfunctioned or caught fire or exploded or something. If that happened right now, they'd all have bigger problems.

He hit the "commence" button on the control panel, then tapped the matching one on his pad screen to confirm. As he turned and walked leisurely back toward the "safety line," trying to look calm but purposeful for the cameras, he felt a huge rush of air, like the wind right before a thunderstorm back on New Atlantis. It kind of made him feel like some holo character who had just outrun a big storm — and maybe some villains.

The whirring noise got louder, the gusting sensation increased, and he had to quicken his pace. Too late, he realized that wasn't going to help. The noise was now so loud he could hear nothing else, and his jacket was ripped off his back by the wind. He ran toward the safety line, wondering if he should have paid a little more attention to that warning. The wind force behind him picked up even more.

As his feet lifted off the floor and he was sucked backward, toward the recycler, he suddenly flashed back to a hideous old Human holo about a bunch of people — well, in this case, Humans — getting caught in a tornado on Earth. Tornadoes were easily predicted on New Atlantis, and few People lived in the regions where they were common, so this sort of thing had been surprising to him. He'd watched the movie, badly written and acted as it was, with a sort of strange fascination. The horrible actors had been screaming and shrieking as they were pulled up into the whirlwind, like crumbs being sucked up into a cleaning crawler.

Flying backward toward the recycler, he felt like one of those crumbs.

But how could this happen? The instructions said it would be safe to cross the safety line five minutes after the startup commenced. Wouldn't the recycler still be running?

He slammed into the outside of the filtration system, the air currents under the safety grid sucking his shirt so tight against him that he felt like he was choking. Suddenly he remembered reading that when a recycler first started, it required a massive intake of air, and that it spun at high capacity for several minutes before resuming a lower cycle level.

At least he was too big to get sucked through the slats and into the recycler's humongous turbines. He just had to hang on here until— until he fell on the ground? Oh, crap. Was this all getting caught on camera? Of course it was.

I'm going to look like such an idiot was the last thought that crossed his mind before his shirt successfully ripped off at the arms and blew out one of the safety screens. He was still too big to fit through it, but the increased air pressure jerked him further back and his head smacked against metal. Then everything went dark.

FORTY-THREE

Samantha's AI woke her with a loud dinging that drowned out the gentle hum of the fans, circulating her—hopefully—clean-ish air. She was dozing under the effects of some sedatives, and the combination of sleeping pills and the alarm left her confused as she struggled to sit up, the pile of heavy blankets trying to push her back down.

"What… is it?" she croaked as she tried, unsuccessfully, to blink the sleep from her eyes.

"Your guest, Mister Warford, has arrived," the AI said. "He passed through station security two minutes ago."

"Why didn't you tell me his ship was approaching?"

"Station security does not regularly update me on that. You were supposed to be monitoring all security traffic from here, which you could have done had you been awake. Note that I was running the security traffic on—"

"Yeah… whatever." She shoved the blankets aside with what seemed like a Herculean effort. "Oxygen in here?"

"Eighteen point eight percent, slightly better than outside this room, where it is hovering at eighteen point six, on average. I'd like to call your attention to the situation in the maintenance room, where—"

"Is Warford installing the recycler? That's great!" Samantha fumbled around in the mess of blankets until she found her purse, a shiny black bag big enough to hold ten pounds of makeup—which she was going to need. "If he's doing the installation, I'll just fix my face before going down there. Point the cameras at the wall or something until I'm done."

"Should I use cover video instead of your face for most of this documentary when editing?" the AI asked.

"Most of it, yes." She opened a compact with clumsy fingers, looked at her pale face and bluish lips, and cringed. "But leave in a few 'gritty realism' type shots, you know, just so it looks authentic."

She rooted through her selection of makeup brushes. The garden trowel stuck in the nearest ugly plant would probably work better for the amount of blush she needed to look human again.

"As you directed, I released some of the earlier footage involving Warford as a teaser, in case he—"

She looked up from her mirror when the AI halted. "What's wrong?"

"There's a problem." Its normally cool tone rose to reflect the Human emotion of concern. "You need to get down to the maintenance room right now before Warford damages the recycler!"

"Fucking *People*!" She dropped her lipstick, jumped up, and headed for the door, the motion making her head throb. Suddenly she couldn't remember why she was supposed to be grateful to this Warford prick.

Dragging herself through the deserted concourse and a twisted maze of hallways seemed to take hours, although it was probably only a few minutes. She stumbled into the maintenance room, her legs feeling like lead, unsure what to expect—the AI's data only said that the new recycler was about to "overheat from misuse." Whatever she'd imagined in her head couldn't begin to compare to what she saw.

Warford was actually hanging on the outside of the recycler by his underpants. Judging by the howling noise and the wind gusts tearing at her own clothes, he'd probably failed to follow the instructions about getting behind the safety line before starting the device. His shirt had mostly been torn off around the shoulders—that had to hurt. Heavier and weighed down by a belt, his pants still clung to his paunchy midsection while the waistband of his Hero brand underpants—their advertising touted "freeing lightweight fabric"—had been sucked up into one of the air filtration grates, where it now clogged the air flow—and, with the rest of his body, contributed to the recycler's overheating, preventing the machine from entering the lower-power state that would reduce the air gusts.

The first thing that occurred to Samantha was if Warford hadn't been unconscious, he'd have one hell of a wedgie.

The second thing that occurred to her was she would probably have to edit her hysterical laughter out of this scene.

The third thing that occurred to her was if she didn't turn off the recycler, it was going to overheat and become useless *fast*.

"Station... Five Alpha!" The station's AI had been programmed to take administrative commands from her while Anna and the others were unconscious, although she was locked out of security overrides. "Shut... that damn thing... down now!"

"I don't have control. Warford was using the emergency installation procedure, in which the recycler's connection to the station's AI is established only after the machine has started cleaning the air."

"Where's the override? It's got to be behind the safety line, right?"

"There's one on the recycler itself, and there's one on Warford's pad, which *should* have been behind the safety line at the time that operation commenced." The AI's designers had done an excellent job of programming it for snarkiness.

Scanning the room, she saw Warford's pad plugging another grate.

"Fuck!" she yelled. "Station, I need you to send in a bot to hit the manual override!"

"It will take several minutes to dispatch one that is properly weighted. The ones already in this wing are not."

Weighted? Samantha looked wildly around the room for something she could attach herself to with a bungee cord—something that was, of course, behind the safety line. There were piles of flexible ropes in the corner, with hooks on both ends and a control for stopping the bungee effect. They were typically used for tourists who wanted to go wandering about in space.

She shuffled to the pile of cords, wondering what she should attach one to—her shirt? Her bra? Her belt loops? That would be a great way to ruin a hundred-credit pair of jeans, and it probably wouldn't save her from flying into the recycler. She'd just be doing it naked.

She was pondering the exhausting and time-consuming experience of going to the concourse and dragging back a table when she saw the old recycler. It sat on the floor, steady as a rock, as the air currents whipped around it. All she'd have to do was loosen one end of the cord, punch through two grates with... something... get the rope through one grate and out the other, hook it to itself, and the other end....

She'd never figured out what to do with the other end. Make a loop, pull the thing over her head and tighten it around her hips? That was probably the best idea, but she had a feeling she'd wind up needing treatment for sciatica, at best, and new vital organs at worst.

So then what? Try to get the other hooked end of the bungee cord looped through the new recycler? While hurricane-force winds tried to suck her into it? How much time would she have? A second or two at most as she blew past? On a good day, when she was getting enough oxygen and all her senses were at full capacity and she didn't have a bunch of sedatives slowing her down, that would be nearly impossible to pull off.

And this wasn't a good day.

She looked around the room, searching for a better idea. According to all the displays, the recycler was dangerously close to overheating right now, and probably would in the next few minutes. By the time she found a heavy piece of furniture in another room and dragged it back here, it would probably be too late. Would she be able to get the respiration pod running again, and how long would that take? It would need to cool down, all the clothing and crap that had been sucked in would need to be removed....

She looked at Warford, dangling ridiculously. Her head was still pounding from the lack of oxygen, the drugs, and the stress.

"You fucking idiot!" she screamed at him, even though he was unconscious. All he had to do was get himself and any large, loose objects behind the fucking safety line—how hard would that have been? Of course all of his equipment, the oxygen tank and the breather and any tools she might have used to weigh herself down, were on the other side of the line, too. Well over the line. Some were also dotting the edges of the recycler, being fanned as the system sucked up dirty air.

She looked around again for something, anything, she could use. Warford had at least seventy or eighty pounds on her, and he'd been pulled in. Of course it didn't help that Haylea had turned down the fucking AG in here to save money....

Something flickered in the back of her oxygen-starved brain.

"Station, can you turn up... the AG?" she yelled over the tremendous noise, which got worse by the second as the giant filter tried to suck Warford in.

No matter how much she inhaled, she never seemed to catch her breath.

"How high would you like it?" the station's AI boomed over the racket. "An increase of two to three percent is usually —"

"Crank it up as high as it will go!" Samantha yelled.

"That's not recommended. Since the wormhole incident, we've been on decreased power usage settings —"

"If you don't crank up the AG in this room... right now... at least two people are going to die, and then probably twenty or thirty more. The station will get sued and lose *millions*!" She was vaguely aware that she was trying to argue with a computer. Had screaming always been so exhausting? No, of course it hadn't. "Use whatever clearance Anna gave me to override... whatever you have to override to get...." She sucked in another unsatisfying breath. "To get... the fucking... AG cranked up... all the way... in here."

"So you are authorizing the charges for going over the recommended power settings on —"

"Yes, I'm authorizing the charges!" Every word reverberated in her skull, along with the thrumming from the new recycler.

And then, after what seemed like hours but was probably only seconds, gravity increased. It began as a sensation of her feet getting heavier, then her legs and arms and the rest of her. Breathing was even more difficult now, and she found herself struggling to catch her breath standing still.

And she still had to get to the old recycler and tie herself down.

She gripped the cable with fingers that didn't seem to be working quite right, then slogged across the safety line, where she finally felt some relief in the form of a wind gust. She let it propel her forward, barely moving her feet at all. With the increased gravity, the draft wasn't strong enough to lift her off the ground, but it did do most of the work of getting to the old recycler for her. When she stumbled within arm's reach of it, she finally had to put some effort into fighting the air current. She grabbed one of the metal ledges surrounding an air grate on the useless system, gripping it as tightly as she could with one hand, and the wind tried to pull her away from it. The other hand still clutched the free end of the cable, which she used to stab out one of the flimsy air screens—it took three tries, but who was counting? Then she plunged her hand through the nearest neighboring grate from the inside, taking that one out in two tries.

As she struggled to loop the cable around the metal ledge one-handed, she risked a glance at Warford. She'd hoped increasing the AG would have freed him, but it hadn't. The air gusts weren't able to pull him so close to the grates anymore, so he no longer looked like a stuffed sock that was way too big for a vacuum robot's extension. Instead, he sagged forward, still dangling from his Hero brand underpants. The shreds of his shirt fluttered behind him, bloody, as the wind tugged at them. The band of his ineptly named underpants dug into his beer belly, leaving angry red marks and accentuating his spare tire, the gold Hero logo rippling as wind gusts still tugged at it, and in turn, Warford.

She was wondering how much Hero Underwear would pay her *not* to use a close-up shot of his bulging belly over their precious logo when she finally hooked the end of the taut cable. She looped the other end loosely around her hips and slogged toward the new recycler.

As the wind continued to tug her forward and the cable dug into the denim of her jeans, like a knife slicing into the hip farthest from the old air cleaner, she slapped her hands at the display screen set into the side of the new recycler. It took four tries, but she finally managed to hit the big, blinking emergency override button.

"Are you sure you wish to override this function?" asked a mechanical voice. "The Breathe Easy 550 will quit recycling air and toxic gases will begin to accumulate — "

"Yes, I'm fucking sure!" Samantha slammed her hand into the display again. "Read my DNA… I have clearance!"

"So you are authorizing the shutdown of this piece of equipment even though — "

"Yes, I am aware of the consequences… and I am authorizing the shutdown… of this piece of equipment!"

Then the noise faded, and the wind gusts slacked off, and the knife slicing through the denim of her jeans disappeared. She fell, stumbling under the sudden lack of air pressure from the huge cylinder. Sinking to the floor, she spent what seemed like an hour disentangling herself from the cables, then dragged herself into a standing position again.

"Crank the AG down to its previous setting," she told the station.

She slogged over to Warford, who now sagged forward even more. His chin was on his chest, his arms hanging limp at his sides, the damn underpants still snagged on something. How was she supposed to get him down?

Sucking in as deep a breath as she could get of the slightly-less dirty air, she reached up, grabbed him by the waist, and pulled as hard as she could, hoping Hero's ads were exaggerating about the strength of their underpants.

Unfortunately, they weren't. After a minute or two of pointless pulling and tugging, first down, then left, then right, she realized the briefs weren't going to give. Letting go of Warford, she dug in her pockets for her old knife/nail file/screwdriver keychain, one of the few relics she kept from her days on Earth. Fumbling it open to the blade, she slashed straight through the Hero logo on the back of the waistband, and ducked out of the way as Warford fell to the ground. Then, cursing at him the whole way, she directed the nearest bots to drag his ass over the safety line. They paused long enough to roll him onto his stomach, presumably to avoid further injuring the bloody stump of his tail, which had fought the air recycler and lost.

The second she followed him across that line, she used the controls on her pad to activate the Emergency Restart sequence.

A few minutes later, still gasping for breath as the air slowly cleared, she remembered to ask the station to send a medical bot for Warford.

FORTY-FOUR

Samantha was being strangled by a size 3X pair of Hero brand underpants. Behind her, someone—she couldn't see who—was trying to drag her into an enormous air recycler, which was randomly positioned in the middle of the Wormhole in the Wall. As she tried to rip the Hero briefs from around her neck one last time, she sat up, twisting a bed sheet in her hands instead of a giant pair of underwear.

"I see you're awake." Vance's voice sounded hollow and far away. She looked around with a start and realized she was in an infirmary bed. The doctor was down at the other end of the room, checking on a row of other sleeping people in beds.

"What the fuck am I doing here?" She vaguely recalled sitting in the maintenance room for a while, breathing deeply as the fresh air finally flowed, pushing away the medical bots trying to poke and prod her....

"No, don't worry about waking the others, they're still sedated." Vance hobbled to her bed. "And yes, our friend Warford is fine."

"Why are you limping?" She looked around the infirmary. "And where are my cameras?"

"You may want to be filmed in all your—what did you call it? Gritty reality? But some of my other patients might not," Vance said. "Your agreement with Haylea about this documentary does *not* give your cameras access to the infirmary."

"Which brings me back to my first question—why the *fuck* am I in the infirmary? I went back to the bar after I activated the thaw-down sequence for you."

"Yes, I'm fine. Being thawed after only three days didn't cause me any permanent harm. Thanks for asking." He glanced at the display by her bed. "But being stuffed into that damn cryocan left me with an awful cramp in my leg."

"Considering all the risks of being thawed early, I guess you got lucky. But why am I here?"

"Because I was concerned about you, and I wanted to give the others an extra day in cryo—except the ones whose cans had gone critical," Vance added, frowning at a bed midway down the row. It contained an overweight woman whose profile looked vaguely familiar, although Samantha couldn't place her without seeing her face. Wait—could that be Ridiculous Red?

"So you had your bots drag me back here? Why didn't they try to wake me up first?"

"You still had a bunch of sedatives in your system, and given that you'd been functioning on an oxygen deficit, I thought it would be better to let you rest. I'd like to keep you here for—"

"What did you give me?" she asked, noticing the patches on her arm for the first time.

"One is a monitoring patch that keeps track of your vital signs. The other is just something to counteract all the drugs I gave you to increase red blood cell production, so we don't have to keep giving you blood thinners."

"Great, I'm going to get out of here now." Samantha shoved the sweaty sheets off and climbed out of bed. She thought she'd feel like crap at this point, but she actually felt pretty refreshed. Amazing what a few hours of decently oxygenated air could do for you.

"I told you, I'd like to keep you here for observation for a few more hours." He put a hand on her arm.

"And I told *you*, I have a documentary to film, and you banned my cameras. I'm leaving, and you can't stop me." She gently but firmly pushed him aside and started for the door.

"You can leave against medical advice but that doesn't mean it's a good idea." Vance followed at what he apparently considered a safe distance. "What good will the cameras do you now, anyway? Who are you going to interview? We're pretty much the only People awake on this whole station."

"I still don't want to be here. I hate infirmaries, and it's too fucking cold in here anyway." She pulled her sweater tighter. At least she wasn't in one of those hideous hospital gowns they had on Earth, although that would have given her a visual aid when telling Vance to kiss her ass.

"You really need to be monitored for several more hours. It's rare, but sometimes after an oxygen deprivation event there can be complications even a day or two later," Vance yammered behind her. "You're still at an increased risk of blood clots, stroke...."

"My medchip will alert you if there's a problem."

"Can I ask you one thing? I mean, since you have plenty of time and nothing in here is being recorded?"

Samantha smiled as she stopped and turned around. "I was right. You didn't forget your request before you went under."

Vance shook his head. He wasn't smiling. "No, I know the answer now. I just want to know who did it."

Samantha blinked at him, her mind drawing a blank. "Who did what?"

He picked up a pad and flicked his fingers across it. "I took some brain scans earlier, to see if you suffered a significant trauma from your experiences the last few days. If so, I was going to offer a memory suppressant when you woke up."

She rolled her eyes, which brought back her headache. "For the last few days, I didn't have to listen to any of the stupid People on this station criticizing me, accusing me of crimes, or telling me to shut up. Why would I find *that* traumatic?"

"You're right, you didn't." He popped up a holo between them, illustrating what she assumed was her brain in vivid detail. "I'll assume you're not familiar with this type of brain scan. Those lit up areas indicate damage caused by trauma. The color indicates the trauma occurred between five and six years ago. Those variations in color denote recurring events over a series of weeks, possibly months. There's a small margin of error, but at least the majority of these changes happened during the time you were supposedly in a cryocan on your way here."

She stepped closer to the door behind her. "You had no right to take in-depth scans of my brain!"

"It's a non-invasive procedure, and I had valid concerns about —"

"Poking around in my brain is pretty damn invasive!"

"Look, I understand what happened now." Vance's brow knit in a look she hadn't seen pointed at her since the don't-call-it-a-war began — pity. "Obviously, you weren't suffering emotional trauma when you were in a coma, so you couldn't have been in cryo when you were supposed to be on your trip here. And you *did* arrive here five years ago, and you *were* from Earth before that."

"I fail to see how any of this is medically relevant to anything you're doing right now." Her head pounded with anger this time.

He shook his head. "Don't worry, I'm not going to tell anyone. I get it, okay? I know why you can't go back to Earth."

She took a deep breath. It had been such a long time since she'd been around anyone who knew the truth, and then it had been a miserable, slippery slope of anger and blame. "What do you know, Vance?"

He limped to the nearest chair and sank into it like a tourist plopping into a hot tub in low-G.

"Who was it?" he asked. "Who had you? What did they want you to do for them? And how did they get you here? Who has the FTL device—your people or mine?"

Samantha stared at him. FTL device? What did that have to do with anything? "What. The. *Fuck?*"

"I told you, I'm not going to tell anyone," he said. "I don't care what you did. Obviously, you were coerced, probably tortured. I just want to know who has FTL, because at some point it could become necessary for our survival here. The Divide could collapse completely at any time. So it's really important that I know—who has the device? Your people or mine?"

Samantha stared at Vance, at his pity-puckered face and his swishing tail and his hands, waving reassuringly in the air as he talked.

"You're wrong," she said calmly.

"No, I'm not, and you know it." He pointed at the brain holo again. "There's no other explanation. You were not in cryo when you were supposed to be, so you must have come here using a device neither of our governments admits to possessing. We are living in the middle of a war zone, and I need to know who has the best weapon—for myself, for my patients, for my friends here on the station, for all the people who got sucked through and are now waiting to get shot at on the Other Side. Just tell me, please. I won't explain where I got my information if I have to use it."

She shook her head. "I can't help you."

"You don't have to tell me everything." He leaned back and spread his hands. "Just say one word—mine or yours."

Samantha stared him down, refusing to break eye contact first. Finally, she walked over to him, took his right hand, and shook it like a job applicant trying to crush a potential employer into giving up a job.

His mouth dropped open in surprise. "What are you doing?"

"Congratulations, Doctor Vance." She smiled at him. "You are officially every bit as stupid as any Human I've ever met."

Then she dropped his hand, turned, and walked out the door.

And right into Anna. She had been placed on the "thaw immediately" list with Vance due to her job as Security Chief, and she did not look happy.

"Hey, we're not the only two People awake on this station." Samantha threw Vance a glare over her shoulder, then turned back to Anna. "Could I interview you about this harrowing experience and how it has shaped your views on the Human-People conflict?"

"Now is not a good time." Anna snapped a set of flexible electronic handcuffs off the waistband of her ancient khakis. "Since I have to arrest and detain you for attempting to sabotage this station."

FORTY-FIVE

"What is it that you think I've done?" Samantha asked for the fifth time. She was handcuffed to a floor-planted metal chair in Anna's office. "What the hell did Vance say to you?"

Anna sat across the trash-strewn desk from her, pawing through piles of data chips, half-empty coffee cups, and food wrappers. Finally grabbing a pad, she swiped the screen a few times and apparently landed on something useful.

"Vance? Nothing. When I got back here after coming out of cryo, my AI alerted me to a level-five security breach." She popped up a display on the desk. It showed the station, the position of the wormhole, and an asteroid cloud farther out. Between the station and the cloud were several rows of lines, each one consisting of arrows pointing in the same direction.

Samantha tried to spread her hands, but the cuffs, now attached to a ring on the chair arm, stopped her. "What's the point? What is this?"

"Those are highly-scrambled, fractionated communications from this station, to the Milliard Field, in the last three days," Anna said. "They were sent outside of Five Alpha's communications system prior to the wormhole event. My AI estimates there is a high likelihood these signals controlled one of the relays that overrode the Protector's programming and allowed the antimatter weapon to get through."

"What does that have to do with me?" She instantly went from irritated but slightly amused by this ludicrous situation to one hundred percent pissed off. "There were thousands of people on this station in the last week and a half, and those signals were probably pre-programmed."

"Well, if someone programmed a communications device to transmit to the Milliard Field, why would they leave it in the bar you run?"

"That's what this is about?" Samantha tried to stifle a laugh. "The Wormhole in the Wall is open to the public every day. Hell, you and your husband have access twenty-four-seven."

"Twenty-four—"

"Sorry, I forget it's twenty-five here. You know what I mean!" The longer this went on, the more her bitch switch got flipped. "How do I know you didn't plant the fucking thing? The bar belongs to you and Frego."

"But neither of us has been there in the last week."

"But other people have! Where was this device anyway? Under a table? On the floor?"

"Behind the bar," Anna said, her face expressionless.

Of course it was. There were no security cameras behind the bar, only one on the door and two spanning the public space, in case of bar brawls. Beyond that, Frego had never wanted too much surveillance. As he'd explained to her once, it wasn't that he didn't want Anna to know what happened in the bar, he just didn't want her to have to look the other way as head of security. For the most part, he always reported crimes. He had a no-tolerance policy for illegal drugs—"too much competition for the beer I sell"—and promptly kicked out anyone who started a brawl. But there were gray areas, so the overhead cameras covering the door and most of the seating area were the only ones set to actively record.

"You're aware there are ways something could get behind the bar without my knowledge or involvement." Of course the security chief would try to blame this mess on Samantha—the People were *always* trying to pin things on the Humans.

Anna stared her down.

"I think I should have a lawyer present," she said, since Anna wasn't saying anything—obviously waiting to see if Samantha incriminated herself. Like a reporter wouldn't know that technique well enough to avoid it.

"I'm not an officer of the People's government," Anna said. "I work for a private company and therefore do not have to follow any procedures for questioning a suspect."

"Then you have no authority to hold me here." She tugged at the unyielding handcuffs for emphasis.

"I *have* shared my evidence with the authorities, as I am legally and morally bound to do." Anna's mouth twitched with what might be the barest hint of a smug smile. "They've asked me to detain you until they arrive to question you themselves. I am *not* questioning you at their request. You and I are simply having a conversation."

Nice of her to explain the rules *before* she started.

"Have you any idea what these transmissions said? I'm curious, since I had nothing to do with them. People have been using the Milliard Field to communicate about everything from secret trysts to corporate espionage for years, you know." Hopefully she sounded snotty with that last part.

"Yes, and I also know that the high metal content of the field interferes with most normal communications devices," Anna said. "Successful transmission requires multiple devices in multiple locations, and sometimes multiple transmissions of the same message. It's expensive and still sometimes unreliable. Decoding a message like that is far beyond anything we can do here at the station."

"So all you know is that someone was trying to communicate something to someone by way of the Milliard Field, using some sort of device they stashed behind the bar. There's no video evidence of anyone doing any such thing, of course." Samantha started to cross her arms, then realized she couldn't because of the damn handcuffs. She settled for giving Anna an even filthier look. "I had nothing to do with whatever it was. And I'm not continuing this *conversation* without a lawyer present."

Anna shrugged. "Very well then. Why don't I tell you what I think happened?"

She said nothing but lifted one eyebrow.

Anna drummed her fingers on the desk. "You used the device to relay the signal to shut down the Protector long enough to get the antimatter weapon through. You knew exactly where the cameras weren't recording in the bar, so you figured you wouldn't get caught hiding the equipment."

"There are more holes in this plot than there are on an Earth soap opera holo." She should have kept her mouth shut, but this story of Anna's was just too ridiculous *not* to mock. "*You* gave me access three days ago to most of the station. It's not like my social calendar was so busy I wouldn't have had time to find a more secure hiding spot. I can name half a dozen other places besides my bar with no recorded surveillance and public access. But why would *I* want to damage the wormhole? Even if I did, wouldn't I want to be on the Other Side before executing a plan to sabotage it?"

Anna shrugged. "Maybe someone had to remain behind. You've been very insistent about staying here ever since the war began."

"That doesn't make me guilty of anything!" Samantha yelled. "I can stay here without blowing up a wormhole, which I wouldn't even know how to do anyway. Hell, your own people don't understand the Divide, and you've had your best scientists studying it for years. You really think a *Human* with no scientific training figured out a way to wreck the damn thing?"

"You could be working with others." Anna picked up a mug with a cartoon guy and "Secure Itty!" plastered on it, took a sip of what had to be tepid coffee, grimaced, and swallowed. "The fact remains that you've been close to a lot of disasters lately."

"You did not just go there." Samantha snarled. "How *dare* you use my boyfriend's death at the hands of some crazy bastard I never met as evidence that I'm a bad person?"

"It's not evidence, but it does seem like a big coincidence." Anna thumbed through something on a display. "First, you go to a lot of trouble to get off the *Traveler* right before it blows up. Then you portray yourself as the victim, *appearing* to be saddened by Brad's death. Then—"

"You bitch, I didn't blow up the wormhole, but I'd like to get my hands on you right now!" Samantha screamed, and she was aware of another voice screaming in the back of her head, telling her she needed to shut the fuck up right now. Once again, she wasn't in the mood to listen.

"Then you call attention to yourself, right before your people orchestrated moving this meeting here," Anna continued. "You take every opportunity to get everyone's attention focused on the bar and the documentary and you as a publicity whore, as your people call it. Sounds like a great cover for someone who's planning something top-secret."

As angry as she was, Samantha had to suppress a laugh again. "For your People, that kind of logic might make sense. Most of my people aren't smart enough to call attention to themselves to hide what they're doing."

"But you're smarter than most of your people, as you're also constantly pointing out."

Samantha felt thoroughly exhausted, despite having woken up a few hours ago. "If I was a spy, a double agent, or an individual bent on mayhem for whatever reason—and you haven't come up with a good one yet, by the way—why wouldn't I have taken advantage when I was alone on this station for three days? Why wouldn't I finish off the wormhole, or contact my cohorts to get me off this oxygen-deprived hellhole? Or blow up the station, or turn it over to the Humans, or whatever you think the plan was? Why would I have done absolutely nothing for three fucking days while gasping for air?"

"You could have done something that hasn't become apparent yet."

Samantha groaned. "This is a witch hunt."

"A what?"

"It means you're behaving like a Human idiot."

"You Earthers have a name for People behaving like Human idiots?"

Samantha sighed. "I'm going to tell you this story even though it makes my people look even dumber than you think they are."

"Go ahead."

"I didn't pay a whole lot of attention in history class, so I don't remember the exact date, but this was hundreds of years ago, okay?" She shifted in the cold, hard chair. "You have to understand that back then, our medical technology was much less advanced than what we have today, which you currently consider primitive."

Anna blinked at her.

"So, to put things in perspective, doctors didn't have microscopes to identify germs or even a stethoscope to listen to a patient's heart. Usually they treated people with some herbs and maybe a religious ceremony."

Anna crinkled up her nose in disgust.

"So there was this city called Salem, and they had a couple teenage girls who started ranting and raving and hallucinating. Today we would think of those things as symptoms of a drug overdose or a neurological problem, but back then...." She sighed. "Look, this sounds as ridiculous to me as it does to you, but back then everyone in this little town thought they were witches. That means, uh, possessed by demons, or having magical powers, like in a fairy tale or something... uh, well, like I said, it sounds ridiculous to me, too. I don't know what was wrong with people—I mean, Humans, back then."

"What was wrong with the girls?"

"No one knows for sure. The three most common theories are that they were faking the whole thing to get attention, it was some sort of mass hysteria, or they were suffering from a type of poisoning people get from eating moldy bread."

"Why would anyone—"

"Because their food production methods weren't any more advanced than their medical establishment." There was a reason she normally avoided discussing the messy history of her planet.

"So what happened?"

"Some women who knew the girls were accused of being witches and put to death."

"With what evidence?"

She shrugged. "Nobody liked them. They didn't exactly have due process back then."

"The lack of logic in the situation is very tragic, but — "

"I'm not finished." She glared at Anna. "After that, a bunch of *other* people were accused of witchcraft, too. Most of them were either put to death or jailed with no evidence. Maybe you were seen talking to an accused witch, and you were guilty too. Maybe someone didn't like you for some personal reason and accused you. That was all it took. Something like twenty or thirty people were killed before the governor of the state finally stopped the witch trials."

Anna folded her arms over her chest and returned the glare. "If you're trying to convince me your people aren't capable of killing others for stupid reasons, I think you may have picked the wrong story."

"Would you have arrested me if I was one of you?"

Anna jerked her head back as if she'd been slapped. "Of course I would have."

"You found the device in a public place. Anyone could have tossed it behind the bar, and you know it. I think if I was one of you, you might have questioned me but you never would have detained me, and the authorities wouldn't have asked you to, either."

"You're not going to tell me anything, are you?" Anna stood up.

"I'm telling you that you're making the same mistake my stupid people made at Salem."

Anna rolled her eyes. "Nobody's putting you to death, and you *will* get due process."

"That's not the point. If you want to keep me here, fine, I don't care," she shot back, as Anna turned and headed for the door. "But I'm telling the truth — I didn't do this, and I don't know who did. That means that whoever shut down the Protector is still out there. So while I'm sitting in here, collecting favorable media attention, you better get your ass out there and start looking for the moldy bread. Or the next time something happens, you might look pretty stupid."

Anna turned around and looked at her for a moment, her face expressionless. Then she turned back and walked out the door.

FORTY-SIX

"Why exactly is she being detained?" Woolerton demanded from Xenia's wall screen. He sat at his desk, flanked by Haylea, a pale, suited guy who looked like he hadn't seen the business end of the sun in decades, and a quiet tech guy from the station whose name Xenia couldn't remember. Haylea looked pissed. The tech guy had his nose buried in a display only he could see. The suit was also busy with his pad.

"My contact in the Federal Investigative Board—the Level One Violent Crimes Division—tells me she is being held on suspicion of several things, including acts of sabotage against a space installation, vandalism of government property, attempts to destroy an historical monument—"

"The wormhole is hardly government property." Woolerton's pet suit finally looked up from his display. "Or an historical monument. There has been no direct attempt to damage Five Alpha or any ships in the area. Those operations sustained collateral damage from the wormhole disaster, and I see no evidence that was my client's fault."

"I assume this is the lawyer you've hired to represent Samantha." Xenia looked at Woolerton, right past the suit.

"So you have no direct evidence that she did anything illegal?" The lawyer looked over Xenia's shoulder at the bare wall behind her. "All you have is a device used to send covert messages into the Milliard Field—something that happens every day, by the way. I'm very curious what evidence you have that suggests these messages were somehow linked to the Divide disaster."

She was in a delicate situation with that. Because of the way ultra-confidential messages were bounced around in pieces, received by multiple devices, reassembled, and then re-bounced to the source, they were very hard to trace under normal circumstances. The interference situation of the Milliard Field, and the necessity for even more devices than normal complicated matters further. In order to prove a message was sent from Five Alpha and received by something in the Milliard Field, one would almost certainly need the receiving device, as well as its access codes. Yes, the codes might be broken eventually, but that could take days. Based on her latest reports, for Anna to have tracked down the signals, she must have been monitoring the bar where Samantha worked far more closely than she should have, and that wasn't something Xenia wanted to discuss in this meeting any more than Anna probably did.

She had reluctantly taken a meeting with the station's lawyers so the Council could look like they weren't covering anything up. It had to be a politician, because the FIB would never comment on an ongoing investigation, and Carlton thought it should be her since she'd been dealing with the political fallout of the Divide disaster anyway. Besides, there was nothing more than she could say on the subject of "We're trying to stop the wormhole from collapsing."

Fortunately, Xenia didn't have to prove anything about Samantha right now—she only had to create cause for suspicion. "The communication equipment in question sent messages into the Milliard Field a few minutes prior to the event. The device also sent—and received—a message from that area every day at the same time. The signals you, ah, intercepted prior to the wormhole event were the only other communications sent by the device in the last twelve days, besides the regularly scheduled ones. That strongly suggests the regular signals were for monitoring an interference device, and the others were activating the device."

"None of that proves who was using this apparatus," the suit said. "You know as well as I do that without the corresponding equipment from the Milliard Field, we'll never know what those messages said, only their approximate size."

"We're searching for it now," Xenia said.

"The device is a People design, not a Human one," Woolerton said, reading something off his pad. "And apparently a very hard-to-find style."

"Hard, not impossible. Really they're just very expensive on the undocumented market," Xenia said. "And why wouldn't the Humans use the best technology possible to sabotage us?"

"I'm confused," the lawyer said, in a tone that suggested he was anything but. "Do you believe this unfortunate chain of events is the work of one Human acting alone, or do you think it's some sort of Human conspiracy? Do you have physical evidence linking my client to something you can *prove* caused the wormhole event?"

"I don't know if it's the work of one Earther or if the Human government was behind it," Xenia said. "I doubt they'd admit it if they were, and it's likely we'll never know. As to your client, the device was behind the bar she runs, in a place she knows isn't covered by surveillance recording."

"That's circumstantial, and you know it," Haylea said. "Since you have no recordings of that area, anyone could have left the device there. Now, why don't we go over how you came to suspect it was in the bar to begin with, and what right Five Alpha's security staff had to conduct a search of the establishment?"

"As I'm sure you've read in the FIB's report, they routinely scan for suspicious transmissions going in and out of the Milliard Field, and after the wormhole event they increased surveillance," Xenia said. "They noticed a suspicious pattern of activity and further investigation suggested the transmissions might be coming from the vicinity of the station. Then they sent a priority-one message to security on Five Alpha, which at the time was mostly automated due to the life-support situation."

"At which time your security chief received the message and took it upon herself to investigate, by tearing apart the bar that her boyfriend owns—I assume she had access and let herself in?" The suit raised an eyebrow at Xenia.

"Yes." Perspiration formed on the back of her neck. They were wading into a high-problem area.

"Sounds like quite a conflict of interest." Suit stared at Anna, saying nothing further.

"Do you have a question?"

"I am curious why Security Chief Anna didn't simply wait for the FIB agents to search the bar. After all, doing so herself leaves her vulnerable to appearances of impropriety."

The implication was clear—Anna could have removed evidence against herself or someone else, or planted evidence.

"As I understood it from her report, she felt there was an imminent threat to the station and wanted to begin her search immediately," Xenia said, as she'd rehearsed. "She searched all of deck one, not just the bar, you know. Also, she recorded her entire search. You've seen the video?"

"We've all seen it," Haylea frowned as the tech guy, silent for the whole meeting, leaned over and whispered in her ear. "When will you be releasing Samantha?"

"If the FIB have no further evidence against her, they can't hold her for more than two days." The lawyer dismissed his display with a slap of his hand.

"Thanks for your time," Haylea parroted at Xenia, in a tone that suggested she was anything but thankful. Then the communication blinked out. How ungrateful could she be? In any other situation, they would have been talking to a government lackey, not a Councilmember. Xenia only agreed to the meeting to quiet the press furor about Samantha being "framed", as the Human journalists called it.

She told her AI to pull up the latest news items on Samantha's detention. As she suspected, the airwaves were filled with reporters—both Human and People—blaming Xenia, the government as a whole, and the FIB for using Samantha as a "scapegoat," another handy Human word. Samantha's *Glass* friends were the most biased, but the other networks still spent time on the "flimsy" and "circumstantial" nature of the evidence.

They were right, for the most part, Xenia mused as she watched the coverage. Unless some real evidence turned up, Samantha would be released in about fourteen hours, the legal limit for detention without sufficient evidence. That was fine—the purpose had never been to convict an innocent woman, merely to make her *look* like she *might* be guilty. If the charges were dismissed and she was released, the media would stop screaming her innocence, and People would suspect she'd gotten away with something. The Human government would certainly suspect something—hell, they might even try to convict her in the court of public opinion, which was, according to them, the highest court in the land.

Either way, she felt confident she'd created exactly enough of a shitstorm in the press to solve the problem. Now, she just had to unite both sides again, so they could work toward a peaceful resolution.

As she was making notes on how to get back to where they were a week ago, her AI suddenly popped up a news update, in accordance with her request for a continuous search on anything new in the Samantha/wormhole situation.

And that was when the real shitstorm happened.

The "Instant News" update came from a red-haired woman named Sara at the *Glass* Network. She stood before their standard backdrop, a peaceful blue abstract painting.

"*Glass* has recently obtained a report from a Five Alpha representative. It shows their own independent tests of the device believed to have interfered with the Divide Protector prove it was not operated by Samantha, or any Human. The appliance was, in fact, a government-issue piece from the People government."

They showed video of the device, a small, innocuous-looking box, as Sara continued. "This item is a government prototype, so new our contacts in the undocumented market trade had never seen or heard of it before. Its design features were identified by an anonymous insider as standard Guard prototype safeties. In short, it could *only* have been used by a representative of the People government.

"Five Alpha's security chief, Anna, contacted the FIB to report she'd traced communications to and from this box and a source out in the Milliard Field. But a recently obtained report from the station's AI department shows she was only able to trace these signals because security programmed its automated device to spy on one of the station's residents—its only Human resident, that is. This same Human, *Glass* journalist Samantha, has been held and questioned for more than twenty hours based on information station security gave the FIB, while the People government most likely knew where the device was at all times, since it was one of theirs. It's unlikely they hired a Human to work undercover for the FIB. That means—"

"That means we're *fucked*!" Xenia screamed at the holo.

FORTY-SEVEN

Roble couldn't believe Haylea was actually hugging him.

"I'm so happy you found proof Samantha's innocent!" she shrieked in his ear. She was also squeezing him so tightly she was practically squishing his face into her boobs, which was fine, but it was a little awkward—especially since she was simultaneously jumping up and down.

"I'm glad," Roble managed to say into her sequined sweater.

They were in her office, watching the *Glass* report about the information Roble had uncovered. It had taken him a few hours, but he'd positioned each signal from the device and discovered the only way it could have been detected was through far more surveillance than the station was supposed to use on any of its guests. The AI had algorithms preventing it from spying, except in sanctioned situations—which this wasn't. So the bots themselves would have had to be reprogrammed to gather data on a particular person.

Technically, he'd been legally bound to turn over that information to the FIB as well—which he'd done, right after sending it to *Glass*.

As Haylea finally let go and turned to read something on her pad, Roble attempted another conversation with her. "What are you doing for lunch today?"

"Obviously, I'm eating in my office so I can respond to any new developments."

"I could bring you a sandwich or something."

"That would be great! Why don't you grab me something from Earth Hearth?"

"I thought you didn't like their food?"

She shrugged. "It's an acquired taste. Did you try the Good Day beer at the party the other night? It was great. Why don't you stop by the Wormhole in the Wall and grab me one of those too?"

Roble trudged down the concourse, wondering if Haylea really wanted to have lunch with him or if she just wanted a free delivery service. Well, at least she wasn't trying to get rid of him anymore, right? If he could just talk to her for a few minutes over lunch, maybe she'd see how much they really had in common. After all, she was the only other person he knew who liked that cartoon about the cranky cat with—

"Roble, there's something I think you should see," his AI interrupted his thoughts.

Roble groaned. He was right outside Earth Hearth, and he didn't want to be late for his lunch date with Haylea. "Is it going to take long?"

"Based on your usual behavioral patterns, probably. But it could help your friend Samantha."

With a sigh, Roble turned away from the eatery and hurried toward his office instead. If he could get Samantha out of detention, that would make Haylea happy, and maybe she'd hug him again.

What could his AI have found to clear Samantha?

STUPID HUMANS

* *

"When are they going to let you out of here?" Hank asked Samantha.

She turned her gaze away from the holo playing on the ceiling and studied him. He looked tired, but no worse for having spent several days on an overcrowded ship. Despite volunteering to stay on Five Alpha, he'd been shoved onto the nearest functioning vessel—probably for the same reason she had been left off the waking list.

"Soon, I hope." She sat up and swung her legs over the side of the cot in her cell. It was surprisingly clean, and very different from the holding cells she'd seen on Earth when covering stories at the local jail. There was no graffiti, no unidentifiable stains, no smells she didn't want to know the origin of. The flat carpeting was clean and bare, since the cot was the only furniture in the room. Two chairs were positioned outside of the cell.

"That's... good." Hank peered around at the empty space where he apparently expected bars to be.

"You can't see them, but they're there." She stood and walked closer to the tiny red dot on the wall that indicated the end of the safe zone. Pointing at it, she said, "I wouldn't test that thing if I were you."

"Yeah, it might zap me and make me forget everything."

"Vance was here earlier. When I told him I knew about your condition, he assured me he's still working on a cure."

"He's assured me of that too," Hank said. "I'm just not sure when I should go back into cryo. Seems like I should go now, before I get too involved with everything here. But Vance says he might be able to find a treatment faster if I'm out."

"If you're comfortable with being a guinea pig, you might as well stay for a few months and let him try to help," she said. "But you didn't come here to ask my advice, did you?"

He shrugged. "I just came to make sure they were treating you okay."

She gestured behind her at the large, empty cell. "This place is bigger than my apartment over the bar. And did you see the latest news report a few minutes ago? They found the device that hacked the Protector, and it belongs to the People government."

"What? No, I didn't." Hank dug around in his pockets. "Sorry, I haven't gotten used to this AI thing. I thought I asked it for news alerts, but I'm still expecting it to beep like my cell phone did a hundred fifty years ago."

"It's okay, good holo equipment is a prisoner's right here." Samantha turned to the back wall of her cell and gestured for the AI to play the news out in the middle of the floor. "Wait, even I haven't seen this."

"In her latest written statement, Council Vice President of Intergalactic Relations Xenia says she was 'shocked' to learn the device belonged to a government agency known as Shade, a sub-agency of FIB. Shade's official position is that it handles matters of security and safety in a background role. Councilmember Xenia also says that FIB agents concealed its ownership of the device to protect governing members of the Council from a potential security risk—in other words, they felt that knowledge could put the lives of the Councilmembers in danger."

"From something no one else knew for sure existed?" Hank snorted.

"Shade never specifically releases statements about its activities. Usually, it gives only vague reports to members of the government for similar 'security reasons'," Samantha said.

"The same spokesperson suggests that the FIB did not and still does not *know if Shade utilized any civilian operatives in this mission, but it is not uncommon for them to do so,' the holo continued. 'The report goes on to say that for security reasons and the need to confirm information contained within the latest report, Samantha will be held*

for another twenty hours at least. In related news, protests have popped up all over the station, and on both sides of the semi-functioning wormhole, as people suspect she was implicated for a crime she never committed."

Video of protesters running around replaced the talking head. *"A joint statement from Five Alpha's Copacetic Communications Director Haylea and attorney Rutherford says that Samantha maintains her innocence, and they are working on finding further evidence to exonerate her completely."*

"At least you still have friends here," Hank said softly, as she muted the holo.

She turned around to face him. "I'm not so sure about that."

"What is Shade, anyway? Is it like the CIA?"

"Yes, but with even less government oversight." She sighed. "They are... honestly, my opinion? I don't think the Council even knows what they do any more. They claim they don't know sometimes for security reasons, but I think it's for deniability reasons. It's a spy organization that functionally operates almost independently from the government that created it."

Hank nodded. "They're not so different form Earth politicians, are they? Deny, deny, deny."

"And blame, blame, blame." Samantha walked back to the cot and sat down, suddenly exhausted. "It's not just them. You should hear the reports coming through from the Other Side, when they're not gar- bled—the wormhole destabilization is causing a lot of interference."

"What do they say?"

She shook her head. "They're screaming that I'm some sort of traitor for staying here. Someone on a talk show actually suggested I blew up the wormhole so I'd never have to deal with Earthers again."

Hank shook his head. "I can see the appeal, but of course you would never do that."

She nodded. "I guess I shouldn't be surprised. I knew when I chose to stay here the decision wouldn't be popular with anyone at home."

"Why did you do it?"

Once again, it occurred to her how nice it would be to tell someone the truth, and she knew pretty much all of Hank's secrets—even the ones he didn't know she knew. But the walls had ears in this place.

"I didn't like dealing with the stupid Humans on Earth," she said. "It was so much nicer here. Even little things that you never think about. Have you noticed they don't put idiot warnings on things? They just expect that people are smart enough to know you shouldn't use your microwave as a hair dryer for your poodle."

Hank nodded. "Well, it sucks that they're keeping you here even longer for no reason."

She shrugged. "It's bullshit so the Council can cover their asses, but they can't keep me here forever. Eventually, they're going to have to face the facts—I didn't do this, and whoever did compromised a People device without their knowledge."

FORTY-EIGHT

"We're absolutely certain we didn't do this?" Xenia asked, loudly enough to halt the other arguments taking place in the closed Council meeting.

There was silence for a moment, then Tom spoke. Because he was Vice-President of Intergalactic Trade, the military, defense, and FIB measures had been shuffled under his purview at some point—Xenia couldn't remember when. No one wanted the job, because it usually meant being uninformed about something that, until recently, had not been a matter of great concern.

"I have gone over this with my sources in the FIB," Tom said, which was how he usually talked about defense matters.

Right before….

"Most of what they told me is classified, and even *I* wasn't allowed to see some of it." Right before he did *that*. "Based on what I know, I see no evidence that we did this."

"Obviously we didn't do it officially without *someone* in this room knowing about it," Sylvia said, her implication clear. If *someone* in this room knew about it, it would almost certainly be Tom.

On the other hand, any Councilmember could give a suggestion to the head of the military or the FIB. They couldn't order large-scale attacks without the Council's full consensus, but tampering with the wormhole could probably be excused as not being an attack if no one was close to it at the time. This rule was rarely invoked, probably because it was rarely remembered and when it was, no one ever wanted to use it. Most Councilmembers knew little about Shade, wanted to know even less, and assumed its leaders knew what they were doing.

"The FIB is usually very cooperative with us after such a public debacle." Xenia wondered who would stand to gain from this mess. Surely not Tom, Carlton, or Harvington? Leonora maybe, or Maylore?

"I have no reason to believe they weren't this time." Tom leaned back, clasped his hands behind his head, and stared at the ceiling, a pose that usually meant he was deep in thought. "Because of the Protector's importance to security, Shade had all sorts of monitoring devices for it. If one of them went offline, it might have been assumed damaged. Any of Shade's people who had knowledge about them were tracked even more carefully."

He sat forward suddenly, tapping his pad and throwing a holo display in the middle of the table. "This is from their deepest-undercover surveillance center. I don't even have a clue where it is. Could be in another dimension for all I know."

Xenia had to admit it was convincing—dark-suited operatives, deep in concentration on various displays, all looking up with surprise within seconds of each other. One spilled coffee, which seeped onto another agent's jacket, and neither of them appeared to notice. Liquid dripped off the second agent's sleeve as she waved at a blurred display. Yes, these people were trained to be convincing actors, and she knew a recording could be faked, but if it was, the timing was exceedingly good.

"Our best tech experts have worked over this repeatedly." Wova gestured at the holo. "They've assured me there's no evidence it was faked. I've also gone over the usage transcript from every piece of equipment assigned to monitor this thing line by line, and so have a dozen of my top experts. We all agree—there's not one word to suggest anything even slightly unusual."

"Good enough for me," Carlton said, his voice staccato and upbeat. "We need to move on, working on the assumption that we had nothing to do with it—or that Human idiot Fisk. Also, we need to stop this rumor that we framed some Human on Five Alpha."

"Obviously, no one here would have done that," Tom said. She hadn't told him, but he probably suspected—and he probably wasn't the only one. "It'll die down eventually when they can't trace it to anyone in our government."

At least she'd been careful about that.

"This is a difficult situation." Carlton's voice was so soft, it almost sounded like a stranger was talking. "Normally, I would recommend open, honest communication, because that's usually the best solution. But we can't share classified information with the public for security reasons, and even if we did it wouldn't prove we didn't do this. The more we deny it, the more people will think we're lying. But if we don't issue a statement, that will look just as suspicious. Either way, a lot of our own People will start sympathizing with the Humans."

"Since they've declared war on us, shouldn't we be concerned with whether we can beat them?" Leonora asked.

Heads turned to look at her. Xenia shifted uncomfortably in her seat. "Most of our tech is better than theirs. We have a few weapons they don't know about, but the same can probably be said of them. Strategically, our top experts should be able to out-think them."

"We also have a military that hasn't dealt with a large-scale war in centuries," Maylore said.

"Dealing with a major attack from the Humans will be a challenge," Tom admitted. "But right now, more than ninety percent of the Human military is on the Other Side. Since the wormhole event, our military has flooded the area — on both sides — with well-armed ships — and a few surprise weapons."

"We suspect they're going to try to fix the damn wormhole themselves," Xenia said. "They claim they're not, but they're not exactly friendly and forthcoming right now. That leads us back to the original topic — how do we deal with the revelation that our monitoring device was corrupted and used to shut down the Protector?"

Someone, she wasn't sure who, made a derisive snort.

Xenia shot an icy look toward the two prime suspects, Leonora and Oliver. "Does someone find this situation funny?"

"It's just that we're talking about Humans here... no matter how hard we try to avoid violence, those people try just as hard to do the opposite," Leonora said. "One of them probably corrupted the device."

Tom cleared his throat. "We've also received several requests from the Humans to extradite Samantha."

She frowned. "Extradite her? The latest evidence suggests she didn't do anything. We're not even pressing charges."

Oliver shook his head. "They want an excuse to get her back. Maybe she really is a spy."

Xenia rolled her eyes. "Ridiculous. We've scrutinized Samantha, probed her past, talked to people who know her. She was alone on Five Alpha for several days and nothing—oh."

"Yes." Wova dragged a finger across his nose and sniffed, a nervous habit of his that never failed to irritate her. "Maybe she has information they need, and with all the scrutiny on her and the device, she can't transmit it back."

This drew another frown. "But she keeps insisting she won't go back. We have no legal cause to make her go, and we can't stick her in a cryo-can against her will. In fact, sending anyone through the wormhole right now could be dangerous—it's probably okay, but if that thing collapses, anyone traveling through it would be killed."

"Their demand says we can wait until the Divide is stabilized or turn her over to Human troops in the area." Carlton drained his coffee cup and slid it down the table for a refill.

"But what could she have found on Five Alpha? We don't have any state secrets stored there," Xenia mused.

"I have no idea. Maybe she was picking up something one of their other spies collected." Maylore rubbed her fingers together, the way she always did when plotting something.

Xenia shook her head. "If there's any chance she knows anything, we can't give her back to the Humans."

"Agreed." Carlton opened his hand as the table's auto server sent the refilled cup back to him. "It is strange how she's stubbornly stayed here all these years, even when this side became an inhospitable place for Humans. I suspect she's too valuable of an asset to hand back to the Earthers. If she wanted to go, I believe we'd need to find an excuse to detain her."

"How do we tell the Humans we're refusing their request without pissing them off further?" Tom asked.

Xenia whipped her head around to face Carlton. "We are fighting a war in the public eye, on both sides. What's *your* plan?"

"All we can do is give them a close approximation of the truth—we were *surveying* the Protector to ensure everyone's safety, but no security measure is infallible." Carlton's voice grew louder, stronger as he continued rambling, finding his narrative. "We needed to protect the device from the small percentage of Humans—and People—who would wish us harm.

"Our investigation suggests one of our monitors was corrupted without our knowledge, most likely by a Human who went missing after the event—Leon Fisk, who further analysis shows has ties with an Earther fringe group called... Rednecks for Reparations, I think. Although this particular group has not been destructive before, it is possible Fisk decided to escalate its protests to a level of violence. We believe Fisk was killed in the explosion, but will continue searching until we're sure. Additionally, we are also trying to determine who helped him corrupt the Protector long enough to get an antimatter torpedo into the Divide.

"Our scientists are still trying to determine if it's possible to re-stabilize the wormhole. As soon as we've discovered that, we will partner with the Humans, if they're willing to cooperate, to keep the wormhole open and safe for travelers on both sides, while we continue to work to resolve this situation peacefully.

"As for Samantha, we can't extradite someone with no charges pending—I assume she'll be released later today, yes? Good. So if the Humans want to arrest her for something, they'll have to do it themselves."

"But—" Oliver started.

Carlton held up a hand. "They won't do it after we talk about how committed we are to justice and a fair trial and all that crap they claim to care about, and after we present our evidence that Fisk was responsible, and Samantha had nothing to do with it. There was never a single communication between them. They never met."

"Sounds good," Xenia said. "But what if they accuse us of lying or trying to protect someone by blaming a dead guy?"

"We'll just have to keep saying it and hope for the best," Carlton said.

"Anyone else?" Tom asked.

Heads turned around the table, looking this way and that, orienting themselves like little satellite dishes. Xenia was about to admit she didn't have a better idea either and call for a vote, when something flickered in the back of her mind. She snagged the idea, kicked it around in her head while the others looked at each other and shrugged.

"Well, if no one else has anything, let's vote," Carlton said finally. "All those in favor of my recommended—"

"Wait," Xenia said. "I know what we need to do."

✳
FORTY-NINE

Samantha lay on her back, watching the news play out on a holo display projected onto the ceiling. She had to admit her cell was comfortable and clean, with temperature controls and full communication access. Of course, any outgoing messages would be recorded and used against her in a court of law, which was why she hadn't sent any.

She sat up at the sound of footsteps, wondering if it was Haylea, the lawyer, or Hank visiting again. The clacking of metal on an alloy floor ruled out Rutherford— he wore boring brown loafers in a PVC-like material that made almost no sound on the floor. Finally the footsteps rounded the corner, and she saw their owner.

She stifled a gasp, jerked her eyebrows down as quickly as they'd popped up, and forcibly relaxed her face into what she hoped was a look of cool composure. Should she call Rutherford?

"Hello, Samantha." Xenia stopped just short of the invisible wall. "I was wondering if we could talk."

"Not without my lawyer present," Samantha snapped.

Xenia shook her head, a lock of her wavy, dark hair swinging across one eye like a thin curtain. "It's not that kind of talk. I know you're innocent."

"I don't believe you." She stood and walked close to where the red line marked off her side of the barrier. They were less than a foot apart now.

Sighing, Xenia looked over her shoulder, and wandered to the wall, where she collected a dingy guest chair in what Samantha had come to think of as puke green. She plunked it down just shy of the red line and sank heavily into it. "I know you have no reason to trust me, but I really am here to help you."

"You're right, I don't." Samantha crossed her arms and took the opportunity to glare down at the politician. "As far as I'm concerned, you're a prime suspect for blaming me in the first place."

A look of surprise flickered around Xenia's eyes like a bolt of lightning, there and gone in less than a second, but she caught it. Was the other woman surprised that Samantha suspected her of something she *didn't* do, or was she surprised Samantha had figured out what she *did* do?

Then the politician's face pinched into concern. She definitely faked that one. "Why would you think that?"

"Let's be honest here—ever since Brad died, you've blamed me for it."

"That's not true!" Xenia protested, too quickly.

"You're not the only one."

Xenia sighed and leaned back in her chair, staring at the ceiling. Was she using her eyeplant to view something on her AI? Those things had never caught on here any better than they had on Earth—it was just too distracting to read things while walking around, and people could tell by the vacant look on your face that you weren't paying attention. So everyone had the eyeplants but rarely used them, except when privacy was a big issue.

Xenia snapped back into an upright position and leveled her gaze at Samantha. "It can't be easy for you here."

She shrugged. "It's been brought to my attention that I made a public spectacle of getting myself off a ship shortly before 'my people'" —she hooked her fingers into quotation marks even though Xenia probably wouldn't understand the gesture— "blew it up. And apparently, despite your *vastly* superior intellect" —she made the quote marks with her voice instead of her fingers this time— "your People are *just* as quick to jump to conclusions as mine."

Xenia swallowed. Was she nervous? Did she *need* Samantha for some reason?

"I'm sorry if some of my people jumped to the wrong conclusion," she said quietly. "I am *not* one of them, nor did I have you framed. If I felt you were to blame for Brad's death, it's because he got on that ship for you. And yes, I realize you made every effort to talk him out of it. The truth is that Brad made his own decision, and it was wrong of me to blame you for that."

"Thank you. Now, why are you here?"

"I need your help."

"With what?" The woman had some nerve.

"With ending the war." Xenia looked like she wanted to puke on the puke-green chair.

Despite the icy façade she was trying for, Samantha couldn't stop herself from laughing.

"How stupid do you think I am?" She funneled the last peal of laughter into a derisive snort instead. "Do you honestly expect me to believe you want help ending the war from someone you've accused of fucking up the wormhole? Someone you admit the public here doesn't trust? And, in fact, much of the public on the Other Side doesn't trust either?"

"Public perception is exactly why you're the perfect choice."

"The perfect choice for what?"

"For heading up and being the public face of our image campaign to end the war." Xenia's expression suggested she'd just coughed up something nasty and was being asked to lick it back up.

"Let me get this straight," Samantha said. "You want the person you not only accused of blowing up the wormhole and starting a war, but also framed for that incident, to forgive you and help you run a campaign to convince both sides to end this nonsense. Did I hear you right?"

Xenia was a good politician, a crafty actor, and owner of one hell of a poker face. But even she couldn't hide her horror at hearing the word *framed*. If she hadn't chased the look off her face so quickly, Samantha might even have reconsidered whether she was right. But she *did* push the look away so swiftly that Samantha would have missed it if she'd blinked.

"I can't believe you still think that. You said yourself that this station is full of people who don't like you, and anyone could have planted that device."

"You have, on more than one occasion, implied I was some sort of Human spy," Samantha snapped. "Now you're suddenly convinced I didn't do it. Sure, you *might* have found out someone else corrupted the device, but it would be hard to prove that person was working alone. So the only way you'd be standing here now, asking for my help, asking me to become a public face of a campaign to end the hostilities, is if you were one-hundred-percent, completely sure that I am not a traitor, a spy, or a threat. And the only way you could be sure of that is if *you* were the one who had me framed."

For a moment they stood in silence, staring each other down. Several times, Xenia looked like she was going to say something, but then she twisted her mouth into a frown and exhaled awkwardly instead. Samantha waited her out, saying nothing more.

Finally, Xenia was the one to break. "You can't prove any of that. If it matters, I do trust you, and I think we can end this war together and advance both our careers at the same time. Do we have a deal or not?"

Samantha took what she hoped seemed like forever to answer. "I'm listening. Tell me more about this plan."

"First, you'll leave with me and attend a Council meeting."

"You mean a kangaroo court?"

"A what?"

"If this is some sort of trial—"

"Don't be ridiculous." Xenia sighed. "Your friend Haylea and that guy who follows her around, what's his name—"

"You mean Roble?" Where was Xenia going with this?

"Well, you heard how he used the station's AI to find evidence that Anna used her crawlers to spy on you—completely against the station's policy, of course."

"And that means what? More fake evidence?"

"No." Xenia gritted her teeth again, obviously hating this conversation. "It means we have constant surveillance of you since the minute you came to the station, three months ago. We also know the device was moved while you were visiting Champagne, based on our tracking of the signals. Now will you help me?"

"After my lawyer confirms that you've given him—and the media—this evidence proving my innocence, then maybe we'll talk."

FIFTY

"Thanks for letting me tag along," Hank said as he followed Frego into his tiny spacecraft. The curved ceiling was just high enough for him to stand comfortably, but the cabin wasn't crowded. The walls were lined with panels and blinking lights, and there were two long, low couches behind the pilot's chair.

"I'm happy to have company, although I am a little curious why you wanted to go on a routine trade meeting." Frego glanced over his shoulder as he approached the control panel and sat down. "I mean, a lot of people want to go on Guard missions. We usually have to say no for safety or security reasons, but occasionally, we make an exception for journalists."

"Like Samantha?"

"*Her*?" Frego's forehead crinkled as he tapped a few displays and a low humming filled the room. "Oh, yeah, she *is* a reporter. Lately, she's been more interested in *being* the story."

"But that benefited your bar." Hank sat on the couch behind the pilot's chair. It had four vertical rows of small studs giving the vague idea of separate seats. As he sat, he realized the studs were actually a type of seat belt, shooting what looked like tiny bungee cords across his chest and lap.

"Yes, it did, and I'm grateful for her help." Frego rubbed his face, as if trying to rub away the fatigue of the last few days. Dark circles underlined his eyes. He must still be tired from his trip through the wormhole and back under less than ideal circumstances. Hank was suddenly grateful that the flyer could and probably *would* run on autopilot.

"I know I was a little suspicious of her at first, but I realize now that I was being stupid. Honestly, I was just annoyed I wasn't there to run the bar myself."

"You enjoyed that job, didn't you?"

Frego nodded, turning back to his displays and swatting a large orange button. The humming increased, and Hank was pressed gently back into his seat as they started to move.

"I loved running the bar." Frego crossed his arms and leaned back in his seat, its bungee cord digging into his beer belly. The displays he'd been examining on the control panel slid into a neat vertical row, taking up maybe a foot of the front view screen. The rest dissolved to an outer view, which wasn't a big change from the total blackness of a moment before.

"Then the *Traveler* exploded, and I lost my brother and a couple friends. One of them was my main supplier, a sales fiend by the name of Parm. That one could close down a bar." A chuckle started, then quickly died in his throat. "He was going through the wormhole to buy more Earth liquor, you know. Said the stuff was unrefined and so awful People couldn't get enough of it. And by the time they'd drunk enough to realize how bad it was, they were too drunk to realize how bad it was!"

"I think I would have liked him," Hank said. "Is that why you're going on this resupply run yourself, on your day off?"

"Yeah." Frego scratched his beard. "I've been putting it off, but with all the business we've had lately, I can't anymore. My AI reorders the standards that sell best every week, but I can't just keep doing that. Parm used to bring new stuff every few weeks. Said bar patrons were easily bored. Besides, the store I buy from is backordered on almost everything because of, well, transport issues." He gestured out at the blackness in the general direction of the wormhole. "So, anyway, you never answered my question. Why the sudden interest in the amenities trade?"

Hank sighed. "The truth is, I'm a little bored. I know how that sounds, with everything going on. But I'm not a part of it. All I do is watch and hear things that are happening. It's driving me crazy, having nothing to do."

"What did you do back on Earth, before you went into cryo?"

"I was a computer repair tech. Problem is, the computers I fixed have been obsolete for more than a century, and what they have today is miles behind what you guys have, so there's about zero chance of me being useful in my field now."

Frego grinned. "I'm sure you could get into a school to learn a tech field. Probably even get a scholarship! Samantha could do a story about the hundred-and-ninety-whatever-year-old Human going back to school to relearn his old job."

"Yeah, but I don't know if I have time for all of that. I'm not as cured as Doctor Vance thought I would be after my treatment." He realized Frego was only the second person he'd told after Samantha.

"I don't understand. I thought you had a simple genetic defect? Those are easy to switch off, and you said you weren't having symptoms yet."

"Apparently this particular bad gene causes a lot of irreversible damage to neurons years before it causes symptoms."

"Sorry man, that's really jagged." Frego scratched his beard. "Is Vance sure it's irreversible though? I know he's working on all sorts of stuff for this woman who had a stroke, trying to repair her brain damage."

"He told me about that," Hank said. "That's the other reason I'm hoping to get a short-term job. Originally, I was just going to have him put me right back in cryo until he had a solution. But he says it'll be easier to find one if I'm here so he can run tests and—well, I guess use me as a guinea pig."

"A what? Is that what you call station rats?"

"Well, back on Earth we use them for medical tests, to determine if treatments are safe before trying them on people."

Frego's eyebrows shot up in surprise and he half-laughed, half-snorted. "Well, no surprise you can't cure anything! You know how different station rats are from people?"

Hank groaned. "Yeah, twenty people have told me that since I woke up. Starting with Doctor Vance."

"I'm sorry, man," Frego said. "I'm no scientific genius myself. I barely understand how this ship works."

"I agreed with your ideas about medical research before I even left Earth," Hank admitted. "I didn't think someone in my position should have to wait five years for a drug that might potentially save my life to be tested, just so some pharmaceutical company could cover its ass."

"Well, if you want something short-term, I have a buddy who needs a new local trader. I'll introduce you when we get to...." Frego leaned forward to peer at the view screen.

"Is that the protected area? The one your government won't let anyone near because of the Protector and the wormhole mess?" Hank strained against the bungee cords. All the news reports said the government had erected warning signs, increased patrols, and expanded the Protector's range to keep anyone from getting anywhere near it.

"Supposedly, we're working to stabilize the wormhole." Frego sounded like he was reciting a line from a press release — which he probably was.

"You don't sound like you believe that."

He gave a one-shouldered shrug, his back still turned so he could look at the view screen. "If you're asking if I know anything, the answer is no. That is way above my pay scale."

Hank watched the glow fade from the corner of the view screen as their ship pulled farther away.

"When can we start using the wormhole again?"

"I doubt they'll let anyone try to use it any time soon, unless there's some dire emergency." Frego stroked his beard. "Too dangerous. We were damn lucky to get back here ourselves. If you're planning on going home, you'll have to wait until they find a more permanent solution."

"You know, I hadn't even thought about going home." Hank was surprised as he said it. "I figure everyone I knew back there is dead, and Earth as I know it has changed so much that... well, it would be home in name only."

"I guess you have it there." Frego reached under the console and opened up a mini-fridge, extracting a cold beer. "You might as well stay and let Vance try to cure you. Want one of these?"

"Um... sure. But should you be drinking and flying?"

Frego chuckled. "The ship mostly flies itself. I don't do much of anything, and it's one beer, not a whole keg. I don't think I've ever heard of someone getting too drunk to fly and having the AI fail, although I *guess* it could hap—whoa, what was that?"

Hank blinked at the view screen. He thought he'd seen something blurring past his peripheral vision for a split second, but it was hard to be sure. "Did the field... expand or something?"

"I don't know." Frego's fingers flew over a display. "No, I don't think that was it. My sensors registered something with the mass of a small ship hurtling past at what had to be its maximum speed. I think it was something—some*one*—passing *through*!"

"Like you just said was too dangerous?"

Whatever Frego started to say in response was lost under the sudden sound of alarms going off. Half the view screen slid to the side and a new image popped up. Judging by the angle of the aura—which, for the moment, seemed to be holding steady—the second image was the view from the back of their ship.

Where a large, well-concealed mass, outlined in blinking lights—the AI's addition, Hank guessed—was following them. Well, gaining on them. Quickly.

And, apparently, shooting at them. Feeling the ship rock with small impacts—lasers, torpedoes, what all did they have here?—Hank grabbed the arms of his chair even as the bungee cords tightened around him.

"Are we going to crash?" he blurted.

Hank, stabbing at his displays, actually chuckled. "You're thinking like a Human from a couple centuries ago, used to flying in planes. On your *planet*." He smacked something and they zoomed upward.

"I guess I'm not finding this as funny as you are. Who the fuck is in that shrouded ship, and why are they shooting at us?"

Hank stared at the view screen in the hopes he'd see something other than the computer-generated outline of a ship... and wavy lines he assumed were the firings of some weapon.

"Relax, we're fine." Frego sounded so much like a bartender telling a patron to forget his troubles and have another drink that it was almost disconcerting. "We can't crash because we're in space, so you have to forget about things like up and down and gravity—"

"But we can still crash into things. Or get blown to bits!" Hank hated that he sounded like a panicked idiot next to Frego's movie-hero calm.

"Don't worry, this is about to end," Frego said as the ship bucked up and down in what Hank assumed was some sort of evasive maneuver. He tapped some display buttons and the left half of the view screen changed to show an eerily nonchalant man dressed all in black. Black t-shirt, black pants, black sunglasses. Seriously, on a spaceship with no *real* windows?

"Frego, buddy, what are you doing?" he asked in a stage whisper, leaning in toward them. "Do you know how much trouble I'd be in if I wasn't burying this transmission in a standard scramble feed?"

Frego spread his hands. "I'm on my way to a trade deal on Hammonds. Why are you chasing me, Anders?"

"You tried to cross the field! I'm supposed to have disabled your engines by now. Please tell me this was a giant mistake and you just got lost."

"No, check my ion trail, I haven't gone anywhere *near* the field. I've stayed well outside the safe zone set for...." His voice trailed off as something moved to the side of Anders's face.

It was like the darkness in the field of space outside had... shimmered, somehow. Or had Hank imagined it? No, he hadn't, because Frego was looking at it too, and so was Anders.

"Get out of here," Anders hissed, leaning into the display again. "I'm sending you coordinates for an alternate route to Hammonds. *Don't* deviate. And don't share this with *anyone*." His image winked out.

"I guess I don't count as anyone." Hank tried to break the ice as Frego furiously punched display buttons.

"He didn't see you. I set my feed to narrow." Frego finished whatever he was doing and flicked a hand to make the displays disappear. "It'll take half a day longer to get to Hammonds, but I have eight days' leave. You in any hurry?"

"No. Are we still moving?"

"Yup." Frego leaned back in his chair, folding his arms over his chest. "Just very slowly."

"But—"

"Anders told me to take an alternate route to Hammonds. He didn't say how fast I had to go."

"Isn't that dangerous?"

"Not really. I've learned a few things from him over the years, you know. This ship has some pretty good concealing enhancements, and he just sent me some frequencies to avoid. We should be fine."

"But what if one of those things we can barely see hits us?" Hank suddenly remembered that the cold, slimy thing in his hands was a bottle of beer with liquid condensing on the outside, and took a swig.

"We're concealed to look like space junk, not vacuum." Frego glanced warily at Hank. "You don't have a problem with spying on a spy, do you?"

Hank nearly choked. "Anders is a spy?"

"Oh, yeah." Frego knocked back a swig of his own beer. "You know, this Good Day crap isn't half as bad as I thought it'd be."

Hank was still trying to formulate a response when the sky lit up with what looked like fireworks. "Are those—"

"Ships passing through the field? Absolutely. One was probably Anders." Frego pointed at the brightest light. "But not that one. That's got to be a *huge* ship. I wonder...."

Whatever he was wondering gave way to a more important question—who had just gone for the wormhole? Did Anders stop them? Did that huge ship belong to Frego's people, or his? Then he realized, with a start, that he wasn't sure which group was which.

FIFTY-ONE

Roble wasn't sure when he became a "leading expert" on the wormhole event, but he somehow found himself on a ship of research scientists, which included some of the leading minds in engineering, AI design, and galactic exploration. Milena, the head of the Wormhole Recovery Operation, had asked for him and Molly after hearing what was probably an exaggerated account of their work during the Five Alpha crisis.

"Do you think we're here to fix the Protector's security problems or work on stabilizing the Divide?" Molly leaned closer to the wall screen they were watching, along with a group of about forty other scientists.

"I was told I'd be working on the Protector's AI, fixing its security holes." Roble stared at the wall screen, which showed an unimpressive array of asteroids.

"What's visible on infrared?" Molly asked. "That one rock is way too hot, is it one of our monitors?"

"I don't know."

STUPID HUMANS

It was shaped like one of those things they served at Earth Hearth. What did the Humans call them? Baked potato?

"This is as far as we go for now," Milena said from in front of the window. She tapped on the potato and it filled the screen. "While examining the security problems this morning, we came across this."

"A malfunctioning monitor? Is that how the damn Humans were able to get into our system?" someone yelled from the back.

"I want you all to listen very carefully." Milena turned her back on the view screen. "You are all here because you're considered trustworthy, but just in case, I'm going to remind you of the confidentiality paperwork you signed. Everything you see and work on here is completely confidential unless you are told otherwise, understood?"

Nods and mumbles all around.

She raked a hand through her limp hair. "This device is not ours, and it's not the Humans', either. Our estimates suggest it's been floating in this field for thousands of years."

"You're not saying the Ancestors left it?" Molly gaped at her.

Milena shrugged. "We always suspected they left tech behind to monitor the wormhole and we just... lost it over the years."

"How come we never found it before?" asked a skinny guy in the front row. "It's lit up like a radioactive crater on Earth."

"The Humans haven't trashed Earth *that* badly," the woman next to him pointed out.

"Because it wasn't lit up two days ago." Milena waved her hand and the view screen dissolved back to a picture of the rock collection. Nothing showed up on infrared, although the same rock was circled. "It's been inactive for years."

"What would have activated it?" the skinny guy asked.

"Our best guess is the destabilization of the wormhole. The ancestors must have guessed what would happen and programmed the device to activate only if it was hit by a significant gravitational wave." She turned back to the view screen. "There go the crawlers."

A swarm of tiny devices appeared on the screen, zooming toward the baked potato. In less than two minutes they were crawling over it like insects on a slice of fruit. Less than half the size of a personal flyer, the artifact was bumpy, shaped to look like one of thousands of rock fragments floating out here.

Roble's AI dinged to let him know he'd received his work assignment. He was to provide support to the ship's AI, which was running a program created by a scientist named Umora—seated somewhere near the back of the crowd, if he remembered correctly—who had spent twenty years teaching Ancient Technology at the premiere university of New Atlantis. While most people thought of her field as obscure, her research had always focused on preparing for the day when an ancient piece of tech would be found and need analysis. She had studied the few pieces of extant tech still around from the time period, in addition to later pieces that were, presumably, closer to the original programming than more modern ones.

A steady stream of data flowed to his display. The bots were accessing the dataport... trying the first set of unlocking algorithms... failing.... Well, they couldn't expect to get through on the first try. As he watched the patterns change, he realized the algorithms had failed at an earlier point than expected—much earlier. Instead of trying to unlock the encryption, it was trying to talk to the program on its most basic level—essentially, it was trying to understand p-a-s-s-w-o-r-d meant password before it could try to guess or get around the password.

That shouldn't be happening. With Umora's help, the AI had worked out an algorithm that was 99.7 percent sure to communicate with the coding languages used at the time of the Great Escape.

"This can't be right," Umora groused, shoving her way through the crowd of scientists to stand at the view screen by Milena. "Our best AI wrote code that would work with more than ten thousand extrapolations on known languages from that time frame!"

"The really odd thing is that it's not even coming close." Roble watched the ever-growing list of dings that indicated a mismatch. "It's as if none of the characters are even the same."

"The crawlers are starting from the most basic level," Molly mused, "attempting to understand the code as it's written, but almost all of it is hidden behind multiple security screens, so they can only work on the visible part."

Milena turned from the window to look at all of them, although she couldn't have had much of a view—almost everyone was hunched over a screen, deep in concentration. "Are you saying we need to break into the secured code in order to get the code that would allow us to break into the secured code? Because that sounds—"

"Like a real conundrum," Molly finished. "And our AI has determined it's the best option."

FIFTY-TWO

"Can't you tell it to do something else?" Milena asked, displaying the fact she'd spent the last ten years more entrenched in bureaucracy than pure science.

"Of course, if we had a better idea. If the AI thinks this is our best option, I'm inclined to agree." Umora's upper lip curled in disgust as she stared at her pad. "I just don't understand why our program failed. We used actual code from the time period."

"No one knows the exact date of the escape," Roble pointed out. "What we used was the only known code from the date closest to the estimated date. What if—"

"We have a bigger problem." Molly's head popped up. "Isn't anyone watching the heat readings from that thing? Have you noticed they've increased rapidly since the crawlers arrived?"

Roble frowned at the numbers. "Is it some sort of defense mechanism? Maybe it's arming a weapon inside the box... that we're trying to get into?"

"It's probably just a periodic fluctuation," Umora said. "Or a malfunction. This thing has been inactive for thousands of years. It's amazing it still works at all."

"But the heat is increasing and has been since we started," Molly said.

"Well, the crawlers are armed, right?" Milena's fingers stroked the wall screen as if she could make the machines work faster from her vantage point.

"As best as something the size of a sandwich can be," Molly said. "And we have no real idea what kind of weapon could be inside that—"

"Wait, I think the heat has leveled off," an analyst named Komar called from behind them. "Maybe it was just a longer than—"

"No, it hasn't leveled," Roble yelled, louder than he meant to, but everyone's attention was on the screens. "It just spiked to—"

That was when Milena screamed. Her hands still pressed against the screen, blue fingernails tearing at the more-or-less indestructible material, frantically clawing at the image of the crawlers.

Or what was left of them. A bright blossom of light had replaced the box, and flying chunks of twisted metal had replaced the hundred-thousand-credit-each crawlers.

"All that research," Milena screamed. "How could anyone approve putting the most expensive automatics in all of academia so close to a hidden monitoring device that could have concealed explosives?"

Roble was pretty sure he'd followed her many public campaigns to the head of research at the University to do just that, but now didn't seem like the time to mention it. Especially when—

"Are we even trying to outrun the shockwave?" Molly asked from behind him.

Everything after that happened in a blur. Roble was slammed back into his seat as the ship took off—or was that the press of the shock-wave? It was hard to tell since both were moving in the same direction.

"Are we getting anything from the remaining crawlers?" Milena screamed, turning around and stumbling toward the seats as the ship zoomed away from the flying wreckage. AIs calmly instructed everyone to sit down so the couches could secure them, but she didn't listen. She ran to a wall panel and frantically pushed buttons, all the while scream-ing for the rest of the team to help her.

"We need to send a cheaper machine to see if there's anything sal-vageable. Why aren't we getting any readings from the area?"

"I just launched a level-five crawler." Molly studied her pad. "But based on the last readings we got, and the video surveillance, I don't think it'll find anything. I'm getting a ninety-nine percent chance of total destruction, not just of our equipment but also the device itself."

Suddenly, all the yelling and groaning and bitching about the cost came to an abrupt halt.

"What?" Milena ran to Molly's seat to study the data. The ship accelerated again, causing her to pitch forward onto the couch. Mol-ly scooted out of her way and the couch clamped its security belts around the director.

Milena thrashed against the cords, shoving them away so she could grab Molly's pad without asking.

"This can't be happening. The Humans will never believe this wasn't our fault." Umora let her pad drop to her lap. Her green eyes bored into the wall screen, which still showed the rapidly-receding wreckage. "They're going to claim we did this on purpose, to keep them away."

"Will the wormhole collapse completely now?" someone asked from the back of the room.

"I don't think so," another scientist said from Roble's right. "Our preliminary analysis suggests the device was meant to monitor, not disrupt, the Divide. The wormhole should function independently of the device... or it should if it hadn't already started to destabilize."

Unfortunately, the Divide wasn't well understood. Most instruments that passed through the wormhole or even came close to the gravity well were rendered useless by the gravitational radiation. Everything the leading scientists in the field knew about exotic matter was based on studying it far from the wormhole, so its function inside the Divide was only best-guessed. Even the guy who was blabbering about how stable it should be didn't really know anything for sure. They could be sitting next to a, what did the Humans call it, a ticking time bomb or something....

One of the ship's crew loudly cleared his throat. "Professor Milena, ah, there's an urgent message for you. It's from one of the nearby Guard ships. They're insisting on escorting us home for our own safety."

"Oh, no," Umora grumbled. "We all know what that means."

"It means the Guard is trying to cover their asses when the Humans start screaming this is our fault," Molly explained to Roble, having apparently decided that technology was his only field of knowledge. "Someone, somewhere, recorded that explosion, and if we don't explain what blew up, they'll start screaming we're testing bombs out here instead of fixing the Divide."

Roble didn't know much about politics because he didn't want to know much about it. He found it dull and pointless and far less interesting than, say, a radiothermic scan of the area surrounding—

"Wait, we can't leave yet," he yelled, and the room went silent. Milena stopped in mid-sentence and gestured for her AI to cut the connection to the Guard officer.

"Why?" she demanded. "I was just convincing that guy it wasn't necessary to escort us home and you just yelled like a sarachi bird!"

Roble shook his head. "Well, go back to convincing him. We have to stay here. There's a piece of debris from the explosion that's putting out an encrypted signal."

"But there wasn't one before. The purpose of that whole thing was to hide itself," Umora said.

"I think this is intentional." Roble sent her the report. "Why wouldn't there be a signal? Obviously, circumstances have changed. They could have rigged something to survive the blast and broadcast only after the device was completely destroyed."

"Why?" Molly asked. "So they could find the debris? It would be obvious this thing was destroyed anyway, right?"

"I think you're on to something." Milena put the data up on the wall screen. "They probably assumed that they'd replace it before its useful life span ended. The signal was in case something happened unexpectedly."

"They thought someone might find and destroy the wormhole, no matter how well hidden it was," Umora finished. "That signal was meant to alert someone the Divide had been destroyed, but I doubt it's being received anywhere now."

"By someone, you mean the Humans?" Molly asked.

Umora shrugged. "Probably not on this side of the Divide. I would say us, but maybe not all of us. There were almost certainly political factions that disagreed with the decision to leave Earth and shut out the Earthers."

"We have to stay here and decrypt that message, no matter what it takes." Roble hoped Umora realized what a unique opportunity this was—when would they ever get the first chance to observe an artifact from the time of the Great Escape?

Molly sighed, her bangs fluttering. "But the Guard...."

"I'll deal with them." Milena gestured to her AI and a peeved-looking Guard captain appeared on the wall screen. "Captain Horvis, we've uncovered some very intriguing info that your people would find interesting. Of course, you can conduct your own search without us, but I think you'd agree it would be easier with assistance from the leading experts in the field. Perhaps we could stay and help. With all these Guard ships around, you'd be assured that we'd be safe from pissed-off Humans. What do you say?"

*
FIFTY-THREE

"We fucking blew up an Ancestors' artifact, after we destabilized the wormhole?" Samantha stared incredulously at the blinking-red-framed report hanging over the table where she was meeting with Xenia and Tom in their well-fortified ship.

"We didn't blow up either of those things. One of your people went after the Divide, and this situation was an accident." Xenia waved a dismissive hand at the display.

"But our poking around probably caused the artifact to self-destruct." Samantha ripped open the package of chocolate cookies she'd requested. Apparently, the catering staff could get pretty much anything here, and it was all on the government's dime.

And it wasn't even technically her government.

"We don't know that for sure," Tom said.

"It's a working hypothesis." Xenia delicately placed her glass on the table, as if she was afraid to mess up anything else. "If it turns out the investigation triggered the explosion, it wasn't intentional. That scientific team consists of the very best people in the business, and they had no reason to believe it was rigged with a self-destruct sequence."

"Bullshit," Tom said around a mouthful of muffin. He swigged some coffee, swallowed, and turned to Samantha. "How are your people going to view this?"

"Your people blew up the artifact to get even with us for the wormhole destabilization."

"She's right." Tom swatted away the classified report and replaced it with the latest *Glass News* feed, where a well made-up anchorwoman was attempting to referee three guests screaming at each other about the latest "attack."

"We'll probably never know what happened because the Humans covered it up," snapped a man in a gray suit.

"I don't know, are they intelligent enough to blow up the artifact, with all its historical significance, and somehow make it look like our fault?" a woman in a green sweater asked.

"We're intelligent enough to fuck you people up bigtime!" yelled an apparently Human redhead. "Keep talking and I'll shove the results of my IQ test up your ass. Maybe I'll even manage to dislodge the stick!"

"Tell me you found the actual criminal who sold the antimatter weapon to Fisk, like I suggested on the way over here," Samantha said to Xenia as she waved the display off.

"We did, and it's really embarrassing—to the Humans." Xenia brushed cookie crumbs off her tailored sleeve. "The FIB picked him up this morning. He says he had no idea it was going to be used on the wormhole."

"Well, of course not."

"You know it doesn't take a large amount of antimatter to damage the wormhole, right? Only a small amount was necessary to interfere with the exotic matter."

"Yes...."

"According to Banfrey's statement, Fisk said he was going to blow up some small asteroids that weren't worth mining. He claimed explosions were sort of a sexual fetish for him, like pyromaniacs and fire?"

Samantha groaned. "And he couldn't use a sim suite because...?"

"Banfrey says he thought the Humans didn't have as advanced sim tech, and he didn't want to embarrass Fisk by implying the Earthers were intellectually inferior—even though they are. I mean, that's what he said, not—"

"I get the idea." Samantha waved for her to continue.

Xenia popped a dossier over the table. "We're not buying Banfrey's story. He was on Five Alpha and visited the Wormhole in the Wall twice during the time period when the device was placed and when Fisk was there, apparently acquiring the capsule. Since there are no recordings from inside the bar, we can just let public opinion do the rest. Once we've linked him to Fisk and the comm box, your people will just assume he sold the weapon that destabilized the wormhole."

"My people won't buy it. They'll say it's part of a government cover-up."

"But he's one of our own people, working with one of your people to blow up the wormhole," Tom said.

Samantha shook her head. "That's exactly why your own people are going to find this hard to swallow. Once they start second-guessing you, my people won't be far behind. They'll say you're blaming an individual to cover a government screw-up."

"Really?" Tom stole one of her cookies. "Our People might, but your People will just be happy it wasn't one of them. Why would they want to... what's that expression... look at the horse's mouth?"

"I think you mean look a gift horse in the mouth."

"Would you stop insulting the Humans?" Xenia gave him a filthy look. "We're all here to improve relations between our peoples."

"Actually, it's because my people are so stupid that they'll know it's a cover-up." Samantha was genuinely sick of the idea of "improving relations" between the Humans and the People. It reminded her of all those idiots running around Earth, painting peace signs on sewer covers, and yammering about world peace... until they started rioting in the streets. World peace was a great idea—in theory. In reality, it was never going to happen. You might as well be in favor of equality for flying pigs and technicolor unicorns.

"You've lost me." Tom reached for his coffee cup.

She sighed. "Our government is just as corrupt as yours. The difference is that our politicians get caught all the time, because they're stupid. One of them sent out a news release that was supposed to be a video of him shaking hands with patients at a new charity hospital. Instead, it was a video of him having kinky sex with a prostitute—and a blow-up doll. He then gave the prostitute five hundred credits out of his campaign account."

Xenia snickered. "I thought that was an urban legend about Humans."

"That's not even the worst one. Another senator actually got caught breaking into his rival's campaign headquarters. When arrested, he said he broke in himself because he was afraid to hire criminals. Thought they'd rat him out or try to extort him."

"Obviously, he was much better off doing the job himself," Tom mumbled.

"Ironically, he hired a really sleazy lawyer who got him off all the charges on technicalities," Samantha said. "He then proceeded to run as the candidate who 'isn't afraid to get his hands dirty.' Called it the

'American Way.' Claimed it proved he would work hard in Congress for his constituents."

"He didn't win, did he?" Xenia's mouth twitched like it couldn't decide whether it was amused or horrified.

"He came pretty close. His opponent only won by a few percentage points." Samantha glanced at Tom. "The point is, our government is run by people so stupid it's even obvious to the other stupid people. The other Earth countries are the same, not to mention the UNE. Nobody trusts the government. And if they don't trust our government, they're really not going to trust yours."

Tom nodded. "I get it now. You're right." He shoved back his chair, sighed like someone who hadn't slept since before the wormhole was rediscovered, and turned toward the wall. "I'll get to work finding another scapegoat."

"No, don't do that," Samantha said, and Xenia looked at her in surprise. "Banfrey is fine, but we want to focus on Fisk, not the low-level criminal who helped him. A Human destabilized the wormhole, and the People innocently destroyed an artifact trying to fix it. Now, someone on the Council has to take the fall for knowing about the Protector's vulnerabilities and failing to fix them."

"We can't—" Xenia started.

"We didn't—" Tom said.

"Doesn't matter. I don't care. My people will believe it whether it's true or not. You can't say the whole Council knew and hid it from everyone, but you can throw one Councilmember under the bus—make them take the fall—say they knew. It doesn't have to be a career-ending move. This person makes a statement that he or she knew and chose not to tell anyone, even those on the Council, for security reasons. They point out the corruption of the device as the precise reason they couldn't tell anyone—including their own people and even other Councilmembers. A Human destabilizing the wormhole will make their actions look excusable and spread the blame around as evenly as possible. Now, who do you want to throw to the wolves?"

FIFTY-FOUR

Vance was enjoying a cold beer in the now-packed Wormhole in the Wall, wishing Samantha was around to freak out the locals, when he heard the news from the holo over the bar. The anchor, hearing something in his earplant, suddenly sat up straight, stopped speaking in the middle of a sentence about the new mining operation in the Fotora sector, waited for the cameras to zoom in closer on his genetically perfected face, then announced that in the space of a few hours, the scientific crew repairing the wormhole had found and accidentally destroyed an artifact from the Ancestors.

While the anchor continued talking, somehow managing to keep a serious look plastered on his handsome face—did he practice that in the mirror?—the bar quickly went from its usual low-level squalor to the next level of Loud, Drunk, and Completely Right. It reminded him of the night that everything changed, when the first Person attacked a Human ship and started this whole fucking mess. Did that moron even know why his girlfriend lost him, that she, also being a moron, thought that dating a doctor would allow her to steal the cancer cure? Truly an idea worthy of a Human. It wasn't like People doctors just left that sort of thing lying around. Anyway, it wasn't a simple formula, it was a complicated treatment plan with several layers and multiple drugs, but being idiots, the Humans involved thought they could just send a spy in to steal something simple.

As the noise in the bar increased, he pushed the memories away and ordered another drink. Two people sat down to his left, talking loudly. One was Haylea and one was a man with squinty eyes who looked like he'd have a hard time believing New Atlantis was round without proof. Unfortunately, he hadn't even started drinking yet and he was already Loud and Completely Right.

"I'm telling you, if Samantha isn't released by noon tomorrow, all hell's going to break loose," he said to Haylea. "Even without this latest issue."

Vance stopped studying the bottom of his glass and tried to unobtrusively give the two a second glance. He'd been wondering what had happened to Sam since her arrest. Haylea's media releases simply said she was being held for questioning and the station was working to get the charges dropped. But Hank said he hadn't been able to visit her since the day of her arrest, and when Vance tried to see her the next day, he was told she wasn't allowed visitors. Against his better judgment, he nudged his stool closer to the two.

"Haylea, the guy's right. If you know why they're keeping her with no evidence, I'd like to hear it." He leaned around her and offered his hand to Loud and Completely Right, who he could now tell was Human. "Doctor Vance. I'm Samantha's friend."

"Oh, so you're the one!" He heartily shook Vance's hand. "Good to meet you. She said you were one of the few People who didn't treat her like an idiot."

"No reason to." Vance waved his hand over the automated menu. "Next round's on me for…." He glanced at the Human.

"My name's Lee—I'm Samantha's old boss from *Glass*. She was doing some freelance work for us here on the station—" He shot a look at Haylea, who was studying the bottom of her glass as if the secret to fixing the wormhole was written on the bottom. "That is, until she was arrested."

"I told you, I don't know anything," she said. "Just that they found some technical reason to hold her for another day or two. We all know she's innocent, and Five Alpha's lawyers are doing everything they can to get her out."

"Knowing Sam, she's probably enjoying the media attention and writing the story of her unjust incarceration," Lee said as their drinks arrived. "I guarantee you, I've done everything I can to keep the story in the spotlight—and not just me. Everyone at *Glass* knows she would never do this."

And that was when things got ugly.

"Oh, look, another Earther defending the tacky Human bartender," boomed the voice of a Drunk and Completely Right idiot. A large man in a station laborer's uniform crowded the three of them against the bar, and he wasn't alone—he'd brought two Drunk and Completely Right friends.

"I'm so sick of you Human sympathizers." One of the friends scratched his ass absentmindedly.

"We don't want any trouble." Vance turned back to his drink and hoped that would be the end of it.

"No, you just want to sit here and deny that the Humans just ruined the wormhole for all of us," yelled the third Drunk and Completely Right Idiot, a woman with a long ponytail and a short skirt. Unfortunately, the revealing clothes suggested she lifted weights a lot more than Vance, who considered himself lucky if he had time to run the around the station twice a week. Vance glanced at Lee, who shrugged and turned his attention back to his own beer.

Unfortunately, Drunk and Completely Right in a Short Skirt had other ideas. She grabbed Vance by the shoulder and jerked him around to face her, yanking him off his stool.

"I don't think you people understand just how much the Humans have fucked things up," she yelled.

"Get your hands off me." Vance shoved her just hard enough to make her back up—he hoped. His aim might have been better before his second beer. Or third.

"No, this dope doesn't appreciate that we're all out of work now because there's no wormhole traffic." The ass-scratcher glared at Vance. Then he grabbed Lee's shoulder and yanked him off the stool, too.

Lee had only just sat down to his drink, and he'd probably been in a lot of emotionally charged situations while gathering news. He stepped toward the ass-scratcher, while the guy tried to yank him forward. This surprised the scratcher and threw him off-balance, or what passed for balance considering his current state of intoxication. He stumbled, taking a swing at Lee, who swiftly stepped aside, leaving the punch to land—

Right in Vance's face, he realized a second too late. As the ass-scratcher's fist connected with his jaw, his first thought was, I hope that guy was scratching his ass through his pants at least.

His second thought was, The next time I get drunk, I'm doing it alone in my apartment.

His third thought was, Haylea has a great aim.

"Funny you should mention dopes," she said, as the scratcher stumbled into the tall Drunk and Completely Right Idiot, who so far had done nothing but watch his friends. "Did you know that's a Human term? I guess you're a sympathizer too, since you've adopted their dialect."

"Whadidyousay?" asked Drunk and Completely Right in a Short Skirt.

"My friend, Samantha, told me about the origin of the word on Earth." Haylea passed her hand under the auto sanitizer mounted on the bar. It wasn't bleeding, but it had touched the ass-scratcher's face, after all. "Dope was slang for marijuana, and when the Humans get stoned, they usually get even dumber—her words, not mine, right? So they started calling people who were acting dumber than Humans usually act dopes."

"So you're friends with a Human, huh?" asked Drunk and Completely Right in a Short Skirt. She took a step closer to Haylea, then looked over at Vance as if she thought he'd be easier to beat up. "Well, have you ever asked why her People want to ruin our economy? It's not our fault they're so stupid they can't cure cancer themselves! Don't they know destabilizing the Divide will only prevent their own people from getting the cure?"

"It's not all of them, it's a small number of idiots," Haylea said. "You're just making assumptions without facts, the way so many Humans do."

"Hey, is that the Human walking in?" asked the tall Drunk and Completely Right, just as Vance worried that Haylea was about to make the situation worse instead of better.

He cautiously glanced back at the door, trying to keep the Drunk and Completely Rights in his line of sight at the same time. There was Samantha, wearing what looked like a brand-new black dress and high-heeled boots. She had a new haircut as well, and didn't look like she'd been mistreated in prison. In fact, she looked more like she'd been to a spa.

Flanking Samantha was Councilmember Xenia on the right, and a guy who looked vaguely familiar to Vance, as his eyes darted frantically around the crowded bar. Councilmember Tom? He'd aged a lot since he was last on holo — two days ago. He pulled his jacket tighter around him, as if it would protect him from a bunch of drunken morons.

Not that he had anything to worry about, since his group was tailed by six dark-suited security people.

Haylea rushed up to Samantha and tried to give her a hug. One of the dark suits stepped between them, and she pulled up short. Samantha flapped her arm at the suit like she was swatting a fly. "She's a friend."

He stepped back but kept his hand on the gun at his hip — an unspoken warning to everyone in the bar not to start any trouble in front of the important political people.

Haylea finally hugged Samantha, who politely hugged her back even though the expression on her face suggested she thought of hugging as a dumb Human custom she wished she'd left behind on Earth.

"Are you okay?" Lee wandered carefully up to the newcomers as the rest of the bar remained silent and staring. Sam shot a glare at the suits and they let him pass as well.

"Are you?" Haylea demanded, jumping back from Samantha and staring at her. "What did they do to you? No one would tell me anything! That lawyer I hired said he couldn't get you out until eight hours from now, and that they'd moved you to a secure location for questioning. I was afraid I'd never see you again, and of course I knew you were innocent — "

"And these people have been telling the media nothing." Lee's eyes flickered from Samantha to Tom to Xenia, as if he wasn't sure what the biggest story was. "I hope you'll take the time to answer some questions for *Glass News*, since you're here. Let's start with the most important question — since I see Samantha is no longer restrained, does that mean she's been cleared of all charges? Did you use your political clout to get the charges dropped, or did the FIB officially — "

"Yes, the FIB cleared her of all charges." Xenia held up a hand to stop the barrage of inquiries. "And we'll be happy to answer all your questions. In fact, we'd like to offer you an exclusive interview, if you're willing to join us right now."

Lee's mouth worked for a moment as he struggled to find an answer. He'd obviously been prepared to start shouting questions as the group left.

"I... I... of course... I'd be happy to accept the exclusive interview," he stammered.

"We'll need to go live very quickly," Samantha said. "I assured them that wouldn't be a problem."

"No," Lee said quickly. "Not at all."

"We'll need you, too," Samantha said to Haylea.

"Great." She looked at Vance. "Need me to punch anyone else for you?"

Vance looked around, but didn't see any sign of the Drunk and Completely Right Idiots. Apparently they'd melted into the background and out the door during the commotion—just when he was planning to kick their asses. Figured.

"I'll be fine, thanks."

"Good, then you'll both need to come with us right now," said Xenia. "We have very limited time."

"I need to stop and check something with Roble," Samantha glanced at her pad.

"Where are we going?" Lee asked.

"Back to jail," Xenia said calmly.

Vance headed back to the bar and ordered a drink to go.

FIFTY-FIVE

The jail cell didn't look any different than it had a day and a half earlier, with a lumpy-looking but surprisingly comfortable cot for the only furniture. The lighting cast a dim, washed out glow than reminded Samantha of every government installation she'd ever seen, from here to the DMV on Earth. And yet, in spite of the fact the protective field around the room was invisible, the space looked bigger and more open today. It was just a trick of the mind, but she couldn't shake the impression.

"What the hell are we supposed to do about the toilet?" Haylea stared at the room like she was visiting an impoverished slum on Earth and wondering how to keep the soles of her hot pink heels from getting dirty.

"I'm sure you'll think of something. That is your area." Xenia dragged two chairs into the room and shoved them in front of the bed.

"This better work." Haylea pushed a chair in front of the toilet. "I hope no one has to go before the show starts."

"I think we can all hold it for fifteen minutes." Samantha sat in the center of the ring of chairs. Haylea plunked down to her right, and Xenia sat stiffly to her left. Lee, as the interviewer, was across from all three of them, pulling up his own chair as a bot rolled into the room with a table. After a few seconds, Samantha realized it was one of the antiques they'd used for the delegates' party. In fact, the chairs had been there too.

Haylea was getting the hang of this marketing thing, after all.

Lee began the interview with the usual bullshit chatter, introducing and thanking everyone for joining him and recapping the circumstances that had led to this "current crisis." That was the part of journalism Samantha liked the least—the dull repetition of the same facts, the thanking people for taking the time to lie to your face, the fact that news was supposed to be exciting but it was mostly boring and predictable. The artful reconstruction of the truth required more skill and presented a more interesting challenge.

And right now, she had one hell of a challenge.

"So we'll get right to the current topic of concern," Lee said after two or three minutes. "The Human/People conflict has degraded considerably in the last few days with a declaration of war from the Humans. We'll get to the Wormhole Problem in a moment, but first I'd like to address another major issue of the last few days—the arrest and imprisonment of you, Samantha, immediately after the Five Alpha air filtration failure in which you could have died."

"As you know, I was cleared of all charges." She'd chosen Lee because she knew he would never sidestep a landmine when he could stomp right on it. As she'd told Haylea three times earlier, a reporter who lobbed softball questions was the last thing they needed if they wanted people to take the interview seriously. "Some evidence was planted in the Wormhole in the Wall, the bar where I work here on Five Alpha."

"You're saying someone wanted you to look guilty?"

"Exactly. What better target than one of the few Humans on the station? And unfortunately, the security personnel here didn't do much investigating before locking me up." She flicked a hand around the cell. "Even though their evidence could have been linked to anyone who visited a very busy bar in the past week, they blamed me. I'm sure it's because I'm Human."

Xenia plowed in at that point, apparently unable to hold her tongue any longer. "For the record, Samantha was cleared of those charges by the FIB and released the day before yesterday. Security personnel on Five Alpha were only instructed to hold her for questioning for twelve hours. They used their own judgment to detain her further. Our government regrets the situation, and I personally ensured her release when I arrived here."

"So where has she been the last day and a half?" Lee glanced back and forth between Xenia and Samantha.

"Xenia asked for my help in ending the current conflict," Samantha explained.

"I'd like to add that no one here wanted her arrested," Haylea jumped in. "After hearing of her detainment, I got our lawyers working on her release immediately. I also helped one of our AI specialists uncover the evidence that cleared her. I never once believed she had anything to do with the wormhole incident."

"Let's talk about that." Lee shifted to face his other camera angle. "We're all aware of the blame bombardment from both sides. Since we've established that you had nothing to do with it, Samantha, do you have any thoughts on who did?"

She nodded. "It's important to remember there are several separate incidents here, Lee. The unexpected destabilization of the wormhole appears to have been the deliberate act of one individual named Leon Fisk. The Guard is interrogating the People individual who sold him the antimatter weapon, by the way.

"The recent destruction of the Ancestors' artifact is a separate event that has been blamed on both sides, but reports from the scientists at the scene suggest it was most likely a tragic accident."

"The most recent report I read showed strong evidence it was rigged to blow up if anyone spent an extended period of time trying to break into it," Lee countered.

"We're talking about a device that was put in place thousands of years ago," Xenia said. "Who knows what our ancestors were thinking? It may have been intended for protection. Tampering with the wormhole could potentially harm people in the area—just look at what happened here on Five Alpha."

"It could also be that the accuracy of the device has been compromised by age," Haylea added.

"Those are all possibilities." Lee nodded and studied his pad, looking up every few seconds to make eye contact with his audience. "But there is another possibility we have to address—the Ancestors wanted to prevent Humans from following us here, at all costs."

"Yes, our ancestors have made mistakes where Earth is concerned, but those were usually based in a desire to help its inhabitants," Xenia said.

"You mean the Humans. None of us knows what our ancestors were thinking four thousand years ago when they programmed the device." Lee shifted his attention to Samantha. "As one of the few Earthers on this side of the Divide, knowing you may be trapped here for some time if the wormhole can't be restabilized, what do you think? Do you believe this was just an accidental detonation of a four-thousand-year-old self-destruct sequence, was it intentionally caused by one deranged individual, or was one of our governments involved?"

"I can tell you that the People'a government had nothing to do with it," Xenia said, even though she hadn't been asked. "I assume none of the Human government officials wished to go on record about their innocence tonight?"

"The Human delegation declined to reveal their whereabouts for security reasons," Lee said. "They've released a statement claiming no responsibility. However, I was speaking to Samantha."

She took a deep breath. "Like you, Lee, I've been a journalist for many years. As a result, I tend not to believe anything without proof. I wouldn't rule out any of the options you mentioned. But I also know how hard the People have been hammered in the press since the wormhole started destabilizing. It doesn't make sense for them to blow up the Ancestors' artifact — it only makes them look worse and increases the likelihood of retaliation from the Humans. The same goes for attacking the Divide."

"But by shutting down the wormhole, they can prevent Human military ships from getting here in a timely manner," Lee said.

"True," Samantha said. "But there are already a lot of Earthers on this side of the Divide, and knowing how transparent my government usually is, if I had to guess I'd say the Humans have hidden ships and weapons over here. The People would be taking a huge risk by shutting down the wormhole, and so would the Humans. As for the artifact, there's no proof it was designed to do anything but alert the Ancestors if there was ever a problem with the Divide."

"Well, on that subject, let's talk about how the Protector was temporarily disabled by a corrupted FIB device."

"I apologize for that," Xenia said. "There have always been security risks where the Protector is concerned. I know I should have brought that particular vulnerability before the Council instead of hiding it."

"Why did you do that?" Lee asked.

Xenia rearranged her face into an approximate facsimile of contrition. "At the time, I was concerned that the Humans would learn of the Protector's weakness and try to gain control. On the one hand, I knew that telling both our peoples the truth was the right thing to do, but I also knew Human/People tensions were... increasing. I couldn't take the risk that the wormhole could become a casualty of a few deranged individuals—on either side. I knew if I brought it before the Council they could vote to release the information, and while I saw the merits in that, I felt I had a duty to protect the Divide for all of us.

"For a long time, I've worried that I made the wrong choice. But after someone found and seized control of the device anyway—a Human named Leon Fisk, who we believe died trying to escape to the Other Side—I realized that my concern to protect the Divide was correct. I may have gone about things the wrong way, and I should have trusted my colleagues to make the right decision, but my worries were not unwarranted. In the end, even Shade couldn't protect the wormhole, despite their best efforts."

"That's an interesting story," Lee said. "How did someone find out about the Protector's flaw and take control of it?"

"We're not sure, but we don't believe Fisk was working alone. In fact, we have a promising lead that he purchased the antimatter weapon from this man—a Person named Banfrey." Xenia gestured and a holo display showed the guy sneering like the evil genius he was now supposed to be.

"You're saying a Person sold this Human fringe group tech to destroy the Divide?" Samantha asked.

Xenia nodded. "We have him in custody now. He may or may not have known what the antimatter torpedo's intended use was, but he's been dealing in undocumented weapons for years."

Lee turned to Samantha. "What do you think? Do you believe Councilmember Xenia's version of this story?"

"I don't think she has any reason to lie at this point," Samantha said. "Obviously mistakes have been made, but I think we all want to end this conflict. Her concerns about someone damaging the Protector to corrupt the wormhole were valid, especially considering the artifact's self-destruction when we got too close. It suggests our ancestors were worried something like this would happen, Protector or not. That leads us to the report the scientific survey team released — there are some interesting things here."

Lee tilted his head in her direction. "Like what?"

"I'd like to show you something." Samantha waved a hand at Lee's bot, which already had the report. Off to the side, on the monitor that showed the audience's current view, a graphic popped up. "Like you, Lee, most people are focusing on the blame game, picking apart this report to see if it makes one side look guiltier than the other.

"But if you aren't looking for that, you'll notice the section that starts on page eighteen. Not being a scientist myself, I wasn't sure what it meant, so I contacted an acquaintance from the station, Roble, who's currently working with the scientific crew trying to fix the wormhole. He was there when the artifact met its untimely demise, and he confirmed what I suspected this section meant."

"And what's that?" Xenia's eyebrows jerked together with concern.

"Roble is an expert on AI and computer systems." Samantha said slowly, knowing much of the audience was reading the report and listening to the show at the same time. "He's the one who discovered the security recordings proving my innocence, by the way.

"But before the device destructed, the crew's bots spent several minutes attempting to access its onboard computer system. Their AI extrapolated hundreds of thousands of possible programming algorithms based on the oldest tech the People have.

"Roble and his colleagues have spent hours analyzing the data obtained before the device destructed. According to this section of the report, the reason they had so much trouble breaking in was because it was radically different than what they expected. So different, in fact, that the probability of the device being designed by the People, even four thousand years ago, is less than two percent."

"You don't mean the Humans designed it?" Xenia said with a loud laugh that cut off after two seconds as she realized how insensitive she probably sounded. "I mean, ah, no disrespect, of course. It's just that the Humans were less technologically advanced at the time that the device was created, obviously. That's all. I certainly didn't mean —"

"That's not what I'm saying at all." Samantha smiled at Xenia, because her insensitivity was about to be forgotten in favor of a much worse slight — she was about to look stupid herself. "What the best Human and People scientists have determined is that there's a possibility this device wasn't created by either of our peoples."

✳
FIFTY-SIX

"Blame it on aliens? Is that seriously the best you could do?" Haylea yelled as they left the security office, in the company of half a dozen of Xenia's guards. "You didn't even run it by me first?"

"I wasn't working for you, I was working for Xenia and there wasn't time." Samantha consulted her pad—*which of the 200 new messages to ignore first? Wait, better see if any of them were important.* "And I didn't make that up. Did you read Roble's report? Someone would have interpreted that and it would have been all over the news within hours anyhow. This way Lee and I broke a big story, and it's a good distraction from the blame game."

"So that's what this is now?" Haylea stopped in her tracks and grabbed Samantha's arm, halting her. "You work for the People? I thought you hated both our governments. I thought you wanted to stay here and continue the Crazy Human bartender routine and get in the faces of all the idiots who didn't like you. Your people have a word for this, don't they? It's sellout."

Samantha sighed. "No, I don't work for Xenia or the People government any more than I ever worked for mine, despite what everyone here thinks. I agreed to help her because she wants what I want—and what you want—for this stupid fucking war to end. Don't you think this station will be busier after it stops?"

"With no functioning wormhole?"

"Again, did you read this report?" She waved at her pad. "The wormhole is still functional. All we have to do is re-stabilize it with exotic matter."

"Oh, is that all?" But Haylea wasn't yelling quite loudly enough to be heard back on Earth any more.

"The sooner we all start pretending to get along, the sooner we can find that out, and business can start flowing to the station again. Pointing out this info about the artifact bought us time, Haylea. Eventually people will realize whoever built the Divide is long gone and probably not a concern to us now. But in the meantime, what we just did will distract everyone for a few days, while the Council tries to make peace with the Humans and the Wormhole Recovery crew tries to fix the wormhole. Now if you'll get out of my way, I'd like to help Roble and the science crew by publicizing their mission."

Haylea shuffled from foot to foot. "So you do want to stay here? I mean, even if you're not stuck on this side of the wormhole?"

"Of course I do. I told you, I want to annoy the People as much as possible." She sidestepped Haylea and started walking again. "I want to remind them why they left in the first place, and why they can't keep up this we-feel-guilty-about-the-Humans thing they have going on. If they start giving my people everything they want, the whole fucking galaxy is going down in flames."

FIFTY-SEVEN

"I'm going to assume you were as shocked by that announcement as I was," Carlton said from the wall screen the second Xenia walked into the living quarters on her ship. Her communication with the Council leader was obscured by various security protocols—her AI automatically heightened its usual strong precautions whenever another Councilmember called. The clock under the holo image showed that Carlton had been waiting for her to arrive—he must be really mad.

"Of course I was." Xenia played along as she tossed her coat in the general direction of the coat closet, where a crawler would eventually collect it.

"I would never have permitted releasing a story like that without first seeking Council approval."

"I didn't want to conceal important information from the Council again." A snipe at Carlton for making her take the blame in the Protector mess.

"How did that reporter latch onto something so obscure in a scientific report, anyway? Why was she even reading that thing when she was supposed to be helping you with this CC crisis? I can't believe you went to all that trouble to implicate yourself and she diverted attention to this Human tabloid tripe!"

"I'm sure she was doing just that—looking for a diversion—and she found one. I thought we were just having an honest discussion about Human/People interaction in recent weeks."

"Right," Carlton said in a tone that suggested it was anything but. "Do you think she made our problem worse?"

Xenia went to the bar and pressed a pre-programmed button for her favorite drink, the Divide and Conquer—equal parts tequila and a spiced drink made popular by the Morovian mining colony Hopper. "Not at all. She got both sides focused on a common problem and made our involvement in the wormhole issue fade into the background, after I explained it in a satisfactory way."

"But the bigger implications...." Carlton stared at something in the corner of his office she couldn't see. "We're still able to communicate through the Divide most of the time, with some interference. All the Humans saw that broadcast, too."

"So?"

"Did you know most of the Human government wouldn't tell their own citizens right away if it found evidence of intelligent life elsewhere in the galaxy? The only reason they know about us is because a civilian found the wormhole and blasted the story to the news media before their government could do anything about it." He drummed his fingers on the desk, a huge monstrosity that was almost a thousand years old. Despite the fact that it was oiled and maintained every day, Xenia worried about fingers drumming too hard on such a fragile piece of history.

"That's a public safety thing, or so they say." She collected her drink as it popped out of the bar.

Carlton spread his hands in a why-do-they-do-these-things gesture. "We've never needed to lie to our People about scientific discoveries for public safety."

She took her drink to the couch, where she flopped down and kicked off her shoes. It was an hour past the new day rollover. "There was an issue. Hundreds of their years ago."

"An issue?"

"Their tech was very limited." She gestured at the empty space between herself and his image. "Their communication was sound only. No images. News came from a radio."

"So, the issue?"

"Radio broadcast. It was an entertainment piece made to sound like a news piece. Said aliens were invading."

Carlton's eyes widened with understanding. "The Humans thought it was real and reacted badly?"

Xenia snorted. "That's sort of the understatement. Some of them were jumping off bridges and buildings. No, I mean that literally—they really committed suicide."

Understanding made an emergency evacuation from Carlton's face. "Because they couldn't stand the idea that there were more intelligent creatures in the universe than them? What hubris! Why didn't this happen when they found us?"

Xenia sipped her drink, swallowed while shaking her head, the tequila burning the back of her throat. "It wasn't that there were more intelligent creatures out there. I doubt they even thought that far into it. The broadcast said they were being attacked and the aliens were going to kill everyone."

"So they jumped off buildings to save these attacking aliens the ammunition?"

Xenia set her drink on the table. "I don't know why they did it. Their people had a lot of strange ideas back then. I would say that their collective intelligence has improved marginally since that time, which is why they didn't react as badly to finding us. Also, they found out we weren't really aliens and weren't trying to kill them very quickly."

"Which leads us back to the wormhole." He started drumming again. "Do you believe this report is accurate? We didn't build this thing?"

She shrugged. "It makes sense. In all these years, we've never been able to build another one, despite all the technological advances we've made since then. There's no historical record of how it was stabilized."

"Data from that time is limited." He studied the display. "Maybe there was an unusually high number of language changes back then —"

"You know that isn't likely." She stared at him until he looked up to meet her gaze. "There would still be commonalities in the language. Our scientists couldn't find one common word between the language of the artifact and our language database, which includes a piece of code from within a few hundred years of the Great Escape."

Carlton nodded. "So what's the threat level for the intelligence that built this thing? Obviously, they're technologically advanced enough to do us significant damage. Do you think they would, at this point?"

She picked up the tumbler, drained her drink, and banged the glass down on the table. "That wormhole has been there at least four thousand years. We've been bumbling around this side of the Divide all this time, and we've found no trace of other intelligent life. Whoever built that thing is long, long gone from this area of the galaxy. I'm inclined to think the risk of them suddenly showing back up and starting another war is very low."

"But?" Carlton had heard the word in her voice without her saying it.

She stared at him over the ancient desk, watched his fingers beat a rhythm on the government's seal, a spacecraft lifting off against a setting sun. "But whoever built the thing put in a self-destruct to prevent tampering, and it was sending a signal just before the device self-destructed."

His fingers froze in mid-beat, middle finger hovering over the seal. For all his Human-sympathizing, he genuinely cared about the safety of his People. "So the builders could show up here soon."

"If they're still around, if the automated signal still works, if I'm right and there was one in the first place, if it still reaches something that can bounce the signal to wherever they are now." Xenia sighed. "There are too many variables to make an accurate assessment of the exact threat level. But my advice is to be prepared."

Carlton nodded. "That will work best with the Humans' help. The broadcast was the right idea, Xenia."

She stared at her empty glass. "Let's just hope we exaggerated our common problem. A lot."

"I'll demand an action plan from the military." Carlton cut the connection, and she was left sitting in a dark living room with a hundred questions and no answers.

FIFTY-EIGHT

Dealing with stress-related illnesses caused Dr. Vance a lot of stress. All day, all he'd done was tell people to calm down and prescribe pills to help them calm down, only to hear that he wasn't taking the "Human attack" or the "alien attack" seriously enough. One patient—an Earther, no less—found Vance's prescription for a mild sedative insufficient to deal with the "Human viral threat that's about to be unleashed."

"What threat would that be?" Vance looked at the clock on his pad.

"My people have been using viruses to kill each other for years." The patient, a pudgy forty-five-year-old named Kurt, leaned forward and lowered his voice, as if he was imparting a state secret. "Anthrax, Ebola, AIDS, Merona Virus. Haven't you done any reading about Earth diseases?"

"You have effective treatments for all those things now." He added "paranoia" to the patient's list of possible symptoms. "And only one of them was ever used as a biological weapon."

"That we know of." Kurt leaned back and folded his arms over his chest, wincing a little. He was still healing from the new heart Vance had put in last month, an hour-long procedure that Kurt had complained bitterly about because it cost "slightly more than three months' worth of hamburger meat from Earth."

"Just because our government got rid of the evidence doesn't mean they didn't unleash a disease intentionally. If someone dumped a new virus into our air supply, something you'd never seen before and had no vaccine or treatment for, what would you do? Prescribe a bunch of happy pills to make everyone feel better as they were killed off?"

"How long have you been on this side of the Divide?" Vance noted his medical assistant had checked in with the infirmary's AI and it was officially time for him to go off-duty—just as soon as he dispensed with this idiot.

"Three years." Kurt looked around the office as if he thought he could see a virus crawling through the air vents. "Been living downstairs since the war started and my company decided it didn't want to mine asteroids in this area anymore. They relocated some of the workers, but not all of us. Guess they didn't want to send a Human anywhere close to New Atlantis. They think we're going to blow up everything! Now I work in a store with no customers."

Vance considered pointing out that Kurt himself had just suggested the Humans were going to attack the station, but decided it would be a waste of his time. "According to your chart, you've been on this station half a year."

"So?"

"So in that time you haven't bothered to educate yourself on our air filtration system or you'd know that it screens for microbial threats. If anyone released a biological weapon it would be detected and isolated immediately, and few if any individuals would be exposed. Anyone who was would be flagged, located, quarantined, and treated."

"You mean imprisoned against their will?"

Vance gritted his teeth. "You'd prefer that the people you think are planning to attack the station walk around and continue trying—ineffectually, to be fair—but trying to spread some sort of deadly virus?"

Kurt started sputtering. "You're... you're... twisting my words. That's not what I meant."

"I don't care what you meant." He pressed a button to finalize Kurt's prescriptions. "The medical establishment here isn't like the medical establishment on Earth. We don't care about your feelings. We know you already think we're jerks, so we don't waste a lot of time trying to change your mind."

"That's obvious."

"So I'm going to tell you the truth. You are paranoid, uneducated, and not physically ill. The best I can do is prescribe medication to ease your anxiety. That will not make the imaginary threat of a biological attack go away, but since it's not real I don't care. If you calm down, you'll feel better and you'll be less likely to aggravate what is a genuinely delicate situation on this station. We are probably safe from large outside attacks, but the threat of inside violence among idiot individuals such as yourself is indeed very high. I can't make you take your medication, but I strongly suggest you do."

He stood up and walked out, leaving Kurt still sputtering in his seat.

Vance went back to his office and peeled off his jacket. Kurt was an idiot, but he wasn't the only one—and it wasn't just the Earthers. When the Humans had first showed up seven years ago, the whole People medical community had been abuzz with rumors that were just as crazy—the Humans were coming to spread a biological weapon that only they were immune to, the Humans were all dosed with anti-Hazing drugs, the Humans were going to dose them with a new Hazing drug and take all their technological info….

Well, at least his people had outgrown *those* paranoid ideas!

Just as he was about to leave his office, the AI chimed. "It's one of your former patients, Merelyn. Would you like me to direct her to the medical station? I'm sure Doctor Falar can—"

"Merelyn?" Vance stopped at his desk. "She's here? She's not alone, is she?"

"Yes, she is. I can direct her to—"

"No, I'll see her."

The door slid open and Vance stared in shock. Merelyn walked smoothly, without a trace of a limp, and both sides of her mouth were turned up in a smile. "Doctor Vance! I'm so glad to see you."

"And I'm glad to see you—like this. You recovered while you were on the *Solara*?"

That was the medical ship he'd transferred her to during the air crisis, along with the other infirmary patients. The ship's doctor was supposed to transfer them back next week, but maybe they'd arrived early.

"I did. The doctor there was impressed with how quickly I improved. I needed therapy to get everything working again, but now I'm just like I was before my stroke—and it's all thanks to you."

"Me?" He had just started a new treatment protocol when the wormhole disaster happened, so he'd only given Merelyn three of ten doses he'd planned to use in combination with regenerative therapy. The crisis forced him to discontinue the treatment, which he'd planned to resume as soon as she returned.

"Doctor Falar said your last treatment must have worked with fewer doses than you thought necessary," she said. "She ran some brain scans and showed me where the neurons were regenerating, making new connections. Then she gave me medication to help them make the right connections again. It would never have been possible without the treatment you devised."

"That's... great." Vance frowned. "But why didn't she let me know?"

"The *Solara* is having major problems with its communications array. It got hit in the wormhole incident." Merelyn took a seat on the couch. "Once Falar cleared me for travel, I transferred to a smaller ship that was heading back here. I wanted to thank you in person."

"Well, I'm glad you're doing better. I'll be very happy to see your records when the *Solara* gets its comm problems fixed." Vance sat across from her. "The treatment I used was designed specifically for your situation, but I believe I can use the same template to help other patients with brain injuries."

"I'm happy to help you in any way I can." Merelyn cleared her throat. "I, uh, also need a favor from you."

"A favor? What is it?"

"You know that my daughter got control of my life when I was incapacitated."

"Ah, yes." Vance tried to suppress a grimace. He remembered the self-centered, greedy woman who dumped her mother in an institution and never once visited, but she was Merelyn's daughter, and Merelyn probably felt obligated to love her anyway.

"While I'm grateful that she placed me in your care, and I was able to get the treatment I needed, my accountant tells me she didn't use such good judgment with my finances." Merelyn took a sudden interest in the geometric pattern of the rug beneath the coffee table. "According to my lawyer, I'll need a statement from you that I'm fully recovered and able to conduct my own affairs now. Doctor Falar already signed one, but the courts will be more convinced by the doctor who's been treating me for the last two years."

"Of course. I'll do a quick exam, then I'll be happy to write a statement for you." He pulled out a scanner and waved it around her. "What do you plan to do now?"

"I'm going to apply to work with the scientific crew studying the wormhole problem." She smiled. "I worked on an FTL research project when I was at the university. We were very close to success when I had my stroke, and my colleagues haven't made any progress since. We were tackling the problem in a different way—not using a wormhole but curving spacetime around a ship."

Vance nodded. "I imagine you could be very useful to Umora's research project. And to be honest, they need all the help they can get right now."

✳

FIFTY-NINE

"Is your intention to inject exotic matter into the Divide to re-stabilize it or create a new stable wormhole?" Merelyn asked Umora, as they sat in her closet-sized office on the research ship. Data pads and holo models rose almost to the ceiling. A display on the desktop updated with new messages every few seconds, its light flickering over the other scientist's face.

"Right now, of course, we're pressed for time. That damn Human and her latest CC stunt have put pressure on us to solve this problem immediately." Umora laughed, but it sounded stressed. "But the truth is we don't have much time before the Divide completely collapses. We need to work fast, but if we inject too much or too little exotic matter, or release it at the wrong time, we could hasten the collapse instead of preventing it."

"I understand the Council named you head of the Wormhole Restoration Project after less than a day of deliberation—and, I assume, they increased your funding exponentially."

STUPID HUMANS

A strangled sound that might have started as humor but ended as pain. "For the first time in my career, funding is not a problem. But now I have a bigger one—those journalists talking about the work we do as if a fix is possible any minute now. We would need years of testing before we could determine if we have the right method for re-stabilizing the Divide. We can't afford to make costly mistakes, as I'm sure you understand. But we don't have years before we lose our opportunity to fix it."

Merelyn lifted her chin. "I do understand. I ensured the safety of my crew and all settlements by conducting the Lightning Project tests light-years away from any inhabited areas. While the project did not go as planned, we learned a lot from the data and no one was harmed."

"I understand the project was flushed after the test."

"Yes." Her palms grew sweaty as they rested on the chair arms. "I suffered some medical problems and had to take an extended leave of absence from the university. My predecessor was unable to find a solution to the unexpected problems we encountered in the test, and he opted to embark on a different area of research. Now, you're probably wondering how my experience with Lightning qualifies me to work on the wormhole project. I believe that my—"

"Actually, that's not why I agreed to the interview." Umora shoved some pads off the nearest pile on her desk, revealing a half-eaten sandwich. She picked it up and took a bite. "I have enough people to argue over how we should attempt to stabilize the Divide. You're here because I need to plan for the worst-case scenario, as the Humans like to say."

"You want me to work on building a new wormhole?"

"No. I want you to go back to working on Lightning. Like you said, I have all the funding I need now. If we fail to fix the wormhole, and there's a strong possibility we might, I need to have other projects in the works to address the problems that will cause. Finding, expanding, and stabilizing a new wormhole is one project, but we've been working on that for years without success."

"You want me to continue my work on Lightning?" Merelyn couldn't believe it. All the time she'd spent studying the data, she didn't think she'd ever get another chance to complete the project. Even if her health problems were cured, the university had not been happy that they'd funded a failure as spectacular as Lightning, and it seemed unlikely they would make that mistake twice.

"If you think you can solve the problems with it, obviously. Let's talk about that." Umora pulled up the data file Merelyn had studied for the past three years. "Have you determined why the protective bubble failed?"

"I suspect the problem was in the design for the bubble generator. Based on these calculations" —she flapped her hand at Umora and her AI sent them to the project director's display— "we could correct the problem by adjusting those parameters."

Umora looked at the data, and her face deepened from a frown to a grimace. "Do you have any idea how expensive that would be, how far away from inhabited areas we'd have to test, and how hard it would be to get approval?"

Merelyn sent more data to the director's display. "I'm sure our approvals will go through much faster with the political pressure to find a travel solution between our solar systems. A recommendation from the Wormhole Restoration Project Director would help, especially if you stressed that the odds of saving the wormhole were small."

She pointed to the display on Umora's desk. "That's a letter from my old associate, Harek, who you've also called in for an interview. He's attached a list of all the equipment we used on the Lightning Project that the university gave him permission to utilize on this research. It's most of what we need, which reduces our costs a great deal. You'll note the final number, which isn't nearly as much as the Lightning Project cost. Also, you just said funding wasn't a problem.

"As for where we'd test, this area is sparsely populated once you get away from the Divide. I can recommend a suitable testing area. Even if this project fails, what we learn could help in more ways than we can predict. Now, what do you say?"

Umora leaned back in her chair, the grimace relaxing into an almost neutral expression. "When can you start?"

SIXTY

Haylea had never seen so many new reservation requests in the entire year she'd worked at Five Alpha as she did within two hours of the broadcast. Now, three days later, she was fully scheduled for the next four months. Apparently everyone, Human and People alike, wanted to look for aliens.

It broke her heart, but she actually had to start turning paying customers down because she was out of rooms.

"Haylea, I've been trying to reach you all day." Roble's voice cut through her haze of juggling rooms and offering to sublet empty apartments.

"I've been busy." She didn't look up.

"I know. I hear you've scheduled every room and apartment on this station for the next year."

"Just four months, but I'm still scheduling people that far out. Everyone wants an alien artifact-hunting vacation now. It's the new thing."

"Well, I just wanted to tell you that the Wormhole Restoration Project—that's what we're calling it now, the team to—"

"Yes, I know." Haylea flapped a hand over her shoulder for him to continue. The sooner he finished, the sooner she could stop ignoring him.

"Well, Umora has refocused our mission and we're leaving tomorrow. One ship is going to stay and work on stabilizing the wormhole or building a new one, while the other is —"

"I've seen the news."

"Right, so I'm going to be on the ship going out to the Halyard Sector. I'll be working with Merelyn —the scientist behind the Lightning Project? I know it didn't work, but it was so close. If her health problems hadn't stopped her work, she could have...."

"Mm-hmm."

"....so I'm going to be gone a long time, maybe a couple months. I just thought I'd stop by and —"

Her head popped up. "Then your apartment will be empty?"

" —and say... what?"

She spun around in her chair to look at him. "Your apartment will be empty for several months while you're gone?"

"Yes, but the automated system will maintain it. Why?"

"Because I can sublet it while you're gone! Don't worry, you'll make a five percent profit." She shoved a pad at him. "Here's the legal form you'll need to sign. It's standard."

Roble gaped at her. "I came to tell you I'm leaving for months and that I'll miss you and all you care about is making money off my apartment? Vance is right. I really am an idiot to care about you." He slapped the pad down on the table. "I will *not* sublet my apartment. It can stay empty —just like your bed, thanks to your scintillating personality and charm."

With that, he turned around and stormed out of her office, leaving Haylea wondering when Roble turned into such a jerk.

SIXTY-ONE

After months with very little work except running the bar and applying Band-Aids to Haylea's CC crises, Samantha suddenly found herself with more freelance jobs than she had time for. Her latest assignment was to cover the Wormhole Restoration Project with a focus on Umora's techniques. The angle was intriguing, but wouldn't be easy, since Umora was notoriously paranoid about people stealing her work. She wouldn't let journalists anywhere near her ship, and although she couldn't forbid her team from talking to the press, she *did* forbid them from discussing proprietary details.

From her research, Samantha knew most of the theories for improving interstellar travel involved building a new wormhole — or, more recently, repairing the one they had. Others called for a new type of travel, either punching a hole in spacetime — which had been attempted many times, resulting in numerous repair bills of a million credits or more — or using a drive that curved spacetime in front of and behind a ship with some sort of protective bubble.

She found some dry technical material released by Umora's university, which said nothing about the current project but described exotic matter in such detail that her eyes glazed over and her brain understood only that scientists were incredibly boring writers. After plodding her way through three pages, she gave up and switched to a Human site, where she downloaded a copy of *Quantum Theory for Dumbasses* on *Glass*'s tab. Unfortunately, it was so simplistic that she failed to learn anything she hadn't already managed to grasp from her research. Calls to every major scientific expert on the subject went to their messaging systems — they were all out working on the problem.

Her last call was to Roble, who she expected to duck her — after all, she'd been hearing about his outburst at Haylea for two days now. The CC director was so pissed, she must like the guy more than she cared to admit.

"Samantha! It's good to hear from you." Roble's face filled the wall screen in front of her couch.

She sat up and shoved her coffee cup onto the nearest table, surprised he'd answered. "It's good to talk to you again. I know you're busy, but — "

"How's Haylea doing? Is she still mad at me?" His eyebrows shot up hopefully. "Did she ask you to call and find out if I was mad at her?"

"Um, no. Haylea...." What was the best way out of this? Tell him the truth? No, he'd get distracted. But if she said Haylea cared, that would distract the dope, too. Shit. Might as well tell the truth.

"Haylea is really mad that *you* got mad at her for asking if she could sublet your apartment... and she's *really* mad that you suggested no one wants to have sex with her. But that's not why — "

"That's great!" He grinned. "If she's mad, it means she cares about me."

Samantha suppressed the urge to bang her head down on the table, mostly because she wasn't finished with her coffee yet.

"I'm glad to hear you're happy about that, but I wanted to ask you about the Wormhole Restoration Project."

Roble's face crumpled into a frown. "You know I'm not allowed to give details to journalists. Or anyone. Umora would shit a wormhole if she knew I was even talking to a reporter."

There was an image she wanted in her head. "I know you can't give me details. I'm just trying to understand the basics so I can explain the general ideas to my audience. I was hoping you could answer some questions about an article Umora published last year on the subject of spacetime curvature methods. Obviously, she's too busy working to talk to a reporter, right?"

Roble stuffed a cookie in his mouth. "Just a few questions. Meal time is almost over, and I need to call Haylea now that I know she's interested."

Great.

"In this paper, Umora discusses the possibilities of curving space-time. She says this method is too dangerous and ends up costing every university that tries it money. But she also adds that it's theoretically interesting, because if it could be made to work, it would solve some of the problems with wormhole travel."

Roble made a halfhearted swipe at the crumbs on his chin, knocking a few off but leaving most of them intact. "It's believed the bubble would shield the ship and its inhabitants from the effects of gravitational radiation."

"That's why we need to be put in cryosleep when we go through the Divide—to protect us from gravitational radiation, right?"

"Right. It's also why stations have to be very far out from the worm-hole. We saw with the destabilization that even—"

"I know." Samantha hoped she was cutting him off in a pleasant tone. "Would the protective bubble completely solve the problem, elim-inating the need for cryosleep?"

Roble shrugged. "No one knows for sure, because no one's ever made it work. It would probably depend on the size of the drive's effectiveness at curving spacetime in both directions without causing the bubble to fail. Listen, I have to go, but if you want to know more about this, you should really talk to your friend Merelyn. She *is* the expert, you know. I'm an AI manager, not a theoretical physicist. My job is to help the crew's automated systems —"

"Merelyn?" It took Samantha a few seconds to figure out who he was talking about. "You mean the woman I used to visit in the infirmary? The one who had the stroke? Vance said he sent her off the station with his other patients after the disaster. But even if she was back, she's in no shape to be working on the repair crew."

"Apparently the last treatment protocol he started her on before the disaster worked better than he'd hoped." Roble glanced over his shoulder as if he expected his boss to catch him taking an extra two minutes for lunch. "She's recovered now, and the first thing she wanted to do was go back to work."

"And her work is wormhole physics?"

"No, her work was the Lightning Project. You've heard of that, right?"

There was a reference to it in the dry paper she'd tried to read, but she couldn't recall the details. "It was a project Umora disparaged."

"She was technically right—it was a disaster. The ideas were sound, and it actually worked at first, but then the bubble failed, causing a massive explosion. They didn't anticipate that problem, because apparently it's one of those situations where the math breaks down at —" He stopped, his head whipping around to look at something off screen. "Crap. I have to go. Anyway, Merelyn is the leading expert in the field. She hates reporters, but she doesn't have enough good things to say about you. You were her only visitor the entire time she was in that infirmary on Five Alpha."

*   *

After saying for the fifth time how much she'd appreciated Samantha's visits, Merelyn promised to speak with her boss about bringing Samantha onto the ship. Samantha thanked her and had just ended the call when her doorbell chime sounded.

"It's Richard from Good Day Beer," said her AI.

"Really?" She thought back to his speech at the party. "He probably wants some free publicity for his stupid beer. Let him in. I'll tell him he's welcome to buy time on *Glass*."

The door slid open, and Richard walked in, wearing a thousand-dollar suit from Saks in New York. She hadn't seen one of those in years.

"What can I do for you?"

He smiled. "Actually, I came to tell you what I can do for *you*."

"What would that be?"

He waved at the window. "You've been here much longer than I have, and as a journalist, you talk to all sorts of people. I'd like you to make a few introductions, point me in the direction of a few... types of people whose services I want to acquire."

"If you wanted services you could acquire legally, you would just ask your AI."

"I assure you I have the best of intentions. I work with a consortium of businesses that want this stupid war to end, and from what I've heard, you want the same thing."

"I'm listening."

"How would you like an exclusive interview with one of the leading businesspeople from Earth?"

"Sounds nice." She stared at him. "You're really trying to end the war?"

"You know we can't leave it to the politicians."

She snorted. "Yeah, you have a point. Exactly what types of people would you want to be put in contact with?"

Richard looked around the apartment, then pulled out a small, cylindrical device and waved it around.

"Just a second, I just have to make sure... yes, we're good." He pocketed the device. "Just wanted to make sure your room wasn't bugged."

"Or that I wasn't recording you."

"Or that. Now, would you happen to know a really good thief?"

She leaned back on the couch. "I might. But first, I might need your help with something."

He raised an eyebrow.

"If you really want to help me end the war, I have an idea. But I'll need your cooperation."

Richard spread his hands. "What do you need?"

✴
SIXTY-TWO

"Absolutely not! No Humans on this ship! Are you as stupid as they are?" Umora glowered over her desk at Merelyn.

"No. I think this would be a good political move for the next Secretary of Education."

Umora raised an eyebrow. "In what way would inviting one of our enemies onto our ship to steal tech secrets be good for any future political career I might he considering?"

Merelyn smiled. "Officially, they're not our enemy."

"They declared war on us. Really, *officially*, with a twelve-thousand word letter explaining why they hate us, signed by a hundred of their fucking politicians."

Merelyn waved a hand. "But we haven't declared war on them. We're officially trying to work things out with a state that's declared war with us but is holding a, what do they call it, ceasefire while we try to work on—"

"I've heard the bullshit. Who cares? I'm not a political operative right now, I'm a scientist, and the best way I can end this whatever-we're-calling-it is to fix the wormhole."

"Officially, that's the best thing you can do. But from a CC perspective, letting a civilian—"

"A civilian *journalist*."

"Exactly. Think how much more civilized we'll look if we invite a Human onto our ship to...." She looked around the overstuffed office, hoping the right word would pop out of a drawer. It didn't. "...to share in an experience that's bigger than both our species'."

"To share our tech secrets with them? That's illegal."

"We won't show her anything proprietary, and we'll block her outgoing communications until we're sure she doesn't have anything her people can use. We'll also make her sign an agreement to be Hazed if she sees or hears anything we don't want to leave this ship."

Umora drummed her fingers on the desktop. "If she shows how hard we're working to fix the problem, maybe Human opinion about our culpability in the wormhole disintegration will improve."

"It will also reinforce the idea that we're trying to make peace."

"And you know this journalist? You trust her not to wait until she leaves and write some horrible exposé describing us as insensitive, anti-Human or, worse, stupid and incompetent?"

"Yes." Merelyn gripped the arms of her chair first with one hand, then with both. It would take time to relearn the habit of using both hands. "I trust her completely, and so can you."

SIXTY-THREE

Hank cringed when he opened the door and saw Richard. "What do you want now? I thought we agreed to forget we ever knew each other."

"Just hear me out, okay?" Richard held up a six-pack of Good Day Beer. "I brought reinforcements."

Hank wanted to slam the door, but that would mean going back into his apartment and trying not to think about his brain turning to mush while Dr. Vance searched for a solution. Maybe if he drank half the six-pack and temporarily turned his brain to *actual* mush, he'd forget about the one thing he didn't want to remember, at least for a while.

"Fine." He crowded Richard out of the way as he stepped into the hall and slammed the door behind him. "But we're enjoying those beers in an actual bar—with witnesses."

Richard rolled his eyes but followed him to the Wormhole, where they sat at a corner table. Hank was grateful the auto-attendant didn't scan guests for outside beverages when they walked in, because Good

Day Beer was, as an import, ridiculously expensive on this side of the Divide. *Especially* now.

"So what *do* you want?" he asked Richard as he opened two bottles.

"I know you have no reason to trust me, but-—"

"You're seriously asking me for help? To do what, get involved with one of your revenge schemes? I'm not helping you go after some poor shmuck like me who desperately needed a cure." Hank knocked back a swig of his beer. "By the way, this stuff tastes like crap."

"I'm done with revenge," Richard said. "When I heard about you, it reminded me of my wife, who I still haven't found. Instead of focusing on my search, I went after you, and I regret that. I really do."

Hank took another sip. "I maintain what I said about this stuff tasting like crap. I'm only drinking it because it's free."

"Understood."

"So you want help finding your wife's cryocan? I don't have any expertise on that. It's not like I found myself! I was unconscious when the Guard found me. If you want help, you should ask them."

"They're in the middle of a war, and after reviewing data on cosmic events, including repercussions of the wormhole event, the area I need to search is huge."

"So what, you want me to help?" Hank was surprised to realize he was actually considering the idea. It would give him something meaningful to do while he waited for Vance.

Richard hunched down over his beer, and Hank realized he wasn't used to asking for help. "We could cover twice as much ground. Some days I can't get away from my business, and I can't just send an employee to work on this for me. They wouldn't understand. And indirectly or not, you were the reason Amy went through that wormhole all those years ago."

"I'm also the reason *I* went through that wormhole, and we still don't have a cure," Hank said. "Not on Earth, anyway. The treatment I stole didn't help anyone."

"But now you've been cured, and if I could just find Amy...."

Should he just tell Richard the truth—that he wasn't cured, that he would probably be going back into cryo in a few months, that if they found Amy there would be no magic cure for her, either? No, he owed Richard, and on the off chance that Vance found a cure, he would feel better knowing Amy's cryocan was somewhere safe.

"I assume you're paying for the ship, meals, and any travel accommodations I might need?" he asked.

"If you help me, I'll buy your meals and provide all the free Good Day Beer you can drink."

Hank groaned. "Let's hurry up and find that can."

Richard raised his beer bottle for a toast.

* *

Before she left Earth, Samantha had once interviewed the head of the CIA, Jim Henderson. He'd agreed to the interview in the hopes of improving his agency's image after several embarrassing gaffes. Probably the worst one was convincing the military to shoot down a spy plane that turned out to be a new kind of aerial advertising for a pizza parlor—"Fly me to the moon, and I'll buy you a half-price pizza!" No one was hurt, but the Agency *and* the Defense Department wasted a lot of money in the attempt to destroy a holo image.

In an effort to impress her with his diligence to detail, the director had his security waste an hour of Samantha's time, frisking her and running scanners over her bra to look for weapons. They didn't find it funny *at all* when she asked if they seriously thought she could fit a nuclear bomb in a D cup. After she passed inspection, Henderson took her on the world's most boring tour, blathering about tight security protocols and safety measures until she wondered if he was hoping she'd fall asleep and look even more inept than he did.

His security measures might have been over the top, but they were nothing compared to the setup on Umora's fortress of a research vessel. Samantha's AI informed her all outgoing communications were being blocked before she even stepped on the ship. Once through the first of three security checkpoints, she had to surrender the device entirely and accept a substitute, which she could take with her when she left—only after Umora combed it for any data she didn't want Samantha to have. The only recording device she could be sure of was her own mind, and Umora even wanted to control that, with the agreement that at any point during her stay she might be told to take a Haze pill.

The situation went against every journalistic principal she'd ever been taught. You didn't let the subject control what you ultimately reported. You didn't give up the right to control your story. You didn't let them stop you from recording the truth accurately.

But if she didn't get onto the ship in the first place, no one would report any of the truth here accurately—so she reluctantly agreed to Umora's terms. Besides, there was one thing the paranoid scientist might not know to check out.

"Can you tell me anything about these security checkpoints?" she asked a guard at the third threshold in thirty minutes.

"Hold still." The slack-faced guard flipped a switch and the vertical ring she was standing still inside hummed to life. "We're checking for weapons, both mechanical and biological. You know, engineered microbes that—"

"I know what biological warfare is. What type of scanner do you use?"

"The standard Quasar Fifty model. One algorithm checks for physical weapons, another scans for unusually virulent microbes, and a third will determine if you're carrying any recording devices you thought we'd miss." The guard looked down his beaked nose at her.

So *that* was what worried them the most. She tossed the guard her most disarming smile. "I wouldn't dream of it."

After a few minutes of staring at the screen as if the secret to understanding women was written on it, he waved for her to step forward. "Go ahead."

Stepping through the final doorway, she breathed a sigh of relief. They had the best security equipment on the market and a highly diligent staff, but no one had thought to look for the one thing she'd hoped they would miss.

"Samantha! It's wonderful to see you again!" Merelyn greeted her with an enthusiastic hug.

"Thanks for helping me get this interview." Samantha disentangled herself as she stepped back. "You look wonderful. I'm glad Doctor Vance's last treatment was such a success!"

Merelyn nodded. "I'm very grateful for his help. But I'm also grateful to you."

"Me? What for?" Her visits weren't *that* great. The scientist had looked bored and annoyed most of the time.

"I had no other visitors, Samantha. Other than Vance, you were the only person who talked to me. You might not have always discussed a subject that interested me, but I appreciated that you were there."

"I'm glad to hear that." She really did like Merelyn, but she was determined to remain as objective as possible until she got off this ship. "Can you show me around?"

The next hour was far more interesting than her time at the CIA. Merelyn introduced her to Umora, who seemed surprisingly happy to see Samantha. Why was that? Political posturing, probably.

Umora conducted the tour herself, showing Samantha a dazzling array of instruments and devices in the main research room. Each wall screen was set to a different angle on the wormhole. They mostly looked the same, dark and empty sections of space interrupted by bright white swirls, but dozens of people were staring at blown-up sections with rapt attention.

At the end of the tour, Umora smiled and gestured to Merelyn. "I'll let her take over from here. If you'll excuse me, I have some reports to study—but I'll check back with you later."

Samantha nodded politely as Umora left, then turned her attention back to Merelyn. "Before you start with the basics, I read about your work on the Lightning Project. As I understood it, you plan to curve spacetime so you can avoid the problems of the Divide."

"Yes." Merelyn's eyes widened. "I'm glad you educated yourself. Did you learn why Lightning failed?"

"My understanding of advanced physics is rudimentary, but most of the articles I read for the layman suggested you overestimated the strength of the bubble and/or the stability of exotic matter in that particular situation."

"Yes." Merelyn grimaced. "I had a lot of time to think about my mistakes when I was in the infirmary, and I'm positive now that the problem was a miscalculation."

"After adjusting your math, you feel confident you can test the project again without another explosion?"

"Yes." Merelyn sat in the nearest chair and changed the wall screen to show... another empty expanse of space. "That's where we're going to test Lightning. And this time, we'll be successful."

"Should we see anything?" She sank into a seat behind Merelyn.

"That's Lightning." Merelyn pointed at a display showing the device, which was shaped like a torpedo. "See the expanding tail?"

"That prevents it from exploding again?"

"No. That allows it to work. When it reaches the appropriate speed, we activate the —"

"Are you showing her the schematics?" Umora screeched behind her. "Are you out of your mind?"

Merelyn gritted her teeth as she turned to face her boss. "We've blocked her communications and we can Haze her. Besides, the schematics for the Bolt have been public for some time, minus this latest improvement."

"We've already filed paperwork on it," Molly yelled from her station, where she was banging away at a display screen. "Your rights to the profits are safe."

She must've been spending a lot of time with Haylea.

Umora shot Molly a filthy look, then turned her gaze back to Samantha.

"Please ignore my colleague." She forced a smile that didn't come within light-years of reaching her eyes. "Money is the farthest thing from my mind. My concern is protecting the integrity of our research. It would be dangerous for the average person to attempt something like this, and a large corporation would only care about profit. They might make dangerous modifications, test unsafely. The ramifications could —"

"Bolt is less than a minute away from reaching test speed," Roble announced from his seat.

Umora sat down on Merelyn's right, turning her back to Samantha. "This better work," she mumbled.

Merelyn smiled. "We've fixed all the problems we know about."

"You see that shimmering directly in front of the pointed end?" Merelyn asked a few minutes later, as she gestured at the wall. "We only see that because we designed a special sensor to pick up exotic matter activity."

"That's fascinating. How does it work?" Samantha asked.

"The beam aims at the area of space we want to reach, an asteroid roughly two light years away." Merelyn tapped a display to her right, her eyes never leaving the screen. "When it reaches a certain velocity, the proprietary device inside the Bolt will create the bubble."

Merelyn looked at Samantha. "Avoiding the expense of cryotreatment, being able to go anywhere, not just where the wormhole—

"The device just activated," Roble announced, and conversation died again. Merelyn and Umora both stared at multiple displays. Samantha peered over their shoulders, trying to understand what she saw. One showed the device's coordinates, while another offered a colorful measurement graph of temperature and pressure gradients. On another, Merelyn had pulled up the schematics for the Bolt again, and this time she zoomed in through the hull to an inside device. Since Umora was so busy with her own displays that she'd forgotten her unwanted guest, Samantha got a good look. The inside device was cylindrical, with about eight components. If it was currently to scale, it wasn't that large.

"Is that what I think it is?" Molly changed the display screen to her right, and everyone turned to look. All Samantha saw was a slight rippling in a V shape under the device.

"According to the Bolt's sensors, yes, it is." Merelyn walked to the wall screen until she was close enough to trace the ripple with her fingers. "The negative mass is starting to curve spacetime here...." She moved her finger to another display. "And here, behind the bubble."

The disturbance intensified, curving from both back and front until the ripples met, forming a ring around the tiny, unmanned craft in the center. Then the shimmering cleared, and the foggy area quickly resolved into clear black. It was as if the small ship and its cargo had never been there.

"The bubble closed completely," said Molly.

"What are we getting from the asteroid sensors?" Umora asked.

"We're trying to establish contact. Any time —now wait, there it is. We're getting the signal." Roble changed the wall screen to their right to show a stream of random numbers. "That's the message we set the asteroid to spit out continuously so we'd know when Lightning got there."

"Proceed to the next level." Umora whipped her head around to look at Samantha. "I'm not giving you back your communications until we're sure it works well. I don't want any false stories bouncing around in the press if there's a problem."

Samantha nodded. "I understand. No *Dewey Defeats Truman* here."

Umora frowned but didn't ask for an explanation.

✳
SIXTY-FOUR

After two days of searching through asteroid fields for Amy's cryocan, Richard announced they were going to make a side trip. Hank hated to admit it, but he was relieved—double-checking an AI's scans of rocks floating in space was mind-numbingly dull. As much as he wanted to help Richard, he was ready for a change of scenery. The beer baron was tight-lipped about where they were headed—until the science research ship *Intrepid* floated into view.

"If I asked how you got your hands on all this top-secret spy shit, would you tell me?" Hank asked Richard. They sat before the sleek, streamlined control panel of a very small, fast, and according to Richard, hard to detect ship, which was a far cry from the luxurious Good Day Beer vessel.

"Would you believe that if I told you, I'd have to kill you?"

"No. You're the head of Good Day Beer for fuck's sake. You don't work for any government I've ever heard of."

Richard shrugged. "I'm a businessman. Sometimes I trade for things."

The wall screens revealed a panoramic view of the vast emptiness outside, including the research ship. Apparently, Richard had traded for the coordinates, but he wouldn't say any more than that.

"Did you get a receipt so you can trade this tin can for a model with a coffeemaker?"

Richard rolled his eyes. "We've got a fridge full of beer in the back and you want coffee?"

Hank couldn't take his eyes off the other ship as it loomed closer. "Are you sure they can't see us?"

Richard hit a square on one of the displays and four smaller ships suddenly appeared around the *Intrepid*. "If they could, those guys would be shooting at us already."

Hank squirmed in his seat, and the safety harness squeezed him tighter. "If we have the same tech they do, why can't they see us?"

"Because we don't. We have much better tech than the ion-masking, heat signature-equalizing crap they're using. Ours does all of that, plus...." Richard frowned at another display. "Ah-ha! That's it!"

"What?"

"Their device works." Richard folded his arms over his chest with a smug grin. "According to my analysis program, they've curved spacetime and moved that ship light years away three or four times in the last hour."

"So maybe now would be a good time for us to get out of here." Hank suddenly realized he had to use the bathroom, and the seatbelt wasn't going to spring him until Richard called off whatever high-alert mode he'd put the ship in when they got close to the *Intrepid*.

"You're right." Richard tapped at another display. Hank watched, because he was trying to catch up on the hundred or so years of technological advancements he'd missed since he'd been fixing these things instead of trying to understand them.

"What are we doing?" he asked as the ship pressed forward. According to the display, they were moving toward the *Intrepid* and its not-so-invisible friends.

"I think they've tested the device enough to ensure its safety," said Richard, as they slid between two of the masked ships.

Hank realized he'd been holding his breath and sucking in his gut, as if that would somehow help them fit in the tight space better. "What the fuck are you doing? You're not seriously going to steal the device now?"

"Why are you whispering?"

"I don't know!" Richard yelled. "We're sneaking around. It seemed appropriate."

"The answer is no, we're not *stealing* anything." Richard popped up another display on the main screen. "See that? That's a full-dimensional schematic of the device they have installed. Using that data, my AI will build a schematic so my people can rebuild this thing. We have to hang around until we have all the schematics."

"Are you sure no one can see us?"

"Aside from the fact that we have the best concealment tech money can buy, they are also *really* distracted. The other Wormhole Restoration group is attempting to fix the wormhole right now. Everyone's watching that." Richard pointed at a display of a news conference.

Hank grimaced at the thought of all the things that could go wrong with wormhole repair. "I heard there's almost as much chance they'll blow it up completely as fix it. They even hired six freighters to haul Five Alpha farther away just in case there's an even bigger gravitational wave when, you know, that thing goes."

"All the more reason to make sure we have the specs for that." Richard pointed back at the Bolt.

"How exactly are we getting those images?"

Richard grinned. "I have a… an employee who hacked the signal they're using to monitor the Bolt, with the help of some special equipment I traded for."

"And you think that device will help you find Angela?"

"Think how much faster I can search with it." Richard put their view of the test area—currently showing nothing but the darkness of space—up on the front wall screen and pointed at a blinking red dot moving into the middle. "That's one of the recovery project's own trackers, which my employee has hacked. In order to protect the Bolt, it can automatically override test parameters if it believes the device is becoming unstable, which is apparently a big concern with these things."

The red dot, which in reality was probably the size of a small Earth car, paused near the center of the screen. After a few minutes, the shimmering that Hank now associated with the spacetime curveball or whatever it was—he wasn't really sure—appeared just ahead of the red blob. Was Richard's expensive spy shit about to be obliterated? Surely a spacetime curveball could do some damage, just look what happened with the wormhole thing—

Then the shimmering cleared and the large, torpedo-shaped ship materialized, snubbing out the red dot.

"Did the curveball break your new toy?" Hank blurted.

Richard chuckled. "I don't think so. Just watch."

The colors around the big torpedo grew brighter, indicating the device was exhausting waste heat. Well, what could you expect from a piece of equipment designed to mess with all of space and time and… what was that?

A display to the right rushed through a rapid-fire slideshow of schematics, things that looked like car parts and furniture assembly instruction pictures and who knew what else — it was going so fast he couldn't even see it.

"Just a few more seconds and we'll have it all." Richard gripped the edge of the console so hard his knuckles looked like oversized, misshapen pearls sticking out of his fingers.

Then the colors bloomed, as they had after the last few times Lightning had reappeared. Hank didn't really understand why, but Richard had blabbered something about the dissipation of the bubble creating a huge energy discharge as the negative energy field collapsed. What it looked like on the display was the torpedo lighting up like a Christmas tree, shortly before one more big shimmer shook the blackness of space. This time, the display to his right abruptly went black.

"What happened? You didn't lose your new toy, did you?"

Richard frowned. "I have no idea, but we got what we needed. And that was just an explorer with enhanced evasion tech. We have more. In order for it to collect the data and override the parameters it had to be close. Lightning can't transmit communications for almost thirty seconds after the bubble goes, and its sensors can't function with all the confusion. The energy drain for powering the device shuts down everything else. They may fix that eventually, but for right now, it's a good opportunity for subterfuge."

"So Lightning doesn't have a record of your device swooping in and getting the final specs?"

"That's right. Our bot wasn't overwhelmed by a power drain, so it was able to transmit back to us." He frowned at the screen. "I wonder why they sent it off again so soon? They always wait at least several minutes for the Bolt to cool down before trying to use it again."

"Great. Now can we get out of here?"

"Absolutely. We just have to duck around a few ships that can't see us."

"By a few you mean... ten or twelve?" Hank looked doubtfully at the displays to Richard's left.

"It's going to be a bumpy ride. Hang on to your seat." Richard tapped a button on the console. "Let's hope my AI really is better than a Human pilot."

"Can I use the can first? I really have to —"

"No time. Right now they're all realizing *their* new toy is gone."

Why hadn't he used the bathroom earlier?

The small ship sped toward the fleet of Guard craft, bobbing up and down to avoid getting too close. They slid under two vessels, then zoomed upward to avoid three more.

"Almost home free." Richard leaned back in his chair. "Just a few more to clear...." An alarm sounded and a blinking light bloomed to the left.

"What's that?" Hank yelled.

"I told you more ships were showing up," Richard said. "Well, twenty of them just appeared on our sensors, and they're all spread out."

"Can't we just... go higher or lower or something and avoid them all?"

"We can't get that far out of the way fast enough," the AI said. "If I try to move above the highest ship, we'll be in danger of hitting several of the lower ones before we clear it. Same with going below. The best calculated course is actually through, if we can avoid hitting those two craft in the middle." Two vessels blinked yellow near the center of the melee.

"I don't have a better idea," Richard admitted.

They zoomed through the field of spacecraft, narrowly avoiding a research boat and two more Guard vessels. Hank thought they were going to make it through without hitting anything when one of the Guard ships near the back of the fleet suddenly shifted downward.

"What the fuck?" Hank yelled. On the wall screen, the ship zipped straight toward them. "Are you sure they can't see us?"

"I hope not." Richard was sweating, and Hank remembered the guy was a businessman, not a pilot or a spy. He had gotten more than he bargained for by doing this task himself.

The AI lurched them away from the new threat, drawing too close to another research vessel.

"Holy crap!" Richard yelled as their ship shuddered from the impact. There was a scraping noise, and everything tilted sideways.

"What's going on?" Hank yelled.

"The AI is trying to get us out of here by maneuvering the craft sideways."

Hank groaned as the ship bucked to the side and the bungee seatbelt dug into his bladder. An empty beer bottle slid off the console and went flying, whacking Richard in the eye.

"Goddamnit, no one's going to believe I walked into a door," he grumbled.

"That's the least of your problems. Can they see us now?" Hank asked. Then it occurred to him he should have asked if they were going to die now. How well could a ship this small hold up, anyway?

"No, our masking tech is still working."

"But they must have noticed we hit them." The shuddering leveled off, but there was a drag on their speed. "Why are we slowing down?"

"We are essentially scraping along the hull of the research ship," said the AI. "Some of our propulsion equipment was damaged. Once we get free of the craft, I can attempt a repair, but it may require unmasking for a time."

"We can't do that!" Richard yelled.

"Then we're going to go home very slowly," the AI said. "And the Guard are going to be looking for the invisible thing that hit the science ship."

"What do we do?" Hank asked.

This couldn't be happening. All those years in cryo, only to wake up and get arrested trying to help a jerk who was pointing a gun at him days ago. How did he get into these messes?

"I have no idea." Richard wiped his brow with a shaking hand. "I guess we glide until we're farther away. How long will the repairs take after we unmask?"

"About thirty minutes," the AI said in its maddeningly calm voice.

"Yeah, we'll be screwed by then." Richard adjusted some controls, putting up the view from behind the ship. "Maybe we can coast for a while. There are only two ships heading toward the one we hit, and they're probably offering assistance."

"Can we at least adjust course?" Hank asked. "That way they won't know which direction the ghost went?"

"That I can do, but we'll still be moving slowly," the AI said. "I will attempt a zigzag course so we are constantly changing direction."

"Crap, one of them is coming after us." Richard pointed to a blinking white dot.

"Richard, I know this is a bad time, but I really, *really* have to use the bathroom."

"Go," he grumbled. "We're not accelerating anymore, anyway."

Hank was almost finished in the tiny bathroom when he heard Richard crow with what sounded like relief.

"What happened?" he yelled.

"The zigzag pattern is working, I think."

Just then, the ship rocked with another impact.

"Don't tell me we hit something else?" He zipped his pants and passed his hands under the automated sink, then walked back into the cabin and crashed on the couch.

"Shit! They're shooting at us!" Richard fumbled with some controls. "Maybe this thing will deflect the lasers. I sure hope so."

"Shouldn't we have been using a deflection shield before?"

"Well, I didn't think it was necessary if they couldn't see us. Besides, the shields would have prevented us from getting the images of the schematics."

The ship bounced around and an alarm sounded.

"I don't think our shields are going to hold up much longer," Richard said with a grimace. "If we shoot at them, they'll know for sure they scraped a ship, and we're completely outgunned anyway."

"Attempting a more aggressive evasive pattern," the AI said. The ship swooped upward, and Hank was finally glad for the bungee cords. He watched in horror as the dark mass loomed closer behind them, laser beams dancing over the ship's hull.

"They can't target too well if they can't see us, so hopefully they won't hit anything important," Richard said as the ship lurched to the right, then down. Hank felt like he was on a roller coaster ride in a tacky theme park back on Earth.

"They're gaining on us, aren't they?" he asked. "If they get any closer, they'll be kissing our ass, whether they can see us or not."

"We can't outrun them, so we just have to keep ducking and dodging," Richard said. "They'll eventually give up, decide they're chasing nothing."

"Actually, they just changed course," the AI said in its ridiculously calm voice. "The lasers are still sweeping in a wide arc behind them, but they are heading back toward the *Intrepid*."

"So we just have to bob and weave for a few more minutes." Richard pointed at the display. "I think they've all been re-routed to deal with Lightning. Look at them swarming back toward the device."

"Why would the Guard stop chasing an invisible ship to help them with that?" Hank asked.

Richard shrugged. "They don't really know it was an invisible ship. Their vessel could have been rocked by some sort of turbulence out here. There were a lot of ships rushing around, too."

"We should be drifting into a dust cloud in four hours," the AI said helpfully. "That should give us the cover we need to make repairs."

Hank settled back in his seat and turned to the nearest news display. "Hey, look, they think they've re-stabilized the wormhole."

Richard glanced at the screen. "That's good. But now both sides know it's vulnerable. If the Protector could be compromised once, it can probably be done again. We need to make sure we have alternative arrangements for transportation home."

Hank stared at the departing Guard vessel. "Do you think maybe something happened to Lightning? Look at all those ships swarming around where it was a minute ago."

Richard shook his head. "You're right. Where did that damn thing go?"

The ship slowed its maneuvering and released Hank from his bungee jail. He got up and went to the front, getting a whiff of Richard as he leaned closer to the view screen. The encounter had apparently made the beer baron sweat buckets, based on the smell.

"You need a shower." Hank pointed at the center of the converging ships. "What are those little things floating around where Lightning was? Is that debris?"

Richard frowned. "If you're right, we just stole a faulty FTL device from these clowns—and they claim to be smarter than us!"

SIXTY-FIVE

"Do you have any idea how hard it is to get the attention of the President of the United Nations of Earth?" Richard asked, as they finally sped back toward Five Alpha a day later.

"You're trying to call the President of Earth from a spaceship with stolen specs of the People's secret tech aboard? Are you crazy?" Hank asked.

Richard looked at him like he was a dumb Human and Richard wasn't. "If I could get in contact with the President of Earth, I think he'd want that piece of stolen tech. Anyway, if we give it to our people, Humans could control travel to the other side *without* the damn wormhole."

"What the fuck, Richard?" Hank stared at his slack-jawed expression. "You said you wanted this device to look for your wife's cryocan. Now you tell me you want to get involved in a war with some people who have been nothing but helpful to me? Who might hold the key to helping your wife, if you ever find her?"

"Hank." Richard's head jerked back as if he'd been slapped. "I found Amy's cryocan. It turns out it was severely damaged by a solar flare, and... she couldn't be revived."

"What?" Hank grimaced, his anger dissolving into sympathy. "Richard, I'm... so sorry."

"I'd like to blame you, but this isn't your fault." Richard shook his head. "The truth is I lost Amy a long time ago, and I need to move on — permanently. I'm going to have a service for her, eventually, but right now I want to focus on this."

"What is this? If we're not looking for Amy, what are we doing?"

"Think about it." Richard rolled up his sleeves and thumbed through something on a display. "The People can build another Lightning, and they haven't declared war on us. If we give the specs to the Humans, it will equalize things. I bet President Howard will have the sense to call off the war and try for peace again."

"What if they take this thing and use it to attack the People instead?"

"Why would they do that?" Richard sighed. "The Earthers have nothing to gain. Attacking the People is only going to convince them that they're right and we can't be trusted with the cancer cure or any new technological advances. We can't beat them in a war if we both have this thing — but they can't beat us either. There's no point in continuing the fight, and I think the president and the UNE are smart enough to see that."

"I think your estimation of politicians' intelligence is a little high." Hank looked at a display that showed the device's design specs. It looked so much smaller and simpler than he would have suspected.

"You know, all the things that have happened so far... they were just excuses. We really got into this non-war over the cancer cure... and *this*." Hank waved at the design.

"I know a lot of whackos from our side of the fence blew stuff up because of that. I know our government would probably like to get its hands on the cure—or the FTL drive—if only because every politician would claim credit for it in the next election." Richard ran a hand through his hair, which was starting to gray. "But you know what else I know?"

"What?" Could he believe Richard? He really wasn't sure.

Richard leaned forward, looking Hank in the eye. "I know a lot of people have tried to steal the cancer cure, and quite a few other medical breakthroughs. Those people all failed, and they will persist for a long time even if this war ends. But I also know the People won't refuse treatment to anyone who shows up here. With this technology"—he waved his hand at the wall screen—"you wouldn't have to be put in cryo and risk dying like Amy did. Do you know how many people are too sick to be frozen in the first place? Once we start mass-producing these things, this type of travel will be cheap within five years. If we have this, we won't need to fight a war over a cure they have—or this new travel tech."

Hank stared at him for a long time. The ship was quiet, with only a low hum emanating from the engines below. He couldn't think of a reason for Richard to lie right now. After all, if he was in this for the profit, he could just sell the device to an Earth company. Giving it straight to the government would make it less profitable, but would end the war faster.

"Okay, Richard," Hank sighed. "Tell me what you want me to do."

Richard's well-preserved face rippled into a smile. "I thought you'd never ask. I was hoping we could use your status as Human poster boy for people who need cures to get our government's attention."

Hank winced, then tried to wipe the expression from his face. "You're one of the richest businesspeople on Earth. Don't you have contacts in the government?"

"I know a couple Congresspeople." Richard scratched his head. "But I don't think they're trustworthy, because—"

"Because they're in Congress. Yeah, I get it, but what makes the president or the people in the UNE trustworthy?"

"Now that's the problem—government bureaucracy and its stifling effect on all forms of progress." Richard rubbed a hand over his face. "Maybe we shouldn't give this thing directly to the government, any more than we should hand it to a private company."

"So what do we do?"

"You're very popular right now, Hank. If you call a press conference, Human reporters will show up in droves. Meanwhile, I'll make sure some of my business contacts in the manufacturing industry know to watch."

"What do you expect me to do?"

"Announce that because you've been in cryo for more than a hundred fifty years, you can look at the situation with more detachment than any Human or Person alive today, and you have a solution for intergalactic peace. A framework for *detente*. The People reporters will assume it's below their intellectual standards and wait to copy something from the AP wire. If they don't, we refuse to give them access. Tell them you just want to speak to the Humans, as it would be presumptuous to speak to the People about this painful transgression of your species. Whatever bullshit you can think of. Be creative. Maybe Samantha can help you with it."

"Is intergalactic peace even a thing? I think we're all in one galaxy here."

"Whatever, Hank, just announce that you have something to say on the subject, and I *guarantee* you every Human reporter in the universe will want in on the feed."

"Then what do I do?"

"Nothing. I'll take it from there."

"What are you going to do?"

"You'll just have to wait and see."

SIXTY-SIX

"What's this about?" Samantha asked Hank, as they stood in the atrium of Richard's spacious spaceship. Bot crews scuttled around, setting up for what appeared to be a huge event. Oddly enough, the Good Day Beer logo didn't appear anywhere, which meant the big announcement was probably personal.

"It's top secret until the presentation starts."

"You said you wanted my help when you called. I can't help you if I don't know what this is about."

"I just wanted you to convince *Glass* to cover the event live. Although I realize everyone is a little distracted with the whole alien thing—"

"It's a vague possibility of aliens. Both governments are spinning it into something more in an effort to dial down the hostilities between our peoples. If you really want a lot of attention, I'd recommend waiting a few days for *that* to die down."

Hank leaned over, his face so close to hers she could smell his aftershave. "This is huge, and it might help *end* the hostilities. I'd appreciate it if you convinced your boss to give me that live feed."

Samantha sighed. "I just spent two days on the research ship, then five or six hours repeating that the wormhole recovery effort appears to be a success. I'm not in the mood for one of Richard's attempts at securing free publicity for his stupid beer. This better be worth my time."

"It will be." Hank's forehead furrowed with concern as he looked around the ship. "It definitely will be. By the way, if I get arrested, can you call that lawyer who represented you after the wormhole sabotage?"

"Arrested for what?"

But Hank was already walking away.

With a sigh, Samantha sent a message to Lee, suggesting the press conference might actually be newsworthy.

✳   ✳

A few hours later, Hank stood next to Richard in Five Alpha's dock, right outside the airlock to Richard's ship. Human reporters milled about, picking at the free food and checking their displays for something more newsworthy.

"You're up in just a minute," Richard said quietly. "Remember, you've got the holo prompter if you forget what to say."

"I won't forget." Hank wasn't going to read what was on the holo prompter, but Richard didn't know that yet.

A display ticked down the seconds and turned green to indicate they were live.

"Hi, I'm Hank. Some of you may know me as the Human who had himself stuffed in a cryocan and shot into space more than a hundred fifty years ago." He swallowed, his mouth dry.

"You may have heard that I've recovered from my illness. The truth is that some very skilled doctors here *did* fix my genetic defect, but they were unable to fix the damage that gene did to my brain cells for the previous years of my life. They're still working on the problem, but I may have to go back into cryo to prevent the disease from progressing."

He heard Richard take a sharp breath, although his face still appeared calm on the display of their feed.

"I'm telling you this because it highlights a problem not unlike the wormhole failure—we don't know everything. Not Humans, and not People. But we have better odds of fixing those problems if we work together. I know it sounds trite, but I really do want to make a difference in whatever time I have here. When I left Earth, my people were embroiled in one war after another. I woke up a hundred-odd years later, and that's still true on Earth—plus now we're in *another* war with people who have been nothing but helpful to me.

"My friend Richard is about to tell you something important. I want you to remember that this is not another reason to continue the war, it's a reason to end it. Thank you for listening to me."

Breathing a sigh of relief that his speech was over, Hank stepped to the side and gestured for Richard to continue.

"Thank you, Hank." Richard shouted to be heard over the reporters screaming questions. He gave Hank a look. It was one Hank recognized all too well—pity.

"Please, please, we will both take questions after the announcement." That quieted the crowd, for the moment anyway.

"Hank is right." He flashed the seasoned CEO's smile that had won over boardrooms and consumers alike. "This war needs to end. What I'm about to say is not a threat. It's an olive branch."

Oh, crap. Hank tried not to wince. This was going to go badly, and not just because the People probably didn't know what "olive branch" meant. Richard was going for every bad high-school-debate argument ever used.

"A few minutes ago, I spoke with a couple old friends in the United Nations of Earth government and informed them that, through a series of unlikely and unusual events that I can't describe for legal reasons, I am now in possession of the design specs for a faster-than-light travel device. It's different from the wormhole in that it can be used to travel anywhere, not just between two fixed points in space. My team of experts is working to determine if it is both safe and effective."

The room seemed to explode with questions. Hank didn't think reporters would get that excited over a politician caught in a kinky sex scandal.

"Let me finish." Richard put on his best self-deprecating smile and dabbed at his totally dry forehead with a handkerchief. "This does *not* mean I stole the specs. They were sent to me from an anonymous source. While my first impulse was to share it with the People, I had to stop and consider the ramifications for all involved. This device could be used against my own people. Just handing it back would be unethical and probably lead to my being brought up on charges.

"It was my patriotic duty as a Human, an American, and a citizen of Earth to inform my people that I have the design and turn it over to them. My friends at the People embassy tell me there is no legal reason for them to arrest and detain me, so I expect that will not be the case when I leave.

"I want to remind the People that my people, the Humans, are only in this war to protect themselves. We want to use this opportunity for peace, not a continued war.

"Now, who has a question? Let's proceed in an orderly fashion, hmm? You first." He pointed at Samantha.

"What do you plan to do with the specs for the device, other than sharing them with your government?"

"I've had my legal team look into the latest intellectual property laws. I can't legally use the design for any commercial endeavor. However, an individual is allowed to use such designs to build a device for personal use. That part of the law is rarely used because most individuals who can afford to build their own spacecraft can afford to buy one and would gladly pay a little extra to avoid the trouble.

"I would like to continue searching for the cryocans of people like my first wife, whose storage units were placed in space and washed through the wormhole." Richard glanced over at Hank, and for just a second he looked sad, but then his face returned to its normal, impassive expression. "Once my government determines the specs weren't stolen, Good Day Beer's corporate attorneys will pursue legal avenues to license the device for use in our fleet of delivery ships."

More questions, fired at Richard like bullets from a gun.

"Did you consider that this may make the tension between our peoples worse?"

"Absolutely. I also considered that handing this device to the People might make tensions much worse. I decided against it."

"Did your contacts tell you what the Human government plans to do with the device?"

"No. You'd have to ask the Human government."

"What do you think this will mean for the war now that both sides have the drive?"

Richard shrugged. "First of all, the Humans only have the specs. I'm not an expert on manufacturing this type of product, and I have no idea how long it will take before my people can build one. I've also heard your government is still testing the device, and I'm sure both sides will be very thorough in making sure the new tech is safe before using it."

Hank couldn't tell if Richard was trying to be ironic or not, given everyone's recent track record in the safety department.

"Can you tell us how it works?"

"Again, I'm not a scientist and can't speak to manufacturing this type of product. I understand it curves spacetime somehow, expanding it behind the ship and decreasing it in front. Meanwhile the ship is in some type of protective bubble. For that reason, this type of travel is less dangerous and wouldn't necessarily require a cryosleep procedure. It would allow one to travel just about anywhere. That's all I know." He affected his best I'm-as-clueless-as-you look, with a crooked grin and spread palms.

"Are you sure you won't face any legal implications from this?" Samantha asked.

Richard smiled. "I'm going to answer that and another question that hasn't been asked yet—but undoubtedly will—at the same time. According to my legal team, I've broken no laws, but it could appear that I have due to the unusual circumstances surrounding my acquisition of the device. For that reason, it's possible the People government has sent someone to arrest me on charges of espionage or something ridiculous like that. After all, look what they did to *you* after the wormhole crisis, Samantha.

"The question that hasn't been asked yet is 'How do you know the device works?' The answer is that I've tested it myself—with the help of a team of cutting-edge technical experts, of course. Now, I hate to be rude, but I really must be going."

Richard spun on his heel and strode straight through the doors of his ship, which closed behind him, leaving Hank standing in a room full of reporters with no answers.

✳

SIXTY-SEVEN

"What just happened?" Xenia screamed. The Council meeting was in its sixth hour of debating what to do about Lightning's destruction. They were discussing whether to continue funding the otherwise successful project when their AI interrupted with another emergency. It proceeded to play a live press conference in which Richard, Human CEO of Good Day Beer, announced he'd accidentally "acquired" Lightning's specs and now felt morally and legally obligated to turn it over to his own government.

Then they watched as he hopped into his spaceship and flew away from Five-Alpha at the speed of a politician fleeing with an undocumented donation.

"What do we do now?" Wova's eyes flicked over every face, searching for an answer—any answer

Xenia shrugged. "Not much we can do. If the Guard can catch him, which is doubtful with all the unauthorized masking tech he has, detaining him will cause bigger problems. And we really can't shoot at him — he'll claim he's innocently trying to promote peace and we're being as violent as we claim the Humans are."

"What a clusterfuck." Carlton's favorite Human phrase.

"So we just let him get away with it?" Tom asked.

"It might be a good step toward peace." Xenia sighed. "I'm sure he's already sent the specs back to his people, and attacking them won't undo that. We have to look at the long-term situation. This war needs to end, *especially* now that the Humans have our tech."

"How do we make peace with them now?" Sylvia gestured at the continuing coverage of the press conference. "Is that your new consultant who was helping you end the war?"

"She didn't know this was going to happen. And her advice about the wormhole disaster did improve our approval ratings by several points."

Tom sneered at the holo. "She's at the press conference. She was one of the first people Hank talked to when he woke up and has interviewed him several times. She also interviewed Richard the night of the peace talks."

"You think she's in on this?" Xenia didn't necessarily trust the Human, but the idea seemed far-fetched. "She was with Umora and her crew when the thing blew up — and I saw that report. They confiscated her recording equipment, never let her near the specs, and Hazed her several times. She didn't get off that ship with anything proprietary."

"That doesn't mean she's innocent," Leonora mused. "I still think she had *something* to do with the wormhole disaster, even if she *didn't* hide the signaling device that shut down the Protector."

"Why would she stay out of cryo and not do anything if she was a spy?" Xenia said. "She could have handed that station to her people. Leaving her out was a terrible idea, but it happened and she did nothing. Five Alpha's still standing and it's not crawling with Humans."

"Maybe she planted something. Maybe she set something else in motion." Maylore hunched forward and pulled up a display. "Something about her is very strange. She came here with the original mission from Earth and randomly announced she wanted to stay here. Talked her way into a job with *Glass*. When the war started and things got unpleasant for her, she *still* didn't go home. She got herself off a ship that was about to explode, and her poor boyfriend got killed."

"Maylore raises a compelling point," Harrington said. "If she went home, she'd get a job immediately. She has no family here, few friends, and her boyfriend is dead now. There's no reason for her to stay. Why would you trust her?"

Xenia gritted her teeth. "Because I knew if she was telling the truth, we still had enemies who wanted control of the wormhole. She was right."

"Or she was working with those enemies."

Xenia shook her head. "We aren't getting anywhere. Her advice about the wormhole incident was sound, and it improved our public opinion ratings. There's no evidence she's a threat, or that she helped Richard and Hank."

"But it's the only thing that makes sense," Carlton said. "She's always around when shit happens with this war. We'd get in less trouble for locking her up again than we would for going after Richard."

"What good will that do now that he has the device?"

"Maybe we can get some info out of her. She'll talk to you, Xenia, under the right circumstances."

"And what would those be?" Xenia was afraid she knew the answer.

"We blame her for this." Carlton gestured at the press conference. "We take her into custody and threaten to send her home if she doesn't tell us what she knows. I know she's too valuable to send back to the Humans, but she doesn't need to know we won't actually do it. And I know one other thing—there's some reason she doesn't want to go back there."

"She was sent here to do something and she didn't do it? Her government wants her dead?" Tom asked.

"It has to be something awful for her to be so insistent on staying here. Maybe it's something personal, not political—but either way, she's scared of something."

"We should have the FIB bring her in," Maylore said.

Xenia shook her head. "No. I will handle this personally."

"Fine, but do it quickly. You have twelve hours, or I'm sending the FIB to do the job."

"I'll get it done," Xenia said through gritted teeth. "I really hope you're wrong. Because if you're not, the Humans have just outsmarted us. And we can never let *that* get out."

SIXTY-EIGHT

President Howard was in an awkward position. He had been pulled off Five Alpha in a mad rush of security guards and screaming aides, only to sit in a masked ship for more than three days, on the hostile side of the Divide, before finally escaping through the damaged wormhole. Once home, he'd spent hours arguing with other politicians about the best way to handle the "People Problem", as the media called it. Then, the final nail in the coffin—the necessity of declaring war after the People attacked the delegation party's ships as they were leaving a peace talk, then deciding to hold off on an official attack while trying to "work things out."

Once home, he went straight to the situation room, where he watched half a dozen generals argue over the best way to defeat their opponents in Earth's first-ever war with another planet. He shot down their plan to send UNE troops to search every ship in the solar system—that would wreck his approval ratings, and Guard ships over here would almost certainly be masked. Their tech for finding "hidden" ships was improving every day, but so was the People's concealment tech.

Instead, he ordered an increased presence of UNE troops around Earth and all its colonies, and promised to reconsider a controversial plan to put nukes in space, something the UNE had firmly voted down for years. With the current situation, however, the minority proponents saw their chance to push the agenda again.

Now he sat in an emergency meeting with his top advisers, representatives of the most powerful countries in the UNE, discussing strategy for ending the situation as quickly as it had begun... and spiraled out of control.

"We need nukes on every UNE ship!" yelled Vladimir Gustov, the UNE-appointed adviser from the Central Soviet States. A real hothead, he was the main instigator of the nukes-in-space movement. Since they had voted to declare war on the People, he'd gone from recommending the weapons on ten percent of the space-going fleet to yelling that every ship needed the power to blow up half the known galaxy.

"Attitudes like that are the reason we've always voted *against* nuclear weapons in space," said Marlena Devenue, the French adviser. "I'd consider putting a small number of these weapons in space, just as a precaution, but you want one on every UNE military ship? Are you crazy? How long do you think it'll be before we accidentally blow up half the solar system?"

"I'm sure there will be many safeguards in place to prevent that from happening." Chairmain Chao of China leaned back, his stony face unconcerned with the heated discussion. If you believed the UNE's latest security reports, his country had a bigger stockpile of nukes than anyone, including Howard's own country, the United States.

"We need to discuss the design specs the beer gentleman gave us," said Bill Holdings, the UK's representative. He was young, very well-liked in his own country, and politically ambitious. It was no secret that he wanted Howard's job. Most days, Howard wanted to tell him he could have it.

Like today, for example.

"Bill is right," he said. "My latest report from our experts shows the specs have merit. This is a design that's already been developed, and if you believe Richard, tested by the People. All we'd have to do is produce one and run our own tests."

"The political implications are complicated, to say the least." Holdings smoothed his hair. He always did that when calculating a delicate diplomatic move. "Our latest intel says they are simultaneously denying having the device and demanding we return any intellectual property that may have been stolen from the People government or one of its citizens."

"So send them back the specs." Marlena smirked. "We've already made multiple copies."

Holdings rolled his eyes. "And then what? When we test this thing, when we use it, are we supposed to claim we came up with it on our own and never looked at Richard's transmission?"

"We can't *not* use it," Gustov snapped. "If it works, this could be the only thing that helps us win the war."

"But they have this, too. And they've already built it and tested it."

"What about demanding they send that Human reporter back? We could say it's for her own safety." Chao rubbed his chin. "She didn't have anything to do with the wormhole incident, so why is she still locked up? They must think she knows something, and I suspect that something would be very useful to us."

"That's a good point, but what about Lightning?" Marlena asked.

"According to Richard, an earlier version of the device blew up spectacularly." Howard rubbed at his gritty eyes. When was the last time he'd slept? Two days ago?

"So we run our own tests," Gustov said. "We've already got our best scientists studying the problem. Can you imagine if we solved their engineering problem? The self-satisfied sons-of-bitches would shit their pants."

"I believe he has a point," Howard said. "We'll research the problem, then conduct tests far away from anything important. It's our only chance."

"But what do we *say*?" Holdings asked. "Damn that idiot, telling everyone in the galaxy he gave us the specs. He couldn't have done this quietly?"

"Apparently he thought he was helping our war effort by making it public. I beg to differ, but it can't be undone now." Marlena took a sip of coffee, grimaced at the taste, and tossed her cup in the recycler. She was a snob who believed all non-French coffee was awful. "What do we say to justify keeping the specs?"

"Safety." Chao spread his hands. "That's why the Americans kept their nukes for so long, right? You justified it by saying you had to protect yourselves. You weren't even at war."

"We are now," Holdings said.

"We declared war but we also declared we will make every effort to resolve things peacefully, and we didn't want to risk sending troops through the Divide when it was unstable." Chao downed his own coffee. "We could now, but we agreed we weren't going to attack them until we try every avenue for peaceful resolution first. We will defend this side of the Divide, nothing more. Let's be honest, in an actual war, they'd probably win."

"But instead of framing it as an act of war, we should say that we're keeping the specs to... protect ourselves from future misuse of the device." Howard smiled for the first time since his last public appearance, and this was a real smile. "Now how much funding can we drum up to research this thing? Who wants to contribute?"

Every hand in the room went up.

* *

The first person Xenia wanted to talk to was Hank, but she had to wait for Anna to finish interrogating him about Richard's exit.

"Could I join the interrogation?" she asked Anna's assistant, a stone-faced guy who looked like he wanted to be at work about as much as he wanted to fly back to New Atlantis without a spaceship.

"She doesn't need help. You can wait, but it's likely to be a while." He flapped a couple fingers toward the wall, where two dilapidated chairs were living out their last days.

"Did you tell her *Councilmember Xenia* was here to see her?"

He heaved a sigh. "She's not impressed with your title."

"Well, maybe she can tell me herself. I am on official business and this is an emergency. Would she be happy if one of her employees was charged with impeding an official investigation?"

He cocked an eyebrow in her direction. "I wasn't aware Councilmembers conducted their own investigations. Isn't that something the FIB would handle?"

She gritted her teeth. "These are exceptional circumstances. If I come back with an officer of the FIB, all of whom report to me, would you let me talk to Anna?"

"I'll send her a message." He said it like one might say, "I'll crank up the AG and run a hundred laps around the station."

His supreme efforts must have paid off, because a few minutes later Anna appeared, looking irritated. "What's this about an FIB investigation?"

Xenia attempted a disarming smile. "I really need to talk to Hank, just for a few minutes. I'd rather not have to involve the FIB, if possible."

"What's this about? Richard's disappearance? I can't believe the FIB *wouldn't* be involved in that."

"They're investigating," Xenia said. "And they'll need to talk to Hank, if they haven't already."

"They're on their way. What are you doing here in person?"

"I need to talk to Hank myself, about a related matter... something I need to handle personally so I can report back to the Council."

Anna studied her face for a minute, then finally shrugged and gestured to the door behind her. "Follow me. You can have five minutes, and I *will* be in the room."

* *

Hank wished he'd never met Richard. Why had he agreed to help the guy in the first place? It wasn't his fault Amy's cryocan got lost, and the treatment he stole wouldn't have helped her anyway. He really needed to learn to control his guilt better.

When Anna left, he assumed she was going to meet the FIB people, which his lawyer, Joe, told him was something like the FBI, only way worse. Apparently intelligence couldn't fix every problem.

Joe technically worked for the station but had apparently been told by Haylea to defend Hank or find another job. He looked even more tired than Hank felt, paging through displays as if he was looking for a Get Out of Jail Free card. Hopefully he could find one for both of them.

When Anna reappeared with a woman he recognized from the news as Councilmember Xenia, Joe nearly fell out of his chair in the process of leaping to his feet, proclaiming how honored he was to meet her, and generally kissing her ass.

Was that good or bad for Hank?

"Due to the unique circumstances of this situation, the Councilmember has asked if she could speak with Hank for a few minutes," Anna said as Xenia gestured for Joe to sit his ass back down.

Anna and Xenia sat as well, and Xenia started right in. "Hank, I'm not here to ask you about Richard."

"You're not?"

"No. I have confidence the FIB will do a thorough job. I can read their report."

"So why are you here?" Joe finally remembered he was here to represent Hank, not set himself up for a political appointment.

"I want to ask you about Samantha."

Hank groaned. "Are you serious? I thought you guys were finally convinced she's not guilty of anything except being Human? Didn't you hire her to help you make peace or whatever?"

"Yeah, that worked out really well," Anna mumbled, just loudly enough for everyone to hear her.

"That's why I came myself instead of sending someone — I *do* trust her. And you can say what you want about the campaign she helped with" — Xenia shot Anna a look — "but we haven't had an attack, official or unsanctioned, from the Humans since that broadcast."

"That's because they're playing with the new toy Richard gave them," Anna pointed out.

"A lot of people think Samantha helped him get it. The Humans just demanded we return her to prove we're not torturing one of their citizens." Xenia looked Hank in the eye. "I'm the only Person on the Council who doesn't think she's a spy for the Humans. I need your help to prove she isn't or they're going to send her back as soon as they build another Lightning Bolt."

Hank felt angry for the first time since he'd been in this questioning room. Getting mixed up with Richard was his own fault, but Samantha had been targeted by these People since the day she set foot on the station, for no other reason than the fact that she was Human.

"I know two things about Samantha," he snapped. "She's not a threat to the People, and the last thing she wants is to go back to Earth."

"They can't legally make her, no matter what they think she's done," Joe said. "That's why her boyfriend couldn't have her hauled back to Earth when he was trying to protect her from just this sort of mess. He had some political friends find a bizarre legal loophole to get her deported for her own safety. But she refused to sign the consent form, and her medchip was set to prevent her from being put in cryo. They could refuse to let her back on New Atlantis, but they couldn't kick her off a space station the Humans jointly own with the People, and they couldn't force her to have a medical procedure without her consent."

"There's no way around that, legally?" Hank asked.

Joe shook his head. "No. Even convicted criminals have the right to refuse medical treatment. And the fact she had a block on her chip makes it almost impossible for anyone to just throw her in cryo against her will, legally or not. The bed would reject her."

"That seems like a convenient way to ensure you can't be deported to the Other Side, no matter what you've done," Anna observed.

"Not really. Most Humans would prefer prison on Earth to coming here."

"It doesn't matter. Preliminary tests with the Lightning Bolt suggest it avoids a lot of problems of wormhole travel, including the potentially dangerous physiological effects. With a few more weeks of testing, we expect it will be cleared for use on People—without cryosleep." Xenia shrugged. "Samantha won't be able to keep us from deporting her, no matter what awful thing is waiting for her on the Other Side. You'll tell her that for me, won't you, Hank?"

Hank felt like he was a pawn in a game too complicated for him to understand. "Why can't you tell her that?"

"I will if I see her. But I'm not sure she'll talk to me. In case she doesn't, you give her that message, all right?"

It hit Hank like a ton of gold bars to the head. "Oh. You think she's going to avoid you because she's guilty, and you want me to deliver your threat, is that it?"

"It's not a threat, Hank. It's a promise."

He shook his head. "You're a piece of work, you know that? All you People are. Samantha's done nothing but sing your praises since she got to this side of the Divide, and all you've done is treat her like shit because she's Human."

Understanding flickered across Xenia's face. "You have feelings for her, don't you?"

Hank looked away. His feelings for Samantha were a complicated jumble he didn't have the luxury of sorting out right now.

"I'm not in the position to get into anything resembling a relationship right now," he said. "But I do care about Samantha, and I'm not going to help you screw her over."

"If you care about her, you'll find out her secret and tell me what it is," Xenia said. "Because I'm the only person on the Council who isn't trying to blame this mess on her right now. And remember Hank, I could be very useful if you want to stay here to continue your treatment."

"What the hell does that mean? Are you threatening to deport me and let the dumbass doctors on my planet deal with my disease?" Hank yelled. "You really are a cold-hearted politician, you know that?"

"I wasn't threatening you at all, Hank. I was, in fact, offering my assistance — to both you and Samantha. I'd be happy to contact any of the best research facilities on this side of the Divide if you think that would help."

"Do you have any more questions about Richard's disappearance for my client?" Joe asked.

"No." Xenia stood and headed for the door. "I meant what I said, Hank. If you want to help your friend, I need to know the truth. Without that, even I can't help her."

✳
SIXTY-NINE

"I'm glad they finally released you for lack of evidence." Dr. Vance flicked a flashlight across Hank's eyes the next morning. "Have you had trouble remembering things lately?"

"No. Have you figured out a way to keep it that way?"

"Not yet." Vance consulted the brain scan images on his pad. His success at helping Merelyn had made him consider Hank's treatment in a new way. "As I mentioned last time, the only really good idea I have is a drug called M Four Fifty-two, but it may not actually exist. The more I consider your case, the more I think it's the best solution."

Hank rolled his eyes. "You still want to give me a drug that may or may not exist?"

"There have been rumors for years about M Four Fifty-two. It was supposedly created by FIB, our government's spy chapter, for use on their agents. They wanted to deal with the problem of Blackout, Haze, and other short-term memory erasers."

"You mean the five-minute rufies? I heard about those. How does that work anyway? How do you target just the last five minutes of memories?" Hank asked.

"Well, they're very similar to traditional memory-blocking drugs like you probably had back on Earth a hundred—" Suddenly Vance realized he had no idea what kind of memory blockers they had on Earth a hundred years ago. Alcohol? "Anyway, they neutralize themselves after being absorbed into the system. That prevents the unreliability of traditional medications, which wear off whenever the liver gets around to neutralizing them. If the drug negates itself, you can control exactly how long it lasts."

Hank stared at him. "M Four Fifty-two prevents these drugs from working, so spies can't be rufied?"

"Supposedly. No one knows for sure." Vance sighed. "If any of it is true, the rumors say the project was cancelled because the drug had some intense side effects. A percentage of people who took the drug ended up with serious neurological problems, including insanity."

"Oh, crap."

"Right, so you see the problem." Vance scratched his head. "Even if the M Four fifty-two existed, and I could get the formula and make it here in my lab—and I have no idea how I'd accomplish that—it would still be too dangerous."

"Even for a patient who's going to lose his mind anyway?"

"Not necessarily. I told you I would keep working on the problem until I solve it, and that's a promise." Vance displayed some images from his latest scan. "These look the same as last week. If they start showing signs of neural degradation, I will recommend a cryo treatment until I can develop a treatment. That's *until*, Hank, not *if*. I never give up on a problem until I solve it."

"So why did you bring up M Four Fifty-two if you don't think it's a good option?"

"I shouldn't have." He sat down, feeling guilty for giving Hank what was probably false hope. "Sometimes I talk before I think when I have an idea. If I could get the formula, I could try to alter it so it still protects your neurons without the potentially serious side effects. There would still be some risk, as there is with any drug that hasn't been thoroughly tested, but—"

"But I'm either going to lose my mind or spend the rest of my life frozen anyway," Hank finished.

"Not necessarily. I would only test the drug on you if I was very confident I'd solved the problem and it would work safely," Vance said.

"But the real problem is you don't know if this thing exists."

Might as well tell the whole story, since he'd opened his mouth anyway. "I asked a colleague who works for the Guard if she could find anything out, but she said they've been getting questions about the 'M Four Fifty-two hoax' for years and there's nothing to it."

"You believe her?"

"I think if it does exist, that information would be held by only a few very high-up people in the organization... and probably someone on the Council."

Hank's eyes went wide. "You heard about my visit from Councilmember Xenia and you think I could ask her for help?"

"Why not? Give her whatever she needs, she might owe you one."

Hank shook his head vehemently. "I don't have what she needs! She wants info on how Richard stole the specs. I really didn't know about that until he'd already done it, and I've already told the FIB—and Councilmember Xenia—everything I know."

"You're not just protecting Richard?" Everyone knew they were old friends after Richard's well-broadcast speech at the delegates' party.

Hank made a noise that was somewhere between a snort and a laugh. "No... that's not it at all. I agreed to help Richard look for Amy's cryocan, and the trip turned into something else entirely. I'm done helping Richard."

"That's the only thing Xenia wanted?"

"That, and she really wanted info about Samantha."

Something flickered in the back of Vance's mind, but he couldn't quite place what it was. "Samantha? Don't tell me Xenia's back to blaming the Human for everything?"

"Actually, the Council is convinced Samantha somehow helped Richard, which isn't true to the best of my knowledge—not that that's very much." Hank frowned. "Xenia says she believes Samantha's innocent, and she's trying to figure out why Sam won't go back to Earth so she can explain all the other circumstantial stuff that makes her look bad."

"You really think that's what she wants? Not to blame Samantha for something?"

Hank's eyebrows rose. "Well, she seems pretty tricky. Who knows? I doubt it, though. That campaign Samantha recommended seems like it kinda worked—since declaring war on you guys, my people haven't attacked, have they? And they have years of experience with wars, Doctor. They've probably had multiple plans for taking you guys out since the second they found that wormhole."

Vance considered for a moment. "So what does she want from you? Information?"

Hank shrugged. "I told her I don't know anything, which is the truth. She thinks Samantha will avoid talking to *her*, so she wants me to deliver a message."

"Which is what?"

"I'm supposed to tell her that once they rebuild the Lightning Bolt and ensure it's safe for Human/Person use without cryosleep, the Council can find a reason to have her sent back to Earth any time they want."

"Ah. She asked you to deliver a threat." Vance swiped the display of scans away with a wave of his hand. "Well, she might be more appreciative if you actually solved her problem."

"You mean, if I found out why Samantha won't go back to Earth and narced on her?" Hank shook his head. "No, I can't—I can't sell her out like that."

"I understand. This whole situation has been unfair to Samantha, and I'd hate to encourage you to make her problems worse. But getting the formula for M Four Fifty-two *is* our best option, and Xenia is one of the few people who could get it for us, or at least tell us if it even exists. Maybe there are other ways, though."

"Well, work on one." Hank's forehead wrinkled. "I've done a lot of things I'm not proud of in the search for a cure. It's hard to explain—what do you say to someone who doesn't have to go through life knowing they're going to lose their mind one day? I usually tell people if they saw what it was like, and knew it was their future, they might bend a few rules too."

He got up and paced around the room. "That doesn't mean I didn't feel bad every time I... did something I'm not proud of. But I felt like I didn't have a choice, you know?"

Vance grimaced. "Look, Hank, Samantha is my friend, too. If you're planning to manufacture evidence or something, I can't encourage that—and I don't think it's what Xenia really wants."

"No, it's not." Hank stopped pacing and finally looked him in the eye.

"Xenia wants the truth. She wants to protect Samantha if she can. But what if I find out the truth and it's bad, Vance? Why do you think she's here?"

"There must be something on the Other Side that scares her. If she was supposed to spy for her government, and she got here and decided she couldn't do it, she wouldn't be able to go back. That would explain a lot of things—and if I can come up with that theory, I'm sure someone on the Council has, too." Something scratched the itch at the back of his brain. "You know, they never found her boyfriend's cryocan. This is probably a lot less likely, but—what if one of the governments has it and they're blackmailing her with it?"

Hank shook his head, a haunted look on his face. "Honestly, I don't know. But whatever it is, I'm going to find out the truth."

Vance watched him walk out the door, wondering if he'd just made a very bad mistake—for all of them.

✳
SEVENTY

Samantha walked down the concourse, weaving her way through a thick crowd of People. Many of them recognized her—and weren't particularly happy about it.

"Stupid Human! Why don't you just go home?" someone yelled from the second floor. "Or do you have to help someone else escape with our superior technology?"

She tried to resist the urge to argue with an idiot, but right now her self-control was taking a mental health day. Stopping, she looked up to see that it was Carlin, the lingerie shop owner who frequently drank at the bar until she fell asleep on her stool.

"If People technology is so superior, how did a stupid Human manage to steal it anyway?" she yelled at the shopkeeper.

Carlin sputtered for a moment, before managing, "Well, they probably had help from a People traitor."

"If the People are so smart, why would they sell out to a group of

Humans who hate them? If you want to sell stolen tech, there's enough of a market among People to make a profit."

Carlin worked her mouth like she hoped it would produce a good answer independent of her brain. Samantha was just about to start walking again when the emergency signals screamed from every direction.

"It was *her*! *She* did whatever's happening!" Carlin pointed at Samantha.

"Oh, fuck me." Where was the nearest exit? Unfortunately, whatever happened had caused the station's emergency protocols to shut down the doors, the same way they had the night of the *Traveler* attack. The way people were running around, screaming like the idiots they thought the Humans were, only intensified her memory of the night Brad had died.

Trying to push the thoughts away, she took out her pad, unrolled it, and pulled up the latest newsbot reports.

EMERGENCY ALERT ISSUED DUE TO A FLEET OF HUMAN SHIPS SURROUNDING FIVE ALPHA.

THIS APPEARS TO BE THE FIRST OFFICIAL OVERTURE SINCE THE HUMANS DECLARED WAR ON THE PEOPLE ALMOST FOUR WEEKS AGO. AN OFFICIAL ATTACK WAS EXPECTED SOONER BUT THE APPROPRIATION OF A HIGHLY PROPRIETARY PIECE OF PEOPLE TECH BY THE HUMANS MAY HAVE PROMPTED A DELAY SO THE DEVICE'S PROPERTIES COULD BE UTILIZED. THE HUMANS HAVE NOT YET CONFIRMED IF THIS IS AN OFFICIAL ATTACK OR ANOTHER EFFORT BY ONE OF EARTH'S MANY FRINGE GROUPS.

Samantha had to hand it to the newsbots, they'd been programmed to be diplomatic. She rolled the pad and tucked it back in her bag, turning to survey the panicking crowd. Should she tell them the doors were locked for their safety, in case of a hull breach? No, they wouldn't listen to a dumb

Human, anyway. Might as well just get footage and send it back to *Glass*.

She dispensed a few floating cameras and ducked into a tiny hallway, knowing it led to the only working door on this level. The stairwells, located in the inner, protected section of the station, remained unlocked in emergencies, so rescue crews could get through.

She could still hear the screaming as she slipped through the door and ran down the stairs.

＊　＊

People doctors weren't required to take a hypocritical oath or whatever it was Human physicians did, but they were required to adhere to a fairly strict standard of ethics. Vance wasn't sure if he'd violated any during his conversation with Hank — he was pretty sure his ass was covered, as the Humans liked to say, from a legal standpoint — but he still felt badly about it. Why did he open his big mouth?

Yes, he was trying to help his patient, but that didn't make it okay. He had indirectly suggested Hank do something unethical that might hurt Samantha. That was what really bothered him — he knew Sam, considered her a friend, and she'd been screwed over enough, starting with her own people. He still didn't know exactly what had happened when she should have been in cryo, but she probably hadn't been a willing participant in whatever crap her people had pulled.

He put down the pad he'd been trying to concentrate on since Hank left and rubbed his eyes. What was it that his brain had been trying to tell him all day? Something to do with Samantha, and where she was when she was supposed to be in cryosleep, either on her way through the wormhole or on her way to... wait, maybe that was it. If she wasn't in cryo, she'd arrived some other way. How did that work?

Her people must have had an FTL device like the Lightning Bolt. How long ago did they steal the specs? Interesting that they'd had it since they first came through the wormhole — but they chose to use the Divide, or pretend to use it. Why?

Well, that was no secret. According to Samantha, the Humans were constantly embroiled in wars and consequently didn't trust each other about things that could be a strategic advantage — like an FTL device that would allow one side to circumvent the need to travel through the wormhole. So they anticipated a conflict with the People. Considering how good the Humans were at picking fights, that was no surprise.

Next question — why pretend to come through the wormhole while actually using the Bolt-like device? Wouldn't it be easier to just go through the wormhole? Maybe they wanted the people on the first mission from Earth to do something during the six months they would have been in cryo? It would have to be important and covert if they couldn't just get someone else to do it while the first visitors went through the standard way.

Planting weapons to use later? No, those probably would have come into play by now. Planting equipment to spy on the People? Possible. Or were they unsure they could arrive undetected using their device? That was a strong possibility. Maybe they needed a ship coming through the wormhole in case their masking tech didn't work as well as they'd hoped. Because nothing could be detected in or near the wormhole, a ship that came through only showed up on scans when it reached a certain distance out.

Maybe they had the device before they had the masking tech they needed to conceal it?

A much less innocuous explanation popped into his head. What if the ship was carrying something that might be dangerous to shove through a wormhole? Would a sufficiently large nuke be a bad idea? Vance wasn't an expert on physics, but he knew People—and Humans—had to be put in cryo to protect them from the potentially dangerous physiological effects of traveling through the wormhole. If the trip could damage the cells of a living organism, it seemed logical that it might make a weapon explode prematurely.

Where was Samantha when this was happening? What happened that she couldn't go back? Probably she only found out about the plan, whatever it was, after the fact, then refused to do whatever her government wanted. If so, why hadn't the Humans taken her out or stuffed her in a cryocan or something? She hadn't exactly made a point to stay out of the public eye....

That was it! She was a reporter, constantly working on stories about how the People government was hiding stuff from the Humans. If she just disappeared, people would notice and ask questions. If she kept quiet about whatever she actually knew, it would be better for her people to leave her alone. That also explained why she *kept* making a public spectacle of herself.

Great. Instead of solving his ethical dilemma, he'd found another one. Was he obligated to tell someone what he knew about Samantha? Patient confidentiality was usually one of the highest ethical standards to uphold, but the ethics committee made exceptions for matters of public safety. Was this one of them?

His musings about weapons and spy rings were just conjecture—all he knew for sure was that Samantha hadn't come through the wormhole five years ago. He still didn't believe she was a threat—in fact, she was probably as much at risk from the Earthers as the People were. She also wouldn't have any insight into the current situation, as her people wouldn't have given her any more information after she defected.

His thoughts were interrupted when the emergency alarms went off, and his AI informed him that the station was surrounded by Human ships.

Oh, great, another layer of complications. All of which could have been avoided if that stupid doctor from the *Traveler* had just gone to the sex sim suite instead of hanging around the medical office and doing his job.

Vance made sure the infirmary was ready to receive patients in case of any crisis and called in extra medical staff. After ensuring the medical center was well-prepared and in the hands of his best assistant, he pocketed his pad, instructed the AI to contact him immediately if any injuries were reported, and headed for the door. He needed more information before he could decide what to do about Samantha.

✳
SEVENTY-ONE

Samantha came around the corner of the stairwell and ran into Hank, who nearly jumped out of his skin when he saw her.

"Oh, crap, Samantha, I was... uh, looking for you."

"What for?"

"I... I need you to tell me the truth. Right now."

That didn't sound like Hank. What was going on?

"About what? I've never lied to you."

He cleared his throat, stuffed his hands in his pockets and stared at the floor. "About why you're here."

"Here? In the hallway?"

"No. Here, on the station, on this side of the Divide." He groaned and finally looked up. "Look... I had a visit from Councilmember Xenia, and she —"

Samantha snorted. "I'm a journalist with years of experience getting people to talk. By your own admission, you were better with computers than people a hundred and fifty years ago and don't know what the fuck is going on right now. She wants *you* to get dirt out of *me*?"

Hank pulled one of his hands out of its pocket and pointed a gun at her. He was back to staring at the ground, and his hand was shaking. "She thought this would help me convince you."

"What the fuck, Hank?" She felt like she was in a bad movie and the punchline was coming any minute. Hank was not cut out for whatever job Xenia had given him.

He rubbed sweat off his brow with his free hand. It wasn't hot. "I don't want to do this. I want you to know that. You were the only person who told me the truth when I got here. I consider you one of the few friends I have. But I have to do this, okay, so if you could please just help me out—"

"Hank, when was the last time you fired a gun?"

"Um, well...." He scrunched his face together, squinting at the ceiling. "When I was in high school, me and my buddies'd shoot beer bottles after we killed a six pack."

"So, a hundred fifty years ago, give or take a few, with an old Earth gun... after a few beers?"

"Uh...."

"Because, you know, you're holding that thing backwards...."

Hank frowned and pulled the gun closer to his face so he could study it.

She took that opportunity to grab it out of his hands. "And you have the safety on." She slid it off, the only sound a slight snick, and aimed it in his general direction. "Or you did. Now why don't you tell me everything Xenia told you?"

"Shit! Was it really backwards?"

"No. I never lied to you before, but I thought this was a special occasion. Why the hell does Xenia want you to threaten me with a gun?"

He groaned. "Please don't shoot me. Xenia just wanted me to get the truth out of you, Richard gave me the gun for protection, I thought it would help and I never would have used it, I swear."

"Oh, for fuck's sake." She slid the safety back on and stuffed the gun in her bag. "Can we just talk about this?"

Hank sighed and sat down on the nearest ledge. "Samantha, I am so sorry. This isn't the first time I've done something stupid because of my—my illness."

"I know all about that, *John Halbrooke*. I told you I was good at finding things out."

His head snapped up. "You know... what?"

"I know about Richard, and why he was pissed at you, and I know what you did. And you know what, I don't care. You had a valid reason. But what does Xenia have to do with fixing your brain?"

Hank shook his head. "Maybe nothing, but... Vance's best idea is to get his hands on a drug that's only rumored to exist, something called M Four Fifty-two. Supposedly some secret government agency *might* have a file on it. Also it was scrapped because it had some nasty side effects, including insanity."

"Have you thought about asking for a second opinion?"

He rolled his eyes. "I've had a second, third, fourth, and fifth. Vance is the only doctor here who's even willing to try to help me. All the others say it's permanent and there's nothing they can do. But if I needed a new heart or liver or something, they could hook me up."

She sat on the ledge next to him. "Back when I was at *Glass*, I heard the rumors about a drug called M Four Fifty-two, but we never looked into them. They were considered conspiracy theories, although the term they have here is Crazy Claims. Same thing though."

"In other words, *Glass* investigating a story like that would be equivalent to the *New York Times* investigating an alien abduction claim."

She snickered. "After that news release on the wormhole's possible creators, they actually *did* run a piece about aliens. But they mostly harped on the fact that there was no definitive proof the wormhole was designed by an extraterrestrial race."

Hank shook his head. "I'm really, really sorry. I swear I wouldn't have used that gun on you. I didn't want to do this—"

"Yeah, I'm sensing some conflict. Why does Vance think the M Four Fifty-two thing that may or may not exist will help you?"

"Rumor says it was designed to prevent rufies from working on people, like spies." He rolled his eyes. "This sounds even more ridiculous when I explain it."

"I see the connection. What did Xenia say?"

"She knows nothing but promises to look into it with some of her colleagues in top-secret places if I get the truth out of you. But no guarantees. I'm really, really—"

"Sorry, I know. It's all right. You did what you had to do. What exactly does she want to know?"

"The truth about why you're really here. She doesn't buy that it's because of the stupid Humans on Earth, like you've been saying for years."

"It's because of the stupid Humans on Earth."

Hank groaned. "Look, I'm sure you have your reasons, and I personally don't care what they are. But there's a time bomb in my brain and I don't have a lot of options, unless I want to be frozen again, wait another hundred years, and hope someone discovers something in that time. So could you maybe make an exception and cut the bullshit?"

Samantha considered, remembering the time she almost told Vance the truth before putting him in cryo. It would have been nice to tell someone after all these years, and of all the people on this station, Hank was the most likely to understand her reasons. Still....

"What Xenia really wants to know is if I'm a threat. She probably thought that about you too, but apparently your story was more believable."

"She believes me but she might find an excuse to have me deported if I don't get the intel on you. Apparently, she thinks you're more likely to tell me the truth than her. She still doesn't trust you because you're Human—and yeah, that sucks. For what it's worth, I already told her I don't think you're a threat."

"And she thinks you're an idiot."

"Well, I am Human."

"It's the stupid Humans."

"Your refusal to go home makes no sense, and it hasn't from day one." Hank stared at his shoes. "Vance has a theory."

"Brilliant. What did he tell you?"

"He thinks you can't go back to Earth because you're some sort of spy, or you were supposed to be, but you turned against your people, and they'd kill you if you went back."

"A lot of people think that. It's crap."

"He also thinks someone might be blackmailing you."

"With what?"

"With..." Hank winced. "He says no one ever found Brad's cryocan, and maybe someone found it and maybe they're using it to blackmail you."

She groaned. "Did he also tell you he'd done an alien autopsy?"

"It makes sense, Sam. It makes more sense than any 'personal reasons' you might have, including the stupid Humans of Earth. I know idiots are annoying, but they're not worth this—staying in a place where people hate you and shit keeps blowing up and everyone thinks you're out to get them and some of them want to kill you."

"Vance mentioned that." She didn't elaborate. "Is that all he said?"

"Those were his two best theories. Thing is, Vance is a scientist. He wouldn't have a theory if he didn't have any evidence to support it." He lowered his voice and scooted closer to her. "If he won't tell me what it is, it must be something he can't talk about, which would probably mean patient confidentiality. So, I'm thinking he has some evidence."

"It's the stupid Humans."

"Samantha, please." Hank was sweating again. "If they send me back to the *stupid Humans*, I'll probably die or spend the next hundred and fifty years in cryo. If they send *you* back, all you have to do is put up with the stupid Humans."

"That is not fucking all that will happen to me!" Her scream echoed around the hallway.

"Then Vance is right, isn't he?" Hank put his hands on her shoulders. "You can tell me the truth. If Xenia knew you weren't a threat to the People, you might actually be safer from the Humans. Please, my chance at having a normal life could depend on this—and yours could too."

She took a deep breath. This was a big mess, but it wasn't Hank's fault, and he was right—he was only trying to protect himself from becoming trapped in a hell inside his own head. She couldn't fault him for that.

"Before we continue this conversation, we need to make sure we're talking privately." She stood and tugged him toward the end of the hallway. "Follow me."

Samantha wound her way through a maze of tunnels, Hank bumbling after her. Finally she found the supply closet she was looking for and dragged him inside.

"What is that thing?" Hank asked as they stared at a large cylinder with a padded slot in the center.

"Something Doctor Vance finally got to put in storage when the Human/People mess exploded," she said. "It was a gift from some visiting Human doctor years ago, and Woolerton told him he had to keep it in his office so as not to offend the Earthers. I saw him directing the bots to move it the other day — he said this ugly thing had been taking up space in his office for years, and he couldn't wait to put it in storage."

"But what is it?"

"An ancient MRI machine from Earth." She climbed into the middle and waved for him to follow. "This thing is a giant magnet. It blocks most communication signals, but just in case…." She took out the little cylinder Richard had loaned her — in exchange for a few favors, like telling him where Lightning was being tested as soon as she left the science ship, and putting him in contact with Jake.

"We're clear of spots," she said, after Hank sat next to her and she scanned him with the device.

"Now can you please tell me the truth?"

"If I tell you the truth, you can't repeat it — especially to Xenia. Just tell her I'm not a threat." She scooted closer to him so she could talk in a very low voice, just in case anyone should be wandering the hallways and blunder into the closet. "If you want info about M Four Fifty-two, forget about involving her — I know someone who can steal anything."

"Even government secrets?"

"He's done it before. He lives for the challenge. This is a society of very smart people, Hank."

"You'll tell me the truth if I promise not to tell Xenia, other than reassuring her that you aren't a threat? And you'll have your friend help me?"

STUPID HUMANS

"Yes."

"Why can't you tell Xenia?"

"Because she probably won't believe you, and she could use what I'm about to tell you against me." She took out her pad and turned off all her recording devices.

He sighed. "Please, just tell me what it is."

"Everything I said was true, Hank. I've never lied about my motives for being here, not since the day I arrived. I didn't go back to Earth because it's full of stupid Humans —"

"Damnit, you promised you'd tell me the truth!" The yelling echoed even louder in the cavernous MRI machine.

"Let me finish!" she snapped. "That *is* the truth, it's just not very specific. Let me tell you a story about the stupid Humans of Earth."

"I've been there."

"Not recently, and you're not me, so shut up."

She took a deep breath and started the story she'd never told anyone in five years.

"Earth is full of stupid Humans, and for reasons I've never understood, it's mostly run by them. I can't say it's much different here after meeting Xenia, but back to the stupid Humans of Earth. One day they blundered their way into a wormhole, found out they're the poor relations of the universe, and you know the rest.

"So the stupid Humans were told how to travel safely through the wormhole, but that they could only send a small delegation for the first visit. They got a list of no's — no politicians, no lawyers, and absolutely no one who worked for *any* government. Academics were allowed, plus a couple journalists and a doctor.

"So these stupid Humans chose a doctor to put everyone safely into cryosleep, because the People warned it was necessary to avoid the potentially dangerous effects of traversing a wormhole. Because the stupid Humans were choosing from people with medical degrees, their choices were limited to mostly people who were even stupider than normal. The one they chose was no exception, and his appointment was made because of his family's connections, not his actual skills as a doctor."

"You're talking about your ex-boyfriend?"

Her fingers squeezed the springy padding in the bottom of the MRI cylinder. The ancient polyurethane was soft and yielding, like the flesh of Michael's neck that day in the infirmary when she wrapped her hands around his throat and wouldn't let go until he dropped the needle.

"Michael. We didn't want to be apart for almost two years. Anyway, it was a good career opportunity for me, being one of the few journalists in the first group to meet the People, so I agreed to go with him. His family connections leaned on someone to get me the job, which was, honestly, completely unfair to some of the other candidates who had years' more experience than I did, but hey, I wasn't going to complain.

"Then the committee did a shit ton of research, to the best of their stupid Human abilities, and determined it was indeed feasible to go through the wormhole in cryo, which had been around for more than fifty years and was considered safe by stupid Human standards. So Michael spent months examining the people chosen for the mission, making sure they had no health problems or genetic quirks that would cause problems. He determined to the best of his stupid Human ability that everyone was as safe as possible, including me.

"So the day we leave, I'm standing in a room full of these things that look like coffins, and I panic. I start thinking maybe I'll be one of those people who go into cryo and never wake up, even though I know that's very rare, especially in someone young and healthy. And Michael says to me, 'Don't worry, I wouldn't let anything bad happen to you.'

"And I think he's right, cryo treatment is very safe and I'm worrying about nothing, so I get in, and he puts patches on me and a mask on my face. He sticks in all these needles, and I think I'm going to wake up looking like a fucking heroin addict with all those marks in my arms. And right before he closes the lid, he says, 'See you soon, Sleeping Beauty.'"

She worked at a rip in the padding, digging her fingers in until it tore open, spilling chunks of polyurethane foam.

"So he closes the lid and I expect to just drift off, like how I always heard it described. I know the drugs are going into me because I felt all those needle sticks, and I'm starting to feel tingly all over and then... and then I am sort of drifting, or at least that's how it feels. I feel like I'm floating, and I'm seeing things I know aren't real, and I know I'm hallucinating. Not dreaming, because I can still hear the hum of the cryocan and the clicking of the cartridges as they keep pushing drugs into me, I can still feel the cold seeping into my skin, the electrodes zapping me. I know I'm not asleep, so I try to jump up and run away, and that's when I discover the scariest thing of all — I can't move. Not a muscle. I can't open my eyes, I can't scream for help, I can't run, I can't hide. I am trapped in a hell inside my own head, and I am painfully aware that I'm losing my mind, and there's not a damn thing I can do about it.

"I stayed like that for more than six months, which was how long the trip took back then."

She gave up on the now-ripped padding, brushing chunks of polyurethane off her fingers, and looked up at Hank. He stared at her, his mouth hanging open. "That's why I don't care what you did, Hank, or John, or whatever your real name is. Because I actually have first-hand experience with losing my mind, and I would do *anything* to avoid going back there—and I have. I refused to go back to Earth with Michael, I had a block put on my medchip, I refused to go back to Earth with Brad, and I made Vance take the last coffin during the air crisis, because I absolutely refuse to be locked in a box and forced to lose my mind again."

Hank rubbed a hand across his forehead. "Why didn't you say anything? Why won't you tell anyone now?"

She gave him her best just-think-about-it look. "The first person I told didn't believe me. First he tried to put me back to sleep, and I told him no, and he wouldn't listen, so I got my fingers around his neck and squeezed until he dropped the damn needle. Then he used that as an excuse to say I had a bad reaction to the drugs while I was waking up and hallucinated *the whole thing*. Hallucinated all those months of hell! Of course, he had a vested interest in not believing me, because he was the stupid Human who fucked up."

"He never figured out what went wrong? I mean, if it was just the stupid Humans, a cryo treatment here might work better."

She shook her head. "No. Michael insisted the bed was working fine and I got the right dose and blah, blah, blah. Bullshit to cover his ass. So I don't know what he fucked up, or what, if anything, could prevent it from going wrong again."

"So you never told anyone the truth, not even Brad?"

"No. After I decided to stay here, I crafted this image for myself. I became someone who chose to stay here and try to find out what the People are hiding from us instead of returning to a crowded, polluted planet of dumbasses, and I liked *that* version of my story better than the truth. I thought if Brad knew, he'd like the first me better, too." She gritted her teeth, wishing she didn't have to say the next sentence. "He died because I didn't tell him the truth."

"No, he died because an idiot blew up a ship."

"I guess so." She put a hand on his arm and looked him straight in the eye. "You get why you can't tell Xenia now, right?"

He frowned. "I get why you don't want the public to know. But Xenia would understand—"

"Xenia might not believe me, and if she thinks I'm telling a half-truth, then someone who thinks I'm a spy would know the perfect way to torture me."

"What?" He shook his head. "No, you have a block on your medchip—"

"The Council probably has a hacker somewhere who could get around it." She realized she was digging her nails into Hank's arm and loosened her grip. "Neither of our governments considers putting someone in cryo torture. No political repercussions. No reason anyone would believe me. She'd be sure it wasn't traced to her and the Council. You can't tell her, Hank."

"I hadn't thought of that." He took the hand that was gripping his arm. "It's okay, I won't tell her. I couldn't do that to my worst enemy."

"Good. Because if you did tell her, I would have to tell everyone about your past, John Halbrooke."

He jerked his hand away as if he'd just touched a hot stove. "You don't have to threaten me."

"You mean like you just threatened me with a gun?"

"Oh... right." He made that cringing face people usually made when they'd just realized they were wrong. "I'm sorry. I told you, I wouldn't have used it."

She sighed. "I understand. People have been screwing me over for so long—Michael, Brad at the end, Xenia—that it's just an automatic response. I believe you, really."

"But... even if I tell her nothing, she's still going to think you're a spy and try to deport you. She said she'd use the Lightning Bolt to have you hauled home to get around the cryo restriction."

Samantha smiled. "So what? If she wants to do that, I don't give a shit, as long as I don't have to go back in a coffin. I'll find some lawyer to fight whatever charges she trumps up and I'll be back—if not soon, then when the war-we're-trying-to-avoid is over."

Hank's face fell. "I'm going to miss you in the meantime."

"I don't think she'll do it, though. Not after you tell her why she shouldn't."

"Why?"

She smiled. "I'm going to announce that I'm keeping a live feed open to *Glass* at all times, which will be available to the public. I will do this to prove that I'm not a spy, and also so the public will know if any of my rights have been violated by the illustrious government here."

"You think *Glass* will agree?"

She shrugged. "I'm not asking them to carry it on their main channel. All they have to do is record it and add a link to their net. They'll have a record even if no one watches."

Hank nodded. "I'll go tell Xenia *that* right now."

"Wait—I need you to get a message to Richard."

He frowned. "Richard? Why?"

"I have an idea about ending this mess, and it requires his help. He said you'd have a way to contact him?"

"I'm only supposed to use it in emergencies, but sure. What's the message?"

"Tell him I have some info he needs, and he should contact me securely. He can do it."

"Okay," Hank said. "Where are you going?"

She climbed out of the tube and hopped down. "To see Doctor Vance. I want to make sure this M Four Fifty-two thing is a viable option before I ask my friend to steal it. That's a major job."

"Don't bother," Vance said, stepping out of the shadows.

She jumped, startled. Why didn't Richard's stupid cylinder check for other people and not just spots? "Shit. How long have you been there?"

"Long enough to figure out the flaw in my logic. I traced the signal from your medchip." He shook his head, staring at her in the dim light. "Why didn't you tell me? I could have helped you figure out what went wrong."

She shrugged. "There's no point. I'm never going to let anyone put me back in one of those coffins. If you want to help someone, concentrate yours efforts on Hank."

Vance looked at the other man, who had climbed out of the MRI machine and was standing by the door. "I think if I could find out anything about M Four Fifty-two—even just confirming whether or not it exists—that might help me determine the course of my research. I'll do everything I can do help you, Hank."

He nodded. "Then I need to go talk to Xenia. Thank you—both of you."

He walked out the door, and Vance started to follow him.

"Wait," Samantha said. "Why were you looking for me?"

He shrugged. "You're a reporter. I thought you might have heard something about M Four Fifty-two, but I see Vance already asked you."

"Mostly what I've heard are conspiracy theories. I'm going to have a—a friend with connections look into the M Four Fifty-two situation, but it might take a while."

"I understand. In the meantime, you might be able to help me with something else. I have a theory."

She sighed. "You're not going to tell anyone, are you?"

"No, of course not." He shook his head. "I can't believe this whole mess with Xenia and Anna and you being locked up happened because you wouldn't just tell the truth."

"Excuse me? I told everyone the truth, over and over. I said I wasn't a threat, I said my reasons for staying here were personal, and I said I didn't know anything. You people wouldn't believe me. If I was one of you, no one would have even asked what I was doing here."

Vance cleared his throat and looked at the floor. "Okay, maybe you have a point there. I'm sorry. Will you help me with something anyway? It's for Hank."

"All right, tell me what kind of help you need."

SEVENTY-TWO

Winding back through the hallways, Samantha pulled up the latest news reports, and saw why she had twenty missed messages from Lee in as many minutes.

THE HUMANS SURROUNDING STATION FIVE ALPHA
HAVE RELEASED A LIST OF DEMANDS:

WE DON'T WISH TO CONTINUE THIS WAR ANY MORE
THAN YOU DO. HOWEVER, OUR GRIEVANCES MUST BE
ADDRESSED. WE WILL NOT ATTACK UNLESS PROVOKED,
BUT WE WILL NOT LET ANYONE IN AND OUT OF THIS STATION
UNTIL OUR DEMANDS ARE MET.

It wouldn't be long until the Humans felt they'd been "provoked."

1) WE WANT THE CURE FOR CANCER, AND ANY OTHER
DISEASES YOU CAN CURE THAT WE CAN'T. WE WILL CONTINUE
TO WORK ON POPULATION CONTROL, BUT YOU CAN'T DENY
US BASIC MEDICAL KNOWLEDGE.

2) WE WANT AN APOLOGY FOR THE WORMHOLE ATTACK. WE WERE NOT RESPONSIBLE, AND WHILE YOU MAY NOT HAVE BEEN EITHER, YOU WERE IN CONTROL OF THE PROTECTOR WHEN IT FAILED AND ARE THEREFORE RESPONSIBLE.

3) WE WANT BOTH OUR PEOPLES TO CONTINUE WORKING TO DECREASE CIVILIAN DESTRUCTION SO THAT ONCE WE'VE OFFICIALLY ENDED THE WAR, BOTH SIDES WON'T HAVE TO CONTINUE FIGHTING OUR OWN CITIZENS.

4) WE WANT FULL DISCLOSURE OF ALL TECHNOLOGY ADVANCES MADE BY THE PEOPLE, AS WE WILL NEVER TRULY HAVE PEACE UNTIL WE HAVE AN EQUAL PLAYING FIELD.

SEVENTY-THREE

"Well, it took several hours of testing, because I wasn't sure exactly what I was looking for." Vance sat across from Samantha in his office, his tail tapping against the chair leg. "But eventually, as I suspected, my AI identified abnormalities in your nerve cells that are consistent with a drug like M Four Fifty-two. That's not conclusive, but it suggests there might be something to my theory, especially since you were Hazed multiple times on the science ship and remember everything. Are you sure it didn't happen here?"

"Michael gave us all a bunch of injections right before we left. They were supposed to be vaccines." She gritted her teeth. "But they could have been anything."

"I have no idea if this caused your problem with cryo or not," he said. "But if half the rumors I've read are true, M Four Fifty-two can have some bad neurological side effects. I've never heard of your government having it though, only mine."

"It's easier for my government to hide stuff from the masses than yours, because people on Earth are idiots."

"I guess that makes sense. Well, I don't think the effects are reversible," Vance said. "I can keep working on it, but it's very difficult to alter neurons without causing more damage. Honestly, you're lucky you didn't suffer any severe side effects from the first dose."

She shook her head. "Don't waste any time on it. I'm not going to let anyone put me in cryo again, and I don't mind the not being rufied part."

"I think I might be able to help Hank, though," Vance said. "That's why I wanted to test you. Now that I have samples of your altered nerve cells, I can try to reverse engineer a treatment for him—but like I said, altering neurons is risky. No guarantees. But I have a place to start now."

"But if the treatment doesn't work, then Hank won't be able to go into cryo while you find another solution."

"No." He smiled. "That's the really good news. My analysis shows your problem with the cryosleep was caused by M Four Fifty-two—and a combination of genes, all of which occur in less than five percent of the Human population and are classified as harmless—because, without the cryo drugs, they are. I can give Hank two of the genes and M Four Fifty-two, and I think it will work. Without the third gene, he should have no problem with cryo."

"You're sure?"

"I found the records for the delegation crew. One of them had the first two genes but not the third. She went back to Earth, so she must not have had a problem."

"What about the insanity part?"

"I suspect that's caused by another gene that Hank and you don't have. But just in case, I'm going to test the treatment thoroughly before I try it."

"Thanks, Vance." She got up to leave just as the door flew open, and Xenia stalked in with three armed guards.

Samantha groaned. "What now?"

✳
SEVENTY-FOUR

"Your people are threatening to blow up our most important asset on this side of the Divide if we don't give them the cure for cancer and every tech secret we have," Xenia yelled over the table in the interrogation room. "Now you need to talk fast, because I don't know when your people are going to make a move. Do you?"

"No! For the last fucking time—"

"Fine," Xenia cut her off. "Then you better answer my questions, or I can't help you. I've made sure your cameras and recording devices are shut down, but I'm releasing a visual-only live feed from the ceiling cameras to your friends in the press, so they can see you aren't being mistreated."

"What do you want this time? More advice?"

"That worked for five minutes, but I no longer have the luxury of time to try the CC approach. Let's move on. Why did you put a block on your medchip for one thing—no cryosleep?"

"Because I didn't want to be put in cryo." Samantha mimicked Xenia's deadpan voice.

"One more smart-ass answer like that, and I will have the guards haul you off without giving you another chance to explain yourself!" Xenia yelled.

"On what charges?"

"Whatever I have to make up. What is wrong with you? If you're so innocent, why do you want everyone to think you're guilty?" So many veins popped out on Xenia's forehead, it looked like a map of New York City.

"If I was one of you, none of the things you think look suspicious would matter," Samantha said. "I just want you to know that before I spend a lot of time explaining things."

"Fine. It's a precarious situation and you may have been judged unfairly, but your… people are trying to start a war with us, and we can't have our heads up our asses," Xenia said. "We did that when the Earthers first came here, and look where it got us! You have three seconds to answer the question, or I'm calling in the guards."

"Fine, but it's a long story. You might want to have a seat," she stalled.

"Talk fast." Xenia flopped down across from her.

Samantha wracked her brain for a solution. There was one story she could tell Xenia that wouldn't reveal anything important.

"My boyfriend Michael and I came here together, then I decided to stay here, and he wanted to go back. So a few days before they were scheduled to leave, he asked me to have coffee with him and slipped me a trank.

"So I want you to picture this—maybe I'm slurring my words a little, but no matter how stoned I get, I always manage to remember my full vocabulary of profanity. So I'm cursing him out the whole way down the hallway to the infirmary where he has all the coffins set up and he stuffs me in one. So I'm lying there, and I'm so angry. I could make it harder for him, but I know something he doesn't.

"He's saying, 'Don't worry, you won't remember anything. I'll tell you that you decided to go back after all and you'll be so relieved that you did.'

"All I can think is, I'm on drugs and I'm thinking more clearly than this moron. I try to explain that to him, but he's not listening.

"So I say, 'Michael, this isn't going to work. I'm going to wake up and hate your guts even more than I do right now.'

"And he says, "Shhh, you'll feel better in the morning,' meaning in six months I guess, and he keeps moving around, doing whatever crap he needs to do to activate the coffin.

'Michael,' I say. 'Do you believe in fate?' And he just stares at me, so I keep talking. 'I don't either. I think people make choices. You make a series of choices and sometimes you get to this point where no matter what subsequent choices you make, everything will always come out the same. Some people call that fate, but it's really just a culmination of choices.

"'We reached that point before we left Earth. We both thought we'd break up if you went without me. We thought the only solution was for me to come, too. But that didn't work either, did it? The truth is, our relationship was dead on arrival here. I've accepted it, and you need to do the same.'

"He shakes his head and says, 'No, that's just the drugs talking,' and shoves me back down in the coffin. He pushes some buttons, then he takes my hand and says, 'Don't worry, I won't let anything bad happen to you.'

"Then he flips a switch and says, 'I'll stay here until you go to sleep.' Like he's doing me this big fucking favor. There's a loud alarm noise, and he looks over at the console.

"'What did you do?' he screams, and I know the bed is telling him I have a cryo block.

"I can actually feel the muscles in my forehead loosen, and I realize that I must have been glaring without noticing it. I smile and it seems to take forever, one muscle at a time, and Michael is staring at me in horror.

"'I wanted to be wrong about you,' I say. 'But I planned to be right.'

"He's shaking his head. 'But how could you know I would do this? I didn't know I was going to do this until an hour ago!'

"I drag myself out of the coffin, and this time he doesn't bother to stop me. I go to the door, and I say, 'You better go back to Earth, because I never want to see you again. If you stay here, I will tell everyone what you did.'

"That's why I had the block put in—because I had a bad feeling Michael would do exactly what he did. I left it in because I didn't know if anything like that would ever happen again, and sure enough, there was the thing with Brad. Different circumstances, but still, he tried to send me back, too. Having that chip has come in handy, because people keep trying to get rid of me for no good reason."

She finally looked up at Xenia, who looked slightly less frozen-faced and slightly more sympathetic.

"I understand," she said finally, her gaze wandering up in the way of people who were watching something play on their eyeplants. "I'm not going to detain you, but I would like your advice about a situation that's come up. Would you mind waiting here for a few minutes?"

Samantha shook her head. "Not at all."

SEVENTY-FIVE

"What did you decide?" Tom asked Xenia when he rejoined her on her ship, which was docked with Five Alpha—and, apparently, going nowhere fast.

"Carlton called. He's seeking support to deport both Hank and Samantha if the FIB can find a shred of evidence that they've done anything wrong."

"By *find*, you mean manufacture."

"That's how the Council works sometimes." She sighed. "It wouldn't be so bad if it was justified, but this time it isn't."

"What can we do?"

"The Humans are demanding all our medical and technological knowledge." She studied her display. "And we're unanimous in rejecting their demands. I know they're stupid, but are they crazy?"

Tom shook his head. "It's not that. They know they won't get everything on the list. They're just hoping they can keep dropping things in an effort to look diplomatic, then when they have only one thing left — I'm guessing the cancer cure — they demand we give them just *one* thing they wanted. If we say no, they wail that we won't compromise."

"The Council will never approve giving them the cure when they have so many starving people already. Not only would we be killing more people, we'd be killing almost all poor people."

"I know." Tom twiddled his thumbs. "But we can't keep calling them ignorant and denying them knowledge."

"You have a solution?"

"No. You?"

"I'm working on it."

"Are you going to do anything about Samantha?"

Xenia shook her head. "We can't find any evidence against her or Hank. I'm going to tell the Council the media will burn us if we do anything to their friend — or their favorite subject. Hopefully, that will encourage them to find a new target. What about the alien angle?"

Tom shook his head. "It was a good distraction a few weeks ago, but we're not sure the wormhole was built by aliens, and if it was, we can't find them. Nobody likes a villain who can't be found and punished. Unless you have an extraterrestrial in your closet, that's a dead end. Plus it's getting us bad press — the Earthers are screaming that if we weren't smart enough to build our own stable wormhole, maybe we're not that superior to the Humans, after all."

She groaned. "We can't blame the probably non-existent aliens, the Humans, or Samantha, and we can't take the blame when we haven't done anything but defend ourselves."

"What about the ships? We're sort of trapped here," Tom said. "I can't believe no one's fired a shot in almost a day."

"No one wants to take credit for starting this fight." Xenia sighed. "We have ships not too far behind, and between Five Alpha and the Earthers. If the Humans start shooting, it won't last long."

"Did you talk to Commander Carroll?"

"Yes. He has twelve plans for blasting them out of our way. Most of them involve heavy losses to the station, and probably loss of lives." Why did she ever want to work in politics, let alone be a Councilmember?

"Did we respond to their demands?"

"We told them we'd need time to consider. They gave us three days."

"Until they do what?"

"They didn't say."

✳ ✳

Vance wasn't sure if he was making things worse or better, but he had a duty to help his patients—all of them.

"What did you call me for? Is there a problem?" Samantha sat on the other side of the desk in his office.

"No, there's no problem, I—"

"Hank said his treatment was going well."

"Yes, it is, but that's not quite what I wanted to talk to you about—not directly, anyway."

He stared at the report on his data pad. Was this the right decision? His inaction had started a toxic chain of events once, and he didn't want to do that again. But Samantha had a right to know, and the AI couldn't find any legal reason he shouldn't tell her the truth.

"When you first came to this side of the Divide with the Human party five years ago, this was where your ship docked. Twenty people.

All brought out of cryo onboard the ship. When you arrived here at the station, after meeting with our welcome party, you were all ushered down here, to the infirmary, where the doctors on duty ran a battery of tests."

Samantha nodded. "Yes, I remember that. It was much less uncomfortable than a Human exam. No poking and prodding and needles, they just kept waving those wands around. They did make us pee in cups and swab our mouths for DNA. Why?"

Vance looked at the shiny metal of his desk, and although he knew he was staring at a distorted reflection of Samantha's face, he saw Iris's instead. The day she left, after he'd discovered what she was after, she'd screamed at him that he was a lousy doctor. *How can you stand by and do nothing when you could help so many people?* He'd tried to explain, all the usual reasons, all the additional Humans who would die, how skewed the deaths would be to the poor and disenfranchised, but she wouldn't listen. He should have told someone after she left, but he couldn't bring himself to do it.

"Vance, do you have some point here?" Samantha startled him out of his memory.

"Yes, sorry." He did the right thing then, and he was doing the right thing now. He could help Samantha without fucking up Earth even worse than his ancestors had.

He hoped.

"So they did take some samples, skin cells and urine and a small amount of blood, although they did it painlessly so you didn't notice. You were the first Humans we'd encountered in thousands of years, Samantha, the medical data was so important—"

"I understand that. What are you getting at?"

He shoved the data pad across the desk to her. "The samples were divided and sent to medical centers all over the civilized sector, and some remained here. They're down in storage, so I retrieved them and repeated the same tests I did the other day. That report shows you had already been dosed with the M Four Fifty-two-like drug. I say *like* because it's not quite the same, based on the, ah, report I got from your, ah, friend."

"So what you're saying is we came up with an anti-rufie drug that isn't quite like yours before we came here, and they dosed me. But why?"

"I'm going to tell you something, but I will never confirm that I said it, because I'm breaking some confidentiality laws. If you tell anyone I won't even remember we had this conversation." Vance took a deep breath. "It wasn't just you. I checked everyone's samples, and you were all dosed."

She turned the pad over in her hands. "I was the only one who had a problem in cryo because of genetic factors?"

He nodded. "In your people's defense, I doubt they could have anticipated this would happen. The drug probably hadn't been tested extensively, and their genetic predictive models are still light years behind ours."

"I was right. It was the stupid Humans." Samantha raked a hand through her hair. "But why? What did they want us to do?"

He shrugged. "My guess is nothing. It was a safeguard, in case we Hazed you after you saw something classified or had some other nefarious plans. Who knows? If I had been in charge of the first People party visiting Earth, I might have made a similar recommendation — but only if I had a drug that was truly safe for everyone. Our systems could have screened for problems."

"I see. My own people screwed me over." She stood up and sighed. "Can't say I'm surprised."

"Look, I can't tell you what to do with this information, but I'd hate to think of this making the current... situation worse."

She shook her head. "I want the war to end, Vance. Because once it does, I'm going to go back to Earth on Richard's ship and raise hell. I'm going to expose and embarrass the bastards who did this to me. Then I'm going to come back here where I belong now."

"I just hope everything's still standing," Vance mumbled as she left.

✳
SEVENTY-SIX

Samantha stood in the deserted docking area of Five Alpha, staring at her pad. It showed a shimmer in the black space before the station, which resolved into a compact ship. She held her breath, hoping Richard's various stolen tech would fool the People ships' sensors—just so long as no one looked at a wall screen. She didn't know what strings Haylea had pulled, but the station's AI guided the ship into one of its bays.

She approached as the airlock slid open and Richard stepped out.

"I'll give you the interview whenever you want," he said.

"Are you sure no one saw you?" she asked.

"I told you, we have better masking tech than anyone on this side of the Divide. And by we, I mean corporations, not the Human government." Richard rolled his eyes as they started down the hallway.

"How did your people do with the information Jake... *acquired* for you?"

He grinned. "I had the best minds at twenty top companies, including Intel, Birnbaum—"

"Stop name-dropping, I know you're rich and powerful. What did the best minds find?"

"They analyzed the info, plus the specs for Lightning, and found there were more mathematical errors than even Merelyn thought. She only solved *one*. Lightning works now, but it will explode one time in about five hundred. If it hasn't happened yet in their testing, they're lucky."

"And your geniuses fixed the problem?"

"Of course. But the People need to stop testing that device, unless they want it to blow up."

"Well, we need to go have a chat with some Councilmembers."

Richard narrowed his eyes at her. "If this was some sort of trick to get me on the station and arrest me, I promise you, my lawyers will make sure the two of you —"

"Relax, it's not a trap. We all want peace." She stepped through the doorway first. "These guards are just here to escort us."

"Mister Swinton!" Haylea came around the corner, Roble hot on her heels. "I hope your stay on Five Alpha will be most pleasurable. If the peace talks cause you any stress, I can hook you up with a half-price massage at Hannah's House of —"

"Thanks, I'm fine." Richard turned to Roble. "I understand you can help with my... situation."

"Yes, and it's an honor to —"

"Save it, we don't have time." Richard handed Roble a chip. "I'm trusting you with this information. You know what to do."

Roble nodded. "I'll get right to work."

Richard turned back to Haylea. "You know, I've been thinking that I need a new trophy wife. How would you like the job?"

Haylea's jaw dropped open and Samantha thought she was going to walk into a wall, but she managed to stop herself in time. She spun around to face Richard. "A trophy wife? What is that?"

"It's when an attractive woman marries a rich man for his money," Samantha helped her out.

"I'm insulted by that offer," Haylea snapped. "Why would you think I'd want to—"

Richard gestured at the walls. "You obviously don't like your job here, and you talk about money and nice things constantly in interviews. Also, you've been ignoring this shmuck—" He pointed at Roble. "Who is obviously, *stupidly* in love with you, so clearly you aren't interested in a relationship with someone who actually cares about you. Your public profile indicates your sexual preference is for men, so what do you say?"

Roble stopped in his tracks, pocketed the chip, and high-fived Richard, a move he'd probably learned from his favorite Earth holo game.

Haylea's face was turning redder than a ketchup stain on a five-hundred-cred shirt. She walked up to Richard and gave him a high-five, too.

Right in the face.

"This shmuck may be annoying and uncoordinated, but at least he's never insulted me like that!" She grabbed a confused-looking Roble and hauled him out the door.

Richard removed a handkerchief from his pocket and dabbed at his jaw, like he thought he could wipe off the red mark she'd left. Then he turned to Samantha. "Well, what do you say we go make some peace?"

"After you, expert."

SEVENTY-SEVEN

Hank walked out of Vance's office and found Samantha waiting on a bench in the main concourse, staring at the outside view on the wall screen.

"Something seems wrong," she said.

"Forget about that. There's nothing more we can do." Hank sat down next to her. "Guess what? Doctor Vance says the treatment worked. My neurons are adapting to resist memory loss."

She smiled. "That's great."

"I couldn't have done it without you."

"Of course you could. It just would have taken Vance longer to figure out what to do."

"You know, I spent a lot of time in my old life being pissed off," he said. "About everything—losing a life with Emily, wanting her to be with someone else instead of me, her lack of cooperation on that, watching my mom degenerate, knowing I would face the same fate, the fact that she didn't get genetic counseling instead of just getting

497

knocked up, drug companies making it so hard for anyone to get a treatment that might not even work."

She groaned. "I'm glad you're cured, Hank, I really am, but if this is a speech about forgiveness and letting go, I'm not into that sort of thing."

"No, it's not." Hank took her hand. "I just wanted to tell you that I'm not pissed anymore. You know why? Because every one of those things ultimately led me to be here with you now."

"I'm glad we're both here, too." She tried to remember the last time she'd trusted anyone as much as Hank. Brad? Well, maybe, until he tried to have her hauled onto the death wagon. Michael? Yeah, until he promised to put her to sleep and didn't do it. "But I don't forgive and forget, and I've been royally screwed over. So if you expect me to hop on this letting-go bandwagon with you, I'm not up for it."

Hank smiled. "You don't get it. I'm not asking you to change. I love you just the way you are, anger and all. And if you want me to help you get even with the people who screwed you over, starting with Michael and ending with the Human government, I will do that."

She tried to think of the appropriate response here. It had been a long time since anyone had given a rat's ass about her, and an even longer time since she'd really cared. And she did care about Hank, despite the fact he reminded her of Earth—or maybe, to some extent, because of it. He had woken up to a world of people badmouthing her, and he never once considered they were telling the truth. He was the first person in a very long time who didn't assume she was a lying, spying, double-crosser from Earth, and she'd responded by threatening to expose his own painful past. But despite all of that, here he was, saying he loved her. Too bad she still couldn't think of the right thing to say.

She decided that a kiss with tongue would be appropriate, and get her off the hook for saying the right thing, so she went for it.

"Save it for later, it's time to go to this disaster of a meeting," Xenia yelled from the doorway.

*   *

Five minutes later they sat in Five Alpha's conference room, waiting for the Human representatives. Samantha was at one end with Tom, Carlton, Xenia, Haylea, Richard, and Hank. President Howard, Morriss, and about a dozen Human security guards walked in and sat at the opposite end of the table.

"Have you watched the news in the last ten minutes?" Morriss asked, not wasting time on small talk.

"No." Xenia's forehead crinkled with concern, and she flicked a hand across the table. A display of *Glass*'s live news bloomed over the table, and Samantha feigned shock as Lee explained the anonymous warning *Glass* had received about Lightning's potential flaw.

"This would really make the situation outside messy," Howard observed dryly.

"We don't want messy," Xenia said.

To her right, Carlton snorted. "Xenia and I are usually at opposite ends of issues on the Council, but we both want to end this standoff without any shots being fired."

"And how do you propose we do that?"

Xenia propped up her cheeks with a fake smile. "We'll give you our tech secrets... if you give us yours."

Howard humphed.

"We'll be more than happy to continue our work toward protecting the wormhole, but I think most people will be using Lightning to get around," she continued. "We won't apologize because we didn't cause the collapse. And we can't, in good conscience, give you the cure for cancer."

"I'm afraid if you can't meet our demands, as laid out, we'll have no choice but to start firing on the station," Howard said. "Your three days are almost up."

"I don't think you really want to do that," Xenia said icily. "You may have anti-masking tech, but we have Lightning, and our ships can pop up anywhere now. I don't think you'll win."

"Lightning isn't safe to use in its current form," Howard said. "You won't get the solution to fix it until we get what we want."

She didn't know it, but Roble's AI was already examining the solution for its feasibility. But he wasn't going to turn it over until the war ended.

Xenia sat in stony silence, calling the Earthers' bluff. Finally, she said, "We're confident our experts can solve the problem."

"Why don't we compromise? We'll let the apology go, and we'll drop the demand for giving us *all* your tech. Just don't fight us over Lightning, and give us all your medical knowledge, including the cancer cure." Howard spread his hands to show they were being reasonable.

"That sounds like a good compromise," Morriss said.

"We can't give you any more medical knowledge at this time, but as you stabilize the population and move into newer habitats in space, that door will always be open," Carlton said, and Samantha knew he, Xenia, and the Council had hashed out where to draw the line earlier. "We'd be doing more harm than good, and we won't do that to you."

The wall screen behind the Humans dissolved into an emergency alert.

"They're firing at us," Tom said unnecessarily.

STUPID HUMANS

Another shimmer in the blackness resolved into several dark, unmarked ships barely visible in the floodlights from the station. Laser beams aimed for the line of Human ships—and the torpedoes they'd just released.

"I thought your ships weren't going to fire on us until we'd finished with the peace talks?" Xenia yelled.

"You think our people are firing on the station with us in it?" Howard yelled.

"Those ships aren't a Human design," Tom said. "But one of your fringe groups could have rented some of ours."

Richard spread his hands. "The specs for Lightning were leaked by someone on our side of the Divide. Could be anyone, and People ships are popular among Humans."

"Why haven't you arrested this guy?" Xenia yelled at Howard.

He shrugged. "As far as we know, he hasn't broken any laws."

"We're thinking it's the Rednecks for Reparations, or the Citizen Soldiers of Solidarity, but we aren't sure yet," Tom said. "Possibly one ship belongs to the RR, and the other the CSS."

"If you can't control your people, we'll shoot them down." Xenia gestured at her military advisors.

Howard's eyes danced around as he read something on his eyeplant. "My people are attempting to contain the situation."

"If they could do that without punching holes in our station, that would be great," Haylea said.

Xenia chuckled as she looked at her data pad. "Good news! These two fringe groups of yours appear to be shooting at each other."

Samantha looked at her pad. The Rednecks were beating the crap out the Citizens of Solidarity. One more good blast with the lasers, and—

"Holy shit, they just hit my ship!" shouted Richard.

"I guess we'll just have to drink domestic beer for a while," Hank mumbled under his breath.

"My experts warned me the spacetime curvature drive could be dangerous if hit with a significant impact." Richard's in-charge attitude rapidly faded from his face. "I'm willing to give you the solution my people found to prevent the drive's destabilization, but only if you agree to, ah, my planet's terms."

"Are you saying your ship could blow up?" Xenia yelled. "That's how you people negotiate?"

"My ship's FTL drive is fixed. I'm saying you better send someone out there to break up the fight before one of those other craft blows up!"

"The Guard Patrol is handling things," Xenia's advisor said. Behind her, the redneck ship shuddered as multiple lasers pulsed on its hull.

"I have a suggestion," Samantha yelled as something, probably a torpedo, hit the station. The untouched crystal water glasses on the table rattled. "Before this gets out of hand."

"Talk fast," Xenia said, beads of sweat popping out on her forehead.

She turned to Xenia. "I think Richard has some information he'd like to share with you."

"This better be good," Xenia snarled.

Richard stood and smoothed his Saks suit. "This is a little awkward. I'm in possession of some information that would be embarrassing to my government, but horrendously humiliating to yours, Councilmember Xenia."

Howard cleared his throat. "May I have a moment with—"

"No," Richard snapped. "Neither of you will do it, so I'm putting all the cards on the table here. This information never has to leave this room if we can all come to an agreement."

He wasn't kidding. Samantha's AI had informed her that all recording and transmitting functions had been disabled when she'd entered the room.

Richard produced a pad and displayed a holo. "Who in this room would be shocked to know that the wormhole wasn't really as lost as the People claim it was until seven years ago?"

Howard whipped his head around. "What did you say?"

Xenia crossed her arms and looked away from his gaze.

Richard swiped at the holo, and Good Day Beer's logo dissolved into a picture of the wormhole. "Not only did they not really lose the Divide, they were using it all that time, or at least most of it. Let's just say they did some tampering."

Xenia's eyes widened almost imperceptibly. Tom stared into space, his eyes flicking back and forth as he read something on his eyeplant.

"Where are you getting this information?" Xenia clasped her hands together in front of her.

Richard smiled. "As with the Lightning situation, I had an anonymous source."

And if you believe that, I have a bridge in Brooklyn I want to sell you.

Samantha let out a breath she didn't realized she'd been holding. Even she didn't know exactly what Richard had up his sleeve, although she knew how he'd looked for it.

"Would you like to know which historical events the People had a hand in, or do you want to guess?" Richard looked at Howard and Morriss. Samantha looked at Xenia, whose poker face grew tighter and more pinched by the second.

"No!" Howard barked and Xenia blinked at him.

"You don't want to know what Richard... thinks he knows?" the Councilwoman stammered.

"Of course not," Samantha said. "Richard's right, that information could be extremely damaging to our people."

"Certainly not more damaging than it is to them." Morriss straightened his tie. "I for one would love to hear what they did to us."

"It's very interesting." Richard's finger hovered over the holo, as if he would reveal the next page at any moment. "They didn't do anything right away. After they left, they spent the first thousand years or so settling in here, before someone got the bright idea they'd abandoned us to our own stupidity. At that point, they started trying to, ah, fix us."

"How insulting." Howard's face crinkled into a sneer.

"Are you saying they experimented on us? With, like, genetics or something?" Morriss asked. "They used us as guinea pigs? This is an outrage, an egregious offense against our Human rights —"

"No, they knew genetic engineering would be limited in such a... an intellectually limited society as Earth." Richard cleared his throat. "They tried to fix us in more of a cultural way."

"We have no knowledge of anything like that," Xenia said. "Are you going to offer us any proof, Mr. Swinton? Or are you just going to keep making baseless accusations?"

Richard flashed an indulgent smile her way. "I have proof, and I'll be happy to reveal it, if the UNE wishes to see how you damaged our society."

"I'm not sure we really want to open that particular can of worms," Howard said softly.

"You already know what they did, don't you?" Samantha stared him down. "And as much as you'd like to politically obliterate them, you know this information would be just as damaging to the Humans, maybe more so."

"Do you know what they did?" Hank asked.

She shrugged. "No, but I've had suspicions for years. Tell you what, why don't I just throw out a theory and we can play hot or cold?"

"Play what?" Tom asked.

"I'm not playing children's games," Morriss snapped.

"I've suspected they tampered with our society since we first made contact," Samantha said. "It's been one of my long-term investigation projects since I've been here, but I was never able to find anyone who knew anything. This isn't general knowledge here—only a few government higher-ups know." Samantha shot a look at Xenia, who remained stone-faced. "It wasn't until recently, when I learned the truth about a secret my own government has been keeping, that I knew where to look for this information. I'm not going to tell you what Richard found, because I haven't seen the data he brought back from Earth—yet. I'm just going to tell you what I've suspected for years."

"Well, tell us your theory," Tom said.

"Given what I know about your society and its capacity for guilt, I figured you were going around trying to fix things. You could have done that in a lot of ways, but my best guess is you started one or more religions before you realized that was a way to make things worse and not better. But if you tell the people of Earth that, you'll just ensure we have one war after another for the next two thousand years, so if that's true Richard needs to bury what he found."

"What religions do you think they started?" Hank asked.

"Take a guess. Given the level of guilt they displayed when we initially showed up, and they're repeated efforts to try to 'fix' us since, I'd say the ones that have caused the most death and destruction."

"I can tell you if you want," Richard said. "But only if everyone agrees."

"I don't think you stopped there." Samantha looked at Xenia. "My guess is your ancestors established a few governments, too. That would be another mess my people couldn't solve without one bloody war after another, which would ultimately make things worse and contribute to the guilt mentality. No wonder you don't want to give up the cure for cancer, given your track record. At least you've gotten better at anticipating the consequences of your help after three thousand years."

"This has gone on long enough," Howard boomed. "What do you want, Mister Swinton?"

Xenia and Tom stared in silence.

"I want this conflict to end. I promise to make sure this information never sees the light of day, which I think we can agree is in everyone's best interest, yes? In exchange, I want this war to end now." He swiveled his head back to look at Xenia. "I know the worst thing that can happen over here is looking as stupid as the Humans. I'm guessing you don't want that."

"What are you implying?"

He shrugged. "I have proof that your People did a lot more to my people than just walking away four thousand years ago. It could be argued that, well-intentioned or not, your actions made things worse, since things obviously aren't going swimmingly on Earth. Not only that, but you covered it up, even hiding it from your own people, something you swear up and down you'd never do here in this enlightened society."

Xenia gritted her teeth and looked at Samantha. "Did you know he was going to do this?"

"I'm as shocked as you are," she said with a perfectly straight face. She didn't add that she knew exactly where Richard had gotten his information, and planned to delve into it herself at a later date. "But I have a suggestion how we can settle this whole thing amicably. Why don't you just give them the cure for cancer?"

"You just said you understood we why can't—"

"Make the situation worse, I know. Not after all your other screw-ups. But now that the Earthers have Lightning, they can colonize other planets, asteroids, whatever. They won't be limited to cramped space stations where they have to fight for air and water. They can find habitable planets and—"

"And wreck them the way they've done to their—*our*—planet?" Tom grimaced.

"Then *you* be in charge of regulating expansion," Samantha said. "Pick a planet for them, tell them what they can and can't do, assign people to ensure they do it. Tell them how many people they have to get off Earth in a certain time frame. They'll go along with it, because they *really want the cure for cancer.*" She shot Howard and Morriss a warning look, and they both shut their mouths. "Besides, they're running out of space on Earth and in their solar system. You might as well take the opportunity to control the situation, because they're going to spread out anyway with Lightning. They'll put up with it, because if they don't, they'll never get any more medical knowledge from you, and they're going to need help when they move to new worlds with new germs and toxins. Most importantly, we will *all* benefit from Richard's information disappearing for good."

"You're okay with this?" Hank looked at Samantha. "You're a reporter. You've spent years trying to unearth what the People have been hiding."

She sighed. "You're right. I believe people should know the truth— except when they're too fucking stupid to use the truth wisely. We've had enough wars over stupid shit on Earth. What's the point of ending this mess with the People just to have a hundred more conflicts back home? I'm not saying continuing the cover-up is going to fix anything, but revealing the truth will definitely make things worse."

"How do we know he'll even keep his word?" Xenia asked.

Richard shrugged. "I don't stand to benefit from that information getting out and the conflict continuing. I want to expand trade on both sides. I want to see us all get along for a change. I want people on Earth to stop starving and dying of cancer. I want my wife's death to mean something. You'll just have to take my word for it. I will never reveal this information."

"What if we just arrest him?" Xenia looked at Howard.

Richard rolled his eyes. "People would notice. Mine would riot in the streets and scream for your heads until you let me go. Peace would be even more of a distant dream. Also, some of my trusted colleagues have this information, and they won't look kindly on your decision to arrest me for trying to make peace."

Xenia stared at him for a moment, then looked at Carlton, her old enemy on the Council. "Well?"

"That's the best idea I've heard all day," he said, as another shot took out whatever camera the wall screen was displaying. "Mister Swinton would have to hand over whatever information he has to both sides, though, and promise it won't leak to the public. He'd also have to agree to a Hazing for the last few days, just to be sure. As would his trusted friends."

Richard put on his best Good-Day-Beer-solves-all-problems look. "Of course. I told you I'm committed to peace."

Xenia looked at the other end of the table. "We've been chosen to make this decision for the Council. Since we both agree, it's up to you."

"Someone is doing something about those ships out there, right?" Richard asked.

"Station security is handling it." Haylea frowned at a display. "But it looks like the Human ships are going after them."

STUPID HUMANS

Morriss and Howard whispered to each other for a moment, then Howard folded his hands in front of him and said regally, "The United Nations of Earth will make a formal vote tomorrow, but we offer a preliminary acceptance of your terms."

SEVENTY-EIGHT

"What are you going to do now?" Hank asked as they wandered down the concourse. "Go back to tending bar? Go back to Earth?"

Samantha smiled. "I do want to go back—for a vacation, and to get answers about what was done to me. Not to mention, I plan to uncover every bit of info Richard dug up—although I probably won't share it right away. Maybe never—Richard had some valid points. Think about it—if it turns out some of our religions were the People's efforts to fix Earth—"

Hank groaned. "Earth would probably be a smoking ashtray by the time that war ended. If it ever did."

She sighed. "That's the thing though—we've been killing each other over religion for centuries anyway. It wouldn't be anything new. Still, I don't know if I want to make the problem worse. I'm not sure I'll sit on it forever, though. There is something to be said for everyone knowing the truth, whether they react badly or not. I wanted to convince Xenia I'd never tell anyone, but I honestly haven't made up my mind yet."

"How did Richard get his info, anyway?"

"I told him where to look." She shrugged. "Once Vance told me we'd all been Hazed, I realized the information I'd been looking for all these years probably went home with one of the other original visitors. I told Richard to start with the team historian, since he was the most likely to have come across some reference in the archives or something. The guy was also good at ferreting out secrets, so he may have investigated a lot more thoroughly than the People expected. They probably figured a good Hazing would solve the problem."

"So you're going to go home on Richard's ship and visit all your old team members?"

"Yeah, there are a lot of people I want to visit on Earth. And I will get to the bottom of what the People did, whether I choose to tell anyone or not. But then I'm coming back here—this place is my home now."

Hank nodded. "It's mine, too. All my friends and family on Earth are gone. I'm going to find a job here, once I figure out what I'd be good at in this society."

"You're welcome to come with me."

"I thought you'd never ask. When we come back, are you going to New Atlantis to work for *Glass*?"

"I think so. There's a consortium of Human and People scientists doing a research project to determine if the People really built the wormhole, or if it was the work of extraterrestrials. If it's the second thing, they want to look for the aliens, although I have no idea where they'd start. Whoever built the Divide hasn't been around for a long time. Anyway, I think that would make an interesting documentary."

"You think *Glass* would go for it?"

"Do you know how much money they made from the air crisis

documentary? At this point, I think they'd go for a story about Haylea's cat cartoon if I pitched it to them. Hey, did you hear Richard flat-out asked her if she'd like to be his new trophy wife?"

"Are you serious?"

"Apparently he pissed her off so much she decided to date Roble, after all. He's moving to Earth to head a new tech company Richard's starting."

"And Haylea's going with him?"

"She heard Human cartoons are so badly written that hers would look great by comparison."

"Well, that makes sense. She'll probably have a big hit. So what happened when Richard asked her to be his trophy wife?"

"It's a long story."

"So tell it to me. I have plenty of time now."

V.R. Craft always heard you should write about what you know, so she decided to write a book called *Stupid Humans*, drawing on her previous experience working in retail and her subsequent desire to get away from planet Earth. She has also worked in marketing, advertising, and public relations, where she found even more material for the book. Now self-employed, she enjoys the contact sports of shopping at clearance sales, slamming on the brakes for yard sale signs, and wasting time on social media, where she finds inspiration for a sequel to *Stupid Humans* every day.